THE OTHER AR

By CONNIE TEAL

Volume Three of 'Threads'

The story continues late February 1928

Also in this series.

Threads. Volume One.

Yes, Sergeant Victor. Volume Two.

Polladras Publishers
Penrose Farm
Trew, Breage,
Helston. Cornwall.
England.
TR13 9QN
writerconnieteal@mail.com

Published 2011.

Connie Teal asserts the moral right to be identified as the author of this work.

A catalogue record of this book is available from The British Library.

ISBN 978-0-9562599-4-3

Printed and bound by the MPG Books Group Ltd

Cover by Knight Design
www.knightdesign.co.uk

CHAPTER ONE

"Wait for Bobby Budgeon mister 'e'll be 'ere, we all agreed, I know 'e'll come." Jack Wainwright, in spite of his few years, nevertheless seemed to act as spokesman for the group of young lads. Just as he'd predicted, a panting Bobby appeared at the top of the pathway, briefly pausing for breath, he ran down to where Joe Spooner and the huddle of boys stood.

"Catch your breath lad, no need of haste, it'll be another five minutes afore the light fades enough."
The evening air had sent the temperature plummeting and even in the advancing gloom the vapour from their breathing hung before their eyes in a mysterious shadowiness. They made for a motley bunch, nine boys aged around 8-10 years, clad in various hand me downs, confirming previous use through the misfitting sleeves, too long and disinclined to remain rolled up, hanging about the wrists in grubby, frayed abandon and trousers, which but for the saving grace of braces would have left long behind the lean waists. Rolls of tired sock crowned every boot and them, too weary to make any attempt at keeping out the wet or cold. One lad displayed the remains of a large boil just above the bridge of his nose, looking for all the world like a third eye, another carried a scab half way up his shin, now at that crusty, campaign medal stage, proclaiming the initial hurt. The shortest of the group wore spectacles, welded to the back of his head by knicker elastic and Charlie Jones' right hand perpetually pointed to the ground beneath him with a thumb and two fingers, like the sign which directed folk to the public urinals at Victoria Station. His little finger and the one adjacent had been bitten off by a frenzied Jack Russell when he was an infant.

"Now listen up," said Joe. "I promised I'd show yer summat you'd allus remember, summat as only fearless folk can see, so I must ask yer now, afore I carry on, 'ave any of yer changed your mind, if you 'ave, now's the time to walk away, no one'll call yer a cissy."

The boys looked sheepishly from one to another but all stood firm.

"Right then," said Joe, "silence, only complete silence, we've got to be still enough to 'ear a pin drop. I shall stand 'ere at the head of the grave and four of yer stand along each side, Bobby Budgeon, you stand opposite me at t'other end o' grave. Now the spirit needs contact wi' us, so all push the toe ends o' your boots tight to the curbstone and keep 'em pressed there."

Joe waited quietly while they shuffled into position. The last light of day seemed to hover behind the church tower and the mop of ginger hair on Bobby's head mellowed to burned copper. Jack Wainwright stood at Joe's right, opposite Charlie.

"Now this is what'll 'appen if you're all dead still an' keep your toes to the curb. I shall count to twelve, like the hours o' the clock, slowly, quietly but just loud enough for the spirit o' the departed to 'ear. It's when I say twelve, the last count, that from this urn below me, a hand'll come, raised, reaching out, a gnarled hand of a tormented soul. Yer must all keep your eyes on the urn and make no movement or sound, do yer understand?"

Nine heads nodded in unison, their eyes wide open like a rabbit's in the beam of the lamp, as the smell of dog grew closer. Bobby's hand inside his pocket clasped his favourite tin soldier, he felt a warm sensation as a dribble of wee reached his leg.

"One, two, three," with five seconds between each Joe counted. "Six, seven."

Inside their boots the soles of their feet arched with every tightening breath.

"Eight, nine."

Bobby turned and fled up the path, startling a roosting pigeon from its perch in the old yew tree.

Joe spoke again, "Ten, eleven."

Their desperation to be gone compelled the boys over the grave, in their haste they collided and tumbled but were out of sight in a trice. Only Jack Wainwright remained. Joe looked into the boy's eyes, deliberately. Jack gave an almighty sniff as if removing any possibility of a troublesome dewdrop causing the uncontrollable swipe of the upper lip with his sleeve, which might interfere with the manifestation.

Now Joe's eyes were trained down at the urn, as he formed his lips to utter the final count, Jack was gone, faster than Joe's delivery of the crucial 'twelve', the poor lad's boots merely glancing the ground in his urgency.

The church clock struck the half hour as a figure stepped out from behind a large memorial stone.

"You're a rotten bugger Joe Spooner, yer frighten 'em 'arf to death every time." Both men laughed roguishly.

"Tis only 'cause o' brother they believe me, they know our Tommy works at Handley's so what I tell 'em about the dead must be true."

"One day a bloody hand'll come out 'o that soddin' urn and scare the shit out o' you Joe Spooner, mark my words."

Ray and Joe laughed their way along Forest Road, they had become mates since finding themselves working similar shifts at the hospital. Disenchanted with the sewage works, Joe jumped at the chance of something more uplifting, many would argue that his current job in the hospital mortuary was far from that but Joe believed that his brother's description of dignity in death was a good enough recommendation for the work, besides Joe found the peace of those in his charge favourable to the unrest on the streets. Ray worked the hospital incinerator, 'I'd rather be in 'ere where I can't smell the bloody chimney than outside where you can' was his verdict on the matter. Often, when they went for a pint at The Standard, some wag would call out, ' 'ere come hot an' cold'.

"That Jack Wainwright's a gritty little bugger, a chip off the old block sure enough. They reckon Steve Wainwright is goin' to speak at the meetin' next week, you got to admire his effort but what good it'll do remains to be seen," said Ray.

"You can't get blood from a stone nor a shred o' compassion from hard hearted bastards neither, that's what I say." Joe sniffed and took a crumpled bag from his jacket pocket." 'Ere 'ave a chunk o' nougat, it's a sight cheaper than a pint an' it'll stop the urge when we walk past The Standard."

Only on a Friday night did they grant themselves a pint of beer, taken in two half measures to spread this small reward for their labours. They were among the lucky ones, each having a job of their own. Some men shared work, agreeing between them who should do the first half of the week and which man should take up the other half. In fact 'arf had become a significant word in 1920's language. Men and women looking across the divide at the healthy, well fed, well heeled of the species, who seemed ever to be immune to those afflictions ailing their 'arf, rounded conversation with a hefty sigh of acceptance and the words, ' 'ow the other 'arf live', rather as those who prayed ended their commune with God, 'Thy will be done'.

Some of the younger men harboured resentment, not yet ready to say Amen, their antipathy created a tension that prevailed the streets like the weather, interludes of calm, periods of storm, a climate described by the weatherworn Winnie Bacon as being, 'every day the same, never two days alike,' a contradiction which made absolute sense.

Whatever folk thought of the miners two years ago, when in the eyes of some, these militant workers were set on bringing the place to its knees, now bearing witness to abject poverty most saw them as victims of unmitigated greed and manipulation.

"They reckon Smithfield'll stand for council again after all, 'e's took a might o' persuadin', some folk thought 'e'd make a good Mayor but 'e flatly refused to be nominated. Looks likely Cheetham'll get that. Why do we suddenly need a Mayor anyroad, we've 'ad a bloody Sheriff for years, I would 'ave thought 'e wer' enough, a dog can cope wi' the odd flea but when the buggers multiply the poor cur gets robbed o' too much blood. Me uncle Sid says, 'parasites lad, nowt but parasites,' if yer manage to scratch 'em off one place they'll 'op straight back on at another. Poor uncle Sid, talk about long sufferin', if I wer' wed to a woman like me aunty Vi, I'd sod off to join Foreign Legion, she'd likely track 'im down even in bloody desert. She's trained their bulldog to sniff 'im out 'o whichever pub 'e's hidin' in. Poor old bugger walked all the way to The Wheatsheaf last Sunday, even paddled across Upton ford to shake Dempsey off the scent, but 'arf past one in 'e come, slaverin' an' pantin', coverin' every poor sod in drivel as 'e sniffed their trouser leg til 'e found Sid, 'arf way through 'is pint an' by all accounts 'arf way down barmaid's cleavage, mind it was Minnie Clegg an' she's known for 'er hospitality."

4

Joe stopped at the entry.

"See you in the mornin' then Ray, 'ow's it goin' wi' Monica? Susie reckons you're in wi' a chance there."

Joe winked and rubbed his hands together. Ray wasn't sure if the gesture suggested Joe was feeling chill or if his friend's imagination raced ahead of them both. Looking endearingly bashful Ray responded with a simple.

"Alright."

Joe slapped him on the shoulder and laughed wickedly.

"When she gives yer one of 'er custard slices, you're in."

Uhm, the latter thought Ray! Monica Salmon worked in the confectionary department of Burton's in the arcade, a job many believed Hannibal Burton had created for the struggling young woman, to ease the tensions following her father's suicide. One of the more vociferous during the disputes, Clifford Salmon had been unable to reconcile his convictions after his nineteen year old son, incited by his dad's rallying cries, joined a scuffle on Alfreton Road and fell under the hooves of a police horse. He died two days later of a brain haemorrhage.

Joe hung his jacket behind the scullery door, the sound of fire crackling and the 'clickety clack' of knitting needles reassured him. Edith Spooner had survived an alarming spell of bronchitis the previous winter, for some weeks afterwards, Joe entered the house with trepidation, ever nervous of what he might find. The three youngest, like him, still lived at home. Tommy, his older brother was married to Rosie and rented a tiny place, close to his work at the undertakers. Kathleen too had married, a chap who worked at Players, Ernie Searle. Joyce had moved with the family from The Ropewalk where she'd worked as a daily, to Loughborough. Joe had always been unconvinced by her explanation that Mr.& Mrs.Fosterjohn had become so accustomed to Joyce that they were reluctant to appoint a stranger to their new home. Joe had witnessed, albeit only the once, Lionel Fosterjohn clamp his palm firmly on Joyce's rump and the excited giggle that had erupted from the dutiful Joyce suggested it was not such a surprise. He couldn't at that time voice his concerns to Tommy. Rosie had recently suffered a miscarriage at the three month stage. Besides, any attempt at dissuading Joyce from her chosen course would have proved futile. She had always been the defiant one, digging in her heels at any opposition. Joe could remember the dreadful scene she'd created when their mam had told her she was too young to wear rouge, it had reduced Edith to tears and his rebellious sister had flounced through the door with cheeks like over ripe plums. These days Joe tried to steer stress away from his mam, one night spent in a police cell some years back, had instilled in him the firm belief that his mam deserved better.

Joe leaned over to kiss his mam's forehead, then moved to stand directly in front of her. Talking slowly, mouthing the words carefully, he asked.

"Where are the others Mam?"

Her deafness after all these years seemed to lull her into a silent old age for which she bore no resentment, her own small world, her own peace. She smiled back at Joe, lay her wool and needles in her lap, took his hands between her own and said.

"You're cold Son, warm yourself over the fire, I've a nice hotpot in the oven. Trevor's at Boys Brigade, Brian's gone to meet Pat off the bus, she's bringing the crib home tonight."

Pat worked in the city centre at Moffat's, the shop sold a variety of goods, all secondhand but in good condition. The sign above the window proudly declared 'nearly new'. The family had all chipped in, sending money with Pat each week until the crib was paid for. Kathleen's baby was due in a fortnight.

Joe held out his hands over the hearth turning them, like Pat turned the pikelets on a Sunday teatime, his fingertips tingled as the heat dispelled the numbness. One day he would sit before his own hearth with Susie, they had grown up always knowing each other and their feelings developed over the years, not ever undergoing any kind of revelation but sure, as certain as day and night. It was only Joe's devotion to his mam that delayed his plans to marry, she needed him, although not once had she told him so. Joe believed it to be, nevertheless.

The back door latch rattled and with a gust of cold air, in came Brian carrying the upended crib, Pat followed with a bag of shopping. She spoke at once, animated by events.

6

"What a miserable bugger the conductor was, 'where do you think you're goin' wi' that', 'e said, 'e stood on the footplate lookin' down at me like I wer' summat the cat 'ad dragged in, if it weren't for Mona Dallymore, I reckon I'd still be standin' there. She picked up the crib, said 'excuse me', pushed 'im aside an' wedged it in the stairwell. Yer know what a size Mona is, 'e wer' leanin' back against the handrail wi' 'is knees bucklin' as 'e tried to put a few inches o' decency between 'im an' Mona's bust. From where I stood on pavement 'e looked like Mona 'ad just spit 'im out. 'Two to Sherwood Road' she said, we're together'! We never 'eard another peep out of 'im."

Having finally hung up her coat and gathered her breath, Pat crossed the living room to stand in front of her mother.

"Are you alright Mam?" She asked speaking slowly as they had all become used to doing. Edith Spooner could lip read if folk were patient enough to allow her the chance.

"You didn't 'ave any bother with the conductor then?"

Pat glanced over at her brothers with a smile.

"No bother Mam, no bother at all." She replied, lifting the knitting from Edith's lap to admire the lace patterned matinee jacket, almost completed. "Rosie called in at the shop this afternoon, she usually works all day on a Wednesday, made out she wer' lookin' for a nice little framed print to give to Celia for 'er birthday but I got the feelin' she wanted to tell me summat. She chose a picture o' two kittens playin' wi' a ball o' wool, I wrapped it up real slow, took time over getting' 'er change an' still she left wi' out sayin' owt. Do yer think she might o' missed, she wer' lookin' a bit pale."

Edith Spooner sighed.

"Poor Tommy, 'e wants nothin' more than to give the lass a baby but 'e's afraid summat might go wrong again, I see it in 'is eyes, like the day 'e started school, that look that said, 'make it alright mam', I couldn't change anythin' then an' I can't now. Lay the table Pat, the boys must be hungry, Trevor'll be home any minute."

After the miscarriage Rosie had been depressed, she seemed to blame herself and trying to convince her it was nothing she had done took several months. Tommy at times, heard her muttering to herself anxiously but he couldn't persuade her to tell him what it was that troubled her so. Eventually her spirits lifted but now she never spoke of motherhood, almost as though in disregarding it, fate would best decide. Only William Eddowes had some insight on Rosie's state of mind. All those years ago when he'd used her so selfishly just to release his own tensions, he'd paid little regard for the consequences. When she'd miscarried Rosie thought it must surely be retribution from God. Tommy, in his distress, had told his old friend William of Rosie's non-sensical ramblings, searching as he was for some reassurance that all would be well. William had responded in a way only William could, insensitive as he was, by sending his own wife Celia to call on Rosie, to offer womanly support and comfort. Celia had proved stoic, unaware of past events she bore Rosie's anguished weeping and wailing with strength and patience beyond her years. Ironically, they had grown close, finding an easy friendship in one another. As often as they could they spent time together.

William and Celia had been married a little over three years, she too craved a baby but William had been quite firm on the subject, declaring it must wait until they had a sensible amount of money behind them. They lived in a small, rented house on Glover Street. Celia was willing Rosie to conceive again in the belief that William would then agree to try for a baby so the two young women might share the duties and pleasures of motherhood.

William had progressed in the employ of Andrew Smithfield at Brassington and now worked as a foreman in the print shop. The factory had fared better than most during the strike period. Smithfield paid well, the workforce recognised their boss's regard, this along with the fact that the textile trade was never to be fully embroiled in the troubles as the mines had become, enabled a steady production with only a slight interruption whilst various authorities conferred.

Andrew Smithfield had somewhat reluctantly, stood for council in the early twenties and been elected but the divisive policies, as he perceived them to be, rendered him disillusioned and he'd stepped down following the disputes. People trusted him, his manner charming, almost self effacing, his smile was given as readily to the elderly woman, shuffling away from the pawn shop, as it was to the well groomed ladies leaving their bridge afternoon. Now the people felt they were without representation, Smithfield had been pressured to stand again. William observed developments keenly, Smithfield was his template, the pattern he had chosen for his own. What he had failed to recognise was the importance of the fabric, too light and the pattern would not hold.

There was to be a meeting in St.Andrews hall the following Monday evening. Moderate members of the union had appealed for an open discussion, inviting pit owners and management, councillors and other employers, in fact all interested parties to attend. William relished the prospect, he'd heard that Steve Wainwright was to speak and that most trades would be represented. Part of him hoped for a noisy showdown, a six of one, half dozen of the other exchange, which resulted in little advancement, a measure of humiliation for those he disliked, a modest feather in the cap of those he favoured and a continuing unrest, which in his lack of wit, he believed gave him more opportunity the climb the ladder unnoticed whilst the rest squabbled. He had instigated a debate between his father and his brothers a couple of weeks ago. Celia had insisted they go to Gregory Street that evening to take a card and gift for Annie. 'Your mother's birthday should be most important to you, never mind all the political goings on!' Celia was very fond of her mother in law, her own mother could be tiresome in her relentless pursuit of intrigue, whereas Annie Eddowes held no such desire for gossip. Charles Eddowes however could be daunting, ill humoured and ungracious. It was not something Celia admitted readily but William did possess a great deal of his father's nature. Love was a strange thing indeed she had come to believe. Celia must force herself to embrace Charles with any feeling, yet William she loved dearly. One day she felt quite sure, such an intrigue so close to home her mother would seize upon with zeal. What a curious melting pot life was, the elements within so diverse, could they ever blend or would some forever resist, 'every day the same, never two days alike'.

CHAPTER TWO

Jack Haynes stubbed out his cigarette end on the gatepost, the light inside the hall, from the open doors at the far end of the path, reminded him of that glimpse of heaven he saw above him, when at the end of a shift, the cage neared the top. Yet the low toned babble of men's voices, drifted out like the beginning of a growl from a wide mouthed predator. As he drew closer he could define more clearly the sound. Intense conversation, interspersed with coughing. Jack was convinced that miners coughed differently to everybody else. So accustomed had they become to the involuntary eruptions, that the convulsed chest, the shaking of the shoulders, the desperate need to spit and the long exhaust of air that followed every spasm, was accepted by all as commonplace. Yet when Robert Cheetham hacked his way through the Christmas Carol concert, some folk declared, 'the poor man was stoic he should have been wrapped up in bed'.

Llewellyn Reece was on the door, determined to get every last satisfaction from the half inch of roll-up, protruding from his fingers like a spent Bengal Match on bonfire night.

"Good turn out Taff?" Asked Jack.

"I reckon, all them as you'd expect anyroad."

He sniffed and contorted his nose as if to clear his airways of the blackened mucous they all seemed to accumulate underground, or at least to shift it from its resting place.

"Me mother, God bless 'er, wer' a professional attender, she went to every wake whether she knew the poor sod or not. Mam allus took 'er black felt hat out o' cupboard and put it over the biscuit barrel on the sideboard the day 'afore the 'do'. The warmth o' the livin' room got rid o' the musty ol' smell. Anythin' that come out o' cupboards upstairs smelled o' damp, if there'd been a healthy spell an' she'd not needed hat for a couple o' weeks, then she'd 'ave to brush the mould off it an'all. Me father used to come in from work an' say, 'Bloody Hell lad, another one for plantin' then'." Amazingly Llewellyn achieved one final draw on his fag. "There's most room over in top corner by the windo', stand over there for very long an' you'll freeze to death, bloody draught enough to cut a man in 'arf."

Jack looked around the gathering, a row of chairs had been set out at the top end of the hall, to one side of the piano. A banner made by The Women's Fellowship hung on the wall behind the chairs. In bright blue and yellow it proclaimed, 'In God We Trust'. No doubt the dignitaries were being kept safely out of sight until the assembly was in place and the church clock struck seven thirty. As much seating as was possible to provide had been positioned about the floor but most men preferred to stand. Jack made his way to the draughty corner, nodding acknowledgement to a small number of men he knew by sight but not well, and smiled to himself at his perfect timing. The sound level suddenly dropped as the invited managers and councillors were led to the front by Robert Cheetham. Llewellyn closed the heavy doors and joined a group of men, which included Steve Wainwright. Andrew Smithfield had declined to take his seat at the top of the hall, instead, he stood quietly, not far from Jack Haynes.

Steve Wainwright heard a voice behind him say in a lowered tone.

"Look up, Shylock's 'ere."

Basil Stanford, owner of Birchdale pit, sat third from the right, a quick scan along the line of faces confirmed the rest were managers, some from the mines, Raleigh, Players, Briggs Engineering and council representatives from various departments.

Cheetham remained standing, he cleared his throat, looked briefly to either side of him and then to the front.

"Gentlemen, any opportunity to exchange views, provided each mind is open and receptive to another, should be welcomed by us all. I would remind you that we are gathered in the church hall, as such, it is expected of every one of us, that differences of opinion be aired in a proper manner, with respect for one another and for The Almighty by whose grace we are sheltered from the biting elements outside. I

11

understand that Mr.Steve Wainwright is to speak on behalf of The Union so I hereby call on him to open the debate."

Cheetham's gaze crossed the hall to where Steve stood.

"Perhaps you might like to move forward to the front Mr.Wainwright?"

"With respect Mr.Cheetham I prefer to stand in the middle."

Steve moved several paces until his position in the hall was more or less central. "The men I work with and those I know well will pardon me if I don't face them when I speak, my back is no insult to them, of that they hold no doubt, but those men I know of, but have no real knowledge for, them I choose to address directly."

Smithfield perceived Steve's diplomacy in taking the middle place, it was ever difficult to hold that position, pulled as one so often was by elements from all quarters. Steve nodded towards Henry Wicks.

"There's one exception to my last remark. Mr.Wicks, you've been manager at the pit for most of the years I've worked there and I started at Birchdale when I left school. I reckon after that number of years you must know my foibles pretty well, an' I'd venture to say that I know yours an'all."

Henry Wicks gave a faint smile and nodded his head in agreement. Steve continued.

"We all forget things from time to time, for the most part it makes little difference. Silly, simple things, like forgettin' somethin' the missus asked us to pick up from shop on the way home, or needin' to post a letter an' findin' the envelope still in jacket pocket at teatime. Just a decade ago our men fought for this land. They fought like dogs to the death to keep this nation free. Well I see their freedom, that same pride that drove their spirit then, drives them now to weep and there are some that would scoff, mistakin' it for weakness, laugh, they even laugh, but whose is the shame?

My brother Henry never come back from France, nothin' unusual about that, scores o families could tell yer the same thing. My brother Samuel did come back. I remember our mam's face, her expression as she wrapped her arms around him. Now some of you will know me mam, tiny she is, yet all us lads are great big blokes. Her arms barely reached Samuel's waist, she clung to him an' in spite of her size, if anybody had tried to prise him away, I don't believe they would have managed to budge him one inch. She wer' that happy yet she cried bitter, the tears were for Henry. That night, mam lay in bed thankin' God but she could hear sound comin' from Samuel's room, he wer' cryin' When she went to him, he spoke almost like a child, 'I can't stand the dark mam, I can't stand the dark'. That's what he said. Mam put a 'nightlite' in his bedroom, it must have been weeks afore he let her take it away, but no one scoffed, nobody laughed. That same pride now makes men afraid o' the darkness o' despair, they can't stand the poverty, the hurt, yet we forget, how soon we forget.

There are children in this city that go hungry, suffer cold. Ask Davey Jones why he looks forward to Thursdays. He'll tell you it's because he gets the boots then, his brother Stewart wears them for the first 'arf the week an' Davey gets 'em back for the other 'arf. A bare ten years ago we gloried in victory. What does this triumphant country declare to the world now? Does winning mean that it doesn't matter that our children are unfed, do we stand so tall as a nation that sharing boots is of no consequence? These men around me aren't fools, they understand that the books must balance an' that labour costs dear but they have eyes and those who scoff do their scofffin' in fine, tailored waistcoats over well fed bellies. They walk with leather enough beneath their feet to protect them from each grit an' gravel that would gall the soles. But every man is a servant of age. Whether five pound notes lay tidily in his wallet or copper jangles noisily in his pocket, when his head falls to his chest at the last, nothin' separates him from the next. No divide, no other 'arf but one an' the same in death.

Today's hungry child is tomorrow's labour, they must surely be as vital an investment as the land and the machinery. Who else will keep it all goin'? 'The labourer is worthy of his hire', not legislation in a Trade's Union rule book but an edict from management, top management, your rule book gentlemen."

Steve paused and looked from one to the other of the seated men at the front of the hall.

"Every pair of idle hands is a loss to this country, idle minds are a threat. Our finest asset is 'The People', in them lays unmeasured opportunity. No machine to create, nor weapon to destroy has the potential of the human mind, use it for the good and we all shall know the benefit, allow it to languish without purpose and we lay ourselves open to a destruction not from outside these shores but from within, of our own makin'. Ponder upon it, I ask that you at least ponder upon it. It is human to forget the incidental, we might be excused that, but to forget and furthermore to disregard the profound is to our eternal shame. The men, their wives and children need to know they are valued. You gentlemen are the only ones able to give them an answer. Thank you."

Steve turned to walk back to his original place. An uproar of cheering and applause rose in volume. Steve raised his arm and shouted above the noise.

No, no, you applaud nothin'."

He stood on a chair and cried out over their heads.

"Quiet, be quiet."

A hush descended and a sea of bewildered faces looked at him.

"I have asked a question, only when it is answered fairly should we respond with any emotion. The answer may not come tonight or even next week but these gentlemen know we are waiting, Mr.Wicks wont forget, will you sir?" Steve directed the question at his boss, willing him to speak to the men.

Henry Wicks rose to his feet, walked forward several paces, casting his eyes around the hall as if mentally recording where stood any likely moral support, aware that he cut a lonely figure.

"You are right Steve Wainwright, we do know one another's foibles. Perhaps by the end of this meeting some of those who know each other merely by name might leave this place feeling they have learned of some character, a measure of substance they can attach to those names. It may take many years to recognise foibles as in the case of you and me but we must begin somewhere. I've lived and breathed the pit, you see me as apart from yourselves," he looked around the gathering once more, inwardly he felt a sudden relief. Unable to spot him until now, his eyes at last caught sight of Andrew Smithfield, "but I'm not so very different."

A murmur of sarcasm drifted among the men, albeit briefly, if Wicks was going to speak then they wanted to hear what he had to say.

"For years the mine workings have woven forth an' back below the surface of this city, like veins threading beneath the skin, carrying life blood."

A voice called out from the floor.

"It took life an'all, it bloody well took life."

Robert Cheetham looked anxious and fingered his watch chain, Stanford gazed down into his lap and fidgeted his feet. Wicks spoke again.

"Yes, it's taken lives and if you asked me to, I could name every single one of them. I went to one house, many years ago now, that envelope, his last pay was in my pocket. Inside that house were his widow Margaret and four kiddies, all close in age. Josh, Ben, Laura and the baby Elizabeth. Margaret looked at me like I'd murdered George, her eyes blamed me as if I'd killed him with my own bare hands. George was my half brother. But despite all that, men have put food on the table and fire in the hearth, kept a roof over their heads, only because of the pit. Now circumstances, external influences, which we in management must answer to but have no power to change, weaken the system, thin the blood, they create the vulnerability. The strength of sterling makes export nigh impossible, reparation policy after the war took free coal from Germany to the allied countries, we consumed so much of our own product to fuel the war effort that others jumped in to fill the void created elsewhere. The mines alone cannot now take up the slack. Employment must come from other sources."

Wicks paused and looked across the hall to Smithfield.

"You must lobby those who represent you, those who have already called for more housing, better roads. All this can only be achieved by an increase in labour. God knows we need housing, while the canal is fine for transporting coal, other goods need to move in and out of the city much faster and the railway is too rigid from one point to the next to enable deliveries to customers not directly along it's route. The ring road needs to be progressed more urgently, council housing should be a priority."

"That's right Wicks, pass the buck." Came one mocking voice, another called out.

"Waitin' for a council 'ouse are yer Mr.Stanford?" Smithfield moved forward between the men, he reached the front where Wicks stood looking despairingly at the ceiling. Someone whistled, a ripple of applause was quickly checked by Smithfield when he spoke.

"What Mr.Wicks has just told you is, for the most part correct."

"What's the part that isn't then, tell us about that?" The remark came from Jack Haynes. The hall fell silent.

"Housing schemes have already begun, yes there is a need for more and the ring road does offer a greater opportunity to the trades, it must move more quickly towards completion. If the mines are the veins, then the ring road will be the lungs, taking congestion from the heart of the city, making it better able to function. However, all these things come at a cost. Men go to work to bring home the pay, women plan and budget. You may disagree with me gentlemen when I say that very soon, I believe, women will be given the vote. In my view it will be none too soon."

"Bloody easy for you to say Smithfield, you've not got a missus!" Llewellyn Reece injected a welcome note of humour, it lightened the mood, Smithfield laughed, easily.

"I would nevertheless welcome female guidance on matters of local authority finance. Women look ahead, they grasp the fact that a long term strategy will often meet the demands of an immediate crisis. They put by whenever they can, often taking from the man of the house more than ideally he wants to hand over. Mother has to feed the children, clothe them, keep them warm, instruct them in good manners and civility. Then one day father sees the reward for his investment, he begins to enjoy the return.

In the council chamber I have heard the term 'City Fathers'. Perhaps it is time the city fathers made their investment. All that is required for expansion and development cannot come from the taxpayers' purse alone. As I approached this hall tonight, someone asked if I was to speak, I answered 'no'. 'You should', they said, 'folk listen to you'. It is not to me that you should listen but to your own conscience."

He looked directly across to Basil Stanford. Cheetham noticed at once and stood.

"Perhaps you would care to say something Mr.Stanford?"

Robert Cheetham extended the invitation politely, hoping for some response that might encourage progress.

Basil Stanford seemed nervous, ill at ease, he shook his head and in a voice barely audible replied.

"No."

Boos and sounds of derision rose from the men, it was Steve Wainwright who once more called them to order.

"There are two other mine owners who could have been here tonight, they were invited but only Mr.Stanford chose to attend. We shall not overlook that in making futile gestures. He came, he listened, he knows we await a response, the men need more Mr.Stanford, more recognition, more pay and more hope, most importantly they need your answer."

As Steve spoke the last few words, bells, urgent bells of a fire engine could be heard in the street, approaching louder, then gone into the distance.

Cheetham seized on the opportunity to call the meeting closed, thanking all those present. Openly relieved that no violence had erupted or verbal abuse reached heights of unacceptability.

Llewellyn opened the heavy doors, the night air rushed the threshold, besieging the first to exit and causing those further back to steel themselves, raising their collars, pulling old woollen scarves across their throats to repel the chill.

William Eddowes had entered the hall, literally as Llewellyn pulled the doors closed, creeping unnoticed to the gloom of a corner, behind a pillar, intent on hearing every word but not choosing to be obvious. Now, lowering his cap and drifting out among a huddle of older men, he made his way to where he had seen Smithfield's car, parked around the corner in Forest Road. He leaned against the driver's door, felt in his pocket for a cigarette, briefly smiled at the packet of Players Navy Cut, lit one and feeling smugly content, waited for his boss. He could detect sounds, noisy activity in the distance. He stood erect, listening, it came from the direction of Winchester Street he felt sure. Banging, like vehicle doors, men's raised voices. The old pot bellied stove at the workshop, had the women not left it safe when they'd gone home. William's thoughts raced ahead of him. Footsteps approaching fired his concern and when Smithfield appeared under the beam of the street lamp William stubbed out his cigarette, throwing half away in the gutter, calling out urgently.

"I reckon the fire is somewhere near the workshop. The sounds are coming from that way. We best take a look don't you think sir?" His hand already gripping the handle of the car door.

"It is not necessary that you should trouble yourself William, the hour is late, Celia will be anxious, so often such gatherings as the meeting tonight lead to tension and agitation on the streets. You go home to your wife. I'll drive by the workshop before heading out to Brassington. It is more than likely to be a chimney fire at one of the houses. Edna is ever thorough in checking the stove before she locks up. The temperature is very low tonight, I dare say that someone has been tempted to make too much blaze in the grate. I have needed to caution aunt Alicia more than once in recent weeks. Rather than move from the hearth to fetch a blanket for her knees she will pile high the logs and coal, it is so easily done, catching alight the soot in the chimney. I'll see you in the morning, goodnight William."

He got into the drivers seat, turned the ignition and revved the engine, it had gone cold in the time he'd spent in the hall, thankfully he'd not needed to resort to the starting handle. Raising his hand to wave, he drove away, leaving William disgruntled on the pavement. It would take him no more than ten minutes to walk to the end of Forest Road where it joined Glover Street. He kicked a bottle top into the storm drain and huffed his annoyance. William's sense of his own importance, of Smithfield's reliance on him had been bruised by the dismissal, albeit courteous.

"It'll be alright Winnie, you come wi' me an' let them take Ted to the hospital. I'll get word to your Elsie but let's get off the street, you're shakin' like a leaf an' so am I."

Edna pulled the blanket around Winnie Bacon's shoulders and led her away from the scene. Winnie's cries of despair hung on the cold air, her breathing raced in her panic, far too quickly for a woman of Winnie's years. The brigade was damping down, it had taken but minutes to extinguish the blaze. Fortunately it had not spread beyond the living room, just a few more minutes and it would have caught alight the curtain at the foot of the stairs trapping Winnie above. A familiar voice spoke out of the darkness.

"What can I do to help Edna?"

"Mr.Smithfield?" Edna was surprised by his presence. "Whatever brings you here at this hour?"

"Never mind that now, shall we take the good lady inside and make her a cup of hot sweet tea."

His concern was entirely genuine, Winnie's appearance was alarming, her feet would scarcely work, so uncoordinated had she become through shock.

At last, by the warmth of Edna's hearth and with the door closed to the curious number, gathered on the cobbles of the street, Winnie calmed and fell silent.

Edna spoke to her daughters.

"Put the kettle on Susie," turning to the other she asked, "has Myra slept through it?"

"Yes Mam, not a sound from her."

Edna had sat Winnie in Billy's chair, poking the grate to send heat to her shivering, frightened old neighbour.

"Stay 'ere with Winnie for a minute Liza, I need to talk to Mr.Smithfield."

Edna led him to the scullery where Susie had the kettle singing on the range and cups with milk and sugar at the ready.

"Their daughter Elsie is the nearest, their son lives at Long Eaton an' the other daughter's at Mapperley. Could yer go to Elsie, to tell 'er what's 'appened."

Edna lowered her voice. "I think Ted's in a bad way, it wer' the look the ambulance man giv' me when 'e said, 'I don't think the wife should go in the ambulance'. 'E shook 'is head like there wer' little hope."

Edna's voice wavered. Smithfield took her hand.

"Would you like me to find Billy at the exchange after I've taken Mrs.Bacon's daughter to the hospital?"

"I'm alright an' there'll be no problem in the mornin', I can find some clothes for Winnie an' our Liza'll be at home 'til dinnertime. Billy's usually 'ere afore I leave to open up anyroad, I can explain it all to 'im then."

"Don't worry about your work in the morning Edna, just unlock the workshop for the others and see to things here. Now where do I find Elsie?"

"Melton Road No.6, next door to Mavis and Eddie. Tell 'er not to worry about 'er mam, Winnie's safe 'ere wi' me."

Edna breathed a sigh of relief as she closed the door on Andrew Smithfield, she trusted his sensitivity, he would do all he could to bolster poor Elsie's spirit.

It was Ted's habit to have one last pipe of baccy before settling for the night. Winnie was always first to bed, not surprisingly, she busied herself between various members of the family constantly, Edna imagined that by 8o'clock of an evening, Winnie's bones demanded some respite. Whether Ted had fallen asleep and dropped his pipe or something more drastic had befallen him Edna could not know but the blaze at his chair, on the far side of the hearth, opposite the foot of the stairs where Winnie most often sat, despite its intense heat had not roused him in time to move from the danger. It had been the smell of smoke that stirred the dozing Winnie and the bright, dancing light, evident through the narrow gap down one side of the heavy curtain when she'd looked down the stairs.

Poor Winnie, she had run outside to the street, clad in just her nightdress, her worn slippers, almost tripping her where the sole flapped loose at the front. Her screams alerted neighbours, looking out from behind the blinds all they could see was a ghost like figure in full length, faded cream flannelette, long grey hair falling about the shoulders, waving their arms franticly.

Bill Shipley from No.12 had managed to decipher the word 'fire' and courageously rushed inside, smothering the burning chair and clothing about Ted, before attempting to douse the flames that crept along the rug and lapped at the table legs.

The fire brigade arrived and the ambulance soon after. Winnie had been frantic as they carried the stretcher through her front door. It was a sad truth that for most families, any use of the front door was almost certainly a source of worry. Debt collectors, the police, school inspector, telegram boy, all knocked at the front. Edna had often remarked that the grim reaper allus banged his fist at the front door. When her mam died, it was James Handley who stood at the step of No.24. For weeks after Edna couldn't bear to answer any knocking at the front of the house, she imagined all manner of destruction and demise following her mam's funeral. It was Annie, her dearest friend who finally reassured her. Edna had declared, 'one whiff o' death, an' afore yer know it, me daft 'ead is up through the clouds, lookin' round for sign to pearly gates'! Annie had taken Edna in her arms and said.

'I remember the day Billy led you over the threshold of your little house, it was an emotional time for us all, so close to Harold's funeral. But Billy used the front door, he was proud that day, Billy is still proud. Goodness rests often by your front step, Annie's scholarship, it was the headmaster who brought news of that to your front door'.

When their eldest daughter Annie had been given a scholarship to Clarendon Girls College, Edna and Billy had been overjoyed. Now working in Boot's offices and married to Reg Yeats' nephew, her prospects were good. It was more than Edna had ever dared hope for any of her girls.

Andrew peered through the gloom at the numbers on the front doors, finally finding No.6 Melton Road he knocked gently, not wishing to alarm anyone but aware of the urgency. After a minute or so, footsteps approached from within, the door opened slightly.

"Who is it?"

"Don't be alarmed, I'm Andrew Smithfield, I have just come from Winchester Street. Edna Dodds has sent me. Your father has had an accident and been taken to hospital."

At once the door was opened wide.

"What about me mother, Is me mam alright? Lillian, Lillian." A young woman now stood behind Elsie. "Tell Jack when he gets back from the meetin' that I've gone to the hospital, grandad's had an accident."

Elsie ran through to the scullery, grabbed her coat from the hook and began to thank Andrew Smithfield for his trouble, expecting him to depart.

"My dear, I shall take you to the hospital, that is the very least I can do, I'm sorry, I don't know your name other than Elsie."

"Elsie Sulley sir, me husband is Jim Sulley, works away at Barrow. Jack our youngest and his wife Lillian live with me."

She sat in the car, gripping feverishly at the buttons of her coat. So much trouble, there seemed always to be trouble, if only Jim were home. Elsie's thoughts kept her silent as they travelled into the city to the hospital and to whatever awaited her there.

Jim Sulley had returned from the 'Front' unscathed, his young nephew also, the war had ripped the heart out of so many families Winnie had declared, 'blessed we are, blessed'. Jim and Elsie were a happily married couple, always content in one another's company, so it was a cruel fate that took him away for much of the time. Having a brother living and working in Barrow enabled him to secure a job with Vickers at the shipyard, the alternative would likely have been unemployment. He lodged with his brother's family and came home one weekend each month. Elsie, being a loyal wife, chose not to tell Jim of the problems their youngest son created.

Through the time of the disputes, while not being a hard liner, leading the rallies, inciting agitation, he had ever been on the edge of troubles, ready to stir, almost as if he enjoyed the friction. He had developed the reputation of being unemployable and was among a number of men, perpetually denied work since the strike was broken. He picked up a few days labouring here and there when he could but the extended period of idleness had taken away any small measure of work ethic

Jack Sulley ever had. When he'd put Lillian in the family way, Elsie had near' despaired and Lillian's father had told Jack that 'he would make an honest woman of her or else'!

Elsie could not keep from Jim this situation but Lillian was a very pleasant, mild mannered young woman and another grandchild, even if earlier than expected, presented no real cause for regret. Jim did his best to bring home a little extra each month and since the young couple's wedding, just over twelve months ago, they had lived at No.6 with Elsie. In fact the baby was a great comfort to her, having the baby and Lillian about the house saved her from lonely nights. Jack often disappeared for hours at a time, both women had discovered it best not to question his whereabouts. As a lad his grandfather Ted had threatened many times to give him a damn good hidin', and Jack indeed experienced Ted's slipper across his backside but when the 'lad' became 'youth' and eventually 'young man' Winnie tried desperately to pour oil on troubled waters, Jack had a temper! Ted's frustration and Winnie's anxiety had taken their toll on the old couple.

"Will you be alright if I leave you at the hospital Mrs.Sulley?" Andrew Smithfield's question drew Elsie from her quietness.

"Yes, of course, you must be anxious to be on your way home. I'd hoped we might pass Jack as he walked back from the meetin', that's where he said he was goin'."

"I was at the meeting myself, the hall was almost full, I didn't linger but I'm sure some of the men would have briefly discussed events and exchanged views before going their separate ways. Lillian will tell him what has happened, he will likely come to the hospital to find you."

He parked the car in the area designated, a few yards from the main entrance and quickly walked around to open the car door for Elsie. He steadied her arm as she stepped out. It was the most incongruous of thoughts and given the circumstances, entirely inappropriate but he could be no other than amazed by the length of Elsie's feet, he had never seen such elongated shoes on any woman!

"I am so very grateful to you sir, so very grateful."

He sensed she was close to tears.

"I shall walk with you to the door of the hospital, I do hope all will be well."
As she disappeared inside, he spoke the words quietly to himself. 'In God we trust'.

At last Smithfield reached Brassington, aunt Alicia would be concerned,
worried at his lateness but she was a tough old bird and would be appalled if when he
told her of this night's events, he could not declare his assistance in the matter.
Sometimes he felt Alicia would live to be 100, still waving her stick in military like
command when Andrew himself had become too tired, too feeble to respond. He felt
exceeding' weary some days. The factory was doing as well as he could hope in the
current situation. It amused him somewhat, that folk obviously believed him to be
very wealthy, up there with the Burtons and Cheethams of this world. When in fact, he
ploughed much of the profit straight back into the business. He kept the bank happy
but added little to his own purse other than in the value of the business itself, which he
was aware, could tumble dramatically if market forces turned.
William Eddowes he felt sure, imagined he was in the employ of, 'a city father'.
Sometimes this young man displayed considerable intelligence, a good brain, an able
mind, which Smithfield admired. At other times William disheartened him through his
lack of discernment, his harsh disregard for his fellow man.

Celia turned her head on the pillow to gaze at her husband, not speaking,
simply gazing. He'd said little since coming home from the meeting, pensive, Celia
deemed him to be. She too held thoughts but was far too inspired to allow containing
them.

"Rosie told me a confidence today, I know you will keep the secret and I
must tell you because it is so significant. Rosie has missed twice, she is sure by her
feelings that she is pregnant."
Celia moved her arm under the covers, working her fingers across his chest, she
played mischievously with the bristly hair that ran down to his belly button. She had
washed her hair and the soft scent of chamomile bathed her pillow.

24

"We are not so badly off, I have some money put by, just a little each week but you would be pleased by the amount. You have impressed Mr.Smithfield most surely, your earnings are more than most of your age. Please William can we try now?"

He turned his head to look into her face, showing no expression, giving her no hint as to his mood.

'Women grasp the need of a long term strategy, to answer problems of the immediate'.

Smithfield's words at the meeting drifted through William's head. He reached for the lamp and under cover of darkness, smiled his accord as he paid allegiance to the 'city father'.

Smithfield sat at his desk but in truth, not entirely present. He had slept hardly at all, the meeting, the fire, his journey to the hospital with Elsie Sulley, all had conspired to keep his mind from rest, his heart was elsewhere this morning.

A knock came at the office door, it was already ajar, William entered with an unusually bright.

"Good morning sir." Followed by the most eager delivery of news. "I thought you would want to hear the latest. Hell up, there's hell up in town."

"Why." Asked Smithfield, feeling obliged to respond with some small degree of curiosity. If there had been trouble after the meeting, he could muster scant sympathy given the miserable events at Winchester Street that he'd witnessed. William seemed animated, almost excited at whatever had caused this 'hell up'.

"It must have been done same time as the meeting, they'd have known that Lenton side of town would be quiet while that was kicking of at St.Andrew's. It was discovered this morning, that somebody stripped a pile of lead off St.Saviour's roof last night. You have to feel amused, there was Robert Cheetham reminding everybody to show respect for the church hall and all same time, somebody was stripping the lead from St.Saviour's. If I hadn't seen him with my own eyes I'd have said it most likely to have been Jack Haynes, he's a chancer, always has been but he was in the hall all the time, it was him asked you the question. You can imagine the fire turned out to be another distraction, they must have thanked their lucky stars when the brigade went out to Sherwood. Of course you'd know that the workshop was alright because of driving by on your way home. It was Ted and Winnie Bacon's house had the fire. The brigade soon had it out but not before Ted was burned, dead apparently. I'll get on with Jessop's order, make way for that batch of Vyella for Griffin's."

William turned to leave but Smithfield called him back.

"I don't think it wise to speculate on the identity of the perpetrator William. God knows there is desperation out there and men with desperate need commit acts they would not otherwise countenance. The constabulary are best equipped to pursue the matter, not ourselves."

William nodded.

"Quite right sir, they must know Jack Haynes' foibles, to use that good word."

He laughed, pulled the door to and took himself off to the print shop.

Smithfield leaned back in his chair, sighed and for a few seconds, closed his eyes but even that could not obliterate the sights that tormented him. When he opened his eyes again, a slight movement to his side caught his attention. A spider was intent on adding a few last threads of intricacy to its web, which attached to the gas mantle.

'The mines weave forth and back under the surface of this city, like veins beneath skin, carrying life blood'.

Henry Wicks' analogy. Here, along with the spider, the looms at his own Brassington factory, weave above the surface. He took his spectacles from their case, picked up the paper knife and opened the post. Whatever bills and demands were contained within, they could carry no misery comparable to that which surely now wove so cruelly about Winnie Bacon and her family.

CHAPTER THREE

"Did yer notice 'ow their Jack slunk off, like 'e couldn't wait to be gone. You'd think 'e'd 'ave stayed wi' Elsie, given that Jim's away. That poor woman runs 'erself ragged to keep 'im an' Lillian, not to mention the baby. At least the others showed some concern. What a state Winnie wer' in, I can't think she'll be stoppin' at Elsie's for long, not wi' that toe rag of a grandson to drive 'er mad. You should see the livin' room over there."

Edna paused in her chatter to look across the street to Winnie's house.

"Landlord don't want to know, I s'pose it'll wait 'til Jim can do summat. Billy's itchin' to get over there an' make a start, if only to give Winnie some heart but I told 'im, yer can't do everythin'. I noticed two brushes were on scullery shelf this mornin' an' a pot o' paint, I wouldn't be surprised if 'im an' Victor wer' in there now scrubbin' down, I know 'e's wheedled a key out of Elsie. God 'elp me, why is it allus Billy, anyroad I'll go an' stick the kettle on, you're stoppin' for a bit surely or won't 'is nibs let yer 'ave an hour off."

Edna turned towards the back yard giving Annie little alternative but to follow.

"I'll have just a quick cuppa then, Freddy is coming for his tea tonight and George won't be late home. I think he's taking Alice to the pictures, I'm not sure if it's to please her or himself. George seems to have lost his heart to Delores del Rio. He has her picture pinned to his bed." Annie chuckled.

"Well Alice'll 'ave to rub 'erself over wi' Cherry Blossom boot polish if she's to stand a chance then, I've never seen a young woman so pale, that del Rio piece is the colour o' toffee, I reckon she'd 'ave most o' the fellas suckin' on summat when their eyes are closed. 'Tis 'er middle I can't get over, talk about wasp waisted. Put a length o' clothes line round it an' tip 'er over, yer could play wi' 'er like a

Diablo. P'raps that's what George dreams o' doin' when 'e's lyin' in bed dribblin' at 'er picture."

Edna burst into raucous laughter, then immediately fell into a sober silence.

"Shame on me, we've only just buried Ted."

The kettle was soon on the range, first hanging her best hat and coat over the stair rail, Edna then made a hasty inspection of the scullery. "There what did I tell yer, me bucket an' scrubbin' brush are missin' an' me packet o' soda. "Edna tutted and shook her head as she took cups from the shelf. "I broke a cup last week, let it fall to the flags, I know it weren't best china or owt like that, but mam bought it for me from Waterfords. I keep the saucer up by me bed now, to put Rennies in."

Annie smiled, both Billy and Edna had the most generous nature. For all Edna's fussing, inwardly she would be relieved that her Billy was doing something to ease poor Winnie's plight. The tea was poured and ginger nuts offering comfort, dipped in the steaming cups, when the back door opened and Myra, home from school, bounced inside with her usual detailed account of the day's events.

"Did you know aunty Annie, that the Romans were the first to have a bath, years an' years ago. Bobby Budgeon reckons he hasn't had one yet, Miss Teague said she couldn't believe such a thing an' that Bobby wer' bein' silly but it is true 'cause he crossed his heart an' hoped to die when I asked him if he'd told Miss Teague a fib. He's afraid o' water because o' what happened when he wer' little. He wer' givin' some of his popcorn to the ducks at the embankment when he fell in, an' somebody fished him out wi' Eli Claythorpe's crutch. His mam got fed up wi' Bobby's tantrums every time she got the bath tub down from the hook so she decided to get him baptised at Ripley Baptist Church, that place where they dunk 'em under, she thought that would cure him once an' for all, safe in the arms o' Jesus. Anyroad, he turned blue in the water an' went stiff as a poker, frightened his mam to death so he's had nothin' but a lick and a promise ever since."

Myra's hand delved into the ginger nuts before planting a kiss on Annie's cheek. Edna had gone through to the scullery for a jug.

" 'Ere take this tea over to your dad, 'e's at Winnie's, walk slow an' don't slop it, tell 'im I said not to make 'isself late."

Myra carried the jug as though she held the magic lamp and was desperate not to wake the genie at rest within. Edna watched her safely through the door, returning to Annie with a hefty sigh.

"Billy'll leave it 'til last minute, gobble down 'is food an' rush off to the soddin' exchange. If I say owt 'e just laughs. 'I sit on me backside all night', that's what I 'ear if I tell 'im to rest up for a bit."

Annie took an envelope from her pocket and handed it to Edna.

"You can read that when I've gone, it's from Mabel, a lovely letter, she asks that I pass it on to you." Annie fastened her coat and pulled on her gloves. "I must go now Edna, the shop does get busy late afternoon when the men come in on their way home. I'll see you on Saturday shall I?"

"I'll be in for all me usuals, put a nice bit o' bacon by for me, Joe's comin' round on Sunday, I'll do a fry up."

Edna waved from the back step as Annie turned the corner of the house, then closed the door with a shiver.

"It'll be brass monkeys again tonight," she spoke aloud to herself, her thoughts returning to Winnie Bacon, hers was the very worst kind of cold. Edna set about making a meal for her family and thanked God.

Annie sat quietly in the bus that would take her to the top of Gregory Street. Funerals seemed always to evoke memories, so many had come flooding back at Bertha's. Charles had declined to attend, even the shop was favourable to an hour spent with those stirrings, deep within, which brought back a hurt no less consuming than the original. He'd suggested Annie represent them both, after all, through latter years it would have been inappropriate for Charles to have called on Bertha, her failing health and problems simply of old age, rendered the situation awkward for any male caller. The boys were now young men, even they had recognised that sad embarrassment an elderly lady suffered when the mind retained it's agility but the body failed in its bid. Only Annie and Hilda had continued to visit as often as they could until, quite unexpectedly, Bertha had passed away in her sleep.

Now it was vivid memories of her time with aunt Bella, as a neighbour to Winnie and Ted Bacon, that pulled Annie's thoughts away from Charles and the shop to that little house in Winchester Street, where she had progressed from childhood to adulthood amid such a mix of emotions it seemed unlikely that her mind would dwell for long on this chapter of her life, yet her heart embraced it, holding on tightly as the conductor's bell summoned passengers on and off the bus and the houses and shops, the gates and railings, passed before her eyes as she stared through the window at her side, not really registering the present but glimpsing scenes from the past. Random, unordered scenes, entirely without sequence or reason.

"Hello Annie." A young, cheerful voice and a sudden burst of activity dispelled at once her remoteness.

"Why Maggie, I didn't see you at the stop, let me help you," said Annie, taking a shopping bag from the struggling young woman and placing it at her feet before patting her lap for Maggie's elder daughter to clamber up, making room for her mother to sit beside them with the baby on her knee.

"You looked to be miles away," said Maggie, "we saw you at the window and Jennifer waved but you didn't notice." Maggie observed Annie's attire. "Oh, you've been to a funeral, was it Mr.Bacon?"

"Yes, I stopped at Edna's for a little while afterwards. What have you been up to then?" Said Annie, directing the question more at Jennifer than at Maggie.

"We've been to granny Hillie's then to see aunty Mavis at the shop. Miss Turpin has a bad cough so she wouldn't say hello."

Jennifer's face gazed up at Annie, a telltale rim of yellow stickiness around her mouth from the sherbet crystals Mavis dispensed in tiny cone shaped bags from the large jars behind the counter. Annie recalled the time when Hilda had occupied herself, whilst she and Mavis chatted, by dipping her finger, time after time, into a bag of deep pink sherbet, licking off the fizzy sweetness, 'til her lower face and right hand were enflamed by cochineal. Before Annie had chance to address the situation, an older

30

woman had come along, appeared horrified at the young Hilda and turned on Annie with a look of condemnation, issuing a stern rebuke. 'The child has impetigo, take her to a doctor'!

"Mavis says Miss Turpin's chest is quite bad, I was going to buy a wedge of cheddar but the shop reeked of camphorated oil and you know how butter will soak up the smell of onions if you peel them close-by the butter dish, so I was afraid that the cheese might taste of camphorated. If Toby liked chutney it probably wouldn't have mattered too much but he always eats his cheese just as it is. I shall get some from you at the weekend," declared Maggie.

Annie smiled and held out her finger for little Amy to grasp.

"I want to get home before she wets, we've only had two nappies today so far. If I put her on the pot and sing 'London's Burning', by the time I've reached the second 'pour on water', she'll be weeing. How is Hilda getting on at Clarendon, I suppose she finishes this summer." Maggie took a hanky from her pocket, licked it and wiped Jennifer's protesting face before continuing. "Edna's Annie loved it there didn't she, I saw her the other day, on her way to Boots. Perhaps Hilda could get a job there too, I imagine every now and then one or more of the secretaries might get pregnant and leave so Hilda would likely stand a good chance."

"I often think how fortunate both Edna and myself have been. Neither of us could have paid for our daughter's education, for the two of them to have won scholarships was so very lucky. Especially now as life for women becomes less confined. It's still very much male dominated I know but before too long I feel sure that a woman, if she so chooses, will be able to use her intelligence beyond the home without incurring the charge of insubordination."

"Toby's mam says that men like the sound of their own voices whereas women just like to be sound."

Jennifer wriggled on Annie's knee. Annie lowered her face to the child's ear and whispered.

"You're fidgeting, do you need to wee?"

"Oh no, it's your coat button it's sticking in me." The two women chuckled.

"Toby can't say much, it's required of him to be discreet, a condition of his employment but last night he did tell me about the refurbishment of the Council House. It must be costing a fortune, Clark and Brown's is doing all the upholstery, two men have been in there for days and the oak panelling goes right round the chamber. Sometimes I wish Toby had stayed at the lace market, I know the money's better but affairs of the council seem to be entirely removed from the working man. I'm sure he feels a conflict of loyalties. Yours is the next stop isn't it, we better organise ourselves."

Maggie stood with Amy on her hip to take the shopping bag from Annie's feet while Jennifer pursed her lips to give aunty Annie a goodbye kiss before quickly moving to the aisle to let Annie by.

It was always a pleasure to see Maggie and her family. Annie stood on the pavement waving 'til the bus was too far away for Jennifer to wave back.

Mavis and Eddie were still childless, after all these years it seemed unlikely that they would have a family. Mavis didn't mention it any more and while everyone still hoped, there remained little expectation. Gertie and Steve had two boys, Jack the first born so much like his dad, Henry the youngest reminded Annie of grandad Boucher, he had Samuel's mild manner and was ever content in his own small world. Jean and Randall continued to enjoy their busy life in London and though they remained childless no one seemed in the least surprised or concerned. Jean loved dearly all her nephews and nieces but displayed not the slightest desire to be a 'mam'. Dear Nora still worked for the Hymers, her duties must have become considerably less, only the genteel couple and herself in a large house that saw little activity outside of the day to day routine. Sarah had been asked more than once by Davina to vacate No.69 Mitchell Street and move in with her lonely old friend. It touched Sarah each time but she'd refused graciously, Annie was perceptive enough to realise why. If Nora at some stage must leave the Hymer's employ, then she would have no other home than No.69. All such things were in the hands of fate but it was human nature to devise a plan 'just in case', even if a greater power ordained the outcome.

As Annie draped her coat over the banister she could hear Charles in conversation with a gruffly spoken man, she recognised the voice, it was Stanley Pagett. He would come into the shop once or twice a week, invite hellfire and damnation to descend upon all the backscratchers and arse-lickers, taking never less than ten minutes to purchase tobacco and matches, leaving behind the most nauseating mix of body odours when he finally took himself off to his longsuffering wife. Emily Pagett was a deeply religious woman, speaking regularly at fellowship meetings. It was difficult to imagine any degree of harmony within the Pagett household. No two people could be so opposite in every way. Stanley referred disparagingly to his wife's unflinching conviction as 'Godswollap'. The shop doorbell at last confirmed his departure and Annie ventured through.

"I'll squeeze a lemon onto the sponge, the next customer shouldn't be subjected to Stanley Pagett's lack of hygiene." Annie kept a sponge under the counter especially for the purpose, the strong but pleasant scent of citrus was the only remedy she had found to work almost instantly.

"I don't know why you bother," said Charles, with his usual indifference. "The next one to come through that door will likely be too preoccupied with their own miserable grouse to even notice Pagett's lingering stink."

"I'll take over whilst you have a cup of tea," said Annie, "I had one with Edna. Maggie was on the bus, she sends her best."

Charles grunted tetchily. "Everyone sends their best, just one day you should try saying so and so sends their worst, I might believe that." He went through to the scullery, asking nothing about the funeral or poor Winnie's state of mind. Annie had long since abandoned any regard for Charles' surliness, convinced as she was that he behaved in this way quite automatically with no premeditation, in fact it meant nothing. She placed the sponge with its lemony smell discreetly between the till and a large glass jar of winter mixture, which she had labelled with a special price for two weeks only. Her policy of selling each week, one or two items with virtually no mark-up, had proved good business sense. It encouraged trade, folk had become accustomed to finding these 'specials' and actually looked forward to them. Customers felt appreciated despite Charles' cool manner and obvious disinterest, like Annie they took it for what it was, unimportant! Eddowes' shop was established and in its small way gave reassurance to those less fortunate mortals, clinging to survival.

The sound of agitated voices alerted Freddy to an altercation between two men about twenty five yards ahead of him. He overheard the words, 'I'm the best judge o' that, it's Jack Sulley's speciality' before they became aware of his approach and fell silent. Freddy nodded a brief acknowledgement, Jack Sulley managed a grudging. "Alright?" The second man Freddy had never seen before, moving swiftly on, he sensed trouble. Sulley was a bold character, devoid of all mirth, his associate stood several inches shorter and shivered with the cold. He had a bald patch on one side of his head, as though a scar prevented the hair from growing. Freddy considered it odd that the man didn't cover it up with a cap, perhaps he simply didn't own a cap. His appearance suggested poverty, everything about him was dishevelled and shabby, the image was depressing. At that moment a gloriously cheerful voice called out from across the street.

"Cooee, wait for me Freddy." Hilda raced across, gave him a hug and said, "Guess what?"

"I don't know Hilda, you'll have to tell me." Freddy laughed at her excitement.

"I am invited to a party at Laura's. It's her birthday and her mother and father are having a 'do' to mark that and her elder sister's engagement. It's at The Park, not all that far from Davina's, I've not let on that we visit there often, I'm sure they think that I shall be completely overawed by the experience. They mean it in the very nicest way when they tell Laura it is good to embrace all society, they're not snobs. Laura's dad cycles to work, she bought him bicycle clips for Christmas and he did loads to help with the pantomime, painting scenery and finding props. He went all the way to Clifton to get an old Ali Baba basket that someone was about to throw away. Laura's sister was at Clarendon at the same time as Edna's Annie and they both got into bother when Miss Lovelace found them in the library, composing a letter of adoration to Andrew Smithfield. It was never their intention to post it but I think it was their graphic English, especially their use of the word 'throbbing', which sent Miss Lovelace into hysteria. Come on, lets run. Mam made a beef pie last night, especially for you, plus she needed something she could heat up for tea today, because of going to Mr. Bacon's funeral. She says we can open a big tin of cling peaches as well, in your honour of course, last night it was sago for pudding, ugh!"

Freddy chuckled at his sister's easy chatter, her brightness. Life with the Cropleys could be very routine, even dull once the day's work was done. Both had a tendency to 'drop off' in their chairs soon after supper so Freddy often found himself sitting on a stool in the corner of the cows house, staring back meanly at the shiny eyes that peeped through gaps in the old stone walls, as rats impatient for his departure, willed him to retreat from their menacing presence so they could emerge to search the floor for stray flakes of barley and enjoy the warmth generated by the expulsion of hot air from their ruminant neighbours. Freddy often contemplated the future whilst he sat in the quietness. Arthur had voiced his need to be freed of work and responsibility, Mrs. Cropley's health was not good and Arthur himself suffered severely with a bad back from all the years of heavy lifting.

Freddy had saved hard, always remembering Annie's direction on matters of finance. The farm had been his working life for the past ten years, perhaps Arthur would consider letting Freddy buy into the business at least, with a view to selling out completely at a later stage. Freddy craved something he could call his own, to feel he achieved. He would seek Annie's advice, his dad would be dismissive of the notion he felt sure but his mam was different, she was able to share a vision and held a sound economic approach to matters of commerce. A farm might be considered by some to be outside the realm of commerce, merely a bucolic attempt at industry that deemed profit to be two blades of grass where previously only one had grown. Freddy now saw a future for farming, it excited him and made him impatient, he would show those pompous men who belittled activities on the land as old fashioned and out of touch. Grandma Sarah had once told him, 'hitch your wagon to a star'. The acres at Bobbers Mill were Freddy's star, he wanted to clear the ditches, cut back the hedgerows, see every potential realised and produce a sound profit to equal the factories. Just because a man had mud on his boots didn't mean his head was in the mire also.

George was in the yard filling the coal bucket. "Hello you two, John has just come and mam's got all the pans bubbling away, come on, it's getting chilly out here."

Annie opened the range door and the appetising smell of pastry cooking filled the room. Hilda laid the table eagerly, the evenings Freddy came home for tea always lifted their spirits, he looked towards the shop aware that Annie would call his dad through to eat before she had her own meal, taking over at the counter until Charles had finished and sat 'to let it go down' as was his way. Freddy wanted to speak with her but she seemed ever occupied, perhaps he might slip away from the others for a few minutes, he could take his mam a cup of tea.

"I nearly forgot, this morning, on the way to Raleigh, I met Tommy Spooner, Kathleen had her baby last night, a little girl. Tommy said all is well, although Ernie was so nervous that he chewed right through the mouthpiece of his pipe." George grinned as he delivered the news, knowing his mam would be pleased.

So often aunt Bella's words came back to Annie, 'For every birth there is a death' and vice-versa. Already the vacancy created by Ted was filled.

"The baby is Edith's first grandchild."
Just like George, a wide smile came to Annie's face, it might have been very different had Kathleen's mother succumbed to the bronchitis, Edith deserved the joy of a grandchild.

"I heard a bit of news today too, it was passed to me as 'rumoured' but no smoke without fire a the saying goes. Colliery has sold a parcel of land out at Bestwood to the council, for development, housing most likely as Woolascrofts have the contract to build." John paused. "It could be idle speculation but Jack Haynes told me and whatever else they say about Jack, he does always seem reliably informed. Perhaps his brother Brian's in the know, it was Brian that told Jack when the colliery sold the land and buildings they'd rented out to the railway following that lightning strike. Toby Hillier would know but I imagine he's obliged to keep council matters confidential, especially those of the treasury department where he works. The plan apparently is to build to the north of the city first but eventually to develop progressively around all four points of the compass, using the ring road just as Smithfield described it at that meeting, like a set of lungs. If you can imagine two big carousels, one inside the other, moving in opposite directions, filtering traffic out and in continually, the same principle as breathing."

"What happens if it sneezes or gets hiccups?" George teased mischievously.

"Then you'd see a road gang administering syrup of figs we all know that cures everything don't we?" Said John, holding out his tongue and pulling a face. Laughter rang out across the room to where Annie stood thrusting a spoon into the pie.

"Ready now, sit down." She placed a meal in front of each, instructing Hilda on the peaches and evaporated milk. "I'll relieve your dad in the shop he won't take long and then I'll have mine."
Freddy sighed, George looked across the table at his brother knowingly. "It's the routine Freddy and a peaceable one so mam sticks with it."

Annie looked around the shop at the various displays and shelving. The winter mixture jar was half empty, there were two more in the cellar and three boxes of brandy snaps on the dresser in the kitchen, they were to be the next inviting offer but would fail miserably if Annie let them get damp, so the warmth from the range was vital.
The doorbell rattled, Annie thought it likely to be Mr.Freeman, his evening post had not yet been collected, she'd noticed it on the ledge beneath the counter. He was a splendid old gentleman who declined to have his paper delivered, believing his legs stood the best chance of enduring if they saw regular use. His philosophy reminded Annie of Catherine Appleyard, many times she had described Robert's mother as being of that same determined nature. However, the customer turned out to be Edwin Garbett.

"Hello Annie, how are you?" Edwin called at the shop not infrequently, purchasing a few simple items. Now living alone since his mother died, he often worked late at Jacobson's.

"I'm well thank you Edwin, the office must be busy if you are only now on your way home."

"I could have left earlier but one or two accounts are very involved at the moment. It sounds silly really but I enjoy the process of making books balance. Perhaps it's because little else in life does. Is that too cynical Annie?" She smiled.

"I know what you mean, given the complexities of human kind I suppose we shouldn't be surprised that cold, soulless figures present less challenge," she replied.

"I shall dine well tonight, two tins of sardines I think and a large slice from that slab of seedy cake please Annie. Mother couldn't abide either so we never had them. I'm sure if I were a child I would ask Santa to put sardines in my stocking." Annie laughed at the notion and cut a generous piece from the cake, placing it back under the net umbrella. Wrapping Edwin's slice carefully in greaseproof paper she said.

"George holds the opinion that seedy cake should be fed to offenders in prison three times a day, every day. That, he says, would do more to bring about an end to criminal activity than any other punishment. Charles will only eat it spread with butter."

"I'm sure it's me that's odd and I can't imagine anyone trying to persuade me otherwise," said Edwin with a deep sigh. "Take care Annie, be cautious of extending credit," he hesitated, "I believe these difficult times will continue and perhaps extend to areas we would not have imagined likely." With that he was gone leaving Annie to ponder his last remark.

Hilda was busy with the washing up, Charles sat in the big chair with the newspaper, Freddy took the opportunity to take a cup of tea to Annie while George and John continued their discussion. If Charles felt any interest in the topic, he nevertheless remained silent. Sometimes George thought the wide-spread Evening Post that hid Charles like a screen, served to distance his dad from the everyday problems which afflicted everyone else, whether intentionally or incidentally George couldn't know but it happened too often and George frowned upon it.

Annie had just helped Mr.Freeman through the door with his paper and two bundles of kindlers.

"Bless you Freddy, a nice cuppa." As Annie made her way back to the counter the door burst open and the bell jangled discordantly.

Mrs.Eddowes, can yer come quick, mam's chokin' on a fish bone an' she's turned colour o' front room curtains, Dolly's tried thumpin' 'er back but it don't work an' I think she's dyin'."

"Alright Elsie, I'll just get a coat, it'll be alright." Annie glanced quickly at Freddy, "Their dad's on nights, tell Charles he must man the shop, I'm sure I wont be long, you drink the tea, there's shortbread in the tin."

Freddy sat at the kitchen table listening to his brothers' banter. Hilda clattered around in the scullery, hanging up saucepans, singing to herself happily, her plea for just half an hour or so of Cribbage had been granted. He would have to wait his time, like his mam's meal must sit drying up in the oven of the range, awaiting her return. But his sister's enthusiasm and John's good company were fine exchange for that hour spent with rats and cows when all was said and done. As for George, well he had a more pressing engagement to attend and it almost certainly involved Alice and Delores!"

CHAPTER FOUR

Billy's work at the exchange was very regular, seldom did anything occur to interrupt the norm', but at nine o'clock he took a call, which began a night of events.

'Ask Wicks if 'e's feelin' the heat'. That was it nothing more and the caller was gone. Billy told the manager, Claude Timmins.

"Don't know what to make of it Billy, could be any one o' the daft buggers, likely worse for drink. We won't rock the boat unless summat else 'appens."
At ten o'clock, Frank, another operator took an alarming call.

'Tell Wicks 'e'll be nowt but a cinder by mornin'.
Timmins at once informed the police. Sergeant Beasley left the station immediately, taking a young constable with him, they made for Langley Drive, to the home of Henry Wicks. Urgent voices alerted Mrs.Wicks to unusual activity downstairs.

"What is it Henry?" Her robed figure appeared on the landing.

"Nothing to worry about my dear, the officer has kindly come to advise of a possible disturbance tonight, unrest among some of the men. Everything is under control." Henry Wicks looked back at sergeant Beasley with an expression that conveyed his desire not to have his wife worried unduly.

"Yes Ma'am, all is well."
She retired with a mutter of annoyance. Wicks lowered his voice.

"I will not be bullied sergeant, a handful of men continue to intimidate a great many others by their unwillingness to listen. Those who suffer genuinely, through little or no fault of their own, I have observed to hold no real desire for conflict, they are too weary, what strength is left in them, be it physical or mental, they preserve for their families. I shall of course be vigilant but you need not disrupt the policing of this city on my account. However, I shall put the foreman at the pit on

40

his guard. You assume this threat to apply to my residence but work requires me to remain at the mine until the early hours on occasions, the men would know that."

"I insist we watch this house tonight. A constable shall be positioned at the front and the rear of the property. I shall also have one drive to Birchdale to take a good look round." The sergeant imposed his authority at least to a certain extent.

"I shall telephone the pit now," said Wicks, "as for the rear of the property, I shall watch over that myself, if you insist on placing a constable at the front then so be it. I would appreciate it if indeed an officer could satisfy himself that nothing untoward occurs at the pit. Whilst I'm sure no harm would be intended of the men working the night shift, any distraction, such as fire, could place them all in peril if matters got out of hand. My feeling sergeant is that morning will break and the inconvenience and disruption to us both will be the satisfaction this limited individual seeks. Whosoever they may be, they are more of a menace to themselves and those around them than they are to me."

The night would be long and vexing, when Henry Wicks explained carefully to his wife the need for him to remain wakeful, she dressed, prepared cocoa for the young constable guarding the front and set about making bread.

Leonora Wicks was not known for her timid approach to life. To everyone's amazement, when the strike was at its height, she had faced Clifford Salmon at one of his impromptu rallies, asking him just one question that almost toppled him from his stand on the brick built gate post at the entry to Player's. Later her words would prove an irony. 'If these were to be the very last words you spoke on this earth Mr. Salmon, would you still employ them to incite these vulnerable men to a futile violence, or would you instead empower your voice to call for the rights of your wife, your daughters, those women who by their intelligence alone, keep the like of you from wallowing in the suffocating swamp of desolation that is the workhouse'.

He could not answer, a hush fell on the gathering, the men, honest at the core, were forced at that moment to acknowledge their reliance on a woman, be it wife or mother, sister or grandmother. It struck a nerve. Women juggled numerous tasks, working many hours at either end of their man's day. They went without themselves, in order to feed him and the children, on a sum artificially reduced through a man's 'right' of a pint, a smoke, a wager. Their strengths day on day were ignored, taken for granted. Leonora Wicks, in forcing the men to recognise the worth of their women defused Salmon's offensive and one by one they drifted away.

Never had a bowl of bread dough been so thoroughly kneaded, or with such strength of hand. At 3am, the constable, near' numb from inactivity and chill of the early hour, received more sustenance and was told by Leonora to, 'at least go inside and take a pee and ten minutes by the stove before you become rigid', she would keep watch at the front. The woman showed no fear whatsoever and while the young constable truly believed any wrongdoer would stand slight chance if up against Mrs. Wicks, he remained at his post but inwardly warmed himself with the fantasy of one day marrying a woman as phenomenally arousing.

As light broke, four splendid loaves sat on a rack in the kitchen, the kettle simmered over the heat and Henry Wicks slept awkwardly in a chair. Leonora had made no attempt to prompt her husband to wakefulness when at around 3-30am, tiredness had overcome him.

"I do believe constable that your shift is at an end, unless we are to suspect the milkman of concealing some manner of incendiary among his bottles of tuberculin tested. Tell sergeant Beasley that both my husband and myself are in fine fettle and thank him for his concern. As for you young man, we are most grateful to you but I do insist that you find your bed as soon as possible and sleep at least until afternoon." She extended her hand to shake his, her grip as firm as any man's. As young constable Peak made his way along Langley Drive the heat that enflamed his nether regions proved the only uncautioned burning of the night!

As he sipped a cup of sugary tea, sergeant Beasley contemplated a barm cake from a batch of Lovatt's early morning baking, deciding whether or not to risk almost certain indigestion. So fresh it was still warm, he would have preferred a slightly staler offering, much less inclined to challenge his temperamental gut. The

42

sense of relief and satisfaction that he and his constables' diligent efforts throughout the night hours had thwarted any attempt on the home of Henry Wicks or the pit, greeted daybreak so confidently that a constable had been despatched to Lovatt's with the purpose of collecting a much deserved breakfast.

The news on his return had completely soured the anticipated pleasure of barm cakes. Henry Wicks was never a target but was, as it turned out, a successful decoy. An area of lead had been stripped from St. Joseph's overnight.

He may have nothing concrete but what some folk said was true, Jack Haynes did always have money in his pocket and seemed well informed on various matters. He worked at the pit, but earnings there were less than they'd been three years ago, other miners declared poverty. Although Haynes had been at the meeting the night St. Saviour's had been stripped, it was just possible he could have crossed town to Lenton and done the deed in time to start his shift at Birchdale, the perpetrator, whoever he was, would surely have had an accomplice. In spite of numerous inquiries two months ago, no amounts of lead had been found where they shouldn't be and no one had seen or heard anything. Sergeant Beasley put the barm cake in the drawer of his desk to mature, this evening he would call on Jack Haynes, routine inquiries. He would nab the blighter who'd made a fool of him, somebody out there would be laughing over a stash of lead, which would doubtless be turned into ill-gotten gain before too long. Sergeant Beasley wrote up his report, impatiently.

"Shockin' news Mrs.Eddowes, shockin', Father Docherty went over from Priest house to St. Joseph's to put the hot brick on his seat in the confessional, 'twas Mrs.Brownridge as told him to do that after he had that bout o' sciatica, apparently it works a treat, stays hot for ages wrapped in newspaper. Well first thing to greet him wer' a bare patch on the roof, somebody's stripped some lead again, like they did at St. Saviour's. Would you believe that folk could be so wicked, stealin' from the house of God. I don't see how they could be Anglican or Roman Catholic do you, should narrow it down for the police anyroad. My Harry says they should bring back the stocks, mind you he spent a night in the cells years ago." Mrs. Lupin cast her eyes to

43

heaven and made the sign of the cross over her ample bosom. "Old Ma Coombe wer'
a miserable piece o' work, they reckon she used to feed her husband on mustard
sandwiches, tis no wonder he succumbed to pneumonia. After he died she ran that
hotel wi' a rod of iron. Harry wer' not much more than a lad when he started there, he
worked as a porter at The Compton. Talk about mean, wintertime, the staff quarters
where Harry and the chambermaids slept wer' perishin' but they weren't allowed any
coal for the grate. Well, every Sunday mornin' Ma Coombe went to church, she'd be
gone for an hour an' 'arf. Harry felt sorry for the girls so he decided to do summat to
cheer 'em up a bit. In the shed out the back there wer' this big chest o' drawers.
Nothin' in it, never had been. Harry said it must have stood five foot tall an' six foot
wide. What he did wer' take the backs an' sides off the drawers, one each Sunday and
burn 'em in the grate, just to give the girls a blaze to warm their knees by afore Ma
Coombe come back from church. Harry put the fronts wi' the fancy brass handles
back in place an' nobody could notice anythin' different. Now would you believe,
later the followin' summer, the wretched woman decided to sell the damn thing, got
this furniture chap to come an' give her a valuation. You can guess what happened,
poor Harry wer' carted off to the police station an' put in a cell overnight. Next day,
they let him go but told him he'd be called up before the beak in due course. Ma
Coombe give him the sack so he had to go home to his mam's an' she give him a thick
ear. Anyroad, Magistrate read the charge an' Harry pleaded guilty. He wer' ordered to
pay twelve shillings. They asked if he needed time to pay, well 'o course he did, Ma
Coombe never give him his last week's wages, it wer' bugger all but better than nowt
so he said yes, a bob a month for twelve months, that was hard you know, really hard,
poor Harry. I've often wondered if it wer' because he did wrong while the old misery
wer' in church prayin', a sort o' divine come uppance. Well if it wer', whoever
pinched lead from St. Saviour's an' St. Joseph's is sure to get more than one night in
lock up an' twelve bob to pay I reckon, don't you." Before Annie had chance to reply
Mrs.Lupin pointed to a stack of clothes pegs. "I better have a box o' them, damn dog
chewed up 'arf a dozen yesterday. I told Harry when he brought it home it 'ould be
nowt but bother but the kids love it an' it keeps them happy."

"I believe the police were busy with another matter. I am not sure of any details but I understand a threat was made against Henry Wicks last night," said Annie.

"I'm not surprised, though Harry reckons Mr.Wicks is a decent sort at heart, but if Basil Stanford throws a stick, Wicks fetches it, an' when Stanford says heel, Wicks does that an'all. Acts on command but Harry says Wicks don't bite an' if somebody come along one day an' threw 'im a bone wi' a bit o' meat left on it, then Stanford would have to fetch the stick 'isself." Mrs.Lupin picked up her shopping bag. "I see your George has found a nice young lady, it wer' awful sad when her mother died, so young. Alice is like her mam to look at, that lovely English rose complexion. Well this won't do, I've got a pair o' curtains home soaking', cheerio Mrs.Eddowes."

Annie had come to realise over the years that a shop counter was very much like a confessional. People seemed ever ready to reveal family secrets or to bare their soul over a pound of broken biscuits. Just the other week, while weighing up pearl barley for a customer, Annie had been forced to listen to the poor woman's account of marital dysfunction. 'I can remember when my Eddie used to look at me wi' that soppy expression an' I'd stop whatever I wer' doin' so he could walk the streets a satisfied man. I allus tried to remind meself of what our mam told me the day afore me an' Eddie got wed. 'Men have needs', she said, 'different to women, don't deny him, 'cause if yer keep 'Dicky' out then 'Dicky' will go in somewhere else'. She spoke all slow an' serious like it wer' the golden rule o' nuptials. Well, I don't know where the bugger's off takin' his needs to these days but 'Dicky' hasn't come anywhere near my door in months'!

Charles had gone to the barber, once away from the shop he seemed reluctant to return, sometimes hours passed before the sound of the back door latch alerted Annie to his arrival. He could be short tempered and snap at the least little thing, at other times, sullen and moody. The boys and Hilda struggled with the tension it created, Annie felt much of her energy was spent in the constant effort of keeping a peaceful household.

John on leaving school, had been fortunate to secure a job at Hamlin's, a firm that manufactured piping for drain work. Just six months into his employment he'd fallen ill with shingles. The burning rash had left him with a number of blemishes on the skin that had followed a nerve along his shoulder and up one side of his neck, they took several weeks to disappear. The inevitable mischief of George and Freddy had taken even longer to fade. 'The pied piper of Hamlin's' had been met at the factory each morning with typical male raillery and in a curious way, had endeared him to all, including the manager. Despite being a comparatively recent recruit, John had survived two rounds of 'lay offs'. The strike had affected Hamlin's, much of what they produced was carried on the railway. The disruption to train services through the involvement of The Transport & General Workers Union, in spite of black leg labour brought in by government, damaged Hamlin's trade for some time. They were not a large company, unlike others that lived off their fat until the hard times eased, Hamlin's carried only modest reserves so survival meant 'doing on less'.

So many households fought that oppressive element which rose from men-folk with nothing to do. Embittered, frustrated and cautioned by police on the streets, they lashed out against the system the only way they could, at home, within those walls that hid their violent eruptions. Annie had witnessed despair many times, standing right there at the counter in front of her. An empty purse, a rumbling stomach proclaiming its void and on too many occasions, that cowed light in a woman's eyes, and the attempt to conceal bruising.

William prospered at Brassington, still worryingly self-centred but nevertheless his progression was steady. Freddy was stoically self-contained, seldom bringing to Annie any cause for her concern. George was simply himself, popular with everyone, his ambition he hid behind that wide grin, his generous nature, aware that for some, visions of attainment were nothing but torment.

The Eddowes household was among the blessed, it might not leap with gaiety and some days may demand a careful tread but they were all fed and no one wept from the pain of physical harm.

Sergeant Beasley stood at the door of No.67 Forest Road. He adjusted his helmet and thrust out his chest in officious posture. His first knock brought no response, he knocked again. Within a few seconds the door was opened, at first slightly. Florrie Haynes on seeing a policeman felt alarm. She had seven sons, only George, Jack and Victor lived with her still at Forest Road. The three eldest were married and William was in the army. It was that mother's dread, bad news at the door.

"Is your Jack here Mrs.Haynes, I need to have a few words with him." Florrie had become hard of hearing over the past couple of years.

"Jack, did you say Jack?"

"That's right Mrs.Haynes, your Jack."

"He's just finished his tea, you best come through."
Jack recognised the sergeant's voice and heard what was said. He got up from the table and went to the door.

"It's alright Mam," he smiled warmly, Florrie, reassured by her son, left the two men and returned to the kitchen.

"Where were you last night?" Beasley stood a good four inches taller than Jack, he held his head back at a slight angle, as if looking down his nose at an offensive deposit on the pavement.

"I wer' here in bed 'til 4o'clock, then I got up, made a mug o' tea, had a slice o' bread an' treacle, picked up me dinner bag that mam got ready the night afore an' left for the pit, shift started 5o'clock. Why do you ask?"

"I suppose there's someone who'll corroborate that?" Said Beasley. Jack sighed, inwardly considering the sergeant's approach pathetic. Did policemen never actually think for themselves. That standard, 'where were you' and that fancy word 'corroborate', most men had no bloody idea what it meant. It was only their own powers of deduction, a bit of nous, that enabled them to answer. Why didn't Beasley just come straight out with it. 'Did you nick the slate from St. Joseph's roof last night'?

"I share with me brother George, he'll tell you I wer' in me bed all night," said Jack.

Beasley smirked, "Of course he will, now why doesn't that surprise me."

"What's the point in askin' me the question if yer disregard me answer," said Jack.

"None o' your cheek, you'll show respect for the law and I represent the law so mind your mouth."

Respect thought Jack, could this mindless puppet of officialdom, who recited a procedure like a kid rendering a nursery rhyme, ever recognise respect.

"When me dad died, a long time ago now, we all stayed wi' mam that first night, George an' me on her bed, Victor in her bed, Eric, Brian an' William on the floor an' Raymond in the chair. If any one of us had left that room, the rest would have known. When you've been that close sergeant, when you've needed each other that much, it don't change. We've all lived that time over an' over since then. If George stirred in the night I'd know an' he'd know if I got up, that's how it is."

"Have you got a shed in the back yard?" Asked Beasley.

"Aye, we have, an' if you want to look inside then I'll show yer."

Jack led the officer through to the back, George sat quietly at the kitchen table, reading the paper. Sergeant Beasley paused, George looked up, expecting some remark, both men's eyes met but Beasley walked on, following Jack through the back door. In the yard, Florrie stood behind a chair on which sat a man with his back to her, having his hair cut.

"Hold your head still Victor, stop fidgetin' or it'll end up with more steps than front o' Council House."

She carried on with her task, not turning to look at Jack or the sergeant. The opened shed revealed an array of items, carefully perched one above the other, so as to make room for the coal.

"I'll answer the question afore you ask it sergeant," said Jack. "It's all bought an' paid for, junk in the eyes o' some but you'd be surprised what folk have a need for. I buy it mostly off Abel at scrapyard, just a few bob, not every week but when I can afford to. I store it in here in the shed an' before long somebody'll ask me if I can get 'em such an' such. Sometimes a thing can sit in the shed for months, other times only a day or two but when I sell it on I make a bit o' money. Yer see, you might find it hard to swallow but women trust me, I'm only a little chap as works at the pit who can usually find what they need if they ask me. Now Abel's likely to look em' up an' down an' if he thinks he can screw em' for double he will. I'm satisfied wi' just a bit for me trouble. Besides, scrapyard fascinates me, it allus did, I couldn't wait to leave school so I could walk in through the gates a man, entitled to be there. I'd bunk off at dinnertime. I weren't goin' to learn owt more, at nearly fourteen unless you were born to the other arf, yer learnin' come from out there." Jack pointed to the street. "I'd shin over scrapyard wall, Abel 'ould be in his office, the men out collectin' stuff. If I kept me head down I could have a real good nosy at everythin'. It wer' like Aladdin's cave to me. I never took owt, wasn't even tempted to, me dad were straight as a die, I wouldn't sully his name, none of us would."

"I suppose you've receipts for all this then," said Beasley, still determined to display his importance.

"You aren't livin' in the real world sergeant, with respect of course! Abel don't waste paper on anythin' under five bob, an' there's nothin' in this shed as cost more than that."

There was certainly no lead. Buckets, bathtubs, bicycle wheels, a dolly tub, even a set of scales but not a single piece of lead.

Jack put the latch back on the shed door. Beasley tapped him on the shoulder, he deepened his tone to emphasise his authority once more before leaving.

"I'll be watching you Haynes."

An echo drifted across the yard, 'Watchin' you Haynes'. The sergeant's eyes flashed as his head swivelled to round on the source of sarcasm. Victor looked directly at the officer of the law, a grin from ear to ear, his freshly cropped hair making his appearance youthful, it portrayed almost a childlike innocence. Beasley was thrown completely off his stride. This was an area of life for which he held no understanding, it was different, outside his jurisdiction.

Florrie gathered the hair clippings into a dustpan, as she stood up, a look of intense weariness fell about her features but she showed no alarm at Beasley's presence.

"Sorry to have bothered you Mrs.Haynes." At first she didn't hear, he moved closer and spoke clearly. "Goodbye Mrs.Haynes I'll leave you to your work."

Florrie smiled vaguely as past his shoulder she could see Victor picking up the chair, not always accurate in his movements, she feared sergeant Beasley might be accidentally struck on his person by a wayward chair leg. Jack walked with him to the street.

"I don't believe I've ever had more than a bob or two in my pocket sergeant, yet there are men walkin' round this city wi' notes in fat wallets, why is it yer never ask them where they were when lead wer' bein' stripped off church roof. It's not havin' a few coins as makes a man a thief. You acknowledge respect when it's shown to you but make nothin' of a man's self respect. When you can recognise the man who has that from the one who hasn't, I'll wager you'll catch your thief."

As Beasley walked away fromNo.67 Forest Road his frustration at making no progress in apprehending the offender was tempered by a curious sense of calm. He felt of all the places in Nottingham, the home of Florrie Haynes was the most unlikely den of iniquity he could imagine. He would keep an open mind, that was his duty after all, but 'Watching you Haynes' had somehow lost vitality.

CHAPTER FIVE

June.

Tommy looked intently at his wife as she moved about the scullery. Rosie hummed a familiar tune and the spoon with which she stirred the pan of soup became vague, blurred before his eyes.

That afternoon he and James Handley had presided at a funeral where the mourners had numbered so many that the church had been filled to capacity and even then, people gathered outside the open doors, standing in solemn rows, not so much in grief Tommy had sensed, but compelled by shock.

Leonora Wicks, that stout hearted, fearless woman, whom most people imagined would endure to a ripe old age, being so emboldened by her commitment to women's rights, had rocked the city to its foundations when on his return from work, her husband Henry had found her at the foot of the stairs, dead from a broken neck.

Henry Wicks' open grief, his anguish too intense to be contained, had moved Tommy deeply. Rosie now carried his child, the baby was due in early September. After losing their first, Rosie had hardly dared think beyond each day but Celia's encouragement and total confidence had at last instilled in Rosie a sense of calm.

"Ready, it's pipin' hot so don't burn your tongue."
She placed a deep bowl of soup on the table by the breadboard, as she leaned forward the telltale swelling at her abdomen confirmed her pending motherhood. Tommy could not comprehend a life without his dear Rosie. Henry and Leonora Wicks had been married many years but what difference did that make, if anything it drove even more harshly the dreadful hurt.

Tommy cut a thick slice from the crusty loaf, breaking it into pieces over his soup. Rosie, now seated to eat her own meal, observed her husband quietly as he took his first spoonful.

"Celia called earlier," she said. "William has been away for a couple o' days, Smithfield needed 'im to go to Sheffield. Celia 'ad some other news an'all, 'er brother Edmund's got engaged."

Tommy paused between mouthfuls.

"Who to?" He asked.

Rosie spread her slice of bread with butter and smiled as if gratified at being able to impart such intriguing knowledge.

"Basil Stanford's youngest daughter Caroline would yer believe."

Tommy savoured a piece of tender knuckle, which Cheetham's well-trimmed bone had miraculously rendered up. He'd heard his mam many times remark 'you'd be lucky to find a morsel o' sinew on a bone that old skinflint Cheetham's worked his knife over'. Tommy's brow furrowed as he puzzled over a random thought.

"That'll make William some sort o' relative by marriage to Stanford won't it?" He said, slightly amused.

"Well, 'is brother-in-law's wife'll be a Stanford," said Rosie.

"Blimey, what a turn up for the books that is, mind you, I've allus thought Will Eddowes wer' destined to move among the elite. There's just summat about 'im."

"Mam's got a sayin' for folk as seem a bit different, 'it must be the way their mother put 'er hat on'. I don't suppose William can remember 'is natural mother, she died when 'e wer' very young didn't she?" Asked Rosie.

Tommy fell silent, his thoughts had returned to events earlier in the day. At the funeral he'd noticed Stanford's reluctance to show emotion. Wicks had worked very many years for Stanford, a kindly hand on the shoulder should surely have come automatically, yet Basil Stanford had kept his distance. Perhaps he'd feared the men might start something but if so, then he was woefully misguided. The men might harbour grievances but not one of those hard working miners, able to attend and represent their mates on shift, would allow any disrespect. Despite all the troubles, most men at the pit held a measure of regard for Henry Wicks and his wife Leonora. They felt for his despair.

Rosie scraped her bowl for the last sliver of carrot, which seemed determined to defy the spoon.

"Celia's mother told 'er that Basil Stanford's father bought Birchdale from Davina Wright after 'er husband died, yer know, she's the lady in The Park who William used to live with. Mrs.Tozer must be in 'er element, I can just picture the two of 'em, 'er an' Mrs.Stanford takin' tea together at 'Barkers', sittin' in the bay window decked up in their finery, all swank. Like the picture on a tin o' Callard an' Bowser from Burton's at Christmas. I've never seen 'er in the Kardoma, far too common, there's another one in Derby, and Leicester." Rosie gathered up the empty bowls and carried them to the scullery, calling back to Tommy, "Mam's made us a bread puddin', I've already 'ad a small piece off the end but I could eat a bit more, do yer want some cheese wi' yours?"

Tommy answered vaguely, his mind still with Henry Wicks. What if he finished at Birchdale who would Stanford appoint then. 'Better the devil you know than the devil you don't', and Wicks had for the most part stopped short of doing devil's work. Change of management at the pit could be detrimental to more than the black faced, wild eyed, bone weary miners who trudged home at a shift's end. Alarmingly volatile still, the slightest friction was sufficient to ignite and just as in the spring of '26, the damage would cover areas far and wide. Through the time of the general strike and some months afterwards, James Handley had discreetly arranged several burials in paupers' graves. Tommy could recall one especially, the widow no more than in her late thirties, stood alone, calm, composed but with ashen complexion. She had removed a pin from her hair and used it to anchor to the ground at the head of the grave, a single rose. She was heavily pregnant and Tommy had offered his arm to help her up from where she knelt. 'I didn't steal it, the rose', she'd said. 'It grew over the wall from next door, I have to gather the hips at the end of the summer and pass them back to Mrs.Willis, she makes rose hip syrup'. Tommy had made sure the pale pink, single bloom remained securely in place before leaving the spot. He looked up at Rosie's face as she placed a mug of tea by his plate of cheese and bread pudding.

"I love you Mrs.Spooner," he said.

She smiled, planted a kiss on his forehead and returned to the scullery, humming a familiar tune.

Edna ran the iron over Liza's blouse with amazing precision, working its tip between the buttons like a mouse along a row of pea shoots.

"I'm that mad I could spit, how you can be so calm about it I don't know, it makes my blood boil."

Edna was annoyed and her ill humour drove her energy, the flat irons, one on the range while the other was in use, had been engaged in perpetual motion for the last thirty minutes and Edna's tongue was equally employed 'til Billy's good ear throbbed from the assault.

"Let it be Edna," he said. "We did what we did for Winnie an' it's still helpin' 'er, she'll feel happy knowin' Lillian's livin' in that house, all Winnie's memories are there, it'll be a comfort, Jack an' 'is family under the roof were 'er an' Ted raised their young ens." Billy tried to placate his agitated wife. "I'll stick the kettle on, make us a nice cuppa'."

"Idle so an' so, that Jack's allus been trouble an' now we've got the bugger livin' on our doorstep. All the hours you an' Victor spent scrubbin' an' paintin', now 'e must be over there wi' nowt to do but sit laughin' at yer."

Edna draped a shirt over the chair back and changed over irons, plucking a petticoat from the shrinking pile of clean laundry in the basket beside her.

Winnie had returned to No.9 at the beginning of May. Billy and Victor had indeed made valiant efforts to restore the little house, making it comfortable and welcoming for poor Winnie's return. In spite of fresh smelling pale cream walls, new curtains of flowered cotton sewn by Edna, a rug from Moffat's secondhand shop and a set of new legs fitted to the table by Joe Spooner, Winnie's strength of spirit, wearied from the many years of daily challenge, just could not rise again and sadly all the pent up emotion got the better of her. She'd put on a brave face when beyond her door, even forcing her tired old knees to bow to the front door step and scrub it with reverence. Yet inside, out of view, the poor woman was haunted by the vision of Ted, that night in his chair, flames all around him. Elsie had eventually found her mam in a collapsed state of nervous exhaustion. Through compassion and the realisation that Winnie could not cope, she had taken her mother back to Melton Road. As a consequence, Jack Sulley, along with his wife Lillian and their young daughter Norma, had moved out of Elsie's and now occupied No.9 Winchester Street, subsidised in rent and housekeeping by Winnie, Elsie and Jim.

Billy put a cup of tea at the corner of the table.

"Can't yer stop ironin' for a bit, sit down an' drink your tea, Liza an' Myra'll be back soon, what time does Susie expect to be home?"

Edna sank down onto a chair with a sigh.

"It don't seem fair, Jack Sulley 'asn't got a workish bone in 'is body, yet there 'e is, a house wi' furniture already in it, coal in the shed an' the whitest front step on the street. Joe Spooner, just like 'is brother Tommy, looks after 'is mam, watches out for 'is sisters, keeps an eye on the two youngest an' treats our Susie as often as 'e can but when the time comes for them to be wed I bet a home won't fall into Joe's lap like manna from Heaven, 'e'll 'ave to struggle for it. Can't be right, the almighty must need 'is eyes testin'. If 'e's lookin' down on the worthy an' givin' 'em a helpin' hand then how do yer explain Jack Sulley's rewards." Edna sniffed her disapproval and sipped the hot tea. "Susie thought they'd be back in Nottingham by 7o/clock," she said, "I wonder what their digs wer' like, it wer' only one night anyroad. Skegness must see more canoodlin' an' all that carry on than just about anywhere in the world I reckon. I hope they behaved the'selves." Edna took another mouthful of tea.

Billy grinned. "Well we didn't, I wer' a virgin 'til you took me to Skeggy. When our mam asked me if we'd paddled, I felt like sayin' we went right in mam, didn't come out 'til we were par' boiled."

Edna picked up a pair of knickers from the laundry basket and threw them at Billy, laughing at the memory.

"Just fancy that," he said roguishly. "All these years an' you're still chuckin' your drawers at me."

Edna stood, crossed to where Billy sat in the big chair and slipped her fingers down inside his shirt as she perched herself on the chair arm.

"Our mam asked me if you'd been a gentlemen. I told 'er that you'd behaved just like me dad would 'ave done. Poor mam, she wer' on edge for weeks." The back door latch rattled and in skipped Myra followed by Liza.

"Annie an' Alec are gettin' a dog," declared Myra excitedly. Edna whispered quickly into Billy's good ear.

"We'll go for a paddle later on, might even go right in!" By now Myra was alongside her mam and dad.

"It's a terrier, Mrs.Allsop's got to get rid of it 'cause it howls its head off every time Sally Army Band plays on the corner of Bingley Street. Nancy Maitland walloped it with her tambourine last week an' Mrs.Allsop was mad, she told 'em Christian Soldiers shouldn't beat defenceless animals an' they could go an' rattle their collection tins somewhere else, but Mr.Allsop said it wer' no good, the miserable mutt had to go. He works with Alec an' told him all about it, so Alec said he'd take the dog, Sally Army never go to Kirby Street, too near the Quaker Meetin' House. Annie reckons Mr.Allsop plays draughts once a week with the woman who cleans The Citadel an' that he wouldn't want to upset her. Alec thought that wer' funny an' laughed. Why's that funny, I didn't understand?"

Myra looked puzzled. Liza cast an amused expression at Edna from the scullery where she'd been emptying her bag.

"Your Sunday treats from Annie, she said to tell you that the cake is a recipe she found in the Woman's Weekly, the soap is a new line at Boots, honey and orange blossom and she couldn't get dad's usual chocolate bar so she bought him some éclairs."

Edna looked down at all the goodies on the scullery table and a lump came at her throat. Every Sunday whether Annie and Alec came to Winchester Street or the family called at Kirby Street, Edna and Billy received 'treats' as their eldest daughter called them.

The home at No.24 ever rang with happiness although over the years, so small the space, so cramped the bedrooms had been, Edna had yearned for a larger house, more for the girls' sakes than for her own. It had not happened, no chance to move had presented itself, so the Dodds family had remained in their limited surroundings, yet not one of their daughters looked back with anything but contentment, it was Annie's way of saying thank-you, the Sunday treats. Edna returned to her ironing and Billy went to the yard to chop kindling for the boiler. The girls now older and more independent, her work regular and for the most part predictable, it had become Edna's routine to change all the bed linen on a Sunday morning, soak it overnight, transfer the sheets to the boiler early Monday morning and light the fire underneath before leaving for work. Billy or Victor would give it a good stir with the dolly at some point during the day and push a few more pieces of wood in the firebox. By the time Edna got home the fire would be out but the linen would have boiled and she could mangle and rinse. If Susie or Liza were home first, they very often began the process which inevitably resulted in a thoroughly wet pinafore and damp cuffs no matter how high the sleeves were rolled. Grandma Dodds would look at them and say, 'soaked pinafore means you'll marry a drunkard'. The old boiler, nevertheless meant a great deal to Edna. When Annie Eddowes had left No.24 to return to her aunt Bella's house following Harold's death, the large, heavy boiler had remained. The only way to transport it across the street to No.11 would have been a horse and cart and then the task of loading and unloading would have required at least four strong men. Annie had felt it rightly belonged in the yard at No.24, she remembered the great delight on Harold's face the day he'd surprised her with the arrival of this valued appliance. To have taken it from that place where so much of her emotion dwelt still, she could not do so instead she made a gift to her dearest friend. Edna had declared it to be, 'just like Harold, strong, dependable and every woman's envy'. Even now, after so many years and events, Edna felt an affinity to that 'long ago'. It seemed to hold them safe, like an anchor, both Annie Eddowes and herself had repeatedly sought its reassurance, almost like the renewal of a vow.

Billy, hampered by the lack of one arm, was intent on splitting the last piece of wood so didn't hear footsteps behind him. When he at last put down the hatchet, a timid voice said.

"I don't know what to do, Jack still hasn't come home."
Lillian Sulley stood with young Norma in her arms, she was close to tears.

"Come inside lass," said Billy, "Edna and the girls'll want to see this little one." Billy rubbed his hand across Norma's curly hair and blew the child a kiss, she came over all shy and buried her face in her mam's neck. Billy chuckled, "I bet Edna could find a nice sweet biscuit for you young Norma, let's see."

Edna had just folded up the old ironing blanket, the pile of neatly pressed laundry sat on the table, she could see Lillian was upset.

"Put all this away upstairs Liza, Myra can help." Edna's glance passed from her daughter to the laundry, Liza understood, gathered it up and called to her sister.

"Sit down Lillian, the kettle's hot."
The young woman could not contain her distress and the tears began to fall.

"Jack went off yesterday afternoon, he never tells me where he's goin' an' if I ask he gets cross. When he didn't come home last night I thought perhaps he was at his mam's but he still isn't here, I don't know what to do Mrs.Dodds."

"Have you been to Elsie's?" Asked Edna.

"If he'd stayed there last night I'm sure that first light his mam would have sent him home, she'd know I'd be worried. I didn't want to make her anxious an'all. I kept thinkin' he'd be back any minute an' he'd be angry if I'd caused a scene."
Edna patted Lillian's shoulder and fetched a dishcloth from the scullery.

"Let's wipe that sticky little hand before you fill those curls with soggy biscuit." Edna laughed as the plump fingers wriggled beneath the damp cloth. She was a pretty infant, her round face and full lips held a great deal of charm. "There, all done," said Edna.

Norma grinned and displayed her pearly white teeth, then immediately let out a sigh.

"Bobba, Bobba, she said.
Edna looked to Lillian to interpret.

"She's asking for her bottle, she still has milk in the bottle yet she'll drink water from a cup."

"Don't fret Lillian, Billy'll 'ave a look around, ask if anybody's seen Jack, won't yer Billy?"
He was already pulling on his jacket.

"Who does 'e knock about with," said Billy.

"I've heard him talk of someone called Swinscoe but I don't know where he lives. I don't think he's a mate either, Jack doesn't speak with much regard. Often when he goes out he'll mutter to himself, 'one day Swinscoe, one bloody day'."
Lillian's eyes were heavy from crying.

"Don't worry lass, I'll find 'im, 'e cant be far away, 'is belly's sure to send 'im home anyroad. In the meantime you best go back to No.9 in case 'e arrives. Let Edna know if 'e does."

Billy walked hastily up the street debating which way to go. The Meadows seemed a likely place to begin, there were always several groups of people on a Sunday watching the antics of the kids, and someone might have seen Jack. George Eddowes and Alice were walking towards Billy when he turned into Ainsley Road.

"No, I haven't seen Jack Sulley since last Thursday," said George in response to Billy's enquiry. "He was outside the labour exchange in the queue, I noticed him because he had a nasty bout of coughing just as I passed by. We're on our way to mam's, if I see Jack I'll get word to you Billy."
The Meadows failed to deliver any news of Jack, no more did the group of people waiting for a bus at the far end of Sherwood Road. Not until Billy cut through the arboretum and bumped into Ernie and Kathleen Searle, pushing the baby in her pram, did he at last hear of Jack Sulley's whereabouts.

"I spoke to 'im," said Ernie, "he were lookin' rough, couple o' days o' stubble, generally scruffy. Kathleen noticed 'is hands looked sore, like they'd been bleedin', women notice things like that I suppose, can't say as I looked at 'is hands meself. Anyroad, 'e should be at Winchester Street by now."

Billy felt relieved. Jack Sulley may not be the most desirable of characters but his wife and child needed him and poor Winnie could not be expected to bear any more heartache. He hurried to give Edna the news, at least now they could look forward to hearing about Susie and Joe's weekend at Skegness, the pair would surely make straight away for No.24 when they got off the charabanc.

All seemed quiet as Billy walked by the house. Just what Jack had been up to he felt it best not to know. There was something about the young man, not obvious but present nonetheless, his attempt at a smile fell short of sincerity, his response to a courteous, 'good morning' seemed ever disinclined to leave his lips in any audible form, so to imagine a future of happiness and contentment for Jack Sulley and his family defied logic. It was an unsettling sense of foreboding, although Billy chided Edna for her condemnation of Sulley, Billy's instinct as a man told him their neighbour at No.9 would trouble their thoughts beyond this day.

Henry Wicks stood at the window gazing at the back garden, an old misshapen elder tree occupied one corner. He recalled the words of his wife from just a few weeks earlier. 'It needs to come down it's an eyesore, we should create a rockery there, some heathers and saxifrage'. Leonora, once she had made a decision, went ahead confidently, trusting in her own judgement. He shook from emotion and tiredness, he'd not slept since the funeral the previous day, the night hours of wakefulness weakened him and even a simple piece of bread defied his appetite. The bell rang at the front door, he felt tempted to ignore it. Leonora would not have ignored it. He walked unsteadily through the hallway, his fingers struggled with the catch.

"Hello Henry, I imagine you seek only your own peace today, I won't keep you but I've been 'sent' and when aunt Alicia instructs, it is altogether best to heed." Andrew Smithfield held a bowl, covered by a cloth. "A meal for you Henry. I think it is the way of the female mind, be it physical or mental weariness, food sustains!" Wicks smiled, a warm, sincere smile.

"Come in Andrew, where would we be without the female mind. I was just thinking about something Leonora said recently, she's quite right, the elder tree needs to be cut down, I must attend to the task."

Smithfield placed the bowl on the table.

"If there is anything I can do Henry, then please say. Your work is not easy, the pit functions as always, machinery can be temperamental from time to time but tried and tested practices redeem any failure. Men however, their mechanics are far more complex, they don't always respond to our best efforts. You will persist in the challenge I trust, we both are aware that Stanford understands little of mechanics and even less of human nature."

"Leonora was convinced that the enfranchisement of women was very close, she perceived a very different society, one that worked as a whole, a continuous process which left no element idle, which by its combined strengths, propelled forward the entire. The principle of one cog fitting exactly another, together a driving force, the need each had for its counterpart to maintain that harmonious cycle. Why could she not have been granted the realisation of her wish before......."

Henry Wicks faltered. Smithfield spoke firmly.

"Perhaps Leonora is now even better placed to impel the wheels that turn. The conscience of a man is more inclined to be influenced from 'above', my humble attempts at this level have ever failed to persuade," said Smithfield.

"Will you take a drink with me Andrew?" Wicks took glasses and a decanter from the bureau. "Have no fear, I shall not turn to the bottle for salvation. I shall be at my desk tomorrow, I will this summer create a rockery where stands the spent old elder tree, and you may tell your aunt Alicia that I shall indeed eat my meal. I am impelled so to do." He smiled, the two men understood each other and conversation flowed easily.

"The development at Bestwood should commence before autumn, the ground work is extensive and will create work for less skilled men initially. Woolascroft's must work within a budget and a time frame, the council has imposed a penalty clause if the development should overrun. I ventured to suggest that if the contract is to be awarded to an established firm such as Woolascroft's, then some benefit should be negotiated in return. They have agreed a number of apprenticeships. It is a drop in the ocean but anything that shortens the queues of unemployed we must pursue," said Smithfield.

Wicks hesitated before speaking. "To the north and west there's a lot of land belonging to the collieries but not utilised, given the current market I can imagine there would be a willing courtship between mine owners and the local authority. In the past I know that mineral rights have complicated schemes, not all are prepared to sell out. Stanford has met with opposition and could do nothing in that situation. Councils, I imagine, have powers of compulsory purchase where the sale of land is opposed. To the south and east of the city there is little colliery land, in that direction any courtship could prove more difficult, the purpose of land in these areas is more agricultural. Farmers view it from above, their value is based on an entirely different set of figures. Below ground, that black economy would seem to govern the purse to an alarming degree."

Their exchange continued for another half hour or so.

"I should be going Henry, I need to stop briefly at the factory on my way home." Smithfield rose to his feet.

"Thank-you for calling Andrew," said Wicks, "I don't suppose you know what saxifrage looks like, now heather I am familiar with but saxifrage escapes me."

Lillian watched as the unwilling eyelids finally closed and her daughter found sleep. Norma, at just over twelve months had teeth coming through at the back, a happy child in the main, especially when home was at peace but her father's moods could make the soreness in her gums seem much worse. Even at this tender age Norma's senses picked up the atmosphere Jack Sulley's ill temper created, his perpetual denial of cheery distraction. The evening was warm, Lillian covered the little girl only lightly before tiptoeing from the room. A wife was entitled to know of her husband's whereabouts, what if their daughter had been taken sick or an accident had occurred. Jack's behaviour was not normal, it was unacceptable. Despite Lillian telling herself these things as she descended the stairs her heart beat wildly, her fingers trembled. Jack sat in the chair by the hearth. He'd washed his face and hands in the cold water, the grate held no fire and his cheeks looked like ivory above the stubble on his chin, no warmth had yet found his circulation. He gripped the poker and drew it up across the bars at the front of the empty grate so that it clattered as it struck each one. He lifted his face toward Lillian for an instant and then repeated the process.

"Don't do that, I've only just got her off. Where have you been, I've a right to know, you could have been lying dead somewhere, what am I supposed to think. I'm your wife, we have a child, other men don't behave like this."

Now Jack's eyes flared, he thrust the poker toward Lillian, she clutched at the edge of the table, moving it slightly, a bottle of gripe water tumbled onto its side.

"No one tells Jack Sulley what 'e can or can't do, where 'e can or can't go, but a wife, my wife, now she does as she's told."

He drew the end of the poker slowly down her apron, leaving a sooty black line, until it reached the area between her thighs. A sickening grin came to his face, he twisted the poker, once, twice, a third time. Lillian began to cry.

"I've not eaten since yesterday," he lowered the poker to the hearth, "food, that's what I need first, food. One day we shall leave this house, be rid of mam's naggin' an' me dad's clutches. I wer' workin' last night, yer should be glad." He stood, put the bottle of gripe water upright and turned away from Lillian, speaking as he walked from the room. "I'm goin' to the lav'."

As he crossed the scullery a bout of coughing erupted, through the open back door she could hear him spitting into the tub. Lillian wiped her eyes with the corner of her apron, then gazed at the sooty stain. She closed the door quickly, shutting out the sound and the dread.

Susie and Joe were back from Skegness, Billy, Edna, Liza and Myra were being regaled with their animated account of the weekend's events, Susie's chatter had barely ceased for a second.

"Our landlady was called Mrs.De'lande, her husband was foreign, he died several years ago from choking on a piece of gristle. As Mrs.De'lande put it, 'he breathed his last over a plate o' mutton'! Apart from ourselves, only an elderly couple were stayin', they were there for a week, for the man's health apparently, although when Mrs.De'lande told them the nature of her husband's demise you could see the man's expression change immediately and we heard his wife whisper, 'for God's sake keep your teeth in'. It was last night that I'm sure I shall never forget. I think Mrs.De'lande considered us too young to be left to our own devices. After the meal, a sort of pot roast, quite nice, the old couple retired to the sitting room to read. 'Now my dears', she said, 'I shall take you to the theatre in town, Saturday is the very best night to attend'.

She explained that through the week the theatre put on productions of drama but every Saturday night was vaudeville, especially for the younger folk who she declared were, 'often away from home and could feel overawed by the sophisticated and cosmopolitan nature of Skegness'. She was so in earnest we could barely contain ourselves.

The theatre was not too far away so we left to walk the distance at a little before seven. Mrs.De'lande wore a fox fur that reeked of camphor and shoes that squeaked. She insisted on paying for our tickets and we supposed that was why we sat right up in the gods where the seats cost less. The stage was quite small, or at least it appeared so from where we viewed it but she was very kind and produced a bag of bonbons to suck. The first turn was announced and the curtain went up to reveal a man and a woman in bathing costume, singing, ' I do like to be beside the seaside', supposedly frolicking in the waves. From where we sat we observed the waves to be two rows of painted board between which they danced up and down in stockin' feet, the man had on suspenders. There was a ventriloquist, a juggler, a man doing tricks with doves, two flappers dancing the Charleston, but they definitely saved the best 'til last. Susie mimicked the master of ceremonies, waving her arm flamboyantly as she announced. "A duet of operatic stature ladies and gentlemen. We are proud, indeed we are thrilled to present the great maestro, Luigi and the magnificent Madame Celeste."

Susie nodded at Joe, who though stifling laughter, obligingly launched himself into a splendid caricature of maestro Luigi, his rendition of the song so firmly set in memory.

Susie quickly grabbed a cushion from the chair and stuffed it up her blouse, then stood by Joe gazing up at him like a lovelorn admirer bearing a tragic obstacle to romance. Joe's unnaturally deepened voice delivered the verse.

> *On yonder hill there stands a maiden,*
> *Who she is I do not know*
> *I'll go and court her for her beauty,*
> *She must answer yes or Noooooooooo.*

Joe held on to the last note with real theatrical emphasis. Now Susie thrust her chest out like a pigeon and postured with her clasped hands held before her bosom. She sang the chorus with all the dramatic gesturing of Madame Celeste.

> *Oooooooooo no John, no John, no John Noooooooooo.*

Myra was near hysterical from laughing,

"Again, do it again," she cried.

Liza clapped enthusiastically and Billy stood with his arm about Edna whistling while Edna called. "Encore, encore."

"I wish you'd all been there," said Susie, "after about five verses we thought this must be the final one but no, it went on and on, at least twelve verses, and each one as dire as the last. Joe was in stitches but I don't think it was meant to be comical. Mrs.De'lande had supped several Sherries before we left and she sank further and further in her seat 'til we could hardly see her face above the fox fur. She was asleep before the man with the doves left the stage. I can't remember ever laughing so much, really Mam, you'd have loved it. "Susie pulled out the cushion and threw it to Myra. "We've got presents haven't we Joe?" She said.

From their bags came sticks of rock, picture cards, a kiss me quick hat for Edna and a small packet of anemone corms for Billy to plant at the allotment.

"Didn't you go to the beach?" Asked Myra.

"Of course we did, we paddled and had a donkey ride. Joe's donkey was called Merle and mine was Poppy," said Susie.

"Guess who was selling the donkey rides," said an amused Joe. "None other than the great maestro Luigi and later we saw candy floss being handed out by the magnificent Madame Celeste! He chuckled.

"There was an ice cream vendor at the top of the beach and as well as vanilla he had coffee flavoured cornets, they were delicious, I had one yesterday afternoon and another just before we caught the coach to come home." Susie kissed Joe's cheek. "I've been thoroughly spoiled," she said.

"I best be gettin' along, I want to call at Kathleen's on me way, we bought a teethin' ring for the young 'en, Susie says that when she's grown up Kathleen'll be able to tell Beth that she cut her teeth on a bit o' Skegness."

All the excitement of the evening at last stilled, the girls in their bed, Edna and Billy sat quietly.

"Where do you suppose Jack Sulley 'ad been all that time," said Edna. "Poor Lillian was nearly at her wits' end."
For several seconds Billy didn't speak, then a smile spread slowly across his face.

"Mrs.Dodds, I've waited since middle o' the afternoon, in all that time the tide's come in, gone out and come in again. When are we goin' to 'ave that soddin' paddle?"

Charles sat staring at the floor, Hilda and John were in bed and George was walking Alice home. Annie had been knitting a cardigan to fit Kathleen's little girl come winter but her eyes had grown tired, now the needles and wool lay idle in her lap.

"Davina would like us all to go for tea next Sunday, she begins to look quite old Charles, she will after all be seventy six in August. Surely to spend a couple of hours at The Park wouldn't be all that taxing, you could read your paper there just as you do here, Davina doesn't expect you to chat endlessly. She has always been such a good friend to us, sometimes I think you fail to acknowledge enough just how kind Davina has been."

Charles sighed, "What has age to do with anything. Leonora Wicks could have been no more than in her early fifties but she's dead and buried, Davina could outlive the both of us, who knows." He stood. "Wicks may not think to cancel it but I can't imagine he'll want her magazine anymore, put this week's on the counter for sale, I don't want to be stuck with it. I'm going to bed, a week seems too far ahead to sensibly plan, next Sunday will be time enough to decide whether or not I'm going to The Park for tea."

Annie waited for Charles to climb the stairs, she put her knitting on the dresser and fetched a small pan of milk to heat for herself. She felt the need of something comforting, a measure of warmth, not for her extremities but to ease the sense of chill somewhere deep inside herself.

The only chance she had to call on Davina was of a Sunday afternoon and then not every week by any means. Walking along The Ropewalk and passed Tamarisk ever prompted a feeling of loss. Robert Appleyard had passed away, very peacefully, at home, Catherine and Annie both present. Charles had raised no objection when Annie had handed him Catherine's note, delivered by a messenger boy. Robert was failing fast, please, please could she come. Remembering Dr Robert Appleyard's efforts when his own mother lay so very ill, Charles took over at the shop and sent Annie on her way at once.

The emotions that tore at the two women as they sat at Robert's bedside, whilst never voiced, were nonetheless so similar. Margaret should have been there but it was too late. All the years removed from her father, yet in actual distance there stood no real impediment. Annie knew that just as herself, Catherine would consider Robert to be closer to his daughter in death than in life. One of those many echoes that travelled along the empty corridors at the convent, following seemingly silent nuns whose inner voices might be heard by their creator and by those abiding in his Heaven.

Following the funeral Catherine had stoically carried on at Tamarisk. Her daughter, memories of happier times, of Philip, all persuaded her to stay in that large, lonely house. Not until a surprise visit by Donald, one of the servicemen she and Robert had cared for during the war, did her spirit find release from its confinement. Donald brought news of life, his marriage, and his two children. He'd held Catherine's hands. 'Dance one more time with me Mrs.A'. He'd sung a cheerful lyric and gently led her about the room, until quite spontaneously and unchecked, Catherine had laughed, open, joyful laughter.

The very next day she had replied to yet another letter from Norman, pleading with his mother to vacate Tamarisk to travel to Durham, where her time could be filled with activity, just as she had ever chosen it to be. Packing her personal belongings Catherine had left The Ropewalk and caught a train north. Her words to Annie had been touching and would forever remain in Annie's memory. 'Dance my dear, however downcast life would have you be, order your spirit to dance. Remember that we must keep our minds from defeat'.

Annie missed Catherine very much, it made all the more disturbing Davina's advancing age. Tamarisk had stood empty for almost twelve months. Norman had come to Nottingham to act for his mother in instructing an agent to undertake the sale of the property. Within five months a buyer had been found. Norman had again travelled to Nottingham to arrange the removal of furniture and other items. Finally the keys were passed to a family from Newark. Annie had seen them once or twice as she passed by on her way to Davina's. It was a curious coincidence that the new occupants of Tamarisk were, mother, father, two sons and a daughter, a replica of the Appleyards, although Annie remembered Catherine saying that Norman had already left home before she, Robert and the two younger moved from a small property close by the hospital, to The Ropewalk. Perhaps that explained why Norman achieved to detach himself so much more readily than his mother.

Catherine wrote to Annie regularly, long, interesting letters, very often three or four sheets of text. As Annie turned each one it was as if between them, musical notes had lain waiting and now freed, they rose up from the paper as cheery encouragement, ordering her spirit to dance.

Not so the last few letters Annie had received from Alice Hemsley. Now irregular, no longer sent at their established stages of the year's progression, but sometimes two, almost identical in content, within days of each other. Alice's writing had become confused. In her last communication she had twice referred to Charles as Nathan. When Annie had cautiously enquired of Davina if Alice had recently been in touch, her reply confirmed the doubts harboured by them both. 'I fear Alice is unwell', Davina had said anxiously. 'I anticipate a letter from Walter when his strength permits. Dementia is a most cruel affliction, I would prefer to drop suddenly, in the midst of a lively endeavour than to exist with a mind that could no longer organise coherently'.

Annie sipped the boiled milk. It began to soothe. Sarah and Davina both in their gentle way bolstered her strength 'til it paid no more heed of Charles' indifference, than it would of any minor obstacle, as she had come to regard it. The back door latch rattled, George was back.

"Haven't you gone to bed yet Mam, I would have been here ten minutes ago but I bumped into Ernie Searle. Susie and Joe had a good weekend at Skeggy by all accounts. Joe called in to see Kathleen on his way home, apparently their landlady took them to the theatre, I'm sure Edna will give you chapter and verse when you see her."

Annie smiled. "I'm glad they enjoyed themselves, they both work hard and deserve a treat."

George was silent for a moment, his mam sat all alone, even when Charles was in the room with her, she may as well have been alone. He stood in front of her.

"There's to be a midsummer dance at the Masonic Hall next Saturday night, in aid of the orphanage at Snenton. Alice won't be able to go, she promised her dad to go with him to visit her grandma in Buxton, they couldn't get back in time." He paused, just for a second. "So, I'm taking you Mam. This shop can manage without you for once, we both know dad wouldn't consider going, so me, your son, George Boucher is taking you dancing, and that's an end to it!"

CHAPTER SIX

September.

Edna put the packet of semolina into her shopping bag.

"That's the lot," she said, as Annie entered the last item in the book.

"It's a weight to carry Edna," said Annie. "Why don't you leave some of it here and I'll send what isn't urgent with George or John tomorrow."

"No I'll be alright, donkeys go best laden they say. I'll 'ave five minutes on a bench in the arboretum. I really thought I'd feel different, yer know, liberated, like some sort o' burden 'ad been lifted from me shoulders. Shows how daft Edna Dodds is, enfranchisement, all I know is if I've been 'enfranchised', then it must 'ave been done under anaesthetic, 'cause I never felt a bloody thing an' still 'aven't."

Annie chuckled. "We are entitled to voice our opinions on local council issues, government polices and we might expect our views to be taken into account. We are now granted the vote, to be recorded alongside the votes of men, to present ourselves at the poll, whatever the election, local or national."

Edna huffed sarcastically. "How are we 'sposed to know owt about any o' that stuff. I'm lucky if I find time to read headlines on the soddin' paper, let alone all that political drivel, even Billy turns to sports page after pretendin' to understand Baldwin's theory on things. His mam reckons there's not one o' them pocket linin' windbags as don't claim to 'ave shit a miracle every day. They'll speechify an' tell yer the ins an' outs of a duck's backside then go home to somebody else's missus to try an' hatch another bugger just like the'selves."

Annie sighed. "I know it seems far removed from our lives but only by minding can we ever change things. Each political party has its own manifesto, spelling out its intentions. We should study them in depth, if the policies of one appear to align with our own then we might vote for their representative, be it at local council level or national government."

Edna sniffed and looked slightly amused. "I wouldn't mind studyin' Smithfield's manifesto in depth, if I wer' a single woman o' course!"

"Shame on you Edna Dodds," said Annie, trying to look shocked.

"I'm only pullin' your leg, but I am surprised that some revitalized widow 'asn't cast off 'er weeds an' shown 'im the benefits o' domestic bliss."

"Why a widow?" Asked Annie, feeling it somewhat unfair to dismiss Andrew Smithfield's chances of finding a single lady.

"Well 'e's not in the first flush o' youth is 'e, an' livin' wi' an aged aunt, I reckon 'e's probably got used to the older woman. 'E comes across as a decent bloke though, even before I wer' 'enfranchised', 'e allus listened to what I 'ad to say, like 'e were actually interested."

Just then the shop doorbell rang and Mrs.Rashleigh's head popped round the side.

"Can't stop but thought you might not 'ave heard. Rosie Spooner's had twins, no more than arf hour ago, don't know what sort."

With that the head withdrew and the door rattled back in its frame.

"God help 'im, Tommy Spooner never seems to get any modest measure o' responsibility, over the years that lad 'as fed an' watered more than 'is share. Joe's the same, thinks the world of 'is family. Edith Spooner might be deaf but them two lads of 'er's must 'ave sounded Hallelujahs in 'er heart, I've said to Billy, our Susie's lucky, when she's wed to Joe she'll never want for owt as matters."

Annie was pensive. "Twins, I hope Rosie is alright."

"If any woman wer' fit to 'ave twins it must be Rosie. 'Er bosom wer' a sight bigger than mine even afore she left school. I don't suppose there's much demand for a wet nurse these days but I reckon Rosie could feed two an' still 'ave plenty left over to nourish another. When she started workin' at The Kardoma, 'er mam spent a small fortune at Drew's on good brassieres. I can remember Audrey Potts tellin' me that if she'd totted up the cost of every corset she'd ever 'ad it wouldn't 'ave come to the amount she'd shelled out on Rosie. 'I'll not 'ave a daughter o' mine waitin' on table wi' a loose bust an' saggin' shoulders', she said." Edna sighed. "I've seen men wi' their noses pressed to the windo' when Rosie wer' takin' a muffin off one o' them fancy glass stands. It's a good job we women don't behave like that or we'd be crawlin' past the queue at labour exchange on all fours eyein' up every crotch." Edna picked her shopping bags from the counter. "God bless 'em, both little babies, whatever sort they are." With a sigh that revealed Edna's concern for Rosie, that new mother, she was gone.

Freddy leant against the ancient wooden gate, he must have repaired it at least four times in recent years and even now it protested his weight. So much of the farm was run down and in need of improvement. The machinery with which they worked was outdated, more modern systems enabled greater efficiency. He'd just finished the last stook of corn, while the scene he now surveyed would doubtless be charming to the eye of the incarcerated factory worker, or the clerk, whose days were spent with his nose poised only inches from his ledger, Freddy nevertheless felt frustrated.

He had spoken with his mam when he'd managed to find her free from the shop and alone for a few minutes. He explained his vision for the farm, telling Annie of his intention to seek additional funds from the bank. Freddy had remembered her instruction on matters of money, 'save all you can, one day you'll need it'. They had discussed the financial implications and Annie's opinion had been encouraging but tempered by her concerns over the wider economic situation. She admired Freddy for his purpose and ambition but he was yet so young, his life should hold more than years of toil. 'We'll ask your dad if he can help' she'd said, 'you should seek as little as possible from the bank. I'm sure Charles will agree and you could let your dad have the money back when you're established, a bit at a time'. Freddy's response had been immediate and firm.

'No Mam, this is for me to do, if William ever learned that dad had loaned me money can you imagine how all my days, he'd taunt me with that knowledge'.

Arthur Cropley had agreed in principle to Freddy buying into the farm but with Arthur's health now imposing severe restrictions on his ability to work, Freddy must secure the means of updating equipment and in the process, enable Bobbers Mill to achieve the greater potential its acreage should present. Arthur would keep a third interest, which Freddy would buy from him progressively over the course of the next few years.

The old couple would retire to a small property closer to town, where they might both find life kinder and less arduous. Freddy would employ a labourer through the periods of lambing and harvest and rely on piece workers if at other times he couldn't manage alone. As he contemplated the future, a struggle for more immediate survival suddenly appeared before his eyes. A rabbit fled between the stooks, chased by a stoat, the undulating motion of the latter seemed to propel it all the faster and the shrill squeal of the unfortunate rabbit, outrun and overcome somewhere behind a corn stook, brought a shiver to even the country-wise Freddy. He picked his jacket from the gatepost and the pike from where he'd rested it against the thorn hedge. His appointment at the bank had been arranged for 10-30 the following morning, he could only hope the manager, empowered to decide his fate might bear no trait similar to that of the stoat. He had heard accounts of men pursued for trifling amounts, overcome and destroyed of spirit, when a sensible deliberation between both parties could have enabled a mutually agreeable result.

His mam had suggested he approach Barclays Bank. Through latter years a number of smaller banks had chosen to merge with Barclays, they were receptive to enterprise and displayed a less stuffy, old school image. Freddy was not aware of his mother's reservations regarding Gerald Birkett, manager at Braithwaites, the bank used by his father. It was human nature to take an impression of character from any individual representing officialdom and Gerald Birkett had not ever inspired Annie with confidence. In fact the opposite was the case, she doubted his integrity. Whether this was wholly justified she could not know but Freddy was a young man, the nature and situation of his work limited his worldliness. He needed advice and measured support. Gerald Birkett worked for no one but himself, as an advisor he was dubious, any support he offered would be measured for his own gain before the furtherance of another. That was Annie's instinctive belief.

As Freddy hung his jacket on a hook behind the door, the smell of onion cooking and steamy vapour emitting from a pan gently simmering on the stove, confirmed steak and kidney pudding was on the menu. He would miss Dorothy Cropley's cooking, other than the good meals he had at Gregory Street, Mrs.Cropley had fed both Arthur and himself for many years. Few occasions offered Freddy any young female company, there was however one young woman whom he'd met at the seed merchants. A query on the Bobbers Mill account had rendered it necessary to call at the office, or what passed for an office. In reality it was a most basic facility, Freddy had considered the young woman busily working within to be truly flexible, answering the telephone, typing up invoices, making tea and bandaging a nasty gash to the hand, sustained by one of the men occupied in loading, all during the ten minutes or so that passed whilst Freddy awaited clarification of Arthur's account. Her smile radiated to all four corners of the simple wooden shed, her hair was the colour of the barley straw he stacked in the barn and her voice remained in his head long after he had returned to the farm, like a catchy tune heard for the first time, which refused to be silenced.

'Just a moment, I'll check the ledger, how are Mr. and Mrs.Cropley'? A simple enough exchange, yet the words lingered and kept Freddy company as he laboured. Eventually he'd plucked up the courage to ask her if she'd like to go for a walk one evening, after work. Her answer had been 'yes', no attempt at coyness or silly dithering to undermine his confidence, just a straightforward 'yes'. Friendship blossomed. Freddy had been close to telling his mam about the developing romance between himself and Francis Ripley when he'd last called at the shop but Celia had been present and for the time he preferred William not to know. If or when he found himself to be living alone at the farm cottage he would propose to Francis. In each other's company they were completely at ease, they had spoken of their families, of interests and hopes. It was a considerable encouragement to Freddy, knowing that their remembered past and perceived future seemed to coincide.

"All done in the top field are yer lad?" Asked Arthur, proceeding to slice a loaf of bread.

"Wash up quickly Freddy, I'm going to serve up now." Dorothy moved about the room so slowly these days, much reduced in weight, she presented a worrying sight for Freddy. She should not be caring for him, attending her husband was as much as should be asked of her and even that warranted some relief. She ate so little herself, Freddy troubled over her balance, at times alarmingly unsteady. He nevertheless washed his face and hands hastily, joining Arthur at the table where they could discuss the morning's activity and appear not to notice Dorothy's slowness. If Freddy offered to help she became distressed as though embarrassed by her decline. Still sharp of mind, she held full awareness of how much her physical ability had waned.

Freddy was quite determined that he would pay Arthur only the best price for the farm. This elderly couple had treated him as if he were their own. They deserved a comfortable old age, free of worry. Dorothy carefully laid a plate of dinner on the table, smiled at Freddy and said.

"It's a good job we've got you or Arthur an' me 'ould be eatin' up the same meal all week. Does my heart good to see a young man feed, I've made a custard for after."

Arthur had still not told his wife of his intention to move closer to town. Freddy had ventured to suggest that it might be sensible to say something, to give her time to get used to the plan, but as yet Arthur resisted. 'Let's know for sure lad, mustn't jump the gun', had been his response. Perhaps after tomorrow morning's meeting at the bank, Freddy might have confirmation to allow Arthur peace of mind.

"Oh my word, aren't they beautiful?" Celia gazed down at the two tiny babies lying at either end of the crib. Two boys, Thomas and Samuel slept obligingly while their mother spread out on the bed the contents of Celia's gift parcel. Matinee jackets, nighties, vests and a cot sheet, embroidered with a Peter Rabbit in one corner all hurriedly wrapped by Celia when she heard of the arrival of twin boys.

"I knitted the jackets myself, I dropped a stitch and didn't realise until I'd done so many more rows that I just picked it up with a bodkin and darned it in, I'm sure that no one could detect it and it's round the back anyway," said Celia proudly.

Rosie was close to tears at her friend's kindness. Through her hanky, which she held to her watery eyes and nose, Rosie sniffled the words.

"You shouldn't 'ave brought all these, they must 'ave cost a fortune, whatever will William say, 'e'll be cross, I know 'e will."

"Nonsense," replied Celia, dismissive of Rosie's anxiety. In truth she would not tell William. Tommy was a very good friend of many years, she had heard William speak often of their youth, growing up together at the same school, on the same streets, it would be a pleasure, one would hope, for William to give to Tommy's young sons. Yet Celia's husband did have a tendency to be ungenerous, there was no need after all for him to be aware of the baby clothes, in these liberated times a wife didn't require her husband's sanction on everything. Besides, he was away again. This time it was to Birmingham Smithfield had sent him with samples of the latest Vyella patterns. He would be back the next day, it was usually just one night but if she must be content alone on these occasions then she was surely entitled to make a gift of a few baby clothes to her closest friend, indeed to William's good friend too for Tommy was the father of these beautiful twin boys, an achievement as yet not reached by William Eddowes.

When Celia one evening over their meal, had suggested she might apply for the part time position, advertised in the window at Drew's, William had been less than agreeable. 'We are doing well enough, why would I want my wife to stand behind a shop counter, to be coughed and sneezed on by all and sundry', had been his response. Celia had though it a most ungracious remark considering his mother's tireless endeavour for all the family.

William had chosen not to add that to allow his wife to go out to work, Celia, their daughter, could send Jessie and Gwendolyn Tozer's impression of him to an unfortunate low. It was William's intention to seek membership of The Lodge. He had waited patiently for promotion, now a foreman at Brassington and on his way up, he felt the time was right to ask his father-in-law to put him forward.

Rosie carefully folded the tiny garments and placed them on the dressing table. "I shall show them to Tommy before I put them in the drawer. Mam'll want to see them an'all, she's gone to the shop for a few bits. I shall be glad when she lets me go meself."

"You must be patient for a few more days," said Celia. "You've given birth twice haven't you really. I've heard mother speak of long confinements in the past. In fact knowing her as I do, I wouldn't be surprised if Edmund and myself had been crawling before mother ventured from the sofa and her essential reading matter. I think she could recite the entire content, cover to cover, of 'Who's Who'. I thought learning Hiawatha all the way through in school was tedious, why did I need to know about a North American Indian, however heroic, but mother could probably tell you the names of all Hiawatha's family right down to second cousins."

Just then, a sound downstairs confirmed the return of Rosie's mam. They heard a 'clomp' as Audrey Potts put her shopping bags down on the flags.

"Whatever 'as she bought, I only asked her to get some bread and potatoes," said Rosie quietly, she called down through the open door, "are you alright Mam?"

"I got a few bits for meself while I wer' there, Miss Turpin an' Mavis send their best," Audrey's animated chatter drifted up the stairs as she moved about the scullery. "Which side o' family do twins come from Miss Turpin asked me. I told 'er it must be on the Spooner's side, all the men in our family are too lazy to make more than one at a time. Twin boys an'all. Accordin' to me dad it took a bit more concentration to make a lad, 'e reckoned if it wer' a girl then the father couldn't 'ave left it soak for long enough."

Rosie turned bright red from embarrassment at Celia having heard such a revelation, she ran out of the bedroom and called down the stairs. "Put the kettle on Mam, Celia's 'ere, she's brought some lovely things for the babies.

Thomas and Samuel slept still, Celia peered down at them then looked back at Rosie, a big grin across her face.

"If William favours a son first then I shall inform him of what is required!" Both young women stifled their laughter so as not to wake the little boys and went downstairs to see Rosie's mam.

"I had no idea you were with Rosie Celia my dear, how are you and your mother, God bless her, you must tell her I asked after her, said Audrey, trying desperately to speak correctly and not to drop a single 'H'. Inwardly she hoped this genteel young lady had not paid any regard to her earlier remark. "I bought some nice biscuits we'll take a cup of tea in a minute." The kettle began to sing and Audrey took down the caddy from the shelf. "I went to Hastilow's to get yer a big tin o' Sanatogen Rosie," she said. Beginning now to relax, her conversation became entirely natural. "Them two little ens'll wear yer down to a shadow if yer don't look after yourself, ask Tommy to get yer some stout when 'beer off' opens. A measure o' tonic every night 'afore yer go to bed an' a drink o' stout wi' your dinner by day'll do yer no harm at all. It'll give yer a bit o' wind but not the sort as bothers babies like cabbage does, just let it go anyroad that's the way, you'll make milk alright."

A bag of malted sweet biscuits now sat on the table. "When I told Miss Turpin an' Mavis these wer' your favourites, they put in an extra arf pound for no charge." Audrey happily dunked a broken biscuit into her tea, Rosie glanced across at her friend for reassurance, this home was very different to anything Celia had previously experienced she felt sure. Celia took a second malted biscuit and just as with the first, she dipped it into the steaming cup, looking happy and content she smiled back at Rosie, thinking but not voicing her notion on the significance of soaking it for just the right length of time!

Celia had felt disinclined to leave Rosie and the babies to return to her own empty house so had stayed until late afternoon, just long enough to say hello to Tommy when he came in from work. Looking tired and seeming rather subdued for the normally cheerful Tommy, he'd embraced his wife, given Celia a peck on the cheek and sunk into the chair without uttering a word. Celia had thought him to be in a state of shock.

'Whatever's the matter'? Rosie had asked nervously.

'I called in to see mam, I wanted to tell 'er that everythin' wer' alright, she wer' that worried after comin' to see you an' the twins, afraid o' summat goin' wrong. It wer' the same when our Kathleen 'ad Beth. It's as if mam can't let 'erself believe the Spooners are due some good luck. When I got there she wer' cryin'. A letter lay open on the table, it wer' from Joyce in Loughborough. Apparently the Fosterjohns dismissed 'er four months ago, she don't say why'. Tommy had hesitated, possibly because of Celia's presence but his torment was too much. 'She's been charged wi' solicitin', the police are holdin' 'er, as it's a first offence they'll release 'er to a responsible member of family to await a court hearin'. Failin' that she'll be transferred to a detention centre for women in Leicester. I'll 'ave to go, there is nobody else, wi' me dad gone an' me the eldest. At least she'll be able to help wi' the twins, washin' an' all that. I won't let mam 'ave the responsibility, besides it wouldn't be fair on the younger ones'.

He'd looked at Rosie with despair in his eyes and she'd wrapped her arm about his shoulders. Celia had heard her whisper, 'It'll be alright'.

She'd felt awkward it was such a personal matter, while Celia bore no measure of judgment, more the contrary, she felt compassion for Tommy and his family but she'd nevertheless considered it only right to leave at once, so husband and wife could talk in private.

As she walked along Forest Road her mind travelled from the company she had just left, to William. Where would he be staying overnight. Hopefully in a cosy boarding house with a motherly landlady who took delight in cooking a good meal for her lodgers. It was strange how a conversation entirely unrelated to herself could still be unsettling. Until now she'd not given the slightest notion to how William might spend his time, she scolded herself for even allowing such unworthy thoughts and hastened her pace, diverting her mind to what she might have for tea.

A voice called out behind her. "Wait for me Celia." She turned to see John, her brother-in-law, running to catch up with her. He gave her a hasty kiss, caught his breath, then asked if she'd been to see Rosie and the twins.

"Celia replied with a brief, "Yes, they are lovely," divulging nothing of Tommy's troubles. No one would hear it from her, no one.

"I'm in no hurry to go home today," said John. "I hate having to give mam bad news but I can't not tell her."
Celia felt anxious, surely word of Joyce's misdemeanour had not reached the streets already.

"Oh dear," she said, "has something happened?"

"Mr.Hamlin gathered us all together at dinnertime and told us he has no other option than to give us a week's notice. I feel sorry for the man, I'm sure he was genuine. Apparently the business never fully recovered from the problems of '26' but orders trickled in and he propped up the firm with his savings. Even then it was proving difficult but when he heard of the development at Bestwood, he secured a bank loan against his house. He felt confident Hamlin's would win the contract to supply all the drainage pipes, he'd done business with Woolascroft's before. It didn't happen and when he queried the situation he was told by the manager at Woolascroft's that they had to work within a tight budget to satisfy the council and that Hamlin's couldn't hope to compete on price with pipes they were importing from abroad."
Celia felt almost guilty at being relieved John's news was not relating to Tommy but she did genuinely hold concern for John's situation.

"What will you do, perhaps William could ask Mr.Smithfield if a job could be found for you at Brassington. He's in Birmingham today, I don't expect to see him until teatime tomorrow but I could speak with him when he gets home."

Celia liked John very much, his regard for Annie, his mother, pleased her especially. That was a big fault on William's part, he ever took his mother for granted. There had been times when Celia could have rebuked him sternly had she mustered the strength of heart. His moods could be so sullen and if provoked he could sulk for days. Celia wanted a baby, keeping him sweet tempered took a great deal of her energy so pointing out to him his lamentable failings not only threatened a protracted spell of gloominess but would almost certainly deny her any chance of motherhood. She threaded her arm through John's.

"Neither of us is in any hurry to go home so at least I can walk with you for company. I'd like to see Hilda, I was pleased to hear she'd been granted another year at Clarendon, I've always recognised her brightness. I can tell your mam all about Thomas and Samuel, I know how much she loves babies and Rosie is proving a splendid mother. It will take her mind off your news and hopefully lessen the dismay. I'm not hungry, a piece of toast will do for me, I don't need to be fed with a full meal when I'm not expected."

John laughed. "Now I can just imagine mam agreeing to you having a slice of toast. You'll be put to the table and made to eat whatever everyone else is having, with an extra spoon of pudding to make up for William's shocking neglect of his wife."

They both chuckled knowing it to be an accurate prediction. Their progress quickened, things didn't seem quite so bad somehow. John remembered it was Thursday, it was nearly always rabbit cooked underneath crispy belly pork on Thursdays. He began to whistle a cheerful tune and Celia's quiet imagination returned to her dream of babies.

Freddy stepped out from the bank feeling he'd achieved some degree of progress but now it was for Arthur to propel things forward. The manager, one James Rothero, seemed a pleasant enough fellow, in his late forties Freddy estimated him to be. His handshake was firm and a brief smile as he'd invited Freddy to take a seat, suggested at least some reason to be optimistic. It was as his face settled back to a more business like composure that Freddy was struck by the manager's moustache. It was so precisely trimmed as to look artificial, too exact to be actually growing, like an ornamental attachment to befit a particular occasion. Perhaps it was to lend an air of importance or to add that distinguished expression which invariably belonged to men of status. Celia's mother had taken to wearing a false hairpiece when outside the house, her own hair having become tiresomely thin. Celia referred to it as her mother's 'snooty snood'. At his side on the desk there was a cup and saucer, he'd clearly taken a cup of tea or coffee prior to receiving Freddy. A telltale smear of

82

chocolate at the base of the cup, revealed evidence of a sweet biscuit having sat in the saucer. There were two pictures on the wall behind Mr.Rothero, a pair of prints in matching frames. One of Wollaton Hall the other of The Castle, magnificent stone structures that rose up over centuries, monuments to man's perpetual endeavour. Rothero had cleared his throat and leaned back in his chair.

'Well now Mr.Eddowes', he'd said 'perhaps you'd like to tell me of your plans, then we can ascertain if the bank is able to assist you'.

He'd listened to Freddy's description of the farm, his vision for the future through more modern methods and his need of additional funds beyond his savings. 'Are you currently with Barclays', had been his initial enquiry. Freddy felt his answer would surely go against him, banking as he was with Braithwaites. Then he recalled Annie's theory on Barclays, a forward looking facility, not displaying that stuffy, old school image. Freddy quickly explained that as a young man, quite naturally, he had followed his father's custom and lodged savings at Braithwaites. Now older and taking a wider view, he considered Barclays to be attuned to more modern enterprise, less bound in tradition. He used his mother's phraseology, adding his own carefully chosen words. 'The brighter premises here at Barclays Bank give a sense of opportunity to someone like myself who is seeking advice'. Flannel, Edna would have called it but if it served the purpose then Freddy had no qualms at using such contrived persuasion.

After twenty minutes of bank manager spiel, to which Freddy listened intently, paying it appropriate homage, it was established that a loan would be offered, but given all the circumstances, not least of these Freddy's age, it must be secured. This required Arthur Cropley to instruct a solicitor on the division of the deed. Freddy's ownership of the two thirds, must be held in title by both himself and the bank until such time as the loan be dispensed. Arthur's remaining third would not then be at risk should Freddy default on his repayments. It all seemed so very unnecessary to the entirely honest Freddy, however his intelligence enabled him to see why it would be a condition of the loan. Whatever it cost Arthur in solicitor's fees, then Freddy would share that cost. The Cropley's must be in a position to buy their house close to town and be comfortable thereafter, he would not countenance any transaction between Arthur and himself otherwise.

It was a little after 11-30 his mam would almost certainly be in the shop. Charles was usually hiding away upstairs or off playing cards with somebody of similar ilk by this hour of the day. His dad behaved curiously, like a nervous creature, venturing out of cover only during first and last light, avoiding predatory others but in so doing, limiting his vision of the world.

Peering through the window Freddy could see two customers within and the figure of his mam behind the counter. He waited patiently until the shop was empty.

"Hello Mam," he said then began to chuckle mischievously. "I've come to buy two thirds of a farm and to ask you to keep a wife under the counter for me until I'm ready to collect her." Annie looked bewildered. Freddy continued. "The bank agreed the loan subject to Arthur's solicitor drawing up the deed and when I've bought that part of the farm and he and Dorothy have moved to their new home," he paused, "then I'm going to ask a young lady to marry me. She's called Francis Ripley and you'll love her Mam. I know you will."

The shop doorbell clanged and in came Mrs.Rashleigh in a state of excitement. "I've got to tell you Mrs.Eddowes, I can't recall anybody in our family ever winnin' owt before but our Steve 'ad the winnin' ticket at the Institute raffle an' 'e took home a bottle o' whisky. 'Is dad'll be round like a shot when 'e knows. That man could smell a tot o' free spirit from miles off. Like me brother's dog, the daft thing went missin' last weekend, gone three days it wer', come back about a stone lighter. Turns out it'd been hooked up to a bitch two miles away in Basford."

Freddy winked at his mam. "I'll tell you all about it when I come for dinner on Sunday."

Annie was perplexed. To have heard such a cryptic account of Freddy's intentions and now having to wait until the day after tomorrow for an explanation seemed unfair. If only Mrs.Rashleigh had arrived just five minutes later. Annie had wanted to tell Freddy of John's situation too, it would all have to wait.

As she politely expressed her delight at Steve Rashleigh's good fortune, she inwardly puzzled over Freddy's remark. The bank loan was one thing but a wife, that was news far too important to be casually delivered across the shop counter. She would tell Freddy, his mam was too old to be teased. As she stooped to take a tin of golden syrup from the bottom shelf for Mrs.Rashleigh's steamed pudding, she smiled from happiness. Her family was expanding, Celia had confided in her that she and William were trying for a baby and George and Alice must surely be close to announcing their engagement.

"Was that a pound of bacon Mrs.Rashleigh or a half?" Asked Annie.

"May as well take the pound, I'd only be back for the other arf by Monday, wait 'til you get grandchildren, they all get sent round to grandma at the weekend." Annie made no reply but as she sliced the rashers, a sense of good things to come drove away those niggling concerns. She looked forward to Sunday.

William was feeling pleased with himself. He'd secured two significant orders whilst in Birmingham and with his confidence riding high he determined himself to speak this weekend with Jessie Tozer about The Lodge. Celia chatted happily from the kitchen where she made ready their meal, content at having her husband home again. William paid little attention, Rosie's babies might charm his wife but they were of no interest to him. Tommy would doubtless work yet more hours to pay the bills and become ever more governed by those two households, his own and his mothers. Why he didn't impose more authority, stamp his own rule William could not understand and he perceived it as weakness. In reality Tommy Spooner was more of a man than William Charles Eddowes would ever be.

Alicia Plowright, Smithfield's aunt, had seen through William's shallow veneer long ago and voiced her opinion quite forcibly to Andrew. He however, persisted in defending the young man, at times almost convincing himself, yet in private moments of contemplation his innate honesty compelled him to admit it was a foolish, irrational loyalty he felt for Annie Eddowes that influenced his thinking. Only by reminding himself of her correct title, Mrs.Charles Eddowes, did he avoid disgracing himself, but it did little to remove the disgrace from his conscience and even less to erase from his mind this futile admiration, stifling his ability to look elsewhere.

Celia placed William's meal on the table in front of him. "John received troubling news yesterday," she said. "Hamlin's are closing down, all the men have been given one week's notice. Perhaps Mr.Smithfield might find an opening for him, you could ask."

William picked up the saltcellar. "You never season the stew enough. I had braised beef last night, my landlady got the seasoning just right. What use is a drainpipe maker to a textile factory, besides, John's like Freddy, too soft for business." He put a potato in his mouth as though that were an end to the matter. Celia felt annoyed and disappointed.

"There's a difference in being kind and being soft, anyway John could learn," she said, turning away to fetch her own meal.

William sprinkled more salt over his food. "Some folk never learn, that's the trouble," he said ungraciously.

Just for that moment Celia wished her husband had stayed in Birmingham with his wonderful landlady. Next time she made stew she would add enough salt to strip the skin from his cruelly abrasive tongue.

CHAPTER SEVEN

Late March 1929

Lillian Sulley watched her daughter as the child played with a toy tea set, a make believe game of pouring from the tiny teapot a cup of tea for her doll and teddy bear. The little fingers carefully placing a raisin in the centre of each toy plate and holding them up to her pretend family. Then Norma, very carefully, carried a cup and saucer to her mam, the concentration on the young face so intense as her imagination urged her not to spill the contents. Lillian's hands trembled as she took it from her, forcing herself to smile back happily at the vision of innocence. As yet not speaking full sentences, only random words passed from Norma's lips but these could be even more potent, undiluted as they were by idle chatter.

"Make better," Norma reached up to kiss away the hurt, just as her mam kissed her when she fell over.

The moisture on Lillian's cheek left a salty taste on the child's mouth, she licked her lips repeatedly. Lillian forced her tears to cease, lifted the tiny cup and pretended to drink the make believe tea. Swallowing hard was easy and tipping the cup at the last with a final gulp, convinced the little girl and sent Lillian's misery down into the pit of her stomach.

Her lower back ached from where Jack had thrust her against the table. Her face still stung from the slap of his hand. Lillian wanted to run from this house, away to anywhere that hid her from Jack Sulley. But there was no such place. Her dad was not a compassionate man, he'd said, 'you made your bed, now you lie in it my girl'. Her mam had cried bitterly from helplessness.

Elsie Sulley was a good woman, she recognised many of the faults displayed by her son but Lillian could not tell her mother-in-law of these violent episodes, not while Winnie lay the bed so poorly and dependent on her daughter.

Jack's grandmother had suffered a severe stroke and barely able to raise a spoon to her mouth, Elsie tended her mother just as she would a baby. A month ago the doctor had said that it could be only a matter of days, that Winnie's body was failing her. Painfully thin and opening her eyes for just fleeting moments she nevertheless breathed still.

Jack had left the house in a rage all because there was no bacon. Lillian had fried two eggs and poured his tea strong as he favoured it but his temper had been foul. A barrage of abusive language had rained down about Lillian and Norma until her motherly instinct of protection empowered her to shriek back at him. 'You're not fit to be a father, you're nothing but a bully'.

He'd slapped her hard, sending her backwards against the table, then he'd struck her again, the thickness of her hair had mercifully cushioned the blow but even then, her ear throbbed from the rush of force that seemed to drive Jack's fury deep inside her head. Norma had begun to whimper, in his frustration he'd picked up her doll and thrown it onto the old sofa underneath the window where it had lain upside down in a bedraggled heap. Jack had begun to shout again but was convulsed with coughing and stormed out of the back door, slamming it in his wake.

After each of her husband's heartless advances, when he turned in their bed to take his 'given right', impaling her on his manhood like some long fought adversary, now spiked and held up as the prize, she'd gone downstairs as he slept and sluiced herself with salt water. The more it stung the more she trusted its consequence. Each month she bled and whether this desperate attempt at protection from pregnancy actually worked or rather it was a merciful intervention from God Lillian could not know, but she shook from relief at the sight of her own blood and the knowledge that nothing of Jack Sulley grew within her.

From where he sat on the low stonewall in front of the Mechanics Institute Jack could observe the congregation, now trickling out of St. Andrew's at the end of the morning service. Smiling, exchanging pleasantries, each one shaking the hand of the Vicar as they left the porch to walk down the path. Jack scuffed his boot over a crack in the paving, intent on destroying a small cluster of leaves that grew from a seed shed by the ash tree outside the Institute building.

This period of inertia, although imposed by himself and vital, as he saw it, to the success of their plans, nevertheless grated away at his nerves.

Two elderly women crossed the road and walked towards where he sat, their very respectable 'Sunday best' taunted him further. So precise, so assured of their ultimate passage to the feet of the Almighty, neither would cast their eyes his way, Jack Sulley was best ignored at all times. He was wrong, one stopped in front of him necessitating the other to do likewise, though Jack could tell by her expression she would have preferred to go straight on.

"How is your grandmother, we said prayers for her in church," said the one. She smelled of lavender, his mam put lavender on the antimacassars when visitors were due.

"Did yer offer one up for me an'all?" Asked Jack in his cynical way.

Undaunted she replied. "We prayed for all of Winnie's family," then, with a glance at her companion they began to walk away.

Jack called after them. "She's still alive, at least she wer' yesterday."

The woman turned to look back. "Don't worry, should Winnie die this week we shall continue to pray for you."

Jack fell silent, even he recognised when he'd been outwitted.

Another month and they could shift the lead on, in the meantime, it lay well hidden in a barn at Swinscoe, a rural area away to the west of the city, where little happened to invite any curiosity.

Jack had never been far away from the confusion and disorder during the strike. Following one of the riots in the street at which he'd observed from the periphery, he'd come upon Horace Clegg, literally crumpled as naught and left behind on the ground. Jack knew him from school days, a slightly built, sickly youth who'd progressed somehow to adulthood without adding flesh to his frame or strength to his constitution. A nasty wound to his head, either intentionally or accidentally caused by a steel toecap, oozed blood that congealed to Clegg's hair. Jack almost carried him to the hospital, unable as he was to walk unaided and by the time two nurses relieved Jack of his charge, so many memories had come flooding back that Jack waited until, bandaged and looking like a rabbit that had miraculously escaped the jaws of a terrier, Horace Clegg stumbled from the hospital doorway.

In school, Clegg had been the goal of every bully, belittled and debased as those, mindless of any consequence, powered their way through the tedious days of learning, using him as amusement at every break-time. Jack had stood enough of it. One dinnertime, within the space of five minutes, he'd bloodied several noses and reduced a number of lads to a snivelling huddle. The headmaster took no account of the wounding inflicted on Clegg, it had produced no blood therefore it was trivial. Jack was punished, made to bend over with his head just below the brass doorknob of the classroom door and in front of all, including the younger class and their teacher brought in to witness, he was caned on the backside, each stroke thrusting his head onto the doorknob. He'd made not a sound and thereafter the bullying stopped. Jack had only to cast a glance at Clegg's tormentors and their eyes would instantly lower. Curiously it won him the admiration of all the girls, indeed adoration might not be too strong a word for their simpering attention. More than this, it earned him the devotion of Horace Clegg who followed him puppy like until the time came for them to leave school and go their separate ways.

Now in later life, the lesson learned all those years ago drove Jack to bully before others bullied him. He'd become bitter and he used that cruel streak as a means to an end, sulking, scheming, arguably more sinister than immediate thuggery.

The biting sting of the cane had not satisfied his headmaster, that man employed to set him an example, to instruct him in the ways of an upstanding gentleman. One pain had not been deemed sufficient, the force of that brass doorknob to his head, adding to his hurt and humiliation instilled in Jack Sulley the only lesson he now considered worth remembering. Defy officialdom, fight only your own battles and never cry.

It was following the encounter in the street two years ago that Jack and Horace renewed their association. This time however, it was to be a partnership in crime. Clegg had an aunt Phyllis living alone on a smallholding at Swinscoe. He'd spent periods living with her, helping out after her husband died. Clegg had the use of a small truck in which his uncle Bill had carried beet and mangolds.

Jack had waited hours at a time outside the labour exchange only to be told 'come back next week'. A dozen or so men had been taken on at the pit, merely a gesture to appease the unions but there had been no increase in pay and save the few improvements in conditions underground, achieved by Henry Wicks through a discreet manipulation of funds, the miners continued to endure that existence of hardship.

Jack was sick of it all, honesty got a man nowhere, well he would make his own way, sod the bloody lot of 'em. He had one skill that set him apart, a fearless ability to climb. Since a child, he'd scaled obstacles with no thought of danger. In fact, being aloft above the rest, brought him a sense of calm, looking down from a height his tormentors seemed so much smaller.

The first job had been St.Saviour's. Since then, five more, the last had been Ripley Baptist Church in late October of the previous year. At the outset Jack had insisted they do only a half dozen jobs, then wait a full six months before attempting to shift the lead on. Horace Clegg had driven the truck and taken the lead, bit by bit from the end of a rope when Jack lowered it down. Never pushing their luck to strip more than a modest amount, Jack had convinced himself that the good Lord would put it down to wear and tear. Each time they had completed their task under the darkness of a moonless night and with impressive speed. Jack required no ladder or climbing aid, he used his feet and hands like a monkey, all he needed was the coil of rope over one shoulder and a bolster to raise the lead. This he carried between his vest and his

91

shirt, a tight belt about his waist prevented it escaping. Sometimes as he climbed, the heavy bolster, even through his vest rubbed the skin beneath leaving reddened welts but Jack's skin had borne welts before, across his backside, they'd stung for days and the scars had never totally faded.

On the back of the truck they kept a tarpaulin, filled and rolled with well rotted manure, like a gigantic cigarette. After laying the lead flat to the bed of the truck, they would unroll the tarpaulin over it and spread the manure. Only once had they been stopped by a constable. 'Bloody Hell, a nosey copper', Clegg had muttered under his breath as he'd brought the truck to a halt and wound down the window. The curious policeman laid his hand on the door and sniffed the air like a bloodhound. 'And what have you been up to, no good I'll be bound'. Clegg sniffed too and answered with such innocence, Jack had been impressed by his subterfuge. 'Been deliverin' shit officer, matured like vintage port, you'd not find better this side o' Newark, could do you a good deal if you're a gardenin' man'. The constable had briefly investigated the back of the truck. 'God Almighty,' taking two steps back he'd waved them on. As they drove up the road his eyes watered, the smell lingered in his tubes. Spitting into the gutter and clearing his nose, one nostril at a time, he'd left the scene muttering to himself. 'Jesus, vintage port! What sort o' fermentin' arsehole did that come from'? In his urgency to remove the stench he'd made no question of the unusual hour and the lead travelled to Swinscoe safely beneath its disguise.

Jack allowed Clegg to inflate himself with an assumed importance, if it kept him happy then why not. On their final run back to the smallholding last October, Horace had laughed out loud. 'Our dad allus reckoned I wer' like me uncle Clem. 'E wer' only a small made up man but they say 'is head wer' screwed on right road, could make a bob where next man 'ould starve'. Jack had asked idly what had become of this uncle Clem. 'Dead, long since, the war, some place out wi' the A-rabs. Somebody's got to fly the flag for Clement Clegg 'aven't they'?

At the end of April, the plan was to take the lead to Derby. Abel at the scrapyard in Nottingham was too obvious. The past six months of inactivity would have cooled the police enquiries. A scrap merchant a distance off, provided the 'no questions asked' price was right, would be sure to strike a deal. Then a similar scheme might be undertaken, not lead, next time they would leave the Almighty in peace. As yet Jack had not finalised his plan but the more he heard those words 'come back next week' and witnessed the power of Basil Stanford and his ilk, the more Jack Sulley festered within, coughing up bitter resentment 'til his mouth was filled with obnoxious bile and his lungs ached interminably.

The congregation had gradually drifted away from St.Andrews. After a few minutes, the Vicar, now minus his surplice and cassock, appeared at the lichgate. He cast a look of surprise across the road to where Jack still sat. The Reverend knew who this man was, Jack Sulley, a troublemaker, never in work and lacking all common courtesy. These days he would normally consign such a man to the place of lost causes, pass the problem along to St.Jude.

He'd been a Vicar many years. When beginning his ministry he would countenance no soul being lost to The Lord, but age wearied a man. 'The cloth' that once defined him as God's own envoy, now served to conceal the tired shoulders, no longer able to bear such weight of responsibility. 'The cloth' granted him easy passage, like a season ticket, he moved about the parish without impediment or confrontation.

Jack Sulley, sitting there on the low wall in front of the Institute, on this day, inexplicably aroused his almost abandoned calling to challenge, to win another man's soul, to take it for The Lord. He walked across the road and sat on the wall beside Jack. He didn't speak and it was the quietness that undermined Jack Sulley's usual brash response to anyone or anything he considered to be invading his space.

Why had the Vicar come to sit by him, why didn't he say something? Jack found himself feeling strangely nervous, intimidated.

Finally the Reverend spoke. "How old are you Jack?"

Jack's uncustomary nervousness lowered his defences and he answered without animosity. "Twenty nine." He replied in a subdued voice.

"I became a Vicar at the age of twenty nine, now I'm fifty nine. All the years you've lived Jack I've been a Vicar." He paused and drew his hand over his brow, letting it rest momentarily in the side of his neck. He spoke again. "When I turned forty, I felt an overwhelming need to spar with a man. In this job you seldom doubt your strength of spirit but it doesn't give you chance to prove your physical strength. I wanted to know if my muscle was as good as that of the next man, if I had a punch, some clout. It didn't happen of course, but if you and I had been born in the same year and if I'd met you here on this wall when I turned forty, I'd have chosen you Jack Sulley to spar with me. Now its too late and I'm too old."

Jack remained silent and his composure puzzled even himself. His usual readiness to lash out with some caustic remark seemed strangely disabled.

The Reverend continued. "It's an irony Jack, that anyone walking by now, observing the two of us sitting here side by side, would likely think us an odd sight. Jack Sulley, keeping company with his tormentor, because that's what they'd imagine me to be Jack, your tormentor. But they'd be wrong, you are my tormentor. You see, I shall never know if I could have held the ground, perhaps even taken some." The Vicar stood and was about to walk away when Jack spoke.

"We could go one round if yer like, an' I could keep one hand behind me back."

The Vicar smiled and held out his hand to shake Jack's. He responded and the two men, for several seconds clasped hands. As he let go his grip the Reverend said. "I do believe Jack, that is what we've just done."

Reg Yeats unfurled his shirtsleeves like the final curtain coming down on a long run play. The small, cluttered room he now surveyed had been his daily environment for the past twenty-eight years. The orchestra of sounds that struck up each early morning, advancing across the factory floor to the door of his office, would ring in his ears long after this day. That once intriguing smell of tobacco, now so familiar it no longer conjured up visions of a new world, a continent of adventure and opportunity but merely hung about his old jacket reminding him of Reg Yeats' lifetime's achievement, his overseeing of other men's lives. For that had been his actual purpose. A well ordered production line dealt with all the elements from the start to an end, but a man's life, at times through no fault of his own, became disordered. When Reg first became manager he viewed his position, his office, as some kind of prestige, like a military rank, but pertaining to civvie street. He'd imagined great things, accomplishments recognised and recorded that he'd wear proudly, the factory manager's equivalent to those worthy 'stripes'. His old jacket bore no stripes, just that ingrained smell of tobacco and a thinning of its cloth from the chaffing and grating of other men's lives.

His successor was to be Raymond Haynes. Reg had considered long and hard, was it fair to burden this comparatively young man with so much responsibility but none other could he recommend with such conviction to his own superiors. Reg had observed Haynes' quiet direction of those in his charge. Made a foreman seven years ago, his ability to encourage, to lead men forward without applying any weight of dominance to stifle the mind of another, had impressed Reg greatly. The two men had spent time together in the office, aware of Haynes' need to be comfortable with all aspects of the business Reg had, in his own quiet way, brought him to command a sound knowledge of the role of manager.

On Monday morning it would be Raymond Haynes who sat at the desk, who opened the office door to that tide of sound rising from the factory floor. He would be the man sharing the delight of another's first born. He would be the one counting the minutes on the clock with some despairing son whose mam lay close to the end, willing her to hang on long enough for him to be there.

Reg recalled the time Stanley Baines had been so sure his mam's death was imminent, he'd sent word to inform his boss that he wouldn't be in to work until the next day. Stanley had stayed at her bedside all that day and every hour of the following three days. On the fifth morning Stanley came to work, too desperate for his pay to risk any more absence. His mam passed away that very morning, faintly uttering his name. Reg had wept with Stanley Baines and advanced two weeks wages so Stanley could respectfully lay to rest the woman who'd reared him alone, against all odds, his father having walked away when he was just a baby.

Reg remembered from years ago a fight that had broken out in the yard one dinnertime. Before he could reach the commotion, a bloody nose, a split lip and ensuing black eyes had been the result. Marching the two offenders to his office and stripping them bare with his tongue, had revealed the source of rancour. Both had bedded the same woman, one had been satisfied without having to 'settle' for services rendered while the other had been obliged to pay five bob. The fight it turned out, was not over the woman but over the half crown which the sorely exploited one, as he'd deemed himself to be, demanded from his younger brother as fair dues, him having utilised the facility first rendering it second hand! Reg had marched them back to the yard and chucked a bucket of cold water over the both of them. In due course he'd been invited to their weddings and was godfather to the daughter of the eldest.

Reg looked at his jacket, draped carelessly over the chair and pictured in his mind one particular morning when an anxious mother had brought her son to apply for work, a memory of a weary woman, doing her best to steer her family through that hideous time of war. The son, William Eddowes, carrying such a chip on his shoulder, its weight prevented him from being upright, so blinded from the glare of his own ego he couldn't see the goodness that stood right in front of him. Reg had gathered up his jacket from the chair for Mrs.Eddowes to sit down. Neither her efforts nor his own had been enough for her son. William Eddowes was the very opposite of Raymond Haynes and now it must be for Haynes to incorporate into his life all those highs and lows, those losses and gains which dictated whether his men truly lived or merely existed. He must be the one to laugh with them, cry with them and through it all, show a tally to the big bosses that endorsed the merit of his own position.

Reg padlocked the heavy gates and looking back through the bars at the factory building sighed at his liberation, he was on his way home. Reg's set of keys would remain with him until his mind drove him to surrender them to Haynes. Already they lay heavy in his pocket, it was unlikely to take his tired mind very long.

George and John had been working together at Raleigh since the new-year. When a job had become vacant due to Charlie Roper enlisting in the army, George had wasted no time in telling his younger brother John. After finishing at Hamlin's John had picked up a few days work here and there, wherever he could. Davina had insisted the scullery at The Park was in dire need of stripping and lime washing. Mrs.Pooley, the housekeeper, had emptied the shelves in readiness and John had undertaken the task with enthusiasm, fixing fresh gauze to the meat safe, a job that had not been done since Frank and Ivy had lived with Davina, and repairing the 'Sheila Maid', that long wooden frame on which Mrs.Pooley hoisted the laundry to air. He gave two coats to the walls and treated the old cupboard doors inside and out with Dutch oil. Finally he'd emptied the trap beneath the sink of accumulated debris and rod the drains. Mrs.Pooley declared the water went away faster than she could blink. Davina, most unexpectedly had burst into tears. John and Mrs.Pooley at first imagined something about the endeavour disappointed her, then Davina revealed the thoughts, which provoked such emotion. Harold, Frank, dear Samuel all such memories had come flooding back and for that moment, Davina longed to see again those long gone friends. When John had told Annie of Davina's distress she'd understood fully. All those years ago, after Harold's funeral, when Samuel had needed work so badly, not just to bring money into the home but also to divert his thoughts from the grief, which would otherwise consume him, Davina had come to the rescue. Whilst John had no such dire need Davina had still insisted the work at The Park was vital and John had saved the day! It was Davina's unique psychology, not so much governed by the head but by the heart.

The closure of Hamlin's had troubled John, it seemed grossly unfair that given all Mr.Hamlin's efforts, it was as a result of decisions made by the local authority that this good man was driven to the verge of bankruptcy. If aunt Bella were still alive, Annie felt sure she would put forward all sides of the debate. Council revenue came from the purse of the ratepayer and when government contributed to the 'housekeeping' it was the taxpayer who enabled the means. So, was it not only prudent to abide by a certain budget? Conversely, if such practice rendered business unviable and resulted in longer queues at the labour exchange, causing grave financial difficulty to many, then which way forward should officialdom go? Either way it seemed unsatisfactory, 'like juggling soot', as Samuel said of making ends meet.

John was bright and a deep thinker, fleet of mind when the occasion required him to be but quiet and ponderous if the situation called for greater deliberation. At his interview with the manager before his employment with Raleigh, it was likely that John's ready perception helped convince the man of John Eddowes' suitability for the job.

Presumably Percy Pollard, the manager, adopted his own standard when interviewing applicants for a position in his factory. When John had related the event to Annie she'd felt amused and they'd shared a chuckle.

Ushered into the office by a foreman whom he knew vaguely from playing cricket down the Meadows, John was greeted with the words, 'now lad, sit yourself down and tell me what, in your opinion, is man's greatest invention'. Mr.Pollard had stood the other side of the desk looking over the top of his spectacles that perched precariously, slightly askew, at the end of a truly bulbous nose. John had responded immediately. 'The wheel sir, beyond all doubt it is the wheel'. Various answers to this question had been delivered across the desk to Pollard over the course of years, the wondrous telephone, the steam engine, that welcome advancement from a candle the miners lamp and on one memorable occasion Cyril Wheatcroft, father of ten, had nominated, 'that bloody marvellous woman's pussary thing', his somewhat confused reference to the contraceptive device, recently discovered by Mrs.Wheatcroft! But it was indeed the wheel, that hub of Raleigh's production that Pollard considered the only correct answer in his assessment of a candidate's suitability to work within his enterprise. John had passed the test, bringing a big grin of satisfaction to the face of his potential boss. It entirely animated Pollard's features and the thin-rimmed spectacles appeared to advance to the left, rather like a bicycle, a miniature of his proud creation. 'Do you ride a bike lad'? Had been his next question. 'Yes sir, I ride a Raleigh Sprite', John had replied.

'Well son you best pedal your way to the factory on Monday mornin' but afore you go can you tell me who it was that invented the wheel'?

'I believe it was the Ancient Egyptians sir'.

Pollard had raised his eyebrows, looked sternly across the desk at John and said, can't you give me the name o' that old Egyptian bloke then'? Well lad, I can see I've got a lot to teach you, half past seven sharp'.

Percy Pollard was aware that John was a stepbrother to George Boucher, in his mind that was recommendation enough.

Today George and John were on their way to Bobbers Mill. Freddy had taken over the reins at the farm towards the end of November, in his excitement at the prospect he'd described the event to Annie as a belated birthday present. In her wisdom she'd pointed out to him that wonderful as the gift might seem, it was paid for by none other than himself, but nothing could dampen Freddy's enthusiasm.

The Cropleys now resided at Bullwell. The small property offered ample accommodation for the elderly couple but not so much as to weary Dorothy with hours of housework. At the back, a long narrow strip of land had brought a glint to Arthur's eye and within a fortnight of moving in, a small chicken coop had been installed at the bottom of the garden to house four bantam hens and one game cockerel. Meek though it was, the presence of those few birds kept the farming blood pumping through Arthur's veins. Freddy visited regularly. Over winter months an hour here and there was just about manageable but he was aware that lambing and harvest, plus all the work he intended doing to improve the farm buildings would very soon keep him virtually tied to Bobbers Mill day and night.

Freddy had written to Harold in Skendleby telling him all about his plans. Ivy and Reggie were so settled in Lincolnshire that even a day trip to Nottingham no longer tempted them. Ivy wrote frequently to Sarah, Davina and Annie. Mrs.Pilkington had become increasingly difficult, making Ivy's visits in the past far from pleasant, often sending her daughter away in a state of misery. The older Ivy's mother became the more cantankerous grew her demeanour, Annie felt it was the likely reason for Ivy's reluctance to visit.

Harold worked on a farm at Huttoft and to his surprise had discovered Alf Shipman the boss's nephew, at one time worked at Players and remembered William starting there. Like Freddy it seemed to be Harold's calling, from school he'd gone straight to the employ of Sidney Shipman and was now fully competent in animal husbandry and working the land. He'd replied to Freddy's letter by return, a wonderful communication of cheerful congratulations and encouragement with a postscript, 'hope to come over soon'.

Molly now almost eighteen was working at the local shop and post office. A bright young thing with a happy nature, which according to Ivy's letters, endeared her to the customers, especially the young men. One in particular had taken a shine to Molly Boucher, sending a posy of flowers and a valentine, which he signed quite unashamedly, 'forever yours, Walter Small'.

Very soon however, Ivy, Reggie and family would receive an invitation to the wedding and Annie felt sure that any possible 'grouse', delivered by Mrs.Pilkington, would simply be ignored, when they travelled to Nottingham on May 4th to be present at the marriage of Freddy Eddowes to Francis Ripley. Sarah and Davina spent time together excitedly planning and assembling a bottom drawer. Annie, unbeknown to Freddy, had almost completed a patchwork quilt, sometimes sewing late into the night. Hilda had determined herself to crochet a pretty duchesse set. A few episodes of frustrated unpicking had made progress slow at the start but now her fingers moved more confidently and only one small, round mat remained to be done. George had sought Billy's help and advice on making a bookcase and this had been an ongoing project in the shed at Billy's allotment with Victor appointed 'master polisher'. So many hours of devoted effort had been applied that the finished article now veritably glowed and was matched only by the big grin of satisfaction permanently adorning Victor's face.

John, working from memory had made a detailed drawing of Bobbers Mill Cottage and had it framed in oak. On the reverse, he'd signed the words, 'Freddy's Farm, 1929'.

It was all very different to the preparation for William's marriage to Celia. Without consulting his wife to be on her wishes he'd intimated to Jessie and Gwendolyn Tozer his expectation of a suitably elaborate affair and with no tact whatsoever had informed the family that an elegant suite of bedroom furniture, on display in Burton's window, would be the ideal gift and entirely affordable if instead of numerous odds and ends, everyone pooled resources in order to purchase it! When Annie had told Edna of William's thoughtless request her response had been immediate and positive.

'As 'e now, well if that's what 'e wants then me an' Billy'll get summat for the bedroom an'all'. Edna had secretly given Celia a package prior to the wedding; to the young woman's delight it contained a beautifully embroidered tablecloth worked by Edna herself. On the day of the ceremony, Edna had presented William with a heavy parcel, carefully wrapped in generous layers of Evening Post within a sheet of thick brown paper. The label read, To William, with love from Billy, Edna and girls. 'From God all blessings flow' and in brackets. (Save the paper, useful in hard times) The large chamber pot, decorated with burgundy coloured peony blooms, had it not been for the mark on the base confirming 'Coalport', would likely have vexed William but he'd recognised its value and put it under Hannibal Burton's bed in the house on Glover Street. He'd surveyed the room with its smart furniture feeling smugly satisfied, the addition of his bride might have made that satisfaction complete had she borne a mark such as Stanford, rather than the name of an everyday maker like Tozer, but Celia would do well enough, William Eddowes would ascend the ranks regardless.

"I bumped into Tommy Spooner yesterday," said George. "James Handley has told Tommy that after Easter he intends taking a back seat, he's been an undertaker all his working life. Apparently, Handley started with his father when he left school but has only three daughters himself. Tommy is almost afraid to think it but he wonders if it's James Handley's intention to let him run the place. The other two men have worked there for several years but not in the embalming room, they just collect the deceased and drive the hearse or bear the coffin if the family request them. If Tommy does get to run things then I imagine there'd be a need to take on someone to do what Tommy now does. He's worked alongside Handley dealing with the corpses as well as presiding at the actual funeral ceremonies. I don't know how the wages compare but his brother Joe might be better off leaving the hospital mortuary to work there. It's not the same, just labelling them and keeping them cold must be easier than embalming but if it's your own brother teaching you it would surely give you confidence."

"What is embalming exactly?" Said John. "We learned all about the ancient Egyptians in school and I remember reading how they preserved a corpse in spices and oil, like mam does pickles but without vinegar, I don't remember Mr.Dunn saying anything about vinegar. Inside the pyramids must have smelled like Burton's food hall at Christmas. Me and Hilda used to ask mam if we could go in there to look at all the fancied-up hams and pies, they'd shine like somebody had painted them with varnish, cherries and slices of orange over the top. But it was the smell that fascinated me, exotic Christmas smells, gold, frankincense and myrrh, that's what me and Hilda thought it was. I've never smelled anything like it on Tommy's jacket though and even Freddy's clothes smell of farmyard."

George chuckled, "I remember sitting in The Standard one night when Jimmy Shields was there having a pint. As the room got warmer so the smell got stronger. Jimmy's worked at the fishmongers on Waverley Street for years. The bloke alongside him said, 'I'm an expert now, one o' them connoisseurs, I can tell each day exactly what wer' the last fish 'e 'ad 'is hands on', and he leaned forward, sniffed Jimmy's hand and said, 'haddock, today it's haddock, yesterday it wer' cod'. Then some bright spark at the next table scoffed and said, 'that's nothin' I can tell yer what 'e'll 'ave 'is hands on tonight, it'll be a little sprat'. Nothing fazes Jimmy, he just grinned and said, 'well, you'll be wrong 'cause it'll be a bloody eel'.

John laughed. "It must be sods law, only bad smells transfer, anything sweet and aromatic keeps to itself."

George said nothing but remembered all the times he'd smelled the sweetness of Celia on William's jacket.

John sighed and exchanged hands on the basket handle. "I don't know what mam's put in here but enough to feed Freddy all week going by the weight of it."

"Do you want to swap?" Asked George, he carried the large parcel of clean laundry and the string that bound it had begun to cut into his fingers.

"Nearly there now anyway." John looked forward to a day at the farm, even if it was to be spent planting potatoes.

"Not long to the wedding either," said George. "I really like Francis and I know mam is pleased, she worries about Freddy living alone with no woman to do for him. Mam won't then feel the need to do all this."

George looked from the parcel of laundry to the basket of cooked food and let out a long sigh. He and Alice had got engaged a couple of months back. He'd hoped to propose last Christmas but Alice's grandma had died just the week before and it seemed entirely inappropriate to ask at such a time. Now, because of Freddy's wedding, George had decided to wait until at least the spring of next year before marrying Alice, a longer engagement was perfectly acceptable and he couldn't expect his mam to be concerning herself with their bottom drawer, which she surely would if he declared his intention to marry sooner rather than later.

Annie looked tired a lot of the time, never complaining, always working. George puzzled over Charles' lack of consideration, while he had been less poor tempered of late, Charles nevertheless took George's mother for granted, and so did William, only Celia redeemed the situation through her regular visits, on occasions bringing a small cake she'd baked herself or some biscuits, a bag of Annie's favourite sweets. Celia would readily take up the iron and make Annie sit for a few minutes, peel potatoes, pick down the washing from the line. George had ever sensed that Celia had developed a great fondness for her mother-in-law, in a curious way it made William's shortcomings seem much less important.

At last the farm gate came into view. Freddy had painted a sign, black lettering on white background and screwed it to the top bar, on it the name, Bobbers Mill Farm and an image of a large bumblebee in black and gold. George imagined it to be rather like his own father's endeavour. Grandma Sarah had shown him the smiley face, scratched into the brick by the front door at Mitchell Street.

'Your dad did that when he wer' just a lad, he said it made this ordinary little house special'. So many times Sarah had told him about the face, George had lost count but he never tired of hearing it, each time he felt closer to his natural dad and strangely reassured, it placed the complex Charles at a sensible distance from where his moods were bearable. Now Freddy had made the farm his 'special' place, the simple sign on the farm gate told the world where Freddy Eddowes' happiness lay, just as that face, scratched into the brick wall all those years ago had declared Harold Boucher's love of home.

As they approached the yard they could hear voices, Freddy was talking with a shabbily dressed, bewhiskered individual whom neither of them had seen before.

"A tramp," said George.

John was immediately intrigued. A would be tramp shuffled about the city centre, one or two more gullible passers by handed him some coppers but most knew him. It could be said that he and his 'wives' of which it was rumoured he had several, shared boisterous relationships. He proudly boast a scar just above one ear, the result, so he claimed, of an altercation with a hatchet, wielded by one concubine on finding him procreating with another. Just how many offspring he'd actually fathered had even been the subject of a sweepstake, organised by the landlord at The Nelson. Numbers ranged from twenty three to nine. The most accurate estimation, based on three weeks diligent enquiry by Morry at the pawnshop, had been written down and sealed in a jar placed behind the bar. Alec Yeats had been spot on with his guess of nineteen, only to be beat at the last by the barmaid, who prior to that moment had kept quiet about her ten year old son. As the pot sat at a little short of a fiver, she'd considered it worth divulging her brief liaison with Wilfred Jennings, declaring if they wanted proof then just give her a hatchet and watch her technique!

Freddy's tramp however, looked like the genuine article, he doffed his cap as they drew near and smiled.

"Good morning to you young sirs," he said while giving a genteel bow. Freddy looked over the tramp's shoulder from where he stood just a few feet behind and winked knowingly at his brothers.

"This is Ernest Birch, Esq, true gentleman of the road." While made in a spirit of fun, Freddy's introduction was entirely sincere.

George tucked the parcel of laundry under his left arm and offered his hand. John put the basket down and did likewise. The fingers escaping from the worn woollen gloves gripped theirs warmly.

"May you enjoy your honest labours in the field and be justly rewarded." The old man delivered the words in a naturally cultured voice, refined, very correct. Placing the cap back on his head he turned, nodded towards Freddy and said, "Pax Vobiscum." Then he walked away down the lane, his back upright, his tread assured, not the slightest lapse into shuffle but rather the 'dignified process' of a statesman. It was a perplexing curiosity, a tramp, no fixed abode, yet his departure left behind a very real sense of awe.

"He sleeps in the barn, comes once or twice a month, stays one night," said Freddy. "I take his smokes and matches off him and give them back when he leaves. He has tea to drink and bread and cheese. I've never felt it proper to ask him about his background and he's not once made any mention of his past but I can't help thinking that Ernest Birch had a previous life, which if we were able to peep inside, would reveal something remarkable. Come on lets have a quick brew before we start."

Freddy led them inside the cottage where the basket was unpacked and a large fruitcake was discovered, within minutes a mug of tea and a wedge of Annie's cake, delivered all the encouragement necessary. By evening all the potatoes would be planted and Ernest Birch, Esq. would have disappeared into the blue yonder, and into the realms of John's imagination.

Three people had made their way down the aisle of the bus to alight at the next stop. Joyce rang the bell and reached under the stairwell for the large box deposited there by one of them. Only four more stops before the terminus and the end of Joyce's shift. She'd be relieved, all day the discomfort of period pain had wearied her and the more tired she became, the more tetchy and intolerant her mood. Waiting to board the No.13 was a group of young men, she knew all but one of them. Normally her own forward character would allow her to go along with harmless banter, recognising it for what it was but this day their rumbustuous exchange as they all piled onto the platform together, their clamour for a ticket so the first to pay his fare could race up the stairs to occupy the front seat, tried her patience and when the pimply faced, runny nosed member of the group cheekily called out as he turned the stair rail 'give us a kiss Joyce', and leaned his face towards her it took all of Joyce's mental strength to resist slapping it.

A conductor on the No.13 bus would not have been her first choice of employment but over the months she'd witnessed Tommy's anxiety. Rosie and the twins were a source of delight and Joyce had so enjoyed looking after them, helping around the house while Rosie shopped or simply took a nap. Breastfeeding the two boys took a lot out of their mother, Joyce could always tell when Rosie was flagging, her pallor would become grey and her movements laboured. By the end of January, sensibly, the infants had been weaned and Joyce knew she must find work to ease the financial strain on Tommy. Their mother too looked so frail, Joyce had been shocked at her mother's decline in the time since she'd left Nottingham with the Fosterjohns and overcome with guilt at the belief that her own behaviour had, more than anything else, contributed to her mam's poor state of health.

Tommy was intuitive and unbeknown to Joyce, he pursued a better situation for his eldest sister. He'd recognised her unnaturally subdued demeanour as unhappiness, he'd taken courage and called on Henry Wicks

Tommy's memory of the day he'd travelled on the train to Leicester, knowing he was about to take on the charge issued by the police, to be responsible for his sister's good conduct, was still sharp in his mind. Joyce had been cautioned and made aware that any fall from grace in the future would be treated very severely. He could recall the exact words the old sergeant had spoken, taking Tommy to one side he'd said, 'clip her wings lad, clip her wings afore she flys too close to the flame'. Joyce was not without intelligence, in fact her abilities she'd proved beyond all doubt while living with him and Rosie. Housework she undertook with a will and her competence in the kitchen had surprised Tommy, he'd not once imagined that the wayward Joyce had observed, with any degree of interest, their mam's cooking and baking skills. He sensed Rosie yearned for their little home to be just that, theirs and their children's. She had lived with her sister-in-law without resentment or animosity but husband and wife felt denied of that special peace.

Tommy had learned that Henry Wicks' housekeeper, due to family problems, had been obliged to leave his employ. As yet, no other had been appointed. Earlier in the afternoon Tommy had sighed deep and long, hesitated for an instant, then knocked firmly at the back door of Henry Wicks' house. Ever truthful, entirely honest, Tommy had told Wicks all of the sorry story. He'd omitted none of the awkward facts, baring his shame and entering his plea on Joyce's behalf, adding in typical Tommy Spooner fashion. 'I'm no Saint sir, but I've grown up, grown wiser, stronger, become sensible, and I know that our Joyce 'as done that an'all'. Wicks had listened, he was aware of Tommy's character, if anyone deserved recognition it was this young man. He'd asked himself, what would Leonora have said, what would his outward looking wife have seen fit to do. Leonora believed in opportunity, not just for the select few but also for the many. 'Perhaps we should agree on a months trial of the situation, as much for your sister's sake as for mine. After all, we may take an instant dislike to one another and find the whole arrangement insufferable. Even that formal relationship between employer and employee is subject to the variance of human nature. Your sister may well run down the path in a month's time rejoicing at being freed from the tedious monotony of keeping house for an old, often miserable individual possessed of a feeble appetite, who never arrives home at the same time two days in a row and cannot keep the sparrows from ripping at the saxifrage, much to his advancing irritability.'

Tommy now awaited Joyce's return from work, he knew that her shift ended at 4 o/clock. Rosie had taken the twins to see her mam, the house was quiet, an ideal time to present Joyce with the opportunity of better work, an offer to which she must afford a great deal of concentrated thought. The back door opened and Joyce walked inside, awkwardly, her breathing seemed short and erratic.

"Are you alright?" Asked Tommy, crossing the scullery to where she stood.

"I don't feel very well, where's Rosie?"

Tommy explained they'd gone to see Mrs.Potts. Joyce burst into tears.

"I'm bleeding too much Tommy, I've a real bad pain." Her face was white and she caught hold his hand, he felt her trembling.

"Come and sit down by the fire I'm going to fetch the doctor." He made her as comfortable as he could before running to the new doctor's house. Dr.Baragruy had retired a year or two back, now they must call on Dr.Anthony Casley. The house sat back from the pavement on Abbey Road. Tommy had heard someone say that Mrs.Casley was foreign, Italian and a striking woman to look at. The door was opened by a girl of about fifteen, she was not a maid Tommy was sure, her clothes were of obvious quality, besides, not as much as a dainty apron hid the elegant embroidery on the belt of her dress and her hair fell loose, all girls in service pinned their hair. Tommy told of his concern for Joyce.

"Father, come quickly, you are needed." She called out to the source of music, playing softly in a room off the hallway. The music ceased at once, the figure of the doctor hurried to a table by the coat stand. He took a jacket from the hook and a black leather bag from the table, paused briefly to smile at the girl, planting a kiss on her forehead, Tommy guessed she was the daughter. Turning to Tommy he spoke urgently but confidently.

"Lead on, tell me as we go."

Joyce looked pitiful, her embarrassment was acute, blood had soaked through her clothes to the cushion on the chair. The doctor's first question filled Tommy with alarm.

"Could you be pregnant Joyce?"

"No, I've bled every month but sometimes between periods too and I've had a pain, a bad pain."

He was about to speak to Tommy when the back door opened. Rosie had arrived home with the twins. Shocked to find the doctor present she panicked, making her well practiced routine of reversing the pram into the scullery, clumsy and awkward.

"Don't be alarmed Mrs.Spooner, you ladies are complex creations, many components to stick or corrode but more often than not, entirely repairable. I shall send for an ambulance, it will be easier to examine Joyce at the hospital and less distressing for her I think".

Joyce sniffled her accord, her anguish and dismay had overcome speech. Bodily she was wet and uncomfortable, mortally embarrassed and despite the doctor's description of her mere mechanical breakdown, she felt terrified. Tommy whispered in Rosie's ear.

"You go with her Rosie, I'll be alright with Tom and Sam, we can't send her off all on her own, besides, it needs to be a woman, men aren't very good around blood."

Rosie's thought's were the very opposite, Tommy dealt with bodies every day, she never asked about his work, preferring not to know the nature of it but her mind carried images of draining blood 'til the cadaver was white as marble. Tommy's stomach churned, the fear showed in his face, love of her husband and genuine concern for Joyce bolstered Rosie's failing spirit and with a tight embrace, husband and wife exchanged strengths.

Tommy had fed his sons, washed them and put them to bed, he'd kept good fire in the grate the night air was cool. He'd looked at the clock so many times it seemed to display its displeasure at his impatience by ticking ever more slowly 'til Tommy began to view the unobliging timepiece with real disbelief. Surely Rosie would return soon, perhaps Joyce too if it was simply 'women's troubles'. Finally at almost 9 o/clock the door latch rattled and Rosie looking tired and strained, hung her coat on the hook.

"What's wrong wi' Joyce, aren't they lettin' 'er come home?" Tommy had hoped that both his wife and sister might come through the door, that all would be well. Rosie flopped down in the chair with a large outpouring of breath. She sniffed, the night air had made her nose watery.

"A doctor examined Joyce, she cried out wi' the pain when 'e felt her, low down, towards her private parts, yer know what I mean. They gave her some stuff to stop it hurtin' an' eventually she nodded off. I sat there for ages, just waitin' for somebody to tell me summat. At last the doctor come, 'e took me out into the corridor, so's not to disturb Joyce I s'pose. 'E said that 'e was confident that the problem was a cyst on 'er ovary, that it 'ad burst an' caused all the bleedin'. Then 'e said that the examination 'e'd done led 'im to believe there may well be another cyst on the other ovary, they might 'ave to remove 'em."

Tommy had listened intently. "Well that's not so bad is it, if they remove the cysts she should be alright after a few days. James Handley 'ad a cyst on the back of 'is neck last year, once they'd drained it an sorted it out 'e wer' like new." Tommy was desperate to find reassurance.

"It's not just the cysts," said Rosie, they'll likely 'ave to take out the ovaries an'all." She wiped the wateriness now about her eyes with her sleeve.

"What does that mean?" Said Tommy, "she'll be alright after won't she. We can live wi'out our appendix, I expect we can do wi'out our ovaries an'all." He tried to sound positive.

Rosie sighed. "The doctor said in a couple o' weeks she'll be on the mend but if they 'ave to remove 'er ovaries it means Joyce will never 'ave a baby." She stood and kissed Tommy's cheek before saying, "I want to see our two, I'll sit wi' 'em for a bit. Make us a cuppa, I'm not hungry, a slice o' bread an' butter wi' a bit o' cheddar'll do. Men don't 'ave ovaries, you've got summat else."

She made her way upstairs, Tommy heard their bed creak as she laid her weight on it. That night neither of them could find sound sleep, waking, napping, on and off until by first light Tommy was glad to dress and go down to put the kettle on.

He'd written a letter to Henry Wicks explaining that his sister had been taken suddenly unwell and would be indisposed for a few weeks. Tommy thanked him for his kind offer to Joyce of work and expressed his regret at her having to decline but wished him well in finding a good housekeeper. Now Tommy was on his way to deliver the note and to send word to the manager at the bus depot. Before going to Handley's he knew he must see his mam, tell her what had happened. Poor mam, every trial, every tribulation took more of her away. Thin, frail, so deaf, old and tired, how much more could she stand. As Tommy walked along Langley Drive towards the home of Henry Wicks he fought back tears. Going around and around in his head were the old sergeant's words. 'Clip her wings lad, clip her wings afore she flys too close to the flame'.

Joyce had done wrong in the past but this punishment was too cruel and the worst part was the fact that he, Tommy Spooner, could do nothing to make it better.

CHAPTER EIGHT

Charles had been very quiet all evening, not an irritable, sullen quietness but a remoteness. While the family were present Annie deemed it most sensible not to disturb his thoughts, directed as they must surely be to some one, some place apart from those immediately around him.

George was walking Alice home, John was accompanying Davina in a taxi back to The Park and Hilda had gone with Sarah to Mitchell Street where it was agreed she would spend the night.

Following the marriage ceremony, a reception had been held at The Conifers Hotel on Aspley Lane. Mr.&Mrs.Ripley had four sons but only the one daughter, Francis. In spite of the fact neither Freddy nor Francis held any desire for a fuss, the Ripleys viewed it as their only chance to marry off a daughter and to do so with some degree of style.

Annie had advised Charles to offer a greater contribution than just the flowers, tradition was all well and good but parents of the bride were subject to limited finances in the same way as those sending a son into marriage. Done diplomatically it could only propagate harmony within the wider family. Francis would inevitably find her days filled with activity at Bobbers Mill. The buxom, rosy cheeked, carefree farmers wife portrayed in children's storybooks, was a stretch of imagination given the difficulties now surrounding much of the population and Freddy's affairs would certainly require his wife to be thrifty.

Only the previous week three men had been laid off at Clark&Brown's. Since the refurbishment of the council house few contracts of size had presented themselves. A possible commission to re-upholster the seating in The Theatre Royal had been thought better of and deferred indefinitely.

Annie witnessed more and more frugality amongst customers to the shop, staples like bread and potatoes they had reduced until the mark up was at an absolute minimum. Beneath the counter, never less than a dozen packets of cigarettes, their eventual owner identified by his name written on one side, awaited the second payment. Of a packet of five, the struggling individual would pay for half, an allowance of two, when he had money enough in his pocket he would come again to the shop and ask for, 'the other arf', the remaining three.

One source of patronage however had surprised Annie to the point of bewilderment. Over the course of the past six or seven months, Basil Stanford's wife had herself come into the shop at regular intervals, presenting Annie or Charles with a list, requesting the items be made ready for collection the following day when they'd been duly picked up and paid for by Stanford's 'man', a very sober character whom Annie had heard referred to as 'Cratchet', assuming the inference was to the unyielding clerk of Dickens' imagination.

Only Sarah and Davina had come back to Gregory Street after the wedding. Ivy and family had left for Skendleby on the latest train but with the promise that during the summer they would visit again and stay overnight.

"I'll make some tea, would you like some toast?" Annie spoke softly to Charles, his quietness made her cautious, reluctant to upset the calm.

"Mother and father were married on this same date 48 years ago, May4th 1881," he said.

Annie paused in her preparation of a simple supper. "Have you told Freddy of the coincidence, I've not heard you speak of it before, I'm sure Freddy would be pleased to learn that he and Francis shared an anniversary date with his grandparents."

"What significance could it possibly have after all these years, coincidence occurs every day in the life of somebody. There are only a given number of days in a month and months in a year, it stands to sense dates will be duplicated. I'd forgotten myself, it was only when I was looking through the deed box, to check the sum of money Smithfield paid for the workshop, that I found their marriage licence. I must have been born very early, yet I can recall mother telling me I was such a bonny baby, plump with skin like silk. Daniel was early, but only by two or three weeks, he was so small his skin was wrinkled, more like stocking hose than silk, even you could not have described him as bonny, so how can mother's memory of me be true?"

Annie had been about to ask Charles why he needed to check the amount Smithfield had paid for the workshop but now, to pursue that enquiry after hearing Charles' puzzlement at circumstances surrounding his birth would appear almost callous. She crossed the room to where he sat, a lonely figure of his own volition. Annie felt compelled to erase his doubts.

"I imagine your mother was not describing to you the infant she first held at birth, but the beautiful child you so quickly became. Babies thrive often at an amazing rate and just as the intense pain of childbirth is forgotten almost at once, so the image of an early born passes swiftly and is replaced by that glorious bundle of soft warm flesh looking up into a mother's eyes, totally dependant. That is the memory your mother held dear and spoke of so proudly to you."

Charles looked up at Annie with impassive expression.

"I've heard rumour that Smithfield is considering selling the workshop. I'm not surprised, with the factory at Brassington to maintain, Winchester Street must be a drain on profits. I was surprised he ever wanted it in the first place."

Annie made no remark but recalled the day Smithfield had come to No.14, to tell her it was not he who'd sought the sale of the workshop.

Charles continued. "Edna could travel by bus, they all could, knowing Smithfield I can't imagine he'd do any other than offer the women work at Brassington, especially Edna, all the experience she's gathered the man would be a fool to let her go. You taught her well, either that or she observed your ways. If he can't have you then I dare say Edna would be a reasonable substitute."

Annie bit her tongue, this day belonged to Freddy, she would say nothing to mar the memory of it.

"I am curious to know how they will compare, the amount he paid me and the figure he will ask now," said Charles. "I will have some toast, with an egg as well, I ate little at the reception."

Celia had been walking on air all day, wearing a particularly pretty outfit, her hat the crowning glory, a deep cerise pink felt creation with soft plumes of purple and cream laid at an angle to one side. Her mother had questioned the choice. 'You can't wear that same hat to Edmund's wedding, you should choose something less striking on this occasion and save such extravagance for your own brother's special day'. But Celia could think of no day more special than this. Just the week before she'd gone to the doctor to seek confirmation. Celia had missed twice and although, unlike most women, she'd not endured morning sickness, her body nevertheless told her it was so, Celia was pregnant. She'd determined herself to await the evening of Freddy's wedding, when all the ceremonies were over. When still in her finery looking the best she could be, while William still stood handsome in his best man's suit, then to tell her husband they were to have a child.

"When?" William's response was precise and urgent. Celia felt suddenly unnerved.

"Around mid November the doctor thinks, why are you so concerned about the date?"

"Uhm, you shouldn't be showing too much then, still able to look elegant with the right style of dress." Said William

Celia was bewildered. "What are you talking about," she was now becoming emotional and close to tears.

William took off his jacket and draped it over the back of a chair.

"Edmund's wedding to Caroline at the end of July, I want you to look especially fine. It is as much a source of wonder to me as I'm sure it is to most at The Lodge but Basil Stanford seeks me out at the close of each meeting and engages in conversation. I can be no other than polite and affable in return. He is puzzled as to why father doesn't join the men of commerce. I told Stanford that I have broached the subject so many times but dad ever declares his disinterest. Smithfield too declines to join, but Stanford is a shrewd man, perceptive and finely tuned to less common knowledge. It would seem Smithfield's father was an out and out failure, lost to drink and women. So it's little surprise he prefers to keep himself to himself. Such a background dogs a man despite, 'the sins of the father' and all that mitigating rhetoric. It explains a great deal, I like Smithfield, he has vision but I've always pondered on why he contains himself with that elderly aunt. Stanford imparted the knowledge to me in confidence of course, he and myself, despite the difference in age, share ideals, view business and industry with similar beliefs. It is important that you shine at his daughter's wedding."

Celia was hurt, all week and throughout the day she had saved her news, expecting William to look on her proudly and match her own delight when he let loose his excitement at the thought of becoming a father.

"I can recall Annie saying of Rosie when she was carrying the twins, 'there's something truly beautiful about a young woman bearing the promise of motherhood'. Didn't I look fine today won't I look beautiful at Edmund's wedding?" Celia's voice wavered from emotion.

"That's a load of sentimental twaddle, mam is full of it." William kicked off his shoes and rubbed his toes. "These socks are too thick."

If he was about to say anything more then Celia was not about to listen.

"You should have married my mother, never mind Basil Stanford, you and mother would have made the perfect match, your ideals are similar to the point of being fused. Stand with her at Caroline Stanford's wedding." Celia ran from the room and up the stairs, angry, upset. She lay on their bed tearful and miserable. If only William had just a shred of Tommy's compassion, he cared for and cherished all of his family. Tommy wasn't influenced by the pompous ramblings of Basil Stanford and his like. Events of the day and tensions of the evening eventually reduced Celia to a tiredness she could no longer resist and she dozed.

William had remained downstairs, not possessing any degree of skill at calming the female in distress, he'd poured himself a whisky and sat staring into the empty grate. He was about to take himself to the privy before bed, when someone knocked at the front door, a glance at the clock confirmed it was almost ten. Again they knocked, louder, persistent, a muffled voice called out something but William couldn't define it. He pushed his feet into his shoes, leaving the laces undone and went to the door.

"A cup o' water, bring a cup o' water, there's a bloke out 'ere in a collapsed state, somebody's gone for doctor, make haste."

The middle-aged man ran back to the street. By now the commotion had roused Celia, she came down the stairs looking confused and alarmed.

"Someone's taken ill in the street, they need water, you stay here I'll go." William hurried to the scullery but Celia took a coat down from the hallstand and walked outside. A huddle of people just a few yards from the front door, stood or knelt over someone on the ground. Celia shivered, the individual lay very still. William reached the scene and held out the cup of water, they all seemed reluctant to take it, to minister to the man at their feet. William knelt, the light from the lamp fell across the man's shoulder and down one side of his face. William's hands shook as he raised the man's head and put the cup to his lips. There was no response, no flicker of the eyes, not the slightest movement of the mouth as the water trickled away down the man's neck. William felt sick, something inside him tore at his senses. He knew this man, years ago he'd wished this man dead, for no other reason than his own mother was dead. She'd died in childbirth, she'd not carried any ailment, unlike Edwin Garbett who's affliction could at times render him mad, like a crazed animal, he lived yet William's mother was dead through the most natural of events, having a baby. Now, here, his head on William's arm, Edwin Garbett was without heartbeat. This very night William's own wife had told him she was carrying their child. Coincidence, of course it was merely coincidence, like Celia being a relative of Cheetham, Edmund marrying Caroline Stanford, life was ever filled with such curiosities. It held no deeper meaning, only what an individual chose to make of it and that was entirely within their own head.

The doctor arrived at last. It took him but a few seconds to establish the gravity of the situation. He too recognised Edwin and calmly suggested a man might help carry the deceased to the shelter of a house. William's front door was still open, the light from inside beckoned the doctor's thoughts.

"You help the doctor William," said Celia, "I'm sure one of the other gentlemen will go at once to inform Mr.Spooner."

It was to Tommy's house that most people now went directly when a death occurred out of hours. Once inside the house with the door closed Celia felt calm, all the agitation of earlier had faded, it seemed trivial now. Dr.Casley noticed William's pallor, colour had drained from his face. Concerned that the young man might be in shock, he spoke quietly to Celia.

"Perhaps you would make some strong, sweet tea Mrs.Eddowes. You seem a little less affected by events than your husband, in spite of your condition." He remembered confirming Celia's pregnancy the week before. She smiled.

"I think perhaps much of this evening has affected William, not every evening does a man learn he is to be a father. I'm sure it must make all the more shocking the sight of death when the mind is filled with happy expectation of new life."

Reassured by her own stoicism, Celia coaxed her husband to drink the tea and offered him comfort, she smoothed her hand across his forehead and kissed his cheek. At times she wondered why she loved William so much and the answer often defied her. He was the father of her unborn child, it was altogether impossible to imagine anyone other than William Eddowes to touch her so intimately. Someone, out there in the city, whoever they may be, must now bear unimaginable heartache when they are told of the death of their loved one. Celia did not know Edwin Garbett but her heart was filled with compassion for this man.

It was almost 1 o/clock. When earlier Annie had asked Charles if it was his intention to attend the funeral his answer had been vague. He showed no sign of preparation, it could wait no longer.

"Charles you really should go, Edwin was a colleague of yours at the bank, he was kind following Enid's death, I know you can remember that time at The Standard, just as I can." Annie willed him to agree.

"It's not necessary for us both to attend, you can represent me, and while you're at that end of town you may as well call in to see Edna. I don't suppose the service will be very long, if he had any family then they must be distant I've never heard of or seen evidence of any."

Charles carried on stacking tins of stewed steak as though the funeral wasn't worth even the slightest interruption. His manner vexed Annie, in fact it offended her. She wished that a regiment of long lost relatives might descend upon St.Andrews, all blessed with wonderful choral voices that would fill the rafters with reverent sound. The reality would almost certainly be very different. Edwin had told Annie a number of times since the death of his mother, that he had no family. If Charles preferred to stay at the shop and sell his tins of stewed steak then so be it. She would go upstairs to quickly wash and dress accordingly then make her way to the church.

Outside the sun shone but beneath the heavily timbered roof of St.Andrews, although the light fell in long shafts through the leaded windows at one side of the church, the air felt quite chill. Annie sat quietly to the back of those already assembled, only few in number, mostly men whom she assumed were clients of Jacobson's and on whose accounts Edwin had worked. Isaac Jacobson sat one row in front of Annie, slightly to the left, Rachel his wife beside him. The dull hum of whispered exchange paused every few seconds to listen for movement on the path outside the open door, it was almost 2 o/clock.

"Do you mind if I sit with you?"

Annie looked up at the source of the quietly spoken request. Andrew Smithfield stood beside her in the pew, she nodded, in truth glad to be less conspicuous, she could see no other woman sitting alone. Now the silence reached all corners of the building, it grew in volume, Annie smiled to herself at the memory. It was dear Winnie Bacon, whose funeral she'd attended just a few weeks ago, who once said to Annie after the funeral of Winnie's uncle, 'we sat there waitin' for Cuth to arrive, 'e wer' allus late, 'e didn't marry 'til 'e wer' forty, an' the silence in church got that loud it made me head ache'. Annie knew just what Winnie had meant.

Now the congregation rose to its feet as the voice of the Vicar induced that deep breath which always began a funeral service for those present out of genuine regard for the deceased.

"I am the resurrection and the life, he who believeth in me shall never die." The Vicar's words so confident, so boldly delivered. Perhaps all the years of his ministry had enabled him to recognise those withering spirits now seated within his church, and his need to raise them through that promise of a life beyond the mortal coil. For some no doubt, it was merely a ritual, to be followed in order to maintain respectability, for others, the last brief moment of closeness on earth.

Annie could detect tears in the eyes of Rachel Jacobson when something compelled the woman to look past her husband at the coffin, as the bearers carried Edwin slowly along the aisle, followed by Tommy Spooner. Jacobson himself fixed his gaze to the front and stood motionless throughout.

The service ended. If Andrew Smithfield had made any move to follow when the Vicar led the bearers from the church to the graveside, then Annie too would have accompanied Edwin at the last. He would likely be buried close by his father and mother. But as herself, Andrew Smithfield, not being family had felt somehow inhibited. People began to walk away, Isaac Jacobson's expression had not changed at any point in the service, Annie supposed his stiffness, his detached manner was due to the contrast in faiths. A Jew finding himself in an Anglican church could be excused for feeling awkward, for feeling not 'at home'. Rachel Jacobson, for an instant caught Annie's eye. At first Annie sensed she was about to speak but simply a smile was the extent of her exchange, yet it held warmth and Annie felt strangely soothed, her thoughts drifted, inexplicably to May Watkinson, to that night when Edwin had found May wandering the streets and brought her to No.14. Smithfield's voice jolted her back to the present.

"Is Charles well Mrs.Eddowes, I rather imagined I would see him here." Annie felt disinclined to fabricate an excuse. "His stomach plays him up at times, nothing serious, I represent us both today." It was not untrue, Charles had no stomach for this funeral.

"Of course, perhaps I could drive you back to Gregory Street."

Smithfield's courtesy was not unappreciated but Annie did want to call on Edna for a few minutes, she felt no urgency to return to the shop.

"It's kind of you but I haven't seen Edna for a little while, her daughter Liza came to collect the groceries last Saturday afternoon. I can walk through the arboretum and be there in no time at all, it would be silly to take you out of your way."

"Not at all, I wanted to speak with you anyway," said Smithfield, "so please let me drive you to Winchester Street, it will make but five minutes difference to my day."

Annie nodded agreement and as they walked to his car she ventured to enquire, "Is it true that you are to sell the workshop?" It was really no business of Annie's whether he sold or kept it but concern for Edna drove her to ask. They reached the vehicle and he opened the passenger door.

"As we travel I shall explain."

He leaned back in his seat for a moment, sighed, then started the engine. "It is true, I need to consolidate the business, orders are reasonable but there's a great deal of competition out there and we seem to all chase a smaller market. I intend telling the women on Friday when I take their pay. All will have a place at Brassington, I know it means a bus fare each day but if I am to protect as much as I can, the long term, then the overheads of the workshop I need to shed and incorporate the activity into the factory. I'm sure you will want to tell Edna but I would be grateful if you'd permit me to explain the situation to her myself at the end of the week. Was it William who told you?"

"No, if William is aware then he's said nothing. Charles heard it rumoured in The Standard. William has other things on his mind, Celia is expecting a baby, not until November but I can imagine it being a sobering thought for William. Once his initial joy at the news fades he will likely begin to question how the event and the responsibility it will bring, might delay his conquest of the city. If William had been born half a dozen centuries ago I'm quite convinced that he would have gazed down upon Nottingham from his castle and repelled any advancing adversary with one swift swipe of his tongue."

Andrew Smithfield chuckled. "Do you think he might have allowed us an audience every once in a while, simply so I could advise him on fabric for his drapes and you could instruct him on matters of public relations. I fear his people might have otherwise risen up in rebellion and only the thickness and quality of his curtains would have saved him from, 'the slings and arrows of outrageous fortune'."

"You know him well," said Annie with a smile, "perhaps you will return the favour and not say anything to William about the baby, I know he will want to tell you himself, he has a great regard for you Mr.Smithfield."

The car pulled up outside the workshop, Annie opened the door and stepped out before he had chance to do the gentlemanly thing. She laughed at his look of surprise.

"I have been too many years living with the instruction of my aunt Bella, 'remember what you are my girl'. Plus I am perfectly able but thank you for the lift, I hope all will be well at Brassington. These are testing times but surely things can only improve. The world seems to advance in cycles, perhaps this current revolution is near' complete." Annie extended her hand, "Goodbye, my regards to your aunt, who I'm quite sure has plied you with just such amount of instruction as aunt Bella did with me."

Annie smiled her gratitude and walked to the workshop door, Smithfield's eyes followed her, the warmth of her hand he felt still on his palm. Under his breath he spoke.

"Goodbye Annie, goodbye Mrs.Charles Eddowes."

Edna looked startled, then remembered it was the funeral of Edwin Garbett that afternoon.

"Stick the kettle on Bessie, me throat's as dry as this wad o' kapok." Edna was engaged in filling cushions, a set of six completed covers, each with a panel of perfectly executed needlepoint awaited their purpose, their eventual display of affluence.

"For Louisa Burton, I've only 'ad one set o' new cushion covers in all the years I've been married an' I made them meself out of aunt Win's old curtains, the other arf don't know they're born."

Bessie produced a cup of tea, it was welcome, several hours had passed since Annie had last drunk anything. Soon Bessie and Maureen were back at their machines, that familiar, constant, clickety click, clickety click, which used to torment Annie's head when she tried to sleep. In those days after Harold's death and those cold, lonely nights when aunt Bella lay upstairs growing more and more frail, when George was but an infant, the sound seemed to summon her from rest as though any lapse in her industry was a shortcoming on her part.

Edna took Annie to the back office. " 'E didn't go then?" Edna was ever forthright.

"He wasn't irritable, he actually suggested that I come to see you whilst I was this end of town. I hoped he'd attend," Annie sighed, "there are times when Charles demands a lot of hope."

"Uhm," said Edna, barely one word but it spoke volumes.

"How's Billy, since George completed the bookcase I've not heard all the usual accounts of Billy and Victor's exploits," said Annie with a chuckle.

Edna let out a long sigh, at the same time picking up a length of ribbon from the desk and winding it round her finger absentmindedly.

"Florrie 'ad a blackout last week, frightened Jack, poor lad thought 'is mam wer' a goner. Doctor's told 'em all that she's exhausted an' needs complete rest for a month. How can Florrie possibly rest wi' Victor around 'er. If 'e 'as tea at our house I can't sit down for ten minutes to let it settle, 'e's got to be clearing away the dishes the minute you're finished. 'E'll be shakin' tablecloth outside the back door afore I've swallowed me last drop o' tea, there's no peace in the lad except when 'e's asleep. Victor's just like that clockwork clown in toyshop window on Parliament Street. That damn thing 'as stood there bangin' them bloody cymbals together for the last ten year.

Our Myra used to love it but lately, if I'm waitin' at that stop for the bus, it grates on me nerves. I feel like rippin' them soddin' cymbals out its hands an' chuckin' 'em over railin's into Oliver Blackmore's for that hoity toity old clown to clatter an' bang of a mornin'. Talk about pompous, I've heard that at every assembly Blackmore makes them boys stand for fifteen minutes, absolutely stock still, while 'e plays patriotic music to 'em, Poor Godfrey Griffin faints at least four mornin's a week but Blackmore won't excuse the lad, reckons it'll make a man of 'im. If I wer' Godfrey's mother I'd tell the old bugger just what does make a man an' it's not standin' listenin' to land of hope an' soddin' glory till the blood drains from 'is head." The ribbon having been wrapped and unwrapped about Edna's finger at least a dozen times was now discarded and a pencil taken up instead. "I've told Billy it can only be for a month, no longer. Florrie's goin' to stay wi' Brian an' Sylvia for a bit. Raymond's got the responsibility o' runnin' Player's now, Brian said it weren't fair to put the worry on Raymond an' Eric's wife is due her third any day. Nellie Draper says I can borrow a single mattress. Victor'll 'ave to sleep on the floor o' livin' room an' understand that when Billy gets home from the exchange at 6 o/clock of a mornin' 'e's got to get 'is head down for a few hours. Billy an' Victor spend most o' the day together anyroad an' the lad does sleep alright at night. Billy loves 'im like 'e wer' 'is own." Edna doodled a little matchstick man with the pencil on a notepad in front of her and looked wistful.

"And you, what about you Edna." Annie looked into her friend's eyes.

"I could never see Victor want for owt, there 'e is, a full grown man yet 'e pulls at your heart strings like a babe."

Annie rose to her feet. "Will I see you on Saturday?" She asked.

"Aye, I sent Liza last week, I wer' too tired to bother but I'll 'ave to come meself this week, wi' Victor to feed an'all I shall need some extra bits."

Annie recognised the stress Edna was feeling and in her mind was already planning one or two ways of helping out. The bacon ends, the last of the cheese block, the older bread, all of which she would normally use up herself could swell Edna's shopping bag. Freddy would gladly give some eggs, she'd bake a cake too. Annie was loth to leave without telling Edna of Celia's news.

"I don't think William has told Andrew Smithfield yet so don't say anything but I thought it would cheer you up to know there's a baby on the way."

"Well it'll be bed socks an' bloomers for you next Christmas then, grandma." Edna gave a roguish grin. "Mam used to say that when the third generation starts comin' along it's time for the first to put on some passion killers. If I'd been married to your Charles all these years I'd 'ave strangled the bugger wi' a pair afore now."

The No.56 ran every twenty minutes, she shouldn't have too long to wait. As Annie walked along Sherwood Road her thoughts returned to Edwin Garbett, the daisy he'd picked and given her at the arboretum. Gathering blackberries at the Meadows when he'd told Annie how his mother sent him each year, how he'd thought it was a ploy on her part, to place him where he might meet a young lady. But in time Edwin had come to believe that it was nothing more than his mother's fondness for blackberry jam.

At the funeral earlier in the afternoon, Annie had seen distress on Rachel Jacobson's face, that smile she'd passed to Annie held more than simply recognition of Annie's attendance. If such thoughts were improper then Annie didn't care. Isaac Jacobson gave no impression of warmth and caring. Annie herself knew what it was to be surrounded by family yet feel indescribable loneliness. Improper or not if her thoughts had any foundation in reality then she was pleased. God failed to bless Edwin in so many ways, if he allowed him that one favour, a few moments of righteous or unrighteous love, it could be deemed nothing more than The Almighty's way of making amends before Edwin's time on earth was done.

When she reached the stop three other people already formed a queue. One man puffed on a cigarette and the smoke lingered long enough to make Annie sneeze. A woman in front of Annie tutted her disapproval but the man paid it no heed and sensing the irritation he caused, relished the antagonism, sending profuse swirls of tobacco smoke over their heads. Annie was relieved when the bus came into view and the man held out his nicotine stained hand to request it. His mischief turned out to be harmless when he stood aside to let the women board before himself, but Annie was surprised to see Joyce Spooner issuing the tickets so thanked him for his courtesy but explained that she wished to speak with the conductress so please, would he go ahead of her.

"Hello Joyce, I've not seen you on the No.56 before," she said.

"New rota, we've all had to change, I'm on this route for the next four months." Joyce handed Annie her ticket and pulled down the flap on her leather satchel.

"It's good to see you looking so much better, how are Rosie and the twins? I saw Tommy, but not to speak to, at the funeral this afternoon. He looked very dignified." Annie was genuinely pleased at seeing Tommy's sister.

"They're alright but I'm not livin' there anymore. It wer' time for me to move out an' let 'em have their home back. Husband an' wife don't want to be forever wonderin' who's listenin' in when they fancy a bit o' fun. Besides, they felt too awkward to be happy cause they thought I wer' miserable. But it's just one o' them things, I've got to get on with it haven't I, make the most of a bad lot. Somebody at the depot put me in the know of a room to let, cheap rent, it'll do me."

"Is it near your mam or Kathleen and Ernie?" Asked Annie with the greatest hope.

Joyce rang the bell as a passenger stood and walked slowly down the aisle.

"It's in a house on Peverell Street."

Annie moved to a seat out of the way with a sense of dismay. Joyce's reply drove hope beyond reach. Poor Tommy.

CHAPTER NINE

Late August

"Ouch, keep your soddin' feet steady Jack, I can feel every nail head on the bottom o' your boots."

Charlie's features contorted from pain and the indignity of being beneath Jack Wainwright's feet as Jack employed his friend's shoulders to support him, somewhat precariously, as he endeavoured to reach a branch of apple tree growing over the high wall at the rear of Henry Wicks' property. At least a dozen blush red apples taunted him and drove his resolve. The muscles in the calves of his legs grew with his determination, spreading the streaks of dried on grubby water over the skin like mottling on marble. A shower earlier in the morning had filled the sunken pavings with puddles and Charlie's mischief in splashing Jack's legs when he'd paused to load his cap gun left a residue of grime from the hem of his trousers to the wrinkled tops of his socks.

"Look sharp, somebody's sure to come through the cut 'afore long, we've been 'ere ten minutes already," said an anxious Charlie.

Jack's fingers reached up and the first apple yielded to his grasp. Wishing he'd not brought the cap gun with him but reluctant to trust the care of it to Charlie, he nevertheless managed to fit the fruit into his trouser pocket and stretched his arm once more into the branch of the tree. A second, third and fourth he achieved to accommodate in the pockets of his trousers, their bulk along with the gun caused such a tightness of the cloth across his nether regions that he protested forcefully.

"Me pecker can't breathe, I'm stiflin' up 'ere."

Charlie's sympathy was slight.

"Just make haste will yer, you've nearly taken me ear off twice wi' your toe cap an' me shoulders feel like they're through to the bone, not to mention the fact that I've had to stand the sight o' your lily white bits disappearing up the leg o' your underpants an' the scab on your knee makes me think o' grandad's ulcer. I know your scab don't stink but just thinkin' about it sets me nose off, if yer don't get a move on I shall puke. Put the rest down the front o' your shirt, not inside your vest though, I don't want to eat the buggers if they've been rollin' around in your sweat." The whole of August had been hot with temperatures well above average, which probably accounted for the apples already bearing reddened skin.

"Yer don't 'ave to look up, cast yer eyes down to yer own knobbly knees," said Jack.

"I've tried but it don't work, 'tis only natural, me eyes want to see what you're doin', you'd be the same if it wer' me up there," Charlie let out a long breath of impatience.

Jack determined himself to secure a group of three fruits that appeared so perfect it would have been a crime to leave them there.

"Make yourself a bit taller can't yer, stand on yer toes Charlie, I only need another inch."

Charlie muttered under his breath, it was always him who had to put up with being trodden on. The shortage of fingers on his right hand denied him a sure grip and Jack, devoid of all tact, reminded him on such occasions of his unsuitability for the task of scrumping apples. He did have the two pertinent digits however and these he raised to Jack defiantly, knowing his pal would be far too intent on Henry Wicks' apples to even notice the affront.

At last Jack was ready to make his descent, Charlie slowly lowered himself by bending his knees and Jack steadied his progress by flattening his hands to the wall.

"Bugger, you're too heavy Wainwright," Charlie rubbed his sore shoulders, "your mam needs to give you less dumplin's." Then he observed his friend's appearance and burst into laughter. Jack stood before him so misshapen by his hoard of apples that he presented a most comical spectacle.

"Well better than bein' all ribs an' willy like you Jones," said the indignant Jack.

They shared out the fruit, placing it more strategically so as not to arouse attention, each eating an apple as they walked along the cut to the street with Jack twirling the cap gun around his finger like he'd seen the cowboys do at the pictures.

"Only one more week afore school starts again," said Charlie, with not a shred of enthusiasm. "When will your dad get back to work, must be six weeks since 'e done 'is leg in, I remember 'e done it just after me grandad come to live at our house."

"Two more weeks," said Jack, between bites of his second apple. "Mam say's if 'e's not out from under 'er feet by then she'll do a bunk wi' the milkman. If me dad 'ad done it at pit mam 'ould be dribblin' sympathy over 'im like syrup on a pancake but because it happened down at the Meadows she's been tetchy from the start. Henry 'asn't helped matters neither, 'e's been a little sod lately. Grandma Sarah reckons it's too much sun on the back of his neck, little bugger won't keep a hat on an' accordin' to grandma it wer' that as sent 'er uncle Moses doolally, they found 'im sittin' naked on top a haystack singin' 'mine eyes 'ave seen the glory'." Jack sighed, the apple, as yet unripe, tasted sour and its bitterness stung the back of his throat like a reprimand, but he ate it down to the core, nibbling with his front teeth 'til the sharp edged casing around the pips offended his gums. It was that sense of satisfaction, as Jack perceived it to be, of getting one over on his dad's boss. That feeling of clawing back, which even at his youthful age, drove Jack Wainright to such exploits. Finally, he stood over a grill in the road and let the core fall between the bars of the drain cover. "Better not eat any more, I'll get the shits," he said.

"Well why did we struggle to pick so many then, I've still got five and you must have at least the same down your shirt. What are we supposed to do wi' the soddin' things now?" Charlie was frustrated.

"Trouble wi' you Jones is you've no spunk an' no nous neither. We'll go down Bobbers Mill an' chuck 'em in to the pigs."

It was only from the tree in Henry Wicks' garden and from one other, overhanging the wall of the vicarage that Jack ever scrumped apples. Fruit of the former he looked upon as unpaid dues to his dad and of the latter, God given!

Steve Wainright had taken a nasty tumble earlier in the summer. Ironically he'd not been a player in the impromptu football match but had merely been spending an hour watching others. When the ball had travelled out of play and Steve had gone to kick it back in, he'd somehow managed to miss it and stumble forward, dislocating his knee cap. Had it not been for the intense pain his embarrassment would have prevailed the situation but onlookers recognised his distress and any likely jest quickly turned to concern.

Worry over their finances, her husband's lengthy absence from work, their two sons' almost constant activity about the home through the weeks of school holiday, all contributed to the tension within Gertie. It was from a totally unexpected source that a welcome diversion came. A knock at the back door sent Gertie into a fluster, her hands engaged by a bowl of pastry at a crucial stage of mixing, she could do no other than call to Steve who sat reading in the living room. Now needing only a walking stick, he made his way across the scullery, chuckling at his wife's chuntering as she propelled her fingers about the mixing bowl at the speed of her growing frustration.

"Mavis, Eddie?" Asked Steve in his surprise.

A big grin straddled Eddie's face and Mavis looked alight from happiness, in her arms an infant of no more than five or six months old.

"Come in," said a bemused Steve.

Gertie had rid her hands of flour and now stood with them safely encased in a tea towel, gazing at the face of the sleeping baby.

"She's ours officially," said Mavis, "we've adopted her haven't we Eddie? She's our own little Marie." Mavis lowered her head down to the child and planted a

130

kiss on the forehead peeping out from under a pink and white bonnet. Eddie still beaming, nodded agreement. "We decided to tell no one just in case. It wasn't easy, I've been dying to say something but we were afraid to tempt fate," said Mavis.

"What about the shop, surely you've told Miss Turpin." Gertie felt anxious.

Now Eddie explained. "The authorities needed a character reference for Mavis and for me, only someone outside the family would do. Henry Wicks wrote one for me and Miss Turpin did one for Mavis but they were both sworn to secrecy. Not even our mams know yet, you're the first we've told. I've got to take Wicks' car back now, he insisted we use it to collect Marie from Snenton. I said we could go on the bus but he wouldn't have it."

"At least stop for a cuppa," said Gertie, "then I can have a hold of her for a few minutes."

The two men exchanged smiles, amused at the outpouring of maternal love, flowing just as surely as new milk, though Mavis could do no other than bottle feed and Gertie's 'baby' was in town with his grandma Clara on the promise of a knickerbocker glory in the café at Griffins if he behaved himself while she had her new dentures fitted.

"How are things at the pit? Asked Steve, lowering himself onto a chair and skilfully flicking a daddy longlegs across the floor with the end of his stick.

Eddie sighed, "Not good. Stanford was in with Wicks for more than an hour yesterday. When he finally left it was like closing the door on a bear, Wicks looked like a man just thrashed. I didn't ask anything but after a few minutes Wicks called me into his office. First he spoke of Snenton, of collecting Marie with the car. Then he related Stanford's latest command. In spite of taking on a handful more of men, production is down. It's level two that's the trouble, shift after shift have sweat the flesh off their bones in that tunnel but if it's not there the poor devils can't dig it out. Jack Haynes says it's that hard down there you can feel the vibrations travelling along the veins of your arms, advancing like a tide, intent on reaching your head and tormenting your brain before it rushes back down to feed another callous on your hands. Only God knows why that layer is different, perhaps he lost concentration on that bit, 'dropped a stitch' as me mam would say. Anyway, Stanford's issued an ultimatum, he wants production up by fifteen percent by the end of next month or there'll be pay cuts and lay offs. The foremen are to stagger breaks to keep all activity perpetual and they must record the names of any men showing signs of age and incapacity and hand the list to Wicks, they'll be first out. Everybody's fed up to the back teeth, I feel sorry for Henry Wicks, caught between a rock and a hard place. I sometimes wonder if Stanford has some sort of hold over him, why else would he put up with it. His wife's gone, he's no offspring, he could tell Stanford to stick it and give himself some peace."

Eddie sipped the tea, Gertie had overheard enough to recognise the nature of their conversation, so had placed a mug of tea by each of them and returned to the comfort and delight of little Marie.

"Tell the lads I'll be back soon, no more than a week, ten days at most. Doctor reckons the knee should be strong enough by then." Not wanting Eddie to dwell on matters of the pit when Mavis was so obviously happy, he shook Eddie's hand.

"Congratulations mate, a dad eh, just wait 'til she reaches our Jack's age, he's out kicking around wi' Charlie Jones. I like Charlie, it's the way that lad shakes my hand before he goes home when Gertie's asked him to stop for his tea. Them two fingers and thumb grip like a vice. I shook Stanford's hand once, I could 'ave been holdin' a lettuce."

"Come on Mavis love," said Eddie, "we need to be goin', I'll drop you home then take Mr. Wicks' car back to Birchdale." Lowering his voice he said to Steve, "I'll be glad when you can speak to the men, they need soothing, there's a lot of unrest."

Gertie waved from the pavement as the car disappeared round the corner. She felt so pleased for Mavis, all the years of waiting and hoping. Marie was a baby born to somebody else but what of it. Their mam always said every baby brought love and deserved love back. Sarah would receive this new grandaughter with nothing but delight and if Samuel were looking down he'd cherish the sight. Despite all the problems that had plagued recent weeks, this day was a good day, Gertie smiled as a memory crossed her mind, 'I wouldn't call the King me uncle' Samuel was never really far away.

"Blimey, look at the bollocks on 'im," said Charlie as he leaned over the wall of the pig enclosure watching a large boar devouring one of Henry Wicks' apples. So sharp and eager were the animal's teeth that small pieces of the fruit fell to the ground from either side of its jaws and were immediately seized upon by the sows, seemingly undeterred by their male companion's noisy objections. One by one, the boys threw in the apples, casting some over the heads of the pigs and delighting in the frantic scrum that ensued. Finally, with their pockets emptied, they shouted 'cheerio' to Freddy who was clearing a barn ready for straw, and to Francis as she picked down a line of washing.

The farm, in just the few months since Freddy took it over, had acquired a fresher look. All the buildings around the yard he'd whitewashed and made good most of the doors. He'd purchased a secondhand grass cutter and seed drill that were infinitely better that the contrary equipment that Arthur had stoically persevered with. He'd taken down two dividing hedgerows to increase the actual area of grazing and bought in six heifers to eventually join the milking herd. Francis had added to the poultry numbers and sold eggs and table birds directly from the farm. Married life agreed with the young couple, happy in their work and content with their brief spells of relaxation, an altogether wholesome nature filled Bobbers Mill with optimism. Even an incident the previous week had failed to disrupt the harmony. Freddy had set about castrating some young males in a litter of pigs. The delicate matter required confidence and speed as the surprisingly strong, thoroughly protesting creatures, squealed and wriggled at an alarming rate. Francis sat on a low bench with one young pig at a time upside down between her legs. Freddy, with a scalpel cut the sack, ripped out the testicle, casting it over his shoulder in any direction, repeating the process until all had been 'done'. Not until late that afternoon when Francis picked in her laundry from the clothes line did she find, adhering to the inside of a sleeve on her blouse, a most forlorn looking pair of balls, removed as they had been, so fast and furious from their place of origin!

An exchange of letters between Freddy and Harold at Huttoft had achieved to encourage both young men and each looked forward to the regular communication. The problem of occasional labour had been resolved by the help of Ernie Searle's brother Royston, or Roy as he chose to be called. A self employed 'odd job' man, Roy proved entirely capable of assisting Freddy with the small building and repair work and equally reliable when out in the fields. The one process he flatly refused to participate in was birthing, be it calves, lambs or piglets his aversion to the sight of blood denied him any involvement with this element of farming.

His first visit to Bobbers Mill had been unfortunate, seeking someone to whom he might introduce himself, he'd followed sounds coming from a low barn at one side of the yard. Stepping inside and turning the corner to the source of activity his eyes had met with a glutinous mass of afterbirth, literally at his feet. Before Freddy could reach him he'd fainted, falling half in and half out of the bloody deposit. To his credit as Freddy acknowledged, he'd returned home, retching every few yards but come back to the farm the very next day, making straight for the house and staying well away from the barns, any possible 'deliveries' out of sight, to declare himself fit and ready for whichever task, provided it produced no blood or cow's innards as poor Roy had described his initiation of the previous day. So far the arrangement had proved successful, Roy was able to meet the demands of Bobbers Mill alongside his other work as and when Freddy needed him just so long as Freddy gave him a day's notice.

Jack and Charlie had left the farm gate, after several minutes swinging on it, to walk along the hedgerows gathering wild flowers to carry home to their mothers. Jack had torn the seat of his trousers on a rusty nail and Charlie's backside was stained green from sliding down a grass bank while he waited for Jack to relieve himself.

"When I get home, if 'e's awake, grandad'll look at me and say, 'who are you'? An' me mam'll shout, 'cause 'e's deaf, 'it's our Charlie Dad'. Happens every day, yet when me dad gets in from work, grandad allus shouts to mam, 'Charlie's 'ere'. Now dad's name is Walter, so mam then shouts back at grandad, 'it's Walter Dad, it's Walter'. But when the soddin' dog comes in grandad gets its name right every time. 'Ere's our Kip' 'e says, so if I'm there I shout 'eureka', then grandad comes over all tetchy an' shouts back at me, 'it's Kip, it's our Kip'. Proper bloody madhouse."

Jack chuckled, "At least you've got a grandad, I've never 'ad one, both died years ago. Grandma Sarah tells me all these stories about grandad Samuel like every word makes 'er happy, yet grandma Clara don't like talkin' about the past, it makes 'er miserable. Everybody's different I suppose." Jack stooped to pick a clump of poppies and added them to his bunch of flowers.

" 'Ere, hold these for me," said Charlie, now it was his turn to take a pee. Walking towards them, but a distance away was a man, as he drew closer Jack could see he was smartly dressed, he was carrying something, a camera, it looked expensive.

"Look sharp Charlie, I feel a right pansy standin' 'ere wi' two bunches o' flowers in me hands."

Charlie returned from behind a tree grinning. "I ought to ask that bloke to take a picture of yer while your lookin' so pretty."

Jack shoved the bunch of flowers back at Charlie and called out,

"Afternoon, fine one for it." Then he raised the flowers, "To give to me mam."

"Do you live here on the farm?" Asked the stranger.

"No mister, but Mr.Eddowes don't mind us pickin' flowers, 'e's sort of related to me mam, but not, if yer know what I mean."

The camera now hung from the man's neck by a strap. "Well I won't tell tales on you," he offered a smile, "live and let live, that's my motto lads. I reckon your mam'll like the flowers, all ladies like to be given flowers." He winked, then walked on, slowly, looking about him at the fields. When he reached the farm gate he paused, put the camera to his eye and appeared to take a photograph. Looking back at the two boys he raised his arm to wave then moved on at a swifter pace.

"Who's that?" Said Charlie.

"Don't know but he looks official. Dad reckons any bloke as wears a trilby on a weekday must be official. Dad says it's not the hat you 'ave to worry about but what's underneath it."

"His soddin' head, what else could be under his hat," said Charlie mockingly.

"Trouble wi' you Jones is you've no nous." Jack sneezed, "Come on, flowers allus get up me nose, let's take 'em home, your grandad'll be waitin' for yer." Jack grinned at the thought.

"Eureka," shouted Charlie, eureka!"

Celia missed the handlebar of the pram, she spent much time in the company of Rosie and the twins and when walking through the arboretum together or to the shops Celia pushed their pram, grateful for the support it seemed to provide. Now walking alone to call on Caroline, her sister in law, she found it more tiring, although showing only modestly, nevertheless her own pregnant state caused her to miss the comfort that pushing a pram strangely offered.

She reached the house, an end of terrace on Purbeck Road. Holding her hands to the pit of her back, she stretched in an attempt to ease a dull ache. A short path and three steps led up to the door, a newspaper was tucked under the boot scraper, Celia supposed it was too thick to go through the letterbox, a magazine appeared to be rolled up inside the paper.

Edmund and Caroline had spent six days on honeymoon in Devon, on their return moving into the property they now named 'Moreleigh' after a village near Dartmouth which had charmed them both. Edmund had progressed at his work and was now qualified as a solicitor with Chaucer, Caffin and Holt. He dealt with all matters of inheritance, Wills and bequests. The stringent code of ethics that bound him to complete confidentiality continued to exasperate their ever-curious mother Gwendolyn but he had once told Celia, 'you would never believe the wholly unexpected and entirely fascinating ways in which man will dispense his chattels!'

Celia could not understand why, when visiting Rosie, she simply walked across the back yard, opened the scullery door and called out 'it's me', yet when visiting the home of her brother and sister in law, her actual family, she went to the front door, knocked and waited patiently. Perhaps it was the orderliness, the absence of nappies, teething rings and general clutter, or the different smells. At the home of the Spooners, baby powder, that lingering smell of warmed milk and a curious aroma, albeit subtle, which Celia had detected as arising from Tommy's jacket when it hung behind the door or over a chair back, might unwittingly calm the senses, whatever the reason Celia felt obliged to attend the front door of 'Moreleigh'. She'd knocked once, then again, about to retrace her steps believing no one to be at home, the door opened and Caroline stood on the threshold. A nervous smile came to her face, she seemed hesitant.

"Hello Celia, come in, mother and I were just saying how good it is to meet and chat together at this place. Mother says it is a true home and Edmund and I must fill it with happiness." As Caroline led Celia through to the sitting room she continued, "indeed just talking about it has made mother so emotional she has shed tears of joy, haven't you Mother?"

Florence Stanford sat by the fireplace but even her distance from the window and the shadow from the large, potted fern on the table beside her, could not hide the blotchy red skin around her eyes.

"We do get so silly as we grow older my dear," she said directing her remarks at Celia, "I can recall my own mother, now dead these many years, weeping from happiness at our wedding. Men have much greater resistance to sentimentality, necessarily so I imagine in the world of the provider, our breadwinners. Mr.Stanford often tells me skin is not sufficient to protect him from the harsh elements prevailing the workplace. He says only hide is tough enough to withstand the rigours of a man's world." Celia noticed how quickly Caroline's expression changed, it donned a sternness and for that instant an atmosphere swept across the room, like a sudden fleeting draught from an unknown source. It passed almost immediately.

"I have some photographs to show you Celia, most have come out very well, the worst one was taken by me of course, poor Edmund is sitting on the parapet of such a picturesque stone bridge looking like some kind of alien creature with three heads. I knew when I clicked the shutter that I'd moved too much but the good ones are really very clear. A kind man whom we met at the village pub took Edmund and me together."

"I shall leave you two sisters to enjoy the pictures, I have seen them already. Caroline is going to have my favourite enlarged at Askew's." Florence Stanford stood, crossed to her daughter, gave her a hug and kissed her cheek. "Don't worry, I shall see myself out, you make the most of your young company. Goodbye Celia dear, William is well I trust?"

"Yes, thank you Mrs.Stanford."

Celia's gaze followed the lady across the hallway and into the kitchen at the rear of the house. Caroline's mother left through the back door and quite inexplicably, Celia felt a measure of relief at this. From now on, Celia would come and go at the back door of this place just as she did at Rosie's. The photographs passed from one to the other of the young women and a more light-hearted chatter developed but still Celia wished that an innocent child's picture book might fall out from behind a cushion or that a pile of laundry, awaiting the iron, would tumble about the table top instead of the stately fern, to relieve this house of its orderliness and that Florence Stanford's tears might be more truly joyful, for Celia sensed a sadness here and this house was after all, the home of her younger brother Edmund.

Lisa Dodds had taken to her work at Turpin's shop like a duck to water. Not as gifted at her studies as her eldest sister Annie had been, since leaving school Liza had done various cleaning jobs and helped in the kitchen at the children's home as a part time post, but her bright personality and willing nature had impressed Lois Turpin. It was Mavis herself who, bearing in mind Miss Turpin's condition had suggested the job might be ideally suited to Liza. Now eighteen, her mental arithmetic was good and her ability to total a list of figures accurately was equally reliable.

Advanced mathematics would have defied her completely but as Miss Turpin observed, the shop while trading at a steady pace, gave 'little' call for 'large' sums. An open lively mind simply developed ability through living, and running errands, regularly helping her mam, had equipped Liza more than adequately for her work at Turpin's shop. Possessing Billy's big hearted friendliness and Edna's shrewd understanding of humankind, Liza could read a situation and apply her own consideration and encouragement. She recognised anxiety even through an attempt to conceal it behind nervous chatter and an enforced smile. She could interpret that curious language of diversion, spoken when times were too bad to use the everyday words which could reveal adversity.

Over the years Mavis had proved popular with customers and not knowing the reason for her leaving, any change was viewed as regrettable but gradually Liza Dodds was winning them over and between her unfortunate spasms, Lois Turpin smiled her relief as she tallied the till each evening and 'danced' to the day's end.

Since Edna began travelling to and from Brassington to work, Susie was usually home before her, Liza often later as Miss Turpin's shop had no set closing time, the hours displayed on the door were perhaps wishful thinking. As it was at Eddowes on Gregory Street, the 'bang bang' on the door just after it had been officially closed, once opened to meet an urgent demand for 'a tin o' luncheon meat for 'is pack-up in the mornin',' then admitted another and another with the cry 'saw your door was still open, I just need……..' until it was accepted that the public sanctioned when a shopkeeper might turn the lock on the door for the night, they were quite undeniably public servants of the most malleable kind.

Myra would return from school knowing that if her dad wasn't at home then he would probably be with Victor at the allotment, young though she was, picking in washing from the line, peeling potatoes for the meal came readily. The household functioned well and would doubtless adapt to the change when they became one less. Soon Susie would be living elsewhere.

Edith Spooner had sat Joe down in the chair opposite her own and while the house was quiet she'd spoken to her second son with real intent. 'I know you think you've to wait 'til I'm gone afore you marry but you're wrong Son. These tired old bones won't give up until me maker decides. I sit 'ere worryin' about you Joe an' I wouldn't fret arf as much if you wer' in your own little place wi' that lass. Marry Susie Dodds, she's a good en, make me happy Joe, then it don't matter when 'e decides. Pat and your brothers are capable o' keepin' house an' Tommy's settled, 'e'll see as Joyce is alright. Kathleen's got 'er own family now. I want to see my boy Joe settled an'all. You're the most like your dad, 'e wer' stubborn, let me see you wed, that's what I want.' Joe had taken his mam's hand in his own, it felt so different to Susie's. The fingers slight and deformed by arthritis, the skin now so thin the veins across the back ribboned in greenish blue and the underside carried lines ingrained from a lifetime spent in that labour of love, which is raising a family in an industrial city where smoke and coal dust define its citizens lest they forget 'their place'. 'If that's what you really want Mam,' Joe had said, smoothing her tired fingers with his love, 'then we'll set a date'.

He'd told Susie of the conversation and they'd agreed to speak with Billy and Edna the following weekend. Susie's parents had been delighted and provided the registry office was available the plan was to marry on September 28th. It was Susie's choice not to have a church wedding, Billy had declared that whatever she wanted, like her elder sister Annie, he'd see that it was done. Susie was anything but vain but whenever she wore anything white, without fail someone would say, ' are you alright dear, you do look peaky'. Blue was her colour and in the window at Griffin's was a lovely blue two-piece. Last April her pay had gone up by half a crown a week when she'd been made manager. After giving her mam keep and taking out her bus fares, Susie had put by regularly and now had a small nest egg, more than enough to purchase the blue outfit. Even if she did look radiant in white, seeing her mam and dad always working, ever struggling, Susie could not have felt happy adding more to their load.

Victor had stayed at No.24 for almost two months, Florrie had much improved through the respite and pestered Billy to bring Victor home to give Edna some relief but Billy relished the lad's company and Edna knew it. Not until her working day was lengthened by the bus journey to and from Brassington did the arrangement cease and Victor return home to his mam.

The workshop was for sale but as yet no buyer had been found. It felt strange to the folk of Winchester Street, walking by those old gates and knowing that all those years of activity within Eddowes' workshop, now were no more. Despite Andrew Smithfield taking over the business and premises more than nine years ago, people had persisted in referring to Eddowes and if it irritated the new owner he certainly didn't show it. In fact, it strangely pleased him. Not ever having known Saul and finding it difficult to regard Charles as 'timeless', it was Annie who ever came to his mind when thinking of his endeavour at Winchester Street. The workshop was a part of Annie, he'd valued it as such. Now circumstances forced him to sell and while the proceeds would be a gain in these troubled economic times, on the other side of his mind he entered a loss that as yet would not balance.

Joe and Susie were to rent a house on Monsall Street, not too far away from Handley's where Joe now worked with Tommy and close to the bus stop for Susie's place of employment, the shoe shop in town, where once the official closing time was reached the door remained closed. The need for footwear was far more ordered and in many cases put off not simply until another day but until there was money enough to pay, the belly must come first.

Tommy and Joe worked well together. James Handley had been agreeable to the appointment of Joe Spooner. He trusted much to Tommy, the reputation of his business, the handling of money but most importantly, that vital requirement of any undertaker, compassion. If Tommy had fulfilled these needs then Handley would trust his judgement and welcome another of Edith Spooner's sons to his employ.

On the 28th September, Audrey Potts would baby sit the twins for Rosie and Tommy to be witnesses to the marriage and so that Tommy could be best man. Only immediate family would be present and afterwards there was to be a simple reception at The Nelson, on the matter of which Billy had been most firm. 'Your dad'll pay for that an' there's an end to it', Susie knew when arguing was pointless. Only one exception had been made to the guest list, Edna had declared, 'I can't marry you off our Susie wi'out Annie there to stop me snivellin'. So an invitation had been extended to Mr.&Mrs.Charles Eddowes in the certain knowledge that Annie would come alone. 'His nibs won't come, God forbid 'e might be expected to smile'. Edna had remarked cynically but accurately as it would turn out.

Annie's mind had been elsewhere since receiving a letter in the post from Walter Hemsley. In fact two letters had arrived on the same day, one from Mabel in Leicester which had pleased Annie so much. Mabel was now engaged to be married, her fiancé, a doctor. Herself a midwife on the district, Mabel's work had frequently placed her in the company of G.P.'s. Now one such had asked her to be his wife and Annie could not be more pleased. Mabel had overcome tragedy and applied herself to study, she deserved happiness and security. Surely Dr. David Terry would grant her both. The other letter however, saddened Annie greatly. Walter Hemsley, himself now approaching eighty years of age, wrote in shaky, emotional hand, that his wife Alice had in latter years become confused of mind. Now her dementia was so advanced that she had been admitted to a mental hospital, the asylum at Handsworth. Every word spelled out Walter's despair, he mourned just as completely, was as utterly bereft as he would be if Alice were dead. A couple so close, their union so 'as one' already his wife was lost to him and his open grief brought tears to Annie's eyes as she read.

Her mind travelled back to those early days at Winchester Street, when each Christmas aunt Bella would receive a card and letter from Alice, her kindness in travelling from Sheffield to attend Bella's funeral and her continuing correspondence with Annie herself for these many years. She would write by return, it would not be an easy letter to compose. Walter would almost certainly have sent word to Davina, she and Alice had been the best of friends. Annie had always found it difficult to understand quite where her aunt Bella had entered this abiding friendship, she'd taught the Hemsley's children but that alone seemed too removed to account for the bond which, whilst Bella had lived Annie had sensed as being significant, indeed relied on by aunt Bella, yet in every other situation Bella Pownall was her own woman, reserved, stern, unbending in her beliefs and fiercely independent.

The back door latch rattled and Charles entered the scullery unusually animated.

"We shall sell every copy of The Post tomorrow I'll guarantee, it's all round The Standard, Fred Woolascroft's son was picked up by the police tonight, kerb crawling. Someone witnessed the whole thing, apparently in his desperation to drive off he knocked the copper to the ground but another bobby saw what was happening and managed to stop him. Woolascroft had been drinking as well, they said his language was diabolical. It won't do his father's affairs much good, it's been rumoured that the council are looking to secure more development land so everyone assumes Woolascroft will tender for the contract. He made the lad a director last year and even the men thought that was a madness. There are three sons but this one has always been favoured, God knows why, they say the lad has a foul temper."
Annie slipped Walter's letter back in the envelope.

"George isn't home yet, Hilda and John have gone to bed, do you want any supper?"

"Who's the letter from," asked Charles?

"Walter Hemsley, Alice's health is poor, I shall get a reply off tomorrow. They were very kind to aunt Bella and me."

"I wouldn't mind a cheese sandwich, I won't have any pickle on it at this hour. It's a shame I couldn't get any extra copies of the paper, we won't have enough spare, folk always want to read about scandal." Charles sat in the chair by the range and loosened his laces.

Annie set about making his supper, the affairs of Fred Woolascroft and his family mattered little to her, she was much more concerned over her oldest friends and their tribulation to dwell on gossip and speculation circulating the bar and tables at The Standard.

Liza bowed her head to allow her long hair to fall free in front of the range.

143

"Perhaps I should have it cut like Jean Tennyson, I wouldn't have all this bother dryin' it then." She shook the tresses with her fingers, natural waves threaded through every strand and even wet as they now were, the intent to curl was already evident. "Why is Susie's hair straight and mine determined to do as it likes," said a frustrated Liza.

Edna laughed, "When you were all little, I used to fret over Susie's hair. I'd try all sorts to put a curl in it but nothin' ever really worked, so instead I'd fill it wi' bows, one on top an' one either side. When she got old enough to care, she made 'er own mind up. One day she come in from school, ripped out the ribbons an' threw em' down on the table in a right old huff. 'I look like Wrenshaw's 'oss she said.' Sometimes the brewery 'ould enter what they considered their finest horse in a show, if it won, then for days after the animal 'ould wear its rosettes as it pulled the waggon through the streets." Edna let out a sigh.

"What's up Mam, you look worried?" Liza had caught sight of the anxious expression on her mam's face, when tired of holding her head down, she'd tossed back her hair and stood upright again.

"I don't know if I've done the right thing, askin' Annie Eddowes to the weddin'. The 28th September is George's birthday, 'e'll be twenty five."

"Surely Mam you don't think George is goin' to want a tea party wi' candles to blow out at his age, he's engaged to be married for goodness sake, George wouldn't want his mam to miss Susie's weddin' just 'cause of his birthday." Liza was genuinely bewildered by Edna's concern.

"Don't pin that up until it's properly dry."

Now Liza let out a sigh and went to sit in the chair opposite her mother. She always said that, mam told her that very same thing every time she washed her hair.

"Your dad an' me were witnesses at Annie an' Harold's weddin', they wer' that happy. 'E wer' Billy's best friend, just like Annie's allus been my best friend. After the registry office we went straight to The Nelson, it wer' our treat to them. A meal an' a drink in celebration. I can remember exactly what we 'ad, even where we sat over in a corner where Annie felt less conspicuous, we still wore our buttonholes an' you know what she's like, never wants to be centre of attention. It wer' beef an' ale pie, in the middle o' the table a plate o' crusty bread an' a pot o' drippin'. Annie an' me 'ad arf o' mild an' the men 'ad bitter. It wer' springtime, I wore me best suede shoes, I loved them shoes, I felt like the bees knees when I 'ad them on. George wer' born the followin' year, September 28th. Harold wer' that proud, 'I wouldn't call the King me uncle', Harold used to say that a lot, allus content, could see no wrong in the world. Thirteen months later 'e wer' killed in an accident at Josiah's slaughter yard." Edna looked deep into her daughter's eyes. "If I can remember all that so clearly, how much more will our Susie's weddin' bring back to Annie's mind?" Tears welled up and began to fall over Edna's cheeks.

Liza took her mam's hand. "Some memories are always there. I can remember the day dad came home. I know he came from the hospital but to me, he'd come straight from that war, that horrible place that grown ups talked about when they thought us kids weren't listenin'. We didn't understand that war was a thing, we thought it was a place, somewhere dads had to go, somewhere a lot of them didn't come back from.

That day in Winchester Street, our place, I saw me dad an' he looked different. I can just remember the feelin', frightened, sad, confused, and yet so happy. I've not felt happiness like that since, it welled up inside me like somebody wer' blowin' up a balloon deep down in me stomach. It got bigger an' bigger 'til I couldn't contain it any more an' it burst at me mouth. I kissed it out all over me dad, pure joy, I kissed my happiness over him an' it wer' wonderful.

Sometimes our dad does kind things, good things that other dads don't think of, an' I remember that day, but it doesn't make me frightened anymore. Nor confused, or sad. I love the memory I wouldn't want to lose it, not ever." Liza leaned forward and kissed her mam's cheek, gently wiped away the salty tears with her fingers and smiled. "Annie Eddowes will enjoy Susie's weddin' Mam, I know she will." Feeling the need to propel their thoughts forward Liza said, "Victor came into the shop today, Florrie sent him for a packet of rice an' a nutmeg, she told him there'd be change. She'd given him a florin and the change came to four pence ha'penny, I gave him a thruppeny bit, one penny and a ha'penny. He looked at the coins in the palm of his hand an' said, 'I want a shiny one, these aren't shiny'. I couldn't disappoint him, he looked that dejected, so I gave him a tanner and put a penny ha'penny out my purse in the till. I reckon Victor could get away with anythin', that big soft grin of his."

"I don't know about could," said Edna, " 'e does, 'e allus does."
At last a chuckle from her mam, and Liza felt relieved.

"What causes St.Vitus's Dance Mam? Miss Turpin must feel wearied by it. Does all the twitchin' an' jumpin' go on when she's asleep an'all?"

"It's summat to do wi' the nervous system, it's all out o' kilter an' the muscles go into spasm. Some say it can follow rheumatic fever if yer get that as a child. I don't know if Lois Turpin suffered from rheumatic fever when she wer' young, it's not summat you feel it proper to ask about is it?"

"She asked me to thread a needle for her today," said Liza. "A button had come off her blouse in the wash an' she wanted to sew it back on. I just stopped meself in time, I wer' about to say, 'I'll do that for you', but then it struck me, if I thought I weren't even able to stitch a button on I'd likely give up all together. She did it, eventually. What would have taken me no more than three or four minutes took Miss Turpin best part o' fifteen. Every time she tried to put the needle to a hole her arm would jump. It wouldn't have been so bad if the button had only two holes instead of four. I made her a nice cup o' tea an' cut a piece from the slab o' marble cake on the counter, we ate arf each. Miss Turpin says she's sure I have an admirer. This young man comes in most days, he could buy everythin' in one go but he just gets one item each day. Miss Turpin reckons he's sweet on me." Liza blushed and Edna's motherly curiosity was aroused.

"Who is he?" She asked.

"I don't know his name, neither does Miss Turpin 'cause I asked her an' she said he must be new about these parts. I reckon he works at Clark an' Browns, he bought a bag o' toffee whirls yesterday an' told me how he needed to suck somethin' 'cause havin' to hold tacks between his teeth all day makes his lips dry. I've heard that's what upholsterers do, when they're coverin' a chair they keep the tacks between their teeth, it's quicker to take them from there than from a box or a bag, speeds up the job."

"Your dad 'ould be good at upholsterin' then, I know 'e don't do it no more but 'e used to keep a roll up in the corner of 'is mouth for ages afore lightin' it, a few tacks between 'is teeth 'ould be no bother." Edna laughed at the notion.

"As Victor wer' about to leave the shop, Robert Cheetham came in," said Liza, feeling her hair and shaking it loose with her fingers. "Quick as a flash Victor held out his hand, 'good morning sir', he said. Cheetham could do no other than take it but he looked irritated. There's Victor, a simpleton in the eyes o' most people, yet his was the courtesy, Cheetham is Mayor of the city, a man of means, upstandin' in the community an' all that pomp but it wer' Victor who showed the good manners, Cheetham would never have offered to shake Victor's hand in a thousand years. It's all hard to fathom Mam. Here, feel if it's dry enough."

Liza leant her head towards her mother for approval. Edna ran her fingers down the curling strands of hair.

"Yes, it'll do, tie it back an' stick kettle on the range."

Edna sat back in the chair and closed her eyes, Annie, Susie, Lois Turpin, Victor all stared back at her even through tight shut lids. 'Every day the same, never two days alike', poor Winnie Bacon, Edna had heard her speak those words many times when she'd been trying to fathom a complexity within the family or settle her doubts over one of Ted's 'certainties' at the bookies. Liza was right, Winchester Street was their place, and good memories were made there. While the kettle boiled, Edna remembered.

CHAPTER TEN

Late December

    This Christmas had been a good one, Annie recalled recent events as she ran the iron over Hilda's new blouse, a gift from Davina. Even Charles had displayed a rare glimpse of happiness at the sight of the plump, seven week old Mathew Eddowes sleeping, blissfully serene in his mother's arms whilst the family, assembled at Davina's house, sang, danced and played games in celebration of a year that delivered so much hope. Freddy's wedding to Francis, George's engagement to Alice, Hilda's diploma from Clarendon and her job at the library, John's progress at Raleigh and most delightful of all, the birth on November 8th of William's first child, a son, healthy, strong, contented Mathew.

    Alongside her own family's good fortune, Annie remembered with tremendous pleasure, the marriage of Susie Dodds to Joe Spooner and the surprise which had brought joy to everyone, the arrival of Marie, adopted by Mavis and Eddie. The ironing, so monotonous and repetitive, relegated almost always to that briefly unoccupied spot at the end of a busy day, this night seemed much less daunting as all the satisfying images of Christmas kept Annie company. She draped the pretty cream satin blouse over the back of a chair and hummed the tune of a carol, Charles had gone to the whist drive.

    Normally held the week before Christmas, this year fate had conspired against tradition when a section of ceiling collapsed in the Masonic Hall and no other venue could be found in time. Indeed the incident could have been tragic as the poor woman whose task it was to clean the premises, escaped the falling masonry with only inches to spare. In her state of shock she had uttered, 'I wer' only dustin', it never 'appens at Citadel, even when I stand in pulpit an' sing Glory Glory Harry Allsop'! Apparently she had been taking a sneaky peek at the regalia, normally locked away but on that occasion left in an unlocked cupboard, when retribution unleashed itself through an almighty descent of Masonic ceiling. A new cleaning lady was now being sought, the previous holder of the post having declared her nerves too fragile for all that 'hocus pocus'.

Tonight the fund raising whist drive had been accommodated in the assembly hall at Blackmore's school, much to the surprise of most everyone. Edna had shed her own inimitable light on the subject, 'Cheetham can't be Mayor forever, it takes a thick neck to stand the weight o' that chain an' Blackmore's got neck enough an' the chest an'all, they could 'ang the bloody shield off council house wall on the end of 'is chain'.

Annie was happy to accept a notion of benevolence, Edna was quite likely correct in her observations but not really understanding why any mortal would desire to be the subject of such public scrutiny, she allowed her thoughts to bypass intrigue entirely and instead to concentrate on her own family's well being. George had told her that he hoped to marry Alice in April. Percy Pollard had taken him quietly aside one day at work and informed him of a 'let' soon to be available on Ainsley Road. Percy's very elderly mother was surrendering the tenancy to move in with him and his wife. 'It'll be a sight easier for Mrs.Pollard than goin' across town to me mother's place every day', had been Percy's explanation, but the hefty sigh that followed and the faintly spoken additional comment, 'Mam'll settle in alright, her little accidents'll likely get less when she can shout to Freda', had felt to George more designed to reassure Percy than to enlighten himself.

Annie was just picking the last item from the laundry basket when a knock came at the back door. She put the iron back on the range and crossed the scullery feeling curious. Hilda was staying two nights at Sarah's. Jean and Randall earlier in the day had returned to London to attend a gathering, a sort of party at Avril's. Buoyant from the successful sale of her work at one of London's top galleries, Avril had extended invitations to all her closest friends expressing her wish that they mark the end of the year and the beginning of the new with a union of hearts and minds. When Jean had so described the event to her mam, Sarah had smiled sweetly but inwardly wondered whatever happened to that simple tradition of bringing in from outside the back door, a nub of coal, a glass of water and a piece of silver on the stroke of midnight before jumping into bed with a union of cold feet and fatigue. Hilda had decided it would ease grandma Sarah's loneliness if she had tea at Mitchell Street and went from there to the library on Thursday morning. George was with Alice, and John, in an attempt to humour his dad and perpetuate Charles' uncharacteristic cheerfulness, had gone with him to the whist drive.

In the darkness Annie could barely make out the individual standing with the collar of their coat muffling their throat from the cold. Not until a familiar voice said, "Sorry to come at this hour but I didn't want to talk to yer in the shop," did Annie recognise Joyce Spooner.

"Come in Joyce, stand by the range for a minute and warm yourself. I was just about to make a pot of tea." Annie felt anxious but determined a smile to hide her concern.

Joyce held her hands over the flat iron. "Can't let 'em get hot, I've got this rash as flares up every few weeks an' it'll itch if me fingers get too warm, doctor reckons it's a reaction to the nickel in coins. I handle 'em all day long, can't wear gloves, not allowed, not even them wi' the finger ends missin', boss says gloves aren't part o' the uniform. Sad don't yer think, bein' allergic to money, I suppose I'd be alright wi' paper money but not much o' that ever stays in my hands. Rent went up last month an' what wi' Christmas an' all that carry on." Joyce sniffed, took her hands from the range, inspected them and sighed resignedly as she pulled out a chair from the table and sat down.

Annie poured two cups of tea, still awaiting the purpose of Joyce's visit to be revealed. "How is your mother? I saw Rosie and the twins last week, my how they've grown, Edith must so enjoy those little boys and young Beth too. Kathleen brought her to the shop yesterday to buy Ernie's coconut mushrooms. He has a quarter of those every week and apparently Beth pretends to cook them in her toy saucepan before tipping them on his plate after he's finished mopping it with a slice of bread." Annie chatted to fill the silence that seemed to hover over them, casting a shadow of foreboding about the room. The brightness of Hilda's blouse now retreating beyond a sense of pending trouble. Not ever before had Joyce called on Annie and her arrival now at Gregory Street must surely suggest some problem, a dilemma Joyce could not confide to Tommy.

"I wer' out treatin' meself to a Christmas drink, it gets lonely sometimes at that room on Peverell Street. You know what folk are like, so I went to The Wheatsheaf, nobody there 'ould take any notice o' me, just a glass o' pale ale an' as it turned out, a sweet sherry an'all, this bloke bought it for me, I think 'e wer tryin' to tuck isself away same as me. Both of us could have been locked up instead o' bein' free to buy a Christmas drink but for family. In my case it wer' Tommy, for him it wer' his dad as saved him from prison, rightly or wrongly, whichever it might be that's how it is. After we'd had our drinks an' dropped summat in the Sally Army tin, he said he'd like to walk me home. Now I know what you must think but it weren't like that, I didn't go out to sell it, an' he weren't out to pay for it. I wouldn't do that to our Tommy anyroad, he's all the things I'm not." Joyce sniffed again and rubbed her fingers together absentmindedly, as though an irritation demanded some relief but was not worthy of any actual attention. "We sat on the bed wi' the eiderdown wrapped around our shoulders, it can be bloody freezin' in that room, landlord don't always put money in the meter, nowt we can do about it, eventually he'll stick a few bob in the slot but it's best to keep quiet. One o' the other tenants complained an' I'll swear for a good week afterwards he kept us perished, just out o' spite. Anyroad, after about an hour I wished I'd sent the bugger on his way when we left The Wheatsheaf. Talk, bloody Hell could he talk, he'd wear the hind leg off a donkey wi' his gabble an' all about isself. His old man read the riot act to him, any repeat o' last summer's disgrace an' he'll be out on his ear. He'd had a few drinks afore I even got to the pub, his tongue wer' well oiled, that loose it ran away from him 'til in the end I couldn't stand it, I come close to stiflin' the bugger wi' the eiderdown so I chucked him out. Christmas, goodwill to all men some folk might say but he could go ring his bloody bell somewhere else, anybody 'ould think Woolascrofts owned this city to hear him talk." Joyce swallowed the last of her tea. "Ta, that wer' welcome, didn't enjoy me cup at home, milk had gone off. His father is preparing to tender for the contract to develop land south o' the city, I heard him say the name Bobbers Mill, plain as day. The council intends to cover Bobbers Mill wi' houses an' that's where your Freddy farms don't he Mrs.Eddowes. The way he spoke I could tell it weren't yet common knowledge. I had to let yer know, I couldn't ignore what I'd heard. You were good to our family when dad wer' killed. I remember you comin' to our house wi' food for mam. After you'd gone she'd put it on a shelf an' say, 'God bless that woman'. Mam allus spoke loud 'cause of her deafness but it felt to me like she wer' makin' sure the Almighty heard. Don't let on to anybody that it wer' me as said owt, folk 'ould never believe I hadn't took Dick Woolascroft back to Peverell Street for money an' I don't want Tommy upset. I don't want landlord to kick me out neither, he might be a miserable, tight fisted old so an' so but I can just about afford it there. It's a strange house, only two other rooms are let out, landlord sleeps downstairs, I reckon he must keep the ghost at bay. Accordin' to a neighbour whose lived on Peverell Street for years, the house we live in is haunted, somebody wer' murdered there, long time ago, beaten about the head wi' a slate fender. I've not heard owt peculiar, seen nowt neither but it does have a creepy feel an' the cyclamen in a pot that mam give me started to wither as soon as I put it on the window sill, like it shrank from summat nasty. Mam said I couldn't have looked after it properly but I didn't have a chance to look after it, the minute it come into that house the poor thing giv' up the ghost 'an that's a fact." Joyce stood and pulled the collar of her coat round her throat. "I'll have to be off now Mrs.Eddowes," she said.

"Please do call me Annie, wait just a moment." Annie went to the scullery and poured some milk into a clean jam jar, screwing the lid on tight. "I am so grateful to you Joyce for coming here to let me know. I promise I won't divulge who it was told me. There's no need for you to sit alone in that room on Peverell Street Joyce, you can come here any evening and be welcome." Annie put the jar of milk in the young woman's hand. "Give your mam my best and thank you."

152

Annie watched as the figure disappeared into the darkness. Touched by Joyce's remark and the memory it had evoked, a tear welled in her eye, suddenly all the joy of recent days and those images of happy events which had helped the iron flow freely over the clothes, now lay crushed beneath a threat so alarming that Annie hardly dare contemplate the outcome.

Annie had pondered on the dilemma as she lay wakeful through the early hours. Charles was Freddy's father, it seemed instinctive to tell him about this worrying situation. Annie knew Freddy would have no desire to sell Bobbers Mill, indeed it wasn't entirely his to sell. Arthur Cropley still held the title to a third and the remainder in principle, was owned jointly by Freddy and the bank, but she'd heard of compulsory purchase, it had been the method employed by the council to secure a parcel of land at Shipley. Freddy's hopes and dreams bedecked the hedgerows and enriched the pasture at Bobbers Mill, his days with Francis eagerly spent in establishing his chosen industry, in proving its right of place alongside the factories and pitheads which dominated the landscape and ordered the lives of men to such a degree, that many of them now confused independent thought and enterprise with militancy and insurrection.

Charles should speak with Andrew Smithfield, he may at least be able to give an honest account of the authority's intention. But Annie had given her word to Joyce, she would not reveal the name of the person who spoke out on the matter and Charles took a pathetic pleasure in intrigue and hearsay. His time spent in The Standard would likely loosen his tongue and the company he kept held little command of discretion. It would inevitably lead to distress for the Spooners, innocent though they were in it all. Tommy deserved better than idle gossip and thoughtless innuendo. Edith Spooner had looked so frail at Joe's wedding to Susie that Annie had feared for her strength to survive the day's celebration. Charles would immediately ask whom it was delivered the information and would not agree to be denied the answer. So, with mixed emotions Annie resolved to go herself to speak with Smithfield, believing that his integrity would allow him to accept her need of discretion and equally disable any attempt on his part to veil facts. Tomorrow, Wednesday, would be New Years Day, it was unlikely that any business of the council could be undertaken until after the weekend. Annie felt sure that Maggie had said Toby Hillier would not be at his desk again until January 6th. On Sunday afternoon instead of calling on Sarah and Davina she would make her was to the home of Andrew Smithfield and his aunt Alicia Plowright. At least when she spoke with Freddy she would be in possession of the facts and Freddy could decide his best course. By then, some patron of The Standard with an ear to the ground might cast the revelation across the card table for public debate. Freddy needed prior knowledge, if only to enable him a dignified composure when the council official stood at his door.

Edna could not find sleep, she muttered to herself, 'shouldn't have had that piece of fruit cake so late', Billy lay beside her, his intermittent snoring confirmed his slumber and it irritated Edna all the more. He had five nights off work from the exchange. So used to the routine of Billy's night work had Edna become that his presence there beyond that customary Sunday interlude for man and wife, now contrarily charged her mind 'til no amount of tiredness could still its determination to ponder and peruse all of life, along with associated problems, even down to an incursion of 'silver fish' in the larder cupboard. She reached for a Rennie from the saucer on the bedside table. New Year had passed quietly at Winchester Street, apart from an unusually late supper due to visiting both their married daughters, and inviting Liza's young man to come for a bite to eat at No.24, little out of the ordinary had occurred.

Edna slipped her legs from under the covers and pushed her feet inside her slippers. It was cold, when she pulled her dressing gown about her, the feeling of relief at the sudden warmth propelled her across the room. She peered through the edge of the curtain, first morning of a new year. The clock showed a quarter past three. Not expecting to see anything but those vague, gloomy shapes of the houses on the other side of the street she was surprised by movement. The sky held little moon, just enough to enable her to distinguish a figure, walking slowly, awkwardly. The man turned into the entry, it could be no other than Jack Sulley, probably the worse for drink. Drunk or sober, he'd be no comfort to Lillian, of that Edna felt certain. His appearance became more abandoned by the week and his frame forever shook from coughing. Lillian hardly spoke, whether her husband's behaviour embarrassed her and drove her silence or whether Jack's temper dominated his wife's tongue Edna could not know, but out there in the darkness, trouble stalked the early hours of 1930. A shiver caused her to step back from the window, as if 'father time' had suddenly rebuked her for harbouring such pessimism, standing as she was at the threshold of his new, untouched, untainted year. Looking towards the sound of Billy's deep breathing, Edna thanked God for what she had and tiptoed down stairs to heat some milk.

The family now numbered so many that Annie had insisted the one large gathering at Davina's over Christmas was more than enough. They would all spend New Years Day in their respective abodes but Annie herself would call on both Sarah and Davina the following Sunday afternoon. Her intention of travelling to Brassington instead troubled her conscience, so with Charles dozing in his chair and John engaged in assembling an intricate cardboard model of London Bridge, a Christmas present from Jean and Randall, Annie decided to go wish, Happy New Year', to those two elderly women so important to her.

George had eaten his dinner, winked at his mother and whispered, 'I'll be back for tea Mam, need to give my Alice a New Year kiss'. His growing excitement at their forthcoming wedding bubbled over. Annie relished his joy, recalling even after all these years, her own impatience, the anticipation that built inside her those early weeks of 1903, when her marriage to Harold in the spring dispelled every cloud which ventured into the sky above Sherwood.

She decided to walk the distance to The Park, any bus service would be irregular given the date. Besides, it had been some time since she had found herself free of the shop on a Wednesday. Tomorrow would doubtless bring that all too familiar procession of humankind through the shop door and with it a grim reality, her tactful glance at someone passing by outside rather than observe the frantic shuffling of coppers in a purse so worn it barely held together, the desperate attempt to gain a couple of eggs, two from their dozen purchased the week before, mysteriously having been addled!

Yet, as was her established routine, just before Christmas Mrs.Stanford had entered the shop, politely enquired after the family's well being, given Annie a short list of items to be got ready for collection by Rex Madden and left in an aura of mystery, just as she had come. Annie sensed the woman's unease, a discomfort, not Annie perceived from anything or anyone within the shop, but from the nature of her custom, almost ritualistic, as if ordered by an authority for which Florence Stanford was obliged to serve. On a number of occasions Annie had bitten her tongue just in time to stop herself thanking Stanford's man with the use of that popular simile, 'Cratchet', rescuing the situation with a hurried, 'Good day Mr.Madden'. No one could say that Eddowes' shop did not have a diverse patronage, in fact if Dickens were alive and living in Nottingham he would likely tuck himself away in a corner, camouflaged by packets and tins, there to create from inspiration a story to endure the generations.

Davina's gate was ajar, perhaps she had already a visitor. Annie walked to the side door, the old oak now so weathered it wore its greyness with distinguished maturity. Mrs.Pooley had recently polished the brass knocker and the contrast of bold bright metal against the retiring, muted complexion of the aged door was as stark as the difference between Florence Stanford and Stanley Pagett, that undesirable, unclean man who'd entered the shop as the good lady left. 'Chalk 'n cheese', as Sarah would say, 'Chalk 'n cheese' Annie dear'. She knocked and waited, the door opened slowly.

"Why my dear I was resigned to a day of solitude, a book, my stitching the only diversion to be allowed this ancient, fragile creature." Davina gave a coy smile but her appearance did suggest her expectation of a New Years Day devoid of company. Her hair was not pinned as correctly as it would normally be and she wore slippers, Annie had never before found Davina in slippers beyond the confines of her bedroom.

"Where is Mrs.Pooley? Asked Annie, feeling concerned.

Davina waved her hand dismissively. "I sent her to her sister's until Friday evening. I have enough logs and coal in the hearth to stoke the Paddington Express and more food than can be justified by one appetite. Indeed a boy came to the door an hour ago asking if I had any job he could do for a shilling. I said don't you know that today is the first day of the New Year. 'Don't make no difference at our house missus' he said, 'mam won't let me ask on a Sunday but today's a Wednesday'. I gave him one shilling, a pork pie and a tin of pilchards and told him to come back tomorrow to chop some kindlers. Now at least I have the distraction of wondering if he'll turn up. Mrs.Pooley would be adamant, 'you'll not see hide nor hair of him again' is what she'd say. Perhaps I'll not see hide nor hair of Mrs.Pooley again either, I gave her a small seasonal bonus and I know she does favour the area around Stanton where her sister lives."

Davina's tongue rattled on as they walked through the hallway to the sitting room. Annie now felt guilty at insisting there should be no gathering of the family so soon after the one just last week. Davina's mood was out of character and disturbing in its cynicism.

"I won't be able to come on Sunday," said Annie, "that's why I'm here today instead."

Davina poked the fire, the room was comfortably warm, on the table a book was open but face down and the crust from some kind of sandwich rested on a plate beside the book, curling at the edges as it dried in the heat from the flames now leaping the back of the grate. Davina sat back in her chair, she looked at Annie intently, disinclined to stir herself she kicked in the damper with her slippered foot in the most unladylike fashion then laughed, amused by her own indecorous gesture of pique.

"I am obnoxious today my dear, truly obnoxious but that does not prevent me sensing your anxiety, what is wrong, I can always tell when something is bothering you."

Annie sighed, and not doubting for one moment her old friend's confidentiality and understanding, she related the events of the previous night when Joyce Spooner had told Annie of the council's interest in Bobbers Mill and begged her discretion over the means in which Joyce had come by the information. Davina's mood was now much more alert, her mind immediately directed away from herself to the potentially ruinous situation threatening Freddy. A letter had come with her last bank statement, the financial situation in America following the Wall Street crash would inevitably affect stock values across the Atlantic and into Europe. The council would be obliged to 'shop' prudently. Freddy's terms of loan with the bank could prove ill matched, conversely, perhaps such unstable economic times might dissuade the authority from spending on anything other than sheer necessities, then Freddy's beloved Bobbers Mill might remain untouched by the so called progressive development of the city bounds.

"Mr.Smithfield has the reputation of being fair, moderate," said Davina, as her mind engaged the problem, "at least he might suggest a way by which Freddy could approach the council, establish dialogue. Only through discussion can any issue, especially one likely to be contentious, have any hope of settlement. The older I become the more convinced I am of the benefit to be gained by an open exchange of opinion. Thoughts bound in silence can often fester and weep, open and aired they find a healthy conclusion." Davina's gaze at that moment went beyond Annie to something or someone influencing her words, she looked remote, distant and Annie felt reluctant to interrupt. "Does Sarah know?" Davina's attention was now firmly back with Annie.

"No, I won't say anything to Sarah, she would feel compelled to ask Toby Hillier the ins and outs of it but that wouldn't be right, it would place him in a very awkward position. I know he is required to maintain neutrality on matters of council revenue. He needs to keep his work, any interference on his part would compromise his security and he has Maggie and the girls to provide for. I shall go to Brassington on Sunday and seek the advice of Andrew Smithfield. My approach on the subject may very well lead to him calling on Freddy, that must surely be the best I could hope for under the circumstances." Annie had observed the shrinking remains of Davina's sandwich. "What have you eaten today, you should have a hot meal inside you this time of year. Mrs.Pooley will have left you with some preparation I hope."

Davina gave a frustrated huff. "I have a list, a set of instructions to save me taxing my brain, lest it fail under the strain. Last night I was to consume the content of a soup pot, tonight I am instructed to eat the pressed beef with a baked potato that has been duly scrubbed and polished to befit this first day of a new decade. Tomorrow evening I am ordered to feast upon a pork pie which by now will be in the belly of my newly found woodcutter friend." She chuckled, "If he returns in the morning I shall make from Mrs.Pooley's list a paper aeroplane and launch it across the hallway at her arrival on Friday." Davina stared down at her slippered feet, "Am I going mad Annie do you suppose, is my brain on that alarming descent into senility or is it merely the prelude to a cantankerous old age. You must not be afraid to scold me if I begin to behave like a peevish child. Mother spoke often of a second childhood." Davina again chuckled and without aforethought said abruptly. "Tell Freddy not to despair, he must never despair."

Annie found Davina's mood altogether curious and not knowing how quite to respond, she spent a few more minutes telling her dear friend about George's excitement before excusing herself through her wish to visit Sarah. Perhaps advancing years brought cynicism, aunt Bella seemed ever to be cynical, but then aunt Bella had always seemed old. Even the chirpy Winnie Bacon had displayed a subdued, preoccupied demeanour in her latter years and some of the more senior customers to the shop were downright contrary. Annie pondered her own likely character if called upon to deal with old age, then burst into laughter at the thought of Edna's rise to this challenge. "Oh, that I might live to see it," said Annie to herself as she turned the corner into Parliament Street and into the New Year with a tangle of emotions only the application of time might unravel.

Davina sat quietly, dear Annie, how fond she was of that young woman. So many problems over the years had tried Annie's resolve, Davina could risk no tribulation to beset Annie as a result of her feeble mindedness. She crossed the room to the bureau where she kept her papers and correspondence. Her fingers travelled along the envelopes until she reached one which several times she had been about to remove but had found herself releasing her grip and slipping it back among the rest once more. This day her action must be determined, she sat back in her chair, took the letter from the envelope and read the words yet again. It was from her old and dear friend Alice Hemsley, the very last letter she would likely receive from Alice. It held a strange account of their past lives, in passages tragically confused, almost like a child's scribbling, yet in others alarmingly accurate. Throwing Alice's handwriting into the flames felt disloyal, heartless, unsympathetic of her sad demise, but to keep the letter, to allow it to sit in the bureau 'til Davina's own forgetfulness , be it borne of age or dementia, ultimately placed it in the path of Annie, another obstacle, another problem to test the young woman's strength, Davina could not permit. She leant forward, her fingers trembled as she let the paper fall into the flames where the fire consumed it with an appetite, which made up for the lack of her own. The envelope and its content had sat in the bureau too long, Davina was not immune to the rigours of age any more than Alice, now she had made certain its destruction could not be too late. "Done", she said to herself, a sudden notion amused her. If the boy turns up tomorrow to chop kindlers, then I shall open the box of chocolates from Burtons and now, as my constitution becomes fickle, I shall eat all except the nutty ones, those I shall save for the cynical Mrs.Pooley!

Annie's thoughts drifted between Freddy and William, the latter so driven to acquire status, dismissive of his younger brother's commitment to his chosen path, that of working the land. Annie worried for Freddy, he seemed ever challenged by William's apparent progress, nothing came easily to Freddy whereas fortune smiled upon William, those curious charms of his ready at a moment's notice to spirit away any obstacle that might stand in his path.

The bus stopped opposite a large billboard displaying a colourful poster designed to entice the population to a pantomime at The Theatre Royal, 'Jack and the

Beanstalk'. Depicted, were a young lad with a complexion which glowed from good health, gazing up at a truly magnificent runner bean stem and his buxom mother, equally proclaiming well being, about to milk the best fed cow Annie had ever seen, its girth wide enough to rival the bus on which she travelled. Freddy prided himself on that glow of health, the stout quarters and full udders to be seen on his herd of cows as they walked across the yard at Bobbers Mill, responding to his call that fell upon their ears twice daily, as regular as sunrise and sunset. He'd wax lyrical about the height and density of his wheat, describing its graceful dance over the field in time to the rhythmic breeze, as the heads of grain rose to the warmth of the sun's rays, each one stretching itself in an effort to see over the shoulder of its neighbour.

William measured success by a different rule, his achievements passed from wallet to bank, entirely rigid with no deviation, elements of nature dared not interfere, neither to aid nor hinder.

The conductor rang the bell and the bus moved forward with that surge of sound from the engine, as though it needed to regain momentum after being made to idle at the stop whilst humankind dithered. A woman lowered herself to the seat in front of Annie, she wore a headscarf, paisley patterned, almost certainly a product of Smithfield's at Brassington. William would likely have worked with Mr.Armistead in the print shop on the bright colours and flowing shapes that now adorned the head and shoulders of Annie's fellow passenger.

She felt surprised that Andrew Smithfield had not seen fit to send word of the council's intent, he must surely be aware that Freddy farmed Bobbers Mill, if only through conversations with William. She could understand his reluctance to involve William, despite the fact that he was now a father and had worked with older men, William's experiences had not achieved to alter significantly that trait which made him unreliable, at times woefully immature. The woman suddenly lowered her head and her hand raised to stifle a sneeze.

"Bless you", said Annie.

The woman turned, "Thank you, I think it's my scarf, it's been in a drawer with a lavender bag and the smell's gone up my nose."

Annie smiled, "Its pretty, lovely colours."

The bus was far from full, Annie supposed that being a Sunday most folk were occupied at home. On a weekday the aisle could hold a number of people standing and between stops small children wriggled impatiently on their mothers' knees, hoping the next stop would produce an exodus and they could reclaim their place by the window where they could draw pictures with their fingers in the condensation coating the glass.

From Brassington gates, where the bus drew up for people to alight, Annie would walk the short distance to the house. She fastened her top button which she'd undone when boarding the bus, remembering aunt Bella's caution, 'undo your coat or you wont feel the benefit of it when you go out again'. In her bag she carried a small slab of Madeira cake and some Lincoln biscuits for Mrs.Plowright. Annie had met the lady only once but had been immediately struck by her brightness, some would say boldness, but Annie had found her most pleasant and approved of Alicia Plowright's confident nature. She thanked the conductor, no one else got off so she stepped back from the pavement's edge quickly and the bus moved swiftly along. Seldom did she come to this area of town, indeed there was little reason to but for the need periodically of Seamus Fitzgerald's services. The old Irishman had for years sharpened scissors, cut keys and capped work boots, from the humble premises of a wooden shed, located half a dozen yards down a cut between Smithfield's factory and a redundant knacker yard. During the period when the factory had been used for munitions, folk had jokingly said, 'one spark from Fitzy's grinder an' the whole soddin' lot'll go up, entrails an'all'. Thankfully no such catastrophic event ever took place and Seamus Fitzgerald endured beyond the need for arms, meeting still the demand for keys, toecaps and sharp scissors, ever refusing to move to a site more central, declaring, 'yer can't uproot old trees begorra'!

As Annie approached the house she could hear voices. A car was parked outside, she felt dismayed, Smithfield and his aunt must have visitors. Had they just arrived or were they about to leave. She hesitated, out of sight behind a privet hedge, men's voices, one was Andrew Smithfield the other she didn't recognise. The

162

exchange sounded urgent, not a relaxed greeting or a cheery farewell but words of some intensity, yet the voices were not raised, if anything they were low in tone. She had come this far, her arrival at Brassington this Sunday afternoon was not without real purpose. "Freddy". She spoke his name out loud. Taking a leaf from Alicia Plowright's book, Annie made bold and started up the side path which took callers to the back door. Smithfield at once noticed her, his expression held a look of bewilderment. The other man whom Annie now alarmingly suspected was a doctor, given the familiar type of bag he clutched, turned on his heel, hurried to the front gate, got into his car and drove off.

"Annie", he called out and beckoned her to join him by the front door, "thank God, however did you hear so soon, there are definitely times when the spread of news is a Godsend, she's too weak to be moved, Dr.Parker's opinion is that her age and the severity of the attack make it too risky to attempt taking her to the hospital." His voice shook slightly, trying to retain his composure in front of Annie seemed to work conversely, the effort weakening Andrew Smithfield's usual calm demeanour. He continued, "Step inside, it is so kind of you to come." As if he trusted Annie to simply follow him he began to climb the stairs, lowering his voice. "Do just peep in on her, she may sense your presence, although Dr. has given her something to make her drowsy, he'll call again later but has to attend an infant with rickets."
Annie could hardly blurt out the fact that she'd no knowledge of their troubles and it was the council's plans for Bobbers Mill that brought her there. She felt tense, this was terrible, Annie had sympathy for anyone in distress but the irony of the situation challenged her own composure. The man was clearly distraught but why did he suppose she had come to the house on hearing of Mrs.Plowright's attack, which Annie could only suppose was to the old lady's heart. The door of the bedroom was ajar, a fire burned in the grate giving that smell of heat on the polished black lead and the scent of wood smoke, as every few seconds a wisp escaped the canopy and curled beneath the over mantel, chased by a back draught the open door created.

Smithfield touched Annie's arm. "What do you think, does she look very bad?"

Annie crossed the room to stand by the side of a very large bed that seemed far too large to accommodate the slight frame, lying very still underneath a pink satin counterpane. The face so aged, so lined and looking as pale as the starched white pillowcase to either side. A clock with an unusually loud tick sat on the cabinet, Annie struggled to overcome the urgent desire to silence it, so intrusive of this lady's need for peace did it seem to be. A trinket, very foreign looking, held a pair of spectacles and two mint humbugs. On the wall above the bed head a picture, obviously her late husband, inanimate though it was, the eyes held a curious light that gave Annie a sense of the man's character, upright, fearless, proud.

"I thought her heart was strong as an ox, she's never shown any sign of failure. It was so sudden, she got up this morning, walked to the lavatory in her dressing gown and collapsed, I heard the thump when she fell, no bones broken, Dr. is quite sure of that but her arm and thigh are black and blue."

As if she'd heard her nephew's account of events her eyes opened, slowly, engagingly. Seeing Annie standing over her she smiled.

"Ah, William." Nothing more, she spoke only a bare two words then the eyelids closed once more.

"I think she should rest Andrew, the medication can serve most purpose if your aunt is still." Annie gave him a look that suggested they talk outside the bedroom. He understood, gesturing with the palm of his hand for her to descend the stairs before him. Each tread tormented Annie's thoughts, this was cruel, how could she possibly reveal the actual purpose of her being there, but what about Freddy?

"It often amazes me how quickly news travels but how grateful I am that you heard and came to us. I shall make some tea, aunt Alicia would be appalled if she learned that I had neglected to give you tea in a cup from the Crown Derby set. It's not a desire to put on airs and graces, there's no side to aunt Alicia, no side at all, but everything must be correct," he paused momentarily, "everyone must be correct. Uncle Josh was just the same, being a military man I suppose that's not surprising. I remember as a boy looking at his uniform and marvelling at the smartness of it. A boy's head is filled with images of battle, of destruction and mayhem at the mere mention of a soldier, but there he was, standing in a state of perfect correctness, groomed from head to toe. I do believe their marriage was correct in every way too, the greatest care taken over every detail. Alicia would prepare for his homecomings, always everything in order. When at that last time he didn't come home, she still remained composed. All who called to pay respect were given tea in a cup from the Crown Derby set."

He chatted nervously. Annie wondered what could have happened to his mother, all his childhood memories seemed to be of his aunt Alicia. She felt sorry for him, a successful man in business, employer of a considerable workforce, now struggling to keep strong in the face of an adversity no ledger nor order book could have predicted, no factory floor unrest incited. At that moment he seemed to Annie as vulnerable as young Freddy and she was helpless to influence the fate of either.

Gregory Street was quiet, other than a group of children playing hopscotch and Mr.Solomon walking his greyhound the pavement was empty. The temperature had fallen rapidly as the afternoon drew toward evening and Annie's toes stung with the cold. The bus had felt chill with even fewer passengers to generate warmth and walking from the stop with little distraction to lighten her thoughts had done nothing to help propel the blood to her extremities. All Annie could do was hope and pray for time. Time to bring about Mrs.Plowright's recovery and time to allow a stay of judgement on the matter of Bobbers Mill.

Hilda sat at the kitchen table, a wide grin on her face. Annie draped her coat over the back of a chair, half expecting some revelation, a vital piece of news, which Hilda could scarce wait to impart. She had seen such eagerness in her daughter many times and been thankful for the child's happiness. Annie had not to wait long.

"Guess what, they wanted to tell you on Christmas day at Davina's but Celia was so proud of Mathew and everyone was 'oohing and aahing' so they couldn't bring themselves to steal Mathew's limelight. I thought they'd want to wait until they could tell you themselves but being New Year and knowing how pleased you'd be they said I could spill the beans. Francis and Freddy are going to have a baby, Freddy is going to be a dad, isn't it wonderful, he'll not be so very far behind William after all. I'll put the kettle on and you shall have a tot of brandy in your tea, you look perished." Hilda skipped to the scullery calling back to Annie, "Francis has sent you some kale and a cabbage, Freddy says you must keep up your strength to cope with your growing family. He reckons that by this time next year George and Alice will likely be adding to the number."

Annie sat down by the range, almost too weary to bother rubbing the discomfort from her toes, a churning in her stomach that had troubled her since leaving Brassington was unremitting.

"Not too much brandy Hilda," she said, "all this good news I need to keep a clear head." Had she spoken her thoughts truthfully she would have asked Hilda to simply bring the entire bottle and a large glass. No wonder those men so long without work, oppressed by poverty and despairing of relief, sought refuge, transportation to that other place where cares were dissolved and the mind mercifully numbed by alcohol, where the senses were distilled to a happy vapour. For no reason she could explain Annie suddenly wondered if the boy had returned to chop kindlers for Davina and if Mrs.Pooley's list of instructions had become airborne. Oh Freddy, don't despair, we must never despair.

CHAPTER ELEVEN

"Is she dead, she looks like she's dead?"

"It's alright Mrs.Rashleigh," said Annie, "the lady has fainted, help me to sit her up if you will."

Mrs.Rashleigh put down her shopping bag. "Don't let me forget me bacon, I need a few rashers o' streaky, that's likely 'er trouble, posh folk don't eat sensible stuff, I'd wager she come out the house this mornin' wi' nothin' more inside 'er than one o' them silly little quail eggs. I've seen 'em in Burton's, you try puttin' one o' them in an egg cup, let alone findin' a spoon small enough to dig the daft thing out with."

"Please Mrs.Rashleigh, if we could just help Mrs.Stanford to the chair." At last Annie managed to position the poor woman with her head below her knees.

"I need to fetch a glass of water, could you stay with her for just a moment?"
The intolerant Mrs.Rashleigh huffed agreement and Annie ran through to the back. Convinced that in her state of semi consciousness Florence Stanford couldn't hear, the opinions of Mrs.Rashleigh became aired.

"You should try livin' on the pittance your old man doles out, you'd 'ave an excuse for faintin' then, chew on some o' Cheetham's gristle an' choke arf to death if yer dared to swallow it, like me nephew did last week. Never mind your petit wotsits' off Burton's fancy counter, yer can join the queue at Lovatt's on a Saturday mornin' when he sells the left over bread cheap. It's well worth gettin' drenched or havin' your feet turn to blocks of ice just so's yer can take home enough crust to go wi' the lard the kids 'ave to spread on it when butter's run out, sprinkle a bit o' salt over it an' yer wouldn't tell the difference."

Annie could hear Mrs.Rashleigh's voice and felt relieved as she returned to the shop, supposing words of comfort and encouragement had been offered in her absence. She put the water to Florence Stanford's lips, raising her head slightly.

"You quite alarmed us, thankfully some colour is returning to your cheeks but you must sit very still for a little while."

"She'll be alright now the bloods come back to 'er head. If I could just 'ave me rashers o' streaky I could be on me way. Rent man's due today, I dodged 'im last week, if I don't come up wi' summat this time there'll be a scene. We wer' doin' well enough 'til Bill got laid off but Henry Wicks sent 'im up the road, Bill an' a score of others. I don't know what they think a man can do, live off fresh air I suppose. I've told the grandchildren, it's no good, grandma can't give 'em best back bacon now an' the streaky 'as to go twice as far."

A faint voice uttered, "Please Mrs.Eddowes, give the lady a pound of best back bacon for her kindness, I shall be pleased to pay for it, I wish to show my gratitude."

Mrs.Rashleigh smiled somewhat feebly. "I only kept yer company while Mrs.Eddowes got some water, yer don't need to give me owt."

Florence Stanford raised her face. "For your grandchildren, a small but sincere thank-you."

Annie sensed an awkwardness on the part of Mrs.Rashleigh and took it to be that display of pride, a reluctance to accept charity. In truth, it was a rush of guilt and embarrassment. The look which had passed from Florence Stanford to Mabel Rashleigh, while benign, nevertheless suggested the latter's remarks had been heard, at least partially. Annie could not know their thoughts so simply spoke her own.

"I am to be a grandma again, Freddy and Francis are expecting their first in June, William's son Mathew is pure delight."

The bacon cut and Mrs.Rashleigh finally departed, Annie turned the sign on the door to closed and locked it. "People can wait while we have a cup of tea, ten minutes will make little difference to their day but I think it might make considerable difference to yours Mrs.Stanford. Come through to the back, you need some measure of fortitude before you go on your way."

"May I call you Annie, do call me Florence, after all we are connected by family, William is Edmund's brother in law and of course Caroline is now Edmund's wife. You must forgive my pathetic weakness, I don't know what came over me, I'm not prone to fainting. Perhaps it was the cold, blood becomes thin as we grow older. Mr.Stanford reminds me often I wouldn't last five minutes in his world, he holds such pronounced views."

Annie put a cup of hot sweet tea in Florence Stanford's hands, smiled and said. "I sometimes think that is what enables 'woman', man's overwhelming conviction of his superiority. While they pontificate and proclaim, we actually 'do' and complete our task before their gesturing allows them to even notice."

"I look forward to being a grandmother," said Florence, "our eldest daughter shows no inclination to motherhood, she leads a busy social life, I imagine Basil considers Patricia far more compatible with that world if thrust and gain. She's married to Anthony Bradshaw, Cynthia Woolascroft's younger brother. Our middle daughter Julia lives in Italy, she has a gift for languages and works at the consulate in Rome, a promising career, I can't think she would choose to interrupt that, not for a few years anyway. Caroline has been unfortunate enough to inherit her mother's unremarkable average. I know she hopes for a baby and I believe Edmund is of the same mind. Are William and Freddy alike as brothers?"

"Goodness no," said Annie, "I would be very surprised if William did not propel himself to some position of importance. I can't imagine that anything less would satisfy him. Freddy on the other hand is ambitious to achieve but he measures his accomplishments by an entirely different standard. I had an aunt, she had very set views. I remember well the discussions, the very many debates she and Harold would have. Harold was my first husband, he was killed in a accident when our son George was a year old."

Florence Stanford intervened with a whispered. "Oh dear, how very sad."

Annie continued, "Aunt Bella would ultimately prove through sound logic and reasoning, that for every positive, there is a negative and vice versa. William sees only one way, his own way. I fear any debate he might have had with my aunt Bella would have ended without agreement. Freddy I feel sure would debate until a sensible accord was reached."

Annie's thoughts at that moment were for Bobbers Mill, more than three weeks had passed since Joyce Spooner's visit and as yet there had been no further word. The temptation to confide her worry to Florence Stanford was abruptly halted when the back door opened and a puzzled Charles entered. His expression prompted Annie to explain.

"Mrs.Stanford became quite unwell, to close the shop for a few minutes was the only solution."

Typically unable to cope with female frailty Charles muttered, "I'll go through then," the sound of the door chime followed by animated chatter confirmed he'd been besieged by the group of persistent women, whom when informed of Florence Stanford's collapse by the over imaginative Mrs.Rashleigh, had waited by the closed sign, determined not to miss any sighting of the lady in her predicament.

Florence looked intently at Annie. "I think my dear I must make a positive move and regrettably, leave you with the corresponding negative."

A chuckle escaped Annie's lips. "Go out the back, that way no one will be disappointed at your recovery."

Both women laughed as they crossed the scullery. Florence stood at the door, opened her purse and pressed money into Annie's hand.

"For the bacon, I wouldn't want you to add that to the list for collection by Mr.Madden, perhaps I can 'do' while the gesturing continues, and not be noticed," she hesitated, "I'm glad we are family Annie, I do feel the connection, albeit through my daughter's marriage, sometimes I earnestly believe that blood does not bind as much as we suppose. Friendship, love outside of duty, can create enduring relationships. I wish your aunt Bella were still alive, I would have enjoyed debate on many subjects, especially if she could help me find that positive, it eludes me Annie, it ever eludes me."

Florence Stanford walked to the street from the quietness of the backyard, turning briefly to wave, then was gone. Annie couldn't help but sense that despite Mabel Rashleigh's many tribulations, it was Florence, Basil Stanford's wife, who day on day knew the greater adversity.

"The Jessops order is finished, all bar the tartan knee blankets, we're still waiting for the midnight blue, Robert Armistead tried the royal on a sample but it clashes. If we despatch the stuff now it will come in on this month's statement." William stood alongside Andrew Smithfield's desk, his impatience was underlined by the swift removal of a pencil from behind his ear and his use of it to tap the appropriate spot on the delivery sheet at which Smithfield needed to initial his endorsement.

"Telephone the manager at Jessops, ask him if he would prefer to wait until his order is complete. If he requests delivery of what is ready then send it out. I have an appointment this afternoon, if I can get back before finishing time, I will, otherwise use your keys and leave any memos on my desk."

Once outside the door William's frustration was vented by waving the sheet of paper in the air like a flag of defiance

"He's losing the plot, God knows she's had a bloody good innings, why can't he pull himself together." William's words were wasted on all but himself, the relentless noise of the machines and various measures of winter coughing, travelled the air in a discordant jumble of sound.

Alicia Plowright clung to a slender thread of life. Nursed privately at home she barely opened her eyes. For the first few days following her heart attack Smithfield dared to hope that his aunt's indomitable strength of mind would overrule her heart's weariness and that she would one morning, raise her head from the pillow, request a generous bowl of porridge and dismiss the 'angel of mercy', hovering at her bedside in anticipation of performing a professional 'laying out'. It was not to be and

171

as each day passed Andrew Smithfield struggled to accept the inevitable. At 3-45 he was to attend a meeting at the bank. Even selling the workshop had not answered sufficiently the question of finance. Brassington was currently running heavy on workforce but light on orders. Customers delayed payment in an attempt to alleviate their own crises of funds, as what started as a ripple of recession, gathered momentum, rolling across industry, seeking solid ground on which to lose pace. Smithfield knew already just what Birkett would say to him. For the third month in a row he'd exceeded his overdraft, pumping in the proceeds of the Winchester Street sale had given the figures a healthier look for a short while but it was the wage bill that left the rest undernourished. Yet to lay off, however few, meant loyal workers would know very real hunger. Some evenings he would sit at Alicia's bedside and voice his worries. Normally he and his aunt would discuss the day's events, enjoying the exchange, Andrew purposefully omitting any reference to financial concerns. Despite Alicia's strengths his fondness for her prevented him burdening her with troubles, yet now his conscience struggled with the fact that his anxiety drove his tongue to use her as a listening ear, aware that she heard none of it, no response, not even a flicker passed to him from his trusted adviser of years.

The previous evening he'd sought the company of Henry Wicks, it had not been his intention to speak of business, merely to pass time with someone he thought of as a friend. Andrew had hoped Annie Eddowes might call again but she had not. He imagined William delivered brief accounts of the situation and Annie was after all, forever occupied with the shop and tending her own family. Conversation that previous evening had been relaxed, neither man doubting the integrity of the other their exchange had developed quite naturally, both baring truths that would have remained covered in less trusted company. It was Henry Wicks' openness that inspired Andrew and somehow rendered the prospect of a session with Gerald Birkett far less intimidating.

It transpired that Henry's father had worked as a foreman at Colver pit, owned by Claude Stanford. One day James Wicks took a bad decision and thirteen men died below ground. There was an inquiry, such as it was in those days, Henry's father was blamed but Claude Stanford stood by him, dreadful though the whole affair was, James Wicks survived the troubles only to die two years later of pneumonia. Henry's mother eventually remarried, her cousin, they had a son, George, Henry's half brother but it was the rest of the story Andrew remembered literally word for word as Henry explained.

'Claude Stanford was a good man, he genuinely cared, however he had one failing, if indeed it is fair to call it a failing. He passed on all his knowledge, good or bad to his son Basil, believing it could only help him in dealing with those many challenges when due to Claude's failing health, he took over the reins at Birchdale, the mine his father had acquired some years previous. Claude Stanford used knowledge as a tool enabling him to create and produce, Basil Stanford uses knowledge as a weapon, enabling him to gain authority and might. All these years I've worked for the Stanford's, even after Claude's death I felt compelled by a curious loyalty. When my half brother George was killed at the pit I went to see Margaret and the children, I wanted to walk away from it all, but Leonora had great powers of persuasion, she feared for the welfare of the men and their families, plus I knew if I quit Basil would waste no time in furnishing Leonora with all the details of her late father-in –law's disastrous judgment that resulted in the death of so many men. I didn't want her to be told, partly because I believed it would prey on her mind and because I felt ashamed of the past. Believe me Andrew, since losing Leonora, so many times I have been tempted to turn my back on the pit, to leave Basil Stanford to his devious doings, but with her gone, all I have is those men, those weary, disheartened men who look to me for hope'.

Andrew looked at the clock, he could put it off no longer, gathering his top coat from the hook, he paused for a moment at the office door, then directed his reluctant steps to the yard, got into his car and made his way to Braithwaites.

"Take a seat Smithfield."

Gerald Birkett gave his usual smile which reminded Andrew of his dentist, that first element of protocol, humility before the infliction of pain. A youth with whom he'd attended class at school once described to Andrew his experience when for whatever reason it had been deemed necessary for him to be circumcised. The unfortunate boy had spoken to Andrew in graphic detail of the event and it was the smile, that odious smile of deception given him by the surgeon, which most haunted the lad's memory. The fact that on coming round from the anaesthetic his realisation was of a sickening, swollen nob that glowed like an illuminated strawberry and throbbed like the mother of all boils, paled alongside the ingrained image, forever stamped on his brain of that satanic smile!

"I would suggest you take immediate measures to reverse this trend to your account. At such a time even we at the bank, especially the bank, cannot ignore the alarming factors dominating all areas of business and trade. Shed some fat, you at least still have some to shed. There are those who now operate with the bare bones of a workforce but in doing so they survive and whilst it is regrettable and undesirable that so many be laid off, it is the only way. Sacrifice some to save the rest, if you do not then inevitably not one will survive and whom do you suppose they will blame, not government, not the banks, not God but you, they will wave their fists and shout damnation at you Smithfield."

Gerald Birkett's rotund middle tried to escape the bounds of his waistcoat, visibly pressuring the buttons to give way as he leaned back in his comfortable leather chair to await his client's response.

Smithfield was sickened by this image of self importance, the carefully crafted immunity against those common ills carried by mortals for whom Birkett held no compassion. Padded against the slightest knock just as the upholstered hide over which he positioned his considerable bulk.

"The account will return to the black before next month," said Andrew, speaking slowly and deliberately. "I assure you that matters are in hand, I shall do what is necessary." He paused before surprising Birkett with a question taken entirely out of context. "If the ring road were to be finished tomorrow and someone loaned you a vehicle, its tank full of fuel saying, 'drive yourself around the entire city until your journey is complete, would you travel from the north, the south, the east, or the west, bearing in mind that wherever you begin you will ultimately end?"

The veiled intimation that all men, regardless of fortune and situation entered this life with nothing and left with nothing was far too profound for the shallow Birkett. In his bewilderment he avoided a definitive answer responding with.

"How we all wish it could be completed tomorrow, what a blessing that would bestow upon the city."

Smithfield rose to his feet and without waiting for the pompous dismissal he spoke sharply.

"Next statement Birkett, by next statement."

He had time to return to the factory before going home, if Jessops wanted delivery of the order minus the knee blankets then he'd sign the despatch sheet.

William caught sight of him entering the office, Smithfield had hardly chance to unfasten his coat before he was enlightened as to events in his absence.

"The midnight blue got here soon after you left, Armistead has everything set up for tomorrow. Jessops want what's ready, I told them first thing in the morning, the delivery sheet is on your desk. Bessie Draper collapsed at her machine same time as the dyes arrived, damn nuisance, anyway she looked grim, Edna said to call the ambulance. They took her to the General Hospital so it's likely woman's trouble. No need to worry though, a machine down will make no difference, probably a blessing in disguise." William pointed to the spot requiring Smithfield's signature on the delivery sheet, his boss took a pen from the old tea caddy that had, at some point in the past, become separated from its lid. The makeshift holder of pens and pencils ever irritated William, it lacked style, surely finances could run to a decent desk set.

Smithfield handed the paper to William saying, "Finish them no later than five and lock up." He turned the key in the drawer of his desk, did likewise at the filing cabinet and walked swiftly past William, wondering how this young man managed to maintain that clinical indifference towards those people with whom he worked every day.

As he drove back to town and to the hospital, a cramp in his left leg tormented his mood. Pain, always some pain or other, be it of body or mind, perhaps that was why his father all those years ago, obliterated it with his excessive indulgence in women and drink.

The receptionist at the desk directed him to ward 9.

"Ask to speak with sister, she'll advise you."

His tread on the hard, polished floor of the corridor began to ease the troublesome cramp but the smell of disinfectant, mingled as it ever seemed to be inside a hospital with people's anxiety and distress, made him long for home and the familiar scent of lavender water, which knowing of his aunt Alicia's great belief in lavender's soothing properties, he'd instructed the nurse to sprinkle over the edge of the pillowcase each evening.

"I'm here to enquire after Bessie Draper, nee Clarke whom I understand was admitted earlier this afternoon."

"Are you a relative?" Asked sister.

"No, I'm her employer, but I was not present when the ambulance came to the factory, Mrs.Draper has worked many years at Brassington, I feel a measure of responsibility for her," he explained nervously, sensing Bessie's condition was serious.

"Her husband is with her, would you like me to tell him that you are here, he may well be glad of some support, Mrs.Draper is very poorly."

Andrew nodded, he felt he was intruding yet to leave and not at least offer what help he could would be too feeble. Bessie had worked ten years for him with little time off other than to give birth to her children.

Sister soon returned with Bessie's husband, she ushered them both into her office and left them alone saying simply, "You will have more privacy in here."

Arnold Draper sniffed and took a deep breath. "I wer' at home when they sent word. I got laid off beginnin' o' December, Christmas don't mean much in business does it, not unless yer sell bloody mistletoe an' soddin' crackers. Our street wer' full o' 'poor men out gatherin' winter fuel' but there wer' no bugger askin' 'yonder peasant who is he'. I've tried Mr.Smithfield, God knows I've tried but there's nothin' out there. Bessie's been lookin' peaky, I've asked 'er more than once if she wer' alright. 'Yes', she'd say, 'how can you expect me to look radiant in winter, I allus look blue in winter, most of us women do'." He sniffed again, "Blue, bloody blue, no wonder. Doctor saw a discharge when they brought her in, smelled it. They're getting' ready to operate on 'er, she never said owt to me Mr.Smithfield, I didn't know." Arnold's voice trembled. "They reckon a baby's died inside 'er, doctor called it summat else but sister explained it to me, 'feet' somethin' or other? It's mortifyin', rottin' inside my Bessie, she's alive, but the baby's dead, dead inside 'er Mr.Smithfield."

Andrew held his arm, not until Arnold's tears ceased did he speak. "Bessie is strong and she's a mother, in my experience through the women at the factory, motherhood drives a woman's spirit like nothing else, I don't believe we men could ever come close to holding that strength with which their children empower them. You know where to find me and I shall find you. Go back to her bedside before they come to take her to the operating room."

"Ta' for comin'." Arnold gave a brave smile but cut a forlorn figure as he turned to walk away.

Andrew felt ashamed of his own pathetic concerns, cramp, what was that but a temporary spasm of pain, a minor discomfort designed to remind him that blood flowed round his body still and he should be thankful he was alive. What of Gerald Birkett's mindless demands, preened, pampered and sheltered inside his warm cocoon of an office. What influence had he ever brought to the reality of the streets where life happened. He took a deep breath but feeling his lungs wither from the intake of disinfectant and dismay he sought the air outside, there at least the mix was changed regularly, from good and bad, cheerful and sad, to sane and mad, it rhymed, he smiled to himself amused by the notion. The smile hid his need of home, Andrew Smithfield so needed to go home.

When he finally pulled up outside the house his legs seemed unwilling to bear him along the path. He'd reached the bottom step when the door opened and the nurse, looking vexed, gabbled words so urgently he was obliged to ask, "Slowly, please more slowly."

"I thought you would be here by six, you are usually here by six. She slipped away, just after five, no sound, nothing changed except her breathing, I could tell it became shallow, until it stopped altogether."

"Have you called the doctor?"

"No, I thought it best to wait for you, so close to the time you would be home it seemed proper to wait for you, but I've done the necessary."

Andrew entered the room, it held no dread, in fact the peace washed over him like the comfort of a caring hand smoothing a fretful brow. He could remember that feeling from childhood, his mother reassuring him when he'd lain in bed suffering from chicken pox.

Alicia looked serene, her expression set as it was, presented not the slightest hint of anxiety, entirely calm. He held her hand, touching the ring, the simple gold band on her wedding finger and swallowed the lump in his throat as his eyes looked up at the picture above the bed head, "Uncle Josh." Andrew spoke to him, quietly seeking from that courageous face which looked back at him with such depths of experience, some small sign that all would be well. "You were a leader of men, I don't imagine it was so very different for you, commanding the fortunes of many, realising the survival of a few." Then one word escaped Andrew's lips, quite without pre-meditation or reason, "Annie." A tremendous sense of loneliness overcame him at that moment, and going round and round in his head were the words spoken by the nurse, so significant following his appointment at Braithwaites and now even more potent trapped as they'd become within his mind, 'I've done the necessary, I've done the necessary'.

"Leave that alone, it's dirty." Rosie ran across the path to where her two little boys were intent on pulling loose the threads from an abandoned glove, which had been placed over the end of a protruding branch of laurel in the hope that its owner might return to find it. The glove itself seemed reasonably harmless, now too weathered to be of any purpose, the faded blue yarn, unravelling by degrees, achieved to entertain the boys for several minutes whilst Rosie and Celia chatted. It was not until the laurel branches parted under the ever increasing efforts of Thomas and Samuel, that an old bird's nest fell to the ground at their feet and Samuel being slightly bigger than his brother, pushed Thomas aside to grab the fossilized remains of a young blackbird and to immediately lift it to his nose to smell it. Rosie shook the tangle of beak and bone from his fingers and cautioned Thomas to stand by Celia while she kicked the debris under the bushes. She took her hanky from her pocket, licked one corner and rubbed it across the grubby palms of Samuel's hands.

"It's his dad's fault, Tommy takes 'em off on a Sunday afternoon an' they eventually come home lookin' like urchins. He can't be content just walkin' 'em along the pavements, oh no, they 'ave to go all the way round The Meadows turnin' over every stone to look for beetles, pokin' at the rabbit holes in the hedge to try an' make 'em run out, then they pick up dead branches an' fir cones to bring back for the fire, I used to bath 'em on a Saturday but now I leave it 'til Sunday night, I've told Tommy that even the fluff in their belly buttons is black, anybody 'ould think I sent 'em up chimney like folk used to years ago."

Celia chuckled and checked that Mathew's eyes were still tight shut. "I sometimes think that William would prefer his son's first word to be sir rather than daddy. He's more likely to take Mathew to his Lodge than to The Meadows."

"They don't let kiddies inside there do they?" Said a confused Rosie.

"I'm only joking but if they did put babies' names down for future membership, like the cradle roll at Sunday school, then William would have enrolled Mathew before the midwife cut the cord."

"Look, there's Susie, it's arf day closin' today, she'll be goin' to 'er mam's. Poor Mrs.Dodds, by the time she gets 'ome from Brassington it's nearly time for Susie's dad to leave for his work at the exchange, so Susie goes to Winchester Street most Tuesday afternoons to do a bit to 'elp out. Cooee," Rosie called and waved to her sister-in-law approaching from another pathway. Recognising their aunty the twins made off to meet her. Celia smiled at the scene as she gently pushed the pram to' and fro'. Susie, with a boy at either side holding a hand, reached the bench where Rosie sat with Celia, she peeped under the hood of the pram and could just about make out the knitted bonnet over the babies head, beyond the curl of woollen blanket and the weather proof cover fixed by poppers to the sides of the pram.

"He must be snug as a bug in there, are you sure he isn't hidin' a felon beneath all those covers," said Susie with a chuckle. "The police are in the city centre, somebody broke into Jessops last night, through a skylight at the back. The manager didn't notice anything untoward until he went into the stock room, apparently nothin' in the shop had been disturbed or stock taken from out the back, but there's a lavatory an' wash up for the staff just off the stock room an' when he went in there it was a scene of demolition. The pipes had been wrenched off the wall, the big brass tap was missin' from the sink an' the tank was in the middle o' the floor minus its brass fittin' for the ball cock. The police told the manager they'd be lookin' for somebody with the climbin' habits of a tom cat who almost certainly had an accomplice, but to his credit the burglar had shown a sense of responsibility in turnin' off the stop cock at the mains to prevent the place floodin'. Sergeant Beasley said whoever did it must be as lean as a weasel to squeeze through such narrow places. It made me think of a lad at school who reckoned he could get between the last railin' an' the gate post outside Players if he sucked a piece o' treacle toffee then put a dollop o' spittle behind each ear an' went through backwards. Sergeant Beasley said the burglar wer' after the metal, lead an' copper, an' the brass, well he said that would have been a bonus. He sent the constables into all the shops off slab square to ask if anybody else had found anythin' unusual, they even went into Moffat's secondhand shop. Pat wer' just sortin' out a box o' kitchen stuff Mr.Moffat bought off some posh folk movin' away from The Ropewalk. It seems Pat held up this strange gadget that looked like a sky rocket an' said, 'unusual yer say, well I don't know what yer make o' this, I've never seen owt like it in me mam's scullery'." Susie burst into laughter, "Turns out it wer' a vibrator, or as the well informed constable put it, 'an aid to climactic intercourse'.

180

Poor Pat wer' none the wiser so she marked it at 1/6d an' displayed it on a shelf alongside a telescope."

The laughter that erupted from all three young women disturbed the dozing Mathew and not even a swifter to' and fro' of the pram achieved to silence his protest.

"Mam used to push our Myra like that to keep her quiet but sometimes she just had to get on with a job that needed both hands, so one day she told Victor to push the pram, gently on the spot, while she went upstairs to change the beds. When she came back down Myra was wide awake suckin' her dummy an' Victor wer' fast asleep standin' up. She wer' afraid to give him a nudge in case he fell over. He stood there like that for ten minutes or more afore he opened his eyes, looked at Myra, then started to push the pram to' an' fro' at a rate o' knots an' Myra began to howl her head off!

Kathleen came into the shop this mornin' to get shoes for Beth, no sooner had they left than Elsie Sulley came in. I suppose it was because one followed t'other so quick that I noticed. I'd put Beth's little foot on the stool an' it looked really dainty then poor Mrs.Sulley stuck hers on there an' it wer' nearly off the end. I managed to fit her with a pair but she didn't have much to choose from. I asked after Lillian an' Norma but she come over all vague an' said 'I don't know, I just don't know'. That Jack's a rum 'en, Joe wer' comin' home from a death, late the other night, after one o'clock. Who should be shufflin' along the pavement but Jack Sulley an' he wer' still a good twenty minutes away from Winchester Street. Mam reckons he's nocturnal, like a bat, flits around givin' everybody the creeps then disappears to nobody knows where 'til it's time to come out again to search the dark for even smaller creepies to feed on.

Jim Sulley's leavin' his work at Barrow to come back here. Elsie didn't want to tell him but she's been havin' blackouts an' the last one frightened her. She came round in a chair by the hearth an' a spark had jumped out o' the fire onto the edge o' the rug, it wer' just beginin' to singe it. After all that dreadful business with her father no wonder the poor woman wer' frightened. Goodness knows where Jim'll find work, she said that in all the years they've been married he's never been

181

unemployed so I suppose if anyone can find a job he can, I hope so for Lillian's sake. I'm sure Elsie must help her with a bit of housekeepin' money. Left to Jack they'd have starved to death by now."

The twins began to fidget and Mathew's crying persisted with only brief intervals when Celia smoothed his cheek with her finger, so they all walked together to the arboretum gates where Susie turned to go along Sherwood Road towards Winchester Street and the others went in the opposite direction.

When the two women and the children approached the bus stop a No.48 was pulling away.

"Isn't that Susie's mam who's just got off?" Said Rosie.

Edna seemed harassed when she reached them, not her usual 'ah well' self. Rosie felt concerned.

"Susie's on 'er way to your place, we only left her a few minutes ago."

"I want to nip home first," said Edna, " I need to tell Billy what's happened, 'e knows Bessie wer' took bad yesterday, I told 'im that afore 'e went to work last night but now there's summat else. Mr.Smithfield's aunt Alicia died, late yesterday afternoon, while 'e wer' at the hospital wi' Arnold an' Bessie. Nobody could expect the man to go to The General again today, not wi' all the business 'e's got to sort out at home so 'e's asked me to go. I'm hopin' I won't be there long but you know what hospitals can be like, when our Ada 'ad her tendon cut to straighten her hammer toe she wer' there for hours. Mam had the kids all day, nearly finished her off. Your Tommy'll not 'ave owt to do wi' funeral, 'e's not usin' Handley's. Williamson's is the nearest undertaker to Brassington, they did Billy's cousin Wilf, only nineteen, kidney failure. Aunt Jessie near collapsed from stress that day, pit siren sounded just as they pulled up outside o' cemetery, spooked the horse an' when the bearers slid the coffin out back o' the hearse the daft animal decided to rear up. Billy said if Jeremiah Williamson hadn't managed to grab end o' coffin' Wilf 'ould 'ave been standin' on 'is head in that box. That wer' the weird thing, when 'e felt like it, Wilf used to do 'is party trick, as aunt Jessie called it. 'E'd do a handstand against the sittin' room wall, in the gap between his mam's china cabinet an' the pianola an' there 'e'd stay, on his head, while aunt Jessie put a mark on the wall to see how much 'e'd grown." Edna hurried off, calling back to them, "E wer' nearly six foot tall when 'e died, last mark his mam made wer' only just below the picture rail."

Not knowing quite what to say following such a revelation, Rosie and Celia continued their walk home in comparative silence. Rosie quietly pondering what to have for tea and Celia wondering in what sort of mood William might be given the sad news of Mrs.Plowright's death.

Celia was in the bedroom feeding Mathew when she heard the sound of the back door latch and footsteps on the scullery floor. She called out, "Is that you William?"

"Who else are you expecting at this time of day?" William's response was an indication of his frustration. The day had begun with confusion when the delivery man had arrived at Jessops the very time the police were asking their questions. It caused a delay and almost an hour of idle time for the unfortunate driver who suffered William's caustic tongue when he finally arrived back at Brassington.

The events of the previous evening could do no other than dominate Andrew Smithfield's thoughts and movements. He'd been out of the office for most of the day and less than attentive when William had tried to pin him down to ask which day Smithfield was expecting him to go to Leicester. A new department store had recently opened there and optimistically the local authority had seen fit to extend Leicester's outdoor market. The factory already supplied a small retail outlet at Loughborough and another of similar size on the edge of Leicester but a large store in the centre of town presented a greater opportunity.

William had enjoyed the few runs he'd made through the countryside between Nottingham and Leicester, the glimpse of aristocracy, as he perceived it, when he travelled by the Duke of Rutland's estate fired his imagination, even the trees seemed to grow more erect and stately, the grass always appeared greener than that at the arboretum and the brief glimpse of distant architecture allowed him just enough vision of elegance on which to work his over active mind, forever in pursuit of more.

There had been an occasion the previous year when circumstances had led to William staying in a boarding house on the Friday night, the fuel pump on the van had suddenly expired in the midst of traffic, a local garage had come to his rescue but a replacement part could not be fitted until the following morning. The job duly completed, William found himself travelling back to Nottingham on a Saturday. Unaware of the traditional activities of The Quorn Hunt, he became intrigued by the numerous groups of people, mostly men, peering over hedgerows and through gateways with expensive binoculars, scanning the open fields, obviously intent on something of considerable interest. Unable to contain his curiosity, he'd pulled into a lay-by, got out of the van and joined a small group of men he'd passed just a few yards back. William, with little effort, could adapt his manner to suit the nature of his company, within the space of five minutes he'd recognised this new elite, of which prior to, William had no knowledge. He'd readily embraced their enthusiasm, offering his own sense of anticipation, a chase, fast and furious across terrain only the most accomplished riders might attempt. His contrived conversation enabled him to shake the hands of landowners and estate managers, to note their well cut attire, their cultured voices, not even Basil Stanford spoke with such resonance, the sound rang in William's ears as he continued his journey back to Nottingham, it intensified his determination to abandon Glover Street, it held not the slightest matter for his imagination, unlike those taunting glimpses of gracious living which drew his eye as he drove through Rutland. Glover Street could neither be altered nor improved. It was as dreary as the hapless mortals who dwelt there, William wanted rid of Glover Street, it was no more desirable than the mangy fox those elegant riders ran to ground. Class, style, to be somebody, that was William's chase, his impatience bayed as loudly as the hounds.

Smithfield needed to concentrate on the business, at least now the old aunt was dead his attention might return to the factory, surely now he wouldn't be so sorely distracted. Since the New Year his mind had been far removed from the predictions of recession discussed by every other businessman, be it casually in the street or at formally arranged meetings. William had overheard conversation between two foremen from Briggs. The one said 'don't the bloody pundits realise we've been shrinkin' here for the past twelve years, recession they call it, they plunged a knife into us when war finished an' now the buggers are twistin' it, that's not recession, it's bloody murder'.

Celia appeared at the foot of the stairs. "He's gone off, he'll sleep for a while now he's fed. Our meal won't be long, it's in the oven, I've made beef pie," Celia declared with a degree of satisfaction. "I was walking with Rosie when we bumped into Mrs.Dodds. I am sorry to hear about Mrs.Plowright, Mr.Smithfield must be upset, I've heard he was very fond of her."

"She was nearly ninety for goodness sake, did he think she'd live forever, she had a bloody good innings is all I can say." William flopped down in a chair as if he had the weight of the world upon his shoulders.

Celia stood by the table folding a basket of ironing before laying out their knives and forks. "It doesn't really make any difference, if you're fond of someone William then at whatever age, their death, the knowledge that they are no longer there causes immense grief," said Celia, now turning her attention to the oven and her proud effort which filled the room with a delicious smell of baked pastry when she opened the range door.

"His aunt had a lifetime, my mother didn't, she had barely any life compared to Alicia Plowright, how can that be fair?" William's mood was volatile and Celia in her young innocence, quite unintentionally made matters worse.

"We can't measure such things William, poor little Danny was on this earth for only four seasons, one winter, the spring, one summer and an autumn, how can that be fair, your mother at least had more than that and I feel sure that after all this time she would be happy for you to think of Annie as your mother, they were friends, either would have wanted their children in such a sad situation to be loved by the other. That fate brought your dad and Annie together convinces me more."

William's eyes flared, he stood, crossed the floor like a man possessed, grabbed his coat from the hook and turned to look back at his wife with contempt.

"Keep your miserable pie, I'm not hungry, it would choke me." He slammed the door that hard it bounced off the latch, drifting open behind him, letting in a blast of air so chill it sent shivers through Celia's entire being. She waited, anticipating a cry from Mathew but surprisingly he didn't disturb. Celia closed the door as tears rolled down her face. She'd made the pie herself, her pastry had much improved since Annie had shown her the difference in sweet and savoury pastry. William favoured a pie over casserole, she tried hard to please him but his lack of gratitude for any effort by herself or his tireless stepmother reduced her to tears often. She should feel anger, resentment at his behaviour yet even now, after his cruel outburst, she worried over his whereabouts, the fact that he would miss his meal and tormented herself with the thought that she'd been uncaring of her husband's memory of his natural mother. Yet his memories were imagined, for William had been far too young to have actual recollection.

Freddy, through the course of conversation had one day said to Celia, 'William believes himself to be ahead of his time, forward thinking, progressive but in truth he wallows in the past, he can't shed the weight of it and clamber out, all his judgements are made there'.

At the time Celia had dismissed the remark as merely that harmless rivalry that occurred between brothers, now she knew its truth.

Sat in a dim corner of The Standard all evening, William had supped his third pint of bitter, soaked up with nothing more than a bag of pork scratchings. Far from under the influence, his better sense told him to seek food. A visit to his brother-in-law's would almost certainly result in the offer of a bite to eat, supper of cheese and biscuits, as was Caroline's habit to prepare for Edmund before bed. It was entirely proper to call on his in laws, to enquire after their good health, now they had Mathew Celia was tied to home in the evenings, they would consider it only natural for William to be alone at this hour.

"William, come in," said Caroline, unable to disguise the surprise in her voice.

"I hope I'm not disturbing your peace but I had to go out this evening and finding myself close by I thought it would be remiss of me not to call for just a few minutes. I always enjoy to chat with Edmund and I know Celia has missed those times she would pop round to see you Caroline, having a baby seems to install an entirely changed routine."

Even William inwardly reproached himself for using such a degree of false cordiality merely to win a bite of simple supper but his stomach rumbled from emptiness and he would not give Celia the satisfaction of permitting hunger to drive him home to feed on her smug offering of a homemade pie. Caroline led him into the sitting room where Edmund sat with a book, he immediately rose to his feet and crossed the room to shake William's hand.

"Good to see you, all is well I trust. Celia was at mothers when I happened to call there a day or two ago, both she and Mathew looked very well I thought. Sit down William, warm yourself," Edmund stirred the coals in the grate, "there, that's better, I wouldn't be surprised at snow by the weekend. One of my clients claims to be accurate nine times out of ten when predicting the weather. He was in the office today warning me to wear shoes with cleats for the next few days so as not to be caught out when the pavements suddenly become treacherous!" Edmund laughed. "That same individual has changed his will three times in the past eighteen months, he obviously finds it much easier to predict the weather than to foresee the elements likely to prevail his demise." He turned to Caroline, "Shall we have a hot toddy my love and perhaps a piece of Stilton with some of that fine fruit cake your mother made."

William's thoughts, now soothed by the warmth, meandered from food to bequests, the mention of a will taking them to Brassington and the affairs of Smithfield's aunt. He would surely inherit whatever she had.

Edmund interrupted his ponderings, "How are things at the factory? I heard this morning that Jessops had been burgled, broke in through a skylight apparently. I dare say such events will become more frequent as the economy squeezes harder."

Now William was more alert. "Yes, our delivery man was there when the police were making enquiries. Not a single item of stock taken despite hundreds of pounds worth just sitting there. Lead and copper pipes and a bit of brass, what's wrong with folk in this city Edmund, not even our thieves aim high."

"That's a very controversial outlook William, whatever brings that on?" Edmund was quite genuinely shocked.

"I sometimes think industry has lost its way, apart from your father-in-law who certainly has his sights on the prize, others seem to be languishing in self pity and it weakens them."

At that moment Caroline entered with a tray.

"I was just saying to Edmund how I admire Mr.Stanford's ability to concentrate solely on propelling the collieries forward, not to allow himself the indulgence of regret and complaint. He focuses on the future, a great mind."

William smiled across at her as she laid the tray on the table. "Indeed father never lets anything stand in the way of his intent, sentimentality is an anathema to him, if they were to bring back death by stoning he would applaud the move, a suitably drawn out punishment! Yes, he does have the ability to concentrate his mind, but how curious it is that I have never before thought of it as ability, more a custom of father's, always to be upheld. Do try the Stilton William, Edmund says it has a real kick to it."

Edmund gave his wife a quizzical look, he detected considerable agitation in her manner yet he could think of no reason for it, William was always welcome, his visit this night might have been unexpected but it created no problem that he could conceive of. If William had sensed anything untoward, then he didn't show it, so Edmund moved conversation swiftly along. "Smithfield surely continues to propel the business forward at Brassington, he retains a large workforce by all accounts."

"You've not heard of his aunt's death then. She's been ill, literally at death's door since the beginning of the month when she had a heart attack. Smithfield I'm afraid allows himself to be distracted by events at home, he's not been concentrating as he should and these are demanding times."

William, not wanting to appear hungry, had waited a polite minute or two before ploughing his teeth into a slice of moist, spicy fruitcake, which made a perfect accompaniment to the crumbly saltiness of the Stilton cheese.

"I'm sorry to hear that, I understand she was a woman of great spirit. I can understand why Smithfield would miss her encouragement," said Edmund.

He probably knows exactly what she's left him thought William, presuming that from the numerous solicitors to be found in Nottingham, Smithfield's aunt had chosen none other than the firm for which Edmund Tozer worked, Chaucer, Caffin and Holt. However he voiced his appreciation of the supper, "A splendid cake, compliments to Mrs.Stanford," William had perfected the craft of speaking whilst simultaneously deliberating on a subject completely removed from the present.

Caroline was unusually quiet but William, already partially numbed from his intake at The Standard and now in receipt of a comforting hot toddy of whisky, lemon and cloves, failed to notice her detachment.

"Come for dinner on Sunday," he said, in a sudden rush of hospitality, Celia shall make one of her pies."

"Pies," said Edmund, "wherever did Celia learn to make a pie, certainly not from mother. I think dear mother would find it beyond her to put a lid on anything, how would she see what was going on underneath and goodness knows, mother needs to see what is going on underneath, bless her." He laughed. "We shall be delighted to come for dinner on Sunday, won't we dear. I dare say Caroline will find something for our young nephew, if indeed there isn't already a package upstairs destined for Glover Street."

Caroline carefully picked up a crumb from the tray and put it on a plate.

"Did you know William that Rex Madden, father's 'man' lives on Glover Street," she said, "he can't be too far away from you, perhaps you should introduce yourself. He's worked for father since he was a young man, he's middle aged now and bears the scars, you're sure to recognise him. At what time should we come on Sunday?" Caroline looked intently at William. His mood of earlier in the evening had by now withered to a weary compliance.

"At one," he replied in a subdued tone, "come at one."

Celia felt a mix of relief and apprehension when at last she heard the door latch rattle downstairs. Her feet were cold, with no William to help warm them she had put on a pair of his socks. It was after 11 o'clock, tired but too anxious to sleep, the past hour had seemed endless. The beef pie sat on the slab untouched, she'd eaten only a small dish of semolina. After a few minutes she heard his tread on the stairs, she could tell from his attempt at quietness that William was not the worse for drink, aware that their son would be asleep he made his footsteps light. He neglected his routine at the washstand climbing into bed beside her without first suffering an assault from the jug of cold water. Despite the stinging chill of her toes Celia resisted contact. She felt hurt and angry but she could not ignore Charles' visit, she was obliged to tell William of that.

"Where have you been, your dad came to see you. I couldn't tell him where you were because I didn't know. He said he'd try The Standard."

"What time was that?" Asked the shivering William, still trying to find a measure of comfort beneath the cold covers on his side of the bed.

"It must have been after nine, Mathew had been settled for a good while."

"I had a drink in The Standard but I'd left there by nine. I went to see Edmund and Caroline, what did he want anyway?"

Celia sighed. "Freddy and Francis have been to talk with your mam and dad. They've had a visit from a council official. Bobbers Mill is on the definitive plan of development. The council need to buy it but Freddy has no wish to sell. All his plans are for the farm, he's already invested a good deal of money and of course their baby is due in June. They are naturally very worried and upset. Your dad wanted to ask if Andrew Smithfield had said anything to you about it."

"No, why would he, I doubt if he even knows Freddy farms Bobbers Mill, I'm sure I've never told him. Freddy just cannot accept progress, he resists change. While forward thinking men grasp more opportunity for industry and housing, Freddy clings to his belief in 'the land' as though from a steaming heap of dung, suddenly will rise up mankind's salvation. A man needs to be ahead of the game, a heap of shit will always be just a heap of shit."

Celia was too tired to argue and Mathew deserved a peaceful household if he was to thrive.

"Do you know someone called Madden on the street?" Said William, he'd at last found sufficient warmth and turned on his side, taking much of the bedcovers with him.

"Doris Madden, she's a very quiet woman, lives about twelve doors down. I believe there is a Mr.Madden but I've not seen him, why do you ask?"

"Not important, it was only something Caroline was talking about. I've asked her and Edmund to come for dinner on Sunday. I think she has something for Mathew. Make another pie, I told Edmund you make a good pie these days, practice makes perfect."

If Celia's toes were to sting all night then so be it, but a distance she would keep between herself and her 'forward thinking' husband. She pulled determinedly at the blankets, turning away from the fast developing sound of his snoring and from her own growing dismay.

Annie ran the clothes brush over the shoulders of Charles' jacket and hung it with his trousers and waistcoat over the top of the kitchen door. The bedroom was cold, a couple of hours in warmer air would render his seldom used best suit more desirable. Charles came through from the shop.

"Mrs.Collett is asking about allspice for some recipe she's found, you best see to her, I don't know what she's going on about. I have to go out for an hour anyway, don't worry, I shall be back in plenty of time to attend the funeral, I won't abscond."

Annie sighed, it was wise to say nothing, Mrs.Collett's allspice seemed the better option.

It had taken Annie most of the previous evening to persuade Charles that he really should be the one to attend Alicia Plowright's funeral service, not Annie herself. His predictable attempt at avoiding any involvement could not be conceded to for William's sake. Annie of necessity, had pointed out that William had been in need of regular, challenging employment when he'd reached eighteen with no established purpose. Reg Yeats at Player's had done his best, Jessie Tozer had been more than accommodating of William's need to be usefully engaged but it was Andrew Smithfield who'd offered him work with opportunity and over the past ten years had advanced William's knowledge and awarded him a greater responsibility. All that aside, when Charles, for whatever reason, had decided to give up the lease at Basford and sell the machines, Smithfield had purchased them and later when the workshop on Winchester Street became available it was Smithfield, who in good faith, bought the entire and to Annie's great relief, had kept on Edna and the other girls.

Charles had countered with a reference to Freddy's troubles over Bobbers Mill but his argument was without foundation. William had told them that it was highly unlikely Smithfield had the slightest notion Freddy farmed the acres at Bobbers Mill. William, by his own declaration had not, as he could recall, ever conversed with Smithfield on the subject of his brother's activities 'on the land', the reference William invariably gave to Bobbers Mill, dismissing it in his mind as being unworthy of further title.

Charles had less than graciously agreed to attend the small Methodist Chapel at Brassington where Andrew Smithfield's aunt Alicia had specified in her notes, that she wished her soul to be received, before interment at the cemetery. Her late husband's remains lay somewhere in South Africa, the conflict of the Boar Wars was possibly one of the most accurately described in the term 'bloody battle', in many cases too little left of what was once a man for the bereaved to be told anything more than, 'died in the service of his country and laid to rest with honour'.

Alicia had a faith which enabled her to believe that only the soul was relevant, flesh and bone could return to the earth wherever fate ordained but the soul travelled to another place and there it found its source of being. If souls recognised each other then Josh and Alicia were together in that place. It was Andrew

Smithfield's belief that they were, such absolute commitment could not be denied by a God of love.

The snow of recent days had almost cleared from the pavements, just a few patches of white huddled beneath bushes and lingered in the gateways and entries that missed any glimpse of winter sun.

Charles travelled on the bus, feeling conspicuous in his dark suit, black topcoat and hat. A child seated on the opposite side of the aisle watched him with concern, Charles, aggrieved at having to endure this mawkish episode, was determined not to let even a hint of a smile pass from his mouth to any fellow human being and the child viewed this expressionless image in black with trepidation. When the mother prompted the young boy to stand, having reached their stop, the poor child physically cowered away from Charles' seated figure.

The Chapel was a short distance away from where Charles alighted the bus, off the main road, about a hundred yards along a quiet side road. A group of people, mostly men, gathered inside the Chapel yard, they nodded recognition as Charles walked nervously towards them. He was relieved when Robert Cheetham took his watch from a pocket and suggested that they now take their seats inside, it was close to time. Charles found himself sitting next to Henry Wicks, who unlike Charles could deliver a smile quite readily. Neither spoke but Wicks' pleasant demeanour softened Charles a little and his breathing became less tight.

The service was comparatively short, a simple but sincere eulogy given by Smithfield himself, not read from preparation but clearly spoken from the heart. One hymn, Love divine, all loves excelling, and The Lord's prayer.

The cortege moved off to Rock Cemetery and those remaining began to walk away, Charles making no attempt to hide his urgency. A voice behind him called out.

"Wait up Eddowes." Charles turned to find Basil Stanford close on his heels. "Don't see much of you Charles, I do see your boy, William. Fine young man, credit to you. We should join one another for a drink sometime. I have daughters, different kettle of fish all together." He laughed, "the eldest could hold her own in a man's world, I suppose I should hope that she never has to, but it's her spirit, crying shame for it not to surface. Mothers, you know how they are Charles, always clucking, but a boy, I can only imagine that a father has more sanction over a boy. I confess to enjoying considerably my conversations with yours." Basil Stanford's hand disappeared inside his coat then reappeared holding a card. "Do make contact Eddowes." He passed the small white business card to Charles. "My regards to your good lady."

From a few yards behind them Henry Wicks had observed the exchange. The service had brought back painful memories but his late wife could yet instil in him some of her own tremendous spirit. He sighed, raised his collar against the cold and returned in thought to Leonora, how he missed her, but she was gone. Listening to Andrew Smithfield speak of his aunt's strengths stirred something in Henry. Leonora was safe now from the like of Basil Stanford, Henry could live without fear or favour. He whispered to his wife, not doubting that she would hear.

"Without fear or favour my dear."

CHAPTER TWELVE

Late March

George opened the small burgundy coloured box to look again at the locket. It had taken him ten months to save enough money to pay Mr.Stillwell at the jewellers. It was around the neck of Delores del Rio, one day at the Odeon that George had first seen the dainty gold trinket, or at least one half of it. The film, a love story, filled George's head with a dream of giving to Alice on their wedding day, a locket, just like the one they had seen at the pictures. Alice had quite innocently commented on the unusual and charming nature of the heart shaped locket, which in fact became two. The small gold heart could be parted down its middle and fitted together again like two pieces of a jigsaw. Each half had its own chain, which simply doubled around the neck if worn as a whole by one individual. On the back of each an inscription, in the film, 'your Carlo' on the one and 'my Rosetta' on the other. George had described in detail to Mr.Stillwell just how he wanted the item to be made and engraved. When they were married Alice would wear her half of the gold heart with the words, 'your George' on the back and he would wear the other inscribed, 'my Alice'.

Since secretly collecting it from the jewellers on Parliament Street, he'd peeped inside the box with a deep sense of satisfaction and excitement at the thought of his wedding in only two weeks time.

He'd secured the tenancy of the house on Ainsley Road, previously occupied by Percy Pollard's mother and working in the evenings he'd created a home fit for his bride to be. It had been a difficult few weeks. The ongoing problems at Bobbers Mill and Freddy's anxieties quite naturally dominated the family's thoughts. It was Alice's nature to be quiet and undemanding at the best of times so George had spared her as much of the troubles as he could, diverting her attention away from controversy and prompting her to sew for their new home and to gather that all important bottom drawer. He'd told no one, not even Annie of the locket, she would only have tried to persuade him to let her share the cost but that would have taken away the satisfaction, it was special, unique, it was George's own inspiration and besides, he'd found his mam a number of times, sitting alone, late at night, searching her mind for a solution to Freddy's plight. If Freddy had to begin again, he would need all the help possible and while George instinctively knew that his brother would stubbornly refuse financial assistance, he was equally aware of their mam's subtle ways of easing a problem. Charles kept Annie in possession of limited funds, a modest sum of housekeeping for meat, which their own shop did not sell, and for small odds and ends, like bus fares and postage stamps. It ever amazed George how thrifty his mam could be and at times of their birthdays or Christmas she produced, like magic, those treats they all so cherished. For herself she sought nothing and it was this total selflessness that enabled her acts of giving.

The council had issued a compulsory purchase order when Freddy had refused to sell, it seemed inevitable that Bobbers Mill would succumb to the developers. The main concern was that Freddy might lose much of his investment. The bank held first charge over the property, Freddy was far too innately decent to allow Arthur and Dorothy Cropley to suffer hardship at their time of life and what mutterings the council had thus far made did little to inspire confidence.

George clicked together the lid and fastener on the box, put it carefully at the very back of the drawer containing his socks and underwear, sighed and followed the smell of onions frying downstairs.

William, Celia and Mathew were coming for tea, he felt a measure of guilt at harbouring dismay, Celia and the child were nothing but pleasure, William however had been in a strange mood of late and the least little thing sent him into a grumpy ill humour. Even Charles had remarked upon it, which George had inwardly considered to be the fire calling the kettle sooty. How his mam managed to keep her quiet dignity he wondered about often. Alice held many of those same qualities. No longer having a mother to help with the wedding, she'd sought Annie's advice and guidance. A comfortable understanding had developed between them. George found comfort in that. Alice's dad too was a good man, he'd done his best since the death of his wife to raise a fine daughter and George felt a great respect for Fred Pearson.

"Smells good Mam." George looked over her shoulder at the joint of pork. "Where are John and Hilda?"

Annie stirred the pan of gravy. "Hilda should be here any minute, she went to see Laura, a practice hair-do before the real thing. Her friend Laura is going to style Hilda's hair for the wedding. John is down the cellar, your dad needed some items brought up for the shelves, I'll relieve him when the others arrive, everything's ready and Hilda and Celia will serve up the pudding."

George bit his tongue, he wanted to say 'for goodness sake Mam have your meal first for a change', but it would have been pointless. His mam stood out there in the shop, very often until closing time, then Charles would wander through to 'cash up', it was the established routine.

If anything was able to cast a shadow over his wedding it was the fact that he'd not be present at Gregory Street to help his mam, to stand close when one of Charles' irritable moods prevailed.

The marriage was to take place at St. Andrew's at 2-30 in the afternoon. Alice had few relatives, just one cousin, one aunt and her father. The shop would be closed from 1o/clock to 4-30 but Charles had insisted the need to open up for the Saturday evening trade, to allow the men to collect their smokes and for the customary late stragglers to buy kindlers and paraffin. Charles would man the shop, no need for Annie to be troubled by it! His selfless gesture had been acknowledged but George knew his stepfather would welcome any excuse to leave the small reception in the church hall before he was obliged to mingle and exchange pleasantries. It ever occurred odd to the openhearted, friendly George, that Charles could sit, sometimes for hours in The Standard, where presumably he was engaged in conversation with others present, yet at any family gathering he was reluctant to remain for very long at all, 'nowt so queer as folk' Edna would say.

John was to be George's best man, after all, they worked together at Raleigh. George had agonised over whether or not to ask Freddy. All their growing up years they'd shared a bond, made stronger by William's contrariness, but George would countenance no ill feeling and if he asked Freddy, then William would surely have been miffed. Besides, Freddy had a lot on his mind, in fact George felt awkward at holding a joyful celebration when for his brother and wife, the future loomed grim. He'd told his mam how he felt but Annie had reassured him. 'Freddy would want you and Alice to be happy, he's man enough to put aside his problems for a day in order that you might enjoy every moment of your wedding. No one escapes troubles, at some point in life we all face adversity. Freddy and Francis will together overcome their difficulties just as you and Alice are bound to do when problems confront you. Remember Winnie Bacon's favourite saying. 'Every day the same, never two days alike'.

The carving knife passed through the belly pork like it cut through butter. George's hand dived in and pinched a small piece of crispy fat from the outside.

"That's as tender as could be Mam."

Annie selected a piece of pork the size of her little finger, laughed and lifted it with a fork to George's mouth. "It's like feeding a fledgling," she said. "I suppose that is what you are about to become, fully fledged and about to leave the nest."

George gave her a wink. "Don't worry Mam, nobody brings to the nest what you do."

Just then the back door opened and in came the family, William, Celia and Mathew in the arms of his aunty Hilda.

"She's got the knack," said William, "Celia has been trying to shut him up for the past hour but he'd have none of it, now look at him." Mathew dozed but his cheeks looked flushed, Annie felt his brow.

"He feels hot, is it his teeth Celia?"

"I think so, I've given him a powder, he keeps biting his ring and his nappies have been a bit strong for the past couple of days."

Celia looked tired and anxious. Annie guessed it would be William's lack of tolerance that tired his wife the most. Babies demanded attention because unable to 'do' for themselves they had no choice. William despite his age and size, could readily revert to the ways of an infant but would dispute any suggestion of it.

Annie pulled the big chair further away from the range, ran upstairs to gather a couple of pillows, lay the sleeping Mathew down at the back of the chair, placing the pillows in front of him.

"There, he won't be too hot like that and he can't roll off. If he's been unsettled, now that he's found sleep he'll likely rest for a while. Keep an eye on him. Call John and your dad, I'll dish up now."

Annie was pleased that her little grandson continued to sleep. From the shop she could hear if he disturbed and all was quiet. Celia needed to have a meal in peace. Annie could remember the traumas of teething, Hilda had been particularly restless and eating and sleeping, for Annie herself had been a virtual impossibility at the times when her daughter's gums pained from that most natural of advancements, teeth! Danny had been the least demanding, that telltale ridge of white evident in his smile yet causing little disturbance by day or night.

Annie swallowed hard and busied herself topping up the cigarette stand. The doorbell chimed and Tommy Spooner entered. Annie knew at once that something was wrong. He sat on the chair by the counter, his breathing was short.

"It's mam, Mrs.Eddowes, me mam's passed away."

His shoulders shook and he could do nothing to hold back the tears. Annie quickly put the lock on the shop door and turned out the light so prying eyes couldn't see Tommy's emotion. She knelt in front of him.

"What can we do to help you Tommy, William's in the back room, shall I fetch him, you and William go back a long way, you've always been his best friend."

Tommy sniffed and drew his sleeve across his face. "Me an' Will' don't move in the same circles anymore Mrs.Eddowes, it's you I came to see. I'm really worried for our Joyce, she wer' there when mam went. I can't pacify 'er, I don't know what to do an' it's makin' it harder for the others. Our mam allus had regard for you

Mrs.Eddowes, will yer talk to Joyce?" Tommy's face, even in the dim light, held a weariness that aged him by years.

"Is Joyce at your mam's house now?" Asked Annie.

"No, she's gone back to Peverell Street. I'm afraid for 'er, she's all mixed up, I know she blames herself for givin' mam such grief. What with all that trouble in Loughborough an' 'er bein' so wilful when she wer' younger, but Joyce didn't make mam die did she? Mam wer' old an' worn out, she never stopped lovin' Joyce no matter what she'd done, mam loved us all the same, I know she did."

"Be strong for the others Tommy, you will have to shoulder the worst of it, you and Joe. I shall go to Peverell Street, William has the van outside, he'll drive me there. He may seem distant, even we, his family, feel left behind at times but William will learn the value of friendship one day. I hope you'll not despair of him Tommy, your character is so much more of a man than his. I still see a boy, I love him dearly but it concerns me that I still see the boy."

William was not in a talkative mood. After their meal and the shop was finally closed for the night, he'd taken Celia and Mathew back to Glover Street. Annie had insisted she would be perfectly alright seated on an old cushion in the back of the van and that it would be entirely unnecessary to run Celia home, then return for her. Peverell Street was not too far from Glover Street, especially in the van. Now as they made their way to Joyce, with Annie sitting alongside him in the front, William's response to his mam's suggestion was less than encouraging.

"I'll go to the funeral but Rosie won't want me calling to hinder her, and Tommy's sure to be busy sorting everything at Handley's. Celia can go to see Rosie and the twins, women are better at dealing with that sort of thing. Mrs.Spooner has been feeble for a long time. I remember you saying how unwell she looked at Susie and Joe's wedding."

"It's just along here, that house, that's the one," said Annie.

"Have you been here before then?" Asked a curious William.

"No, but May and her family lived on Peverell Street before they moved to Melton Road and one day when I met Joyce, in chatting she told me about the house where she rented a room. Someone many, many years ago, under tragic circumstances, met their death in that house. I remembered hearing the same story when I was living on Winchester Street so I knew to which house Joyce referred."

"The whole bloody street looks tragic to me," said William. "How long will you be? If I go to The Standard for half an hour then come back, will you be ready by then?" His manner was impatient so Annie assured him that would be ideal.

To say that Peverell Street had not changed would be untrue. One or two of the small properties now had pretty lace curtains at the windows and the occupants had applied paint to the front doors. One even had a brass letterbox, recently polished, it was evidence of hope and pride.

Since the day Annie helped May to move from No.28, no occasion for her to return had ever presented itself. Her eyes scanned the other side of the street, the old gate where Shawcross would sit to observe all the comings and goings had gone from the mouth of the entry. Even now after all these years, a shiver ran down Annie's spine, she dare not think of Enid, she turned around quickly to knock at the door. After a minute it was opened by a man with so much stubble on his face it was impossible to judge whether he was young or old, native or foreign, welcoming or otherwise. When he spoke, just a single word.

"Yes?"

It held not the slightest trace of pleasantry but at least enabled Annie an accurate perception of his character.

"I have come to see Joyce Spooner, I believe she is at home," said Annie.

He opened the door wider, stood to one side and pointed to the stairs. The cuff on his shirt had become unstitched and hung below his hand, flapping loose as he directed her.

"Top of the stairs, first door on the right, watch yourself on the seventh tread, bloody woodworm."

The landing had a smell about it, behind one of the doors someone inhaled Friars Balsam for their cold. Her gentle tapping brought Joyce to the door, eyes swollen from crying, the young woman looked truly bereft. Joyce sank into Annie's arms and the sobbing began again.

"Hush Joyce, don't upset yourself so. Sit by me on the bed, you feel cold." Annie wrapped her around with a crocheted knee blanket that had lain at the foot of the bed. For a few moments they sat in silence, the air in the room was heavy with that musty smell of damp, evidence of rot in the skirting boards added to the general sense of disrepair and though Joyce had tried with a scattering of simple ornaments and small framed prints, which proclaimed their origin as Moffat's, the room bore nothing to grant this young woman even the fleeting glimpse of a home. Annie took Joyce's hand in her own, determined not to let emotion weaken the purpose of her words, she spoke.

"I was reared by my aunt Bella, mother died when I was a baby. You would have likely considered aunt Bella to be a most undesirable guardian, so stern and strict." Annie squeezed Joyce's fingers, not entirely to reassure the fragile young woman but to feel the warmth of another as she recalled her own early days. "There was only the two of us, she never married. Sometimes I would have a doubt, a moment of uncertainty. Perhaps aunt Bella didn't really want the bother of me, she may not even love me at all. I came to know, beyond all doubt that neither was the case, she did love me and I miss her still. I am, who I am because of her. I hear aunt Bella often, the things she would say to me ring in my head. I can still see her, just as she was, so thin and pale towards the end but possessed of a strength few ever achieve to hold. Your mam was strong Joyce. I remember the way she would create wonderful meals from the most diverse ingredients. The world was at war, your dad, her husband, had been killed but Edith, in her world of little sound, bound you all together, kept you safe from harm. You will always miss her, the fact that she is no longer in the room, no more to cast that smile over her children, but you will still hear her words and picture her just as she was, I promise you Joyce that you will. Any mistakes you made, just as it was for your brothers and sisters too, your mam forgave before she ever went to sleep at the end of the days you made them. Edith loved you Joyce and now she would trust you, her eldest daughter, to keep the family safe from harm. You don't belong here in this place, go home to your mam's house Joyce, be there for Pat, Brian and Trevor. Do for her what she did for you and be proud of the family. William will be back for me soon. I want you to promise me that by the end of next week you will have left Mr.Miserable downstairs, he can find a new tenant, and you will carry on where your mam left off."

Joyce managed a weary smile. "I think I might have a young man, I haven't said anythin' to the others. I met him a few weeks ago when he wer' home on leave. He's in the army. His name's William, William Haynes, he knows Billy Dodds. He's back on camp now but he writes." Joyce paused, as if unsure whether or not to tell Annie. "He signs his letters 'love Will'. Do yer think he'll forgive me an'all, somebody's sure to give him chapter an' verse of me mortal sin." Her hand trembled, Annie held it tighter.

"I know the family, although William is probably the one I have seen least of. You've moved on Joyce, left behind that confused period of your life. Florrie Haynes is not unlike your mam, don't fret, a lot of love dwells in Florrie's house. Have you met Victor, William's youngest brother?" Asked Annie.

"I've not met any of 'em, is Victor nice, William's nice." Joyce had found some calm at last.

"Oh yes," said Annie, "Victor is lovely and he has the gift of putting everything into perspective without realising he's doing it." Annie chuckled. "I'm pleased for you Joyce and I know your mam would be, so no more tears tonight. Be strong for the others, especially Tommy and Joe, they have such hard days ahead." A car horn 'parped' outside in the street. "That will be my William. I shall let you into a secret Joyce. I dream of the day that my William might find the gift of putting things into perspective, he could learn a great deal from Victor Haynes, be sure to remember that when you meet Victor for the first time." Annie kissed Joyce's cheek. "Now mind what I said, leave this place by the end of next week, go home to your mam's."

Annie climbed into the seat alongside William, he began to laugh, his demeanour was changed, completely animated, eager to speak.

"Well I've seen it all now, what a turn up for the books. Our very own 'steady Freddy', in The Standard, drunk." William laughed again, his manner annoyed Annie but his words alarmed her.

"Has Freddy really had too much to drink?" She hoped William might be exaggerating.

"He couldn't walk the white line if his life depended on it, you've got to hand it to Freddy, he's true to his belief, if you're going to get drunk then at least make sure that you're legless. Freddy's always gone the whole hog hasn't he." William chuckled again as though he found it endlessly amusing. Annie spoke sharply.

"And you left him there like that, how can you be so thoughtless?" She was despairing of his nonchalance.

"Well what would you have expected me to do, Freddy's a grown man, he can please himself, I'm not his keeper." William was tetchy.

"Go back to the pub, we'll fetch him out, poor Francis shouldn't be having these worries in her condition. Something must have happened to have driven Freddy to such measures." Annie's tone stilled William's tongue and within a few minutes they were parking just a few yards away from The Standard.

Annie dreaded what they must now do, the smoke and noise, the amused expression on the faces of men too high on drink to recognise anxiety, Freddy's likely bewilderment and eventual embarrassment, but Francis was six months pregnant, this was not fair on the young woman. The problems already surrounding them at Bobbers Mill could not have come at a worse time, Freddy needed to be taken home. Annie walked between the tables to where William pointed. Freddy's head and chest lay over a table top, his arms outstretched, his hands falling over the edge, looking as lifeless as the empty, worn out gloves that begged 'a penny for the guy' each fifth of November. Annie smoothed her fingers down the back of his shoulder, he murmured something inaudible. She lowered her face and spoke softly in his ear.

"Let's go home Freddy."

He raised his head. "Home." One word, then his face fell once more to the table.

Annie beckoned to William, he'd stayed by the door talking with another man. "Help me get him to his feet, you go the other side, when we reach the van I'll go in the back with him." She was about to put her arm beneath Freddy's when she felt a pat on her shoulder.

"Ere, you let me Mrs.Eddowes, 'tis like dead weight when a man's out of it, I'll 'elp William, appen the lad wer' tryin' to ease 'is mind. I've 'eard how council want to build on Bobbers Mill, cryin' shame it is, good lad your Freddy."

"Thank-you Mr.Rashleigh."

Annie stepped aside and together William and Bill Rashleigh managed to steer the helpless Freddy to the door. She recalled the time, long ago, when she'd struggled to help Charles from his place of despair in a dreary corner of The Standard. Then the men had taunted and provoked, only Edwin Garbett had come to her aid. This night no one made the task harder. A hush had descended and the silence was only broken when a voice from somewhere in the room said simply.

"Goodnight Mrs.Eddowes." Annie felt grateful for their display of understanding and respect for their control. By the time they reached the van Annie was shaking from nervousness and cold.

"He'll be alright in the back on his own for God's sake, you sit in the front Mam." William was getting tired and agitated.

"I'm very grateful to you Mr.Rashleigh, I won't forget your kindness." Annie ignored William's remark, waiting until Bill Rashleigh had returned to the pub. "Freddy's not ever been so ill from drink, I shall stay with him, just in case." She said.

"In case of what? He's not ill, the daft bugger's legless that's all, you don't really think he's likely to undo the back doors and jump out, he couldn't even find the latch the state he's in."

Annie sighed, "If he vomits he could choke, it happens William. I shall be perfectly alright in the back but drive carefully."

Annie clambered into the van and William closed the doors, muttering his objection at the suggestion he might drive in any other fashion. Freddy lay still, Annie had put the old cushion under his head, the farm lane was rutted, the thickness of her coat she tucked beneath her bottom, Annie carried little spare flesh. From inside the van it was impossible to know how far they'd travelled, Freddy called for Francis, just once but without opening his eyes. At last the van pulled up and given the jolting passage of the previous few seconds, Annie was relieved to believe they'd reached the farmyard.

Annie smiled reassuringly as William helped her out. "When we have Freddy safely inside you should go home to Celia, it's getting late and she'll begin to worry. I need you to call briefly at Gregory Street, to tell your dad that I'm staying here tonight, to keep Francis company. You can explain what's happened, I shall be back first thing in the morning to help him with the papers."

"Anybody would think Freddy was still in short trousers but if that's what you want then who am I to argue." William climbed inside the back of the van, put his hands under Freddy's armpits and propelled him forward until his legs hung over the edge and his feet were just inches from the ground.

"Come on farmer Freddy, lets get you inside before a cow sees your disgrace and tells all the others."

"Your dad doesn't need to hear an embellished version of tonight's events William. Your brother drank too much, we both know the drink wasn't taken out of merriment, show some compassion, if not for Freddy's sake then for your dad's. It's too easy to mock, it takes character and consideration to recognise a man's despair and to acknowledge it with kindness. Thank-you for driving me to Peverell Street and for helping me to bring Freddy home." Annie gave William a kiss on the cheek, then thread her arm through Freddy's. "Ready," she said. William nodded and they pulled Freddy to his feet.

The cold air stirred him to utter, "All gone, it's all gone." Annie looked across at William, a shaft of light helped them negotiate the path, Francis had heard sound and stood at the open door.

"It's alright Francis," said Annie, "he's had too much to drink, it was fortunate that William found him in The Standard and rescued him, otherwise he could have been there, asleep, until the landlord put him out at closing time. We'll sit him down in the armchair, I think that will be best."

William was quiet, the sight of Francis, swollen from pregnancy and ashen with worry reached his own sense of alarm. Women died in childbirth, his mother died in childbirth, now William's flippant attitude changed to one of concern. He remembered his anxiety following the night Edwin Garbett lay dead in their house, Celia having just told him that she was expecting. Not until Mathew came into the world, healthy and strong, did William lose that dread of something going badly wrong.

"I best get home to Celia, you'll manage now won't you Mam? Don't worry Francis, Freddy will have nothing more than a sore head by morning and that will be enough to stop it ever happening again. He wouldn't play conkers any more after Joe Spooner struck him on the knuckles, Freddy's sensible like that, isn't he Mam?"

Annie saw the look in his eyes, that plea for her assurance that all would be well, Annie saw the boy. "Yes, that's true William," she replied, "don't alarm Celia, tell her that everything is alright, you won't forget to call briefly at Gregory Street?" Annie's tone of request was acknowledged and kissing Francis on the cheek, William left.

Annie unfastened Freddy's laces and pulled off the heavy boots. "Put the kettle on Francis, I think we both need some hot, sweet tea." Freddy mumbled something impossible to decipher. Annie pulled the footstool closer and lifted Freddy's feet, propping his head by a cushion she stroked his brow, he slept. The sound of tea pouring into the cups somehow comforted Annie, they were safe, behind the doors of home. "Don't think too badly of him Francis, all the worry of these past weeks must have proved too much, even for Freddy."

Francis picked up an envelope from the mantelpiece and passed it to Annie. "This came today, I told him to go to the bank on Monday and speak with the manager, it can't be right but the council must surely be obliged to take notice of Mr.Rothero at Barclays."

Annie's head was tired, she read slowly and carefully the content of the document, it sickened her, such blatant disregard for any honest, hard working individual was contemptible, the fact that Freddy, inoffensive, unselfish Freddy Eddowes was the recipient of this cruel and calculated communication from the local authority filled Annie with angry resentment.

"It's only two thirds of the value, the bank loan has to be cleared and Arthur still owns a third of Bobbers Mill, there'll be virtually nothing left of Freddy's investment, it will all be gone." Francis began to cry. As if something at that moment penetrated his sleep Freddy stirred in his chair, mumbled, sighed, then returned to his intoxicated unconsciousness.

"When you've drunk your tea, you go up to bed," said Annie. "I shall stay down with him in case he wakes." She patted Francis on the arm. The young woman made protest but Annie was firm. "Give way to age and experience Francis, when Freddy wakes he will almost certainly want to pee with urgency, he'll be unsteady on his legs for a few hours yet, I don't want you taking his weight. What time do the cows need to be milked in the morning?" Annie's thoughts travelled ahead to the work that could not be ignored or delayed.

"Usually Freddy calls them in by half past six." Francis cast her eyes to her husband, a shadow of stubble darkened his face. "He's lost a button from his jacket, I don't know if I can match it from the button box, I might have to get a card of new ones, he favours that jacket." She leant over him and fingered the tuft of thread at the spot where his top button should be. Annie felt so sorry for Francis, this ought to be a happy time, their first child due early summer, the farm beginning to develop as they'd planned, now all confused and in many ways unknown. Where they would be when then the baby was born dominated Annie's concerns but it was the immediate on which Annie must concentrate.

"I need you to at least lie down, hopefully you will doze Francis, but it is important that you take some rest. I shall leave here at about half past five in the morning, to wake George and John, that will give them time to get here by milking. If the cows are half an hour later than usual I can't imagine it will make that much difference to anything. Freddy will be the worse for wear but should still be able to tell them what to do. You must promise me not to undertake any lifting or bending yourself, it's sure to take George and John longer but thankfully it's Sunday tomorrow so they've nothing to rush off for. Now off you go, I'm quite alright here by the fire."

Annie pulled the other easy chair a little closer to the hearth and Francis finally surrendered to tiredness, walking slowly from the room and up to bed. Through the early hours Annie sat opposite Freddy, she didn't sleep. The fire burned steadily in the grate, her feet were warm but even with her coat around her shoulders, bodily she could find slight comfort. Not until some time after 4 o/clock did Freddy open his eyes. Just as Annie had predicted, his first and immediate need was the bucket. She tried to limit any sound, hoping Francis might have drifted off but within minutes she appeared in the doorway, dressed and openly relieved to see Freddy in an improved state.

"I'm going home now Francis," whispered Annie, "get him to drink some water, as much as you can, stay with him, George and John will come soon."

"It's still pitch dark, you ought not be walking alone," said Francis emotionally.

"It's a quarter to five, probably the very safest time of day, I doubt if I shall meet a single soul." Annie gave her a hug. "There's nothing we can do about the letter today, try not to become stressed, it's not good for the baby. Tomorrow the men will decide what to do. I'll explain it all to Charles, let's get through this day first.

Annie turned the corner into Gregory Street, other than half a dozen men making their way to the pit for the morning shift and a hungry looking fox, her progress had been without company. The van had just pulled up and was dropping off the bundles of newspapers outside the shop door. One day followed another with little reprieve. Whatever would aunt Bella have made of it all. Annie had tried to bolster

Francis's spirit but inwardly she truly feared for the young couple, perhaps that would be the saving grace, the fact that they were young, years ahead of them. Weariness allowed doubts and insecurities to invade Annie's thoughts. 'Remember what you are my girl', even those unforgettable words which so often cautioned her formative years, words which had strangely steeled her against life's blows, now echoed too distant to be compelling. As she stepped inside the back door Annie's mind yearned for peace.

Freddy fidgeted, although he had been waiting only minutes, it felt like hours. No sound came from the manager's office, what could he be doing in there. At last a shuffle the other side of the heavy door and the sudden appearance of James Rothero brought Freddy to his feet as forcefully as if he were sprung.

"Come in Mr.Eddowes, sorry to have kept you waiting, documents needing to be signed are as urgent here as I imagine feeding and watering of stock ever proves to be at Bobbers Mill. Take a seat, what can I do for you?"

Freddy related the whole story to Rothero, scarcely drawing breath between sentences, as if getting it off his chest would result in some measure of hope, a lifeline thrown to him by this official of the bank. Freddy was small fry but Rothero, the council must have regard for James Rothero, manager at Barclays.

"When did you receive the first letter from the council Mr.Eddowes?"

"Late January, I had a visit from an agent, he gave his name as Bradshaw. I asked in what capacity he worked for the council, he told me he was from the legal department. He delivered that first communication by hand. I read it and told him there and then that I had no wish to sell. He advised me to consider very carefully and not be too dismissive in the first instance."

"What is Mr.Cropley's view on the matter, as I recall a solicitor was instructed to amend the deed, protecting Mr.Cropley's interest should you fail on your repayments to the bank. I've looked at your account, certainly there has been no lapse, no delay in any agreed transaction since I endorsed the loan, in fact your account is sound."

"I asked Arthur if he'd been approached by the council," said Freddy. "No one has called on him and he's received no written word."

"Uhm," said Rothero, pausing to think, "that suggests that the council presumes that you bought all of the farm, they haven't been thorough with their enquires. It may be possible to secure a more realistic sum for Mr.Cropley's one third. He can yet name his price. The authority will beat that down somewhat, over the past few months all property values have dropped but not by more than thirty percent, which is what they propose to pay you. It is regrettable that you didn't come to see me when you were first made aware of the authorities' intentions. If you had agreed to sell, in that circumstance you could have quoted the current market value and although the council would have secured it at a lower figure, nevertheless they would have been obliged to offer within reason. As I understand it, when any individual refuses to sell their property to the council, having been given the opportunity to do so, the local authority is empowered to issue a compulsory purchase order and whatever they then offer, the unwilling and subordinate vendor can do no other than accept. Unfortunately and unreasonably, I venture to add, there is no recourse in law."

"So they don't realise that what they have offered me relates to only two thirds of the farm, well that's good isn't it?" Freddy's thought's moved quickly along. "Arthur can quote current market value for his third so that brings it up considerably."

"It won't work quite like that I'm afraid," said Rothero with a sigh. "The necessary legal process, land registry searches, deeds and so on will reveal the division, the council will be entitled to adjust their offer accordingly but they must by law give Mr.Cropley the opportunity to agree the sale of his title, I'm sure you will make certain he does so. I'm afraid I must point out that Barclays holds the first charge over the property, the money owed to the bank will be repaid by the solicitor before you receive the remainder. I am sorry Mr.Eddowes, the sum of five hundred pounds does not represent the current value of the entire property at Bobbers Mill, not even in these times of recession. I am not without concern, the bank tries wherever possible to assist young men such as yourself, to be sympathetic of unforeseen difficulties and to encourage progress. When are you required to vacate?"

"The letter states the council's intention to be in ownership by the end of May." Freddy's voice faltered. "We're expecting our first child in June."

Rothero recognised the depth of emotion behind Freddy's words. "The fact that Mr.Bradshaw and his department have neglected to prepare thoroughly will inevitably delay proceedings. The outcome will be no less sorry, but for Mr.Cropley's improved expectation. Come to see me again, you will have to arrange a sale of live and dead farm stock, there will be something left on which to build. We don't simply cut you adrift Mr.Eddowes, where we see enterprise it would be foolish not to encourage it. Events around the world dictate that the bank must be cautious at this time but we must continue to advance within acceptable parameters." Rothero rose to his feet. "Speak with Arthur Cropley, he is not a young man, for him the situation is even more crucial, I'm sure you agree."

Freddy nodded. "Arthur and Dorothy Cropley are thoroughly decent people," he said.

Freddy offered his hand to Rothero who took it firmly. "Come and see me Mr.Eddowes, that is all I can say, do come to see me, and my congratulations, a baby in June. I always wanted a family but sadly it wasn't to be. My wife and I are happy, but happy in an empty house and that unoccupied space creates an echo of regret." He smiled, it raised the two ends of his immaculate moustache and softened his features.

Freddy, ever polite thanked him before turning away, tears of frustration were now too pressing to be denied.

"Did yer notice Jack Haynes peepin' through the railin's at your Hilda," said Edna, "I know that look, 'e's smitten, I'm not surprised, the lass looks lovely, that colour suits 'er, what did yer say they called it?"

"Coral," said Annie, "both dresses, Alice's and Hilda's were off the peg at Jessops. I'm glad Alice chose the cream satin, she's so very fair, white wouldn't have done her justice. George looks very happy, poor Sarah has wept her way through countless hankies."

"And you 'aven't I s'pose?" Edna looked at Annie with a wry smile.

"A few," said Annie, "I confess to a few."

Edna reached into her pocket and slowly pulled out first one, then two, a third and a fourth, holding them up to reveal all were damp. She laughed. "We're all soft in th'ead, we do it every time, our Annie and Susie, even your William, mind you I weren't sure if the ceremony that day brought on the waterworks or if it wer' pity for poor Celia. Billy's heard as Basil Stanford's been sniffin' round William, it's not a good time for 'im to be on the prowl. Smithfield put it off as long as 'e could but since 'e let ten women go 'e's been wanderin' round the place in some sort o' stupor. 'E kept Bessie's job for 'er, she started back last week, thank God it's summer facin' 'er an' not winter, she's lost over a stone in weight, 'er clothes hang on 'er shoulders, I told 'er, get some o' that Bengers from Hastilows, they reckon that'll put flesh back. I think all that business 'wi Bobbers Mill preys on Smithfield's mind an'all. William gets frustrated but it wer' him as told Smithfield as Freddy wer' in a right old state so 'e's only got 'isself to blame for the boss's lack o' concentration. I s'pose Smithfield would 'ave heard it from somebody else anyroad. It all come too soon after 'is aunt's funeral. If 'e could only find a woman it might help, do yer think we ought to put an advert in The Evening Post. 'Lonely bachelor, plenty o' money, needs unchaste lady to tickle his fancy'. Edna chuckled roguishly.

"Hush Edna," said Annie," "the vicar will hear you, he's coming this way."

"A lovely service ladies, surprisingly it's the first wedding this year. St.Andrew's needs more weddings, sadly we experience funerals far more often, but a christening, now that is one of my favourite occasions. Celia has asked if Mathew can be christened here next month. I imagine many of those gathered today might be present at that service too." He smiled warmly, then left them, feeling it polite to mingle and chat with others whilst the photographer took the last few shots of the bride and groom.

"Well, your lot's in his good books, regular customers, an' if Jack Haynes has his way, then Hilda'll be needin' his Holiness an'all you mark my words. I could do wi' a cuppa. I daren't 'ave one afore we left, I wer' out three times in the night to pee. Look at Billy, allus playin' the fool, that's the second time 'e's tickled Maggie's Jennifer an' pretended it weren't him. That little Marie over there wi' Mavis reminds me o' one of them cherubs they allus put on Sunday school certificates, makes yer wonder why she wer' giv' up for adoption. You'd think as somebody in the family'd 'ave wanted a lovely little thing like 'er."

"I know what you mean but Mavis and Eddie make good parents, they've always longed for a child. I think that must be the last of the photo's done, we should make our way to the hall, Davina and Sarah will need to sit down. John has charge of them, best man's duties and escort to the elderly bless him. Sarah tells the same stories over and over, Davina is getting hard of hearing but John never loses patience. I must speak with Charles, he'll be leaving early to re-open the shop. I hope Freddy and Francis will managed to drive the troubles from their minds today and enjoy themselves. He's had a letter from Harold at Huttoft, it could be a mixed blessing. They exchange letters once a month, Freddy told him what was happening and now Harold is trying to persuade him to move with Francis to Lincolnshire. Farming is the main industry there, with Freddy's experience Harold believes he'd stand a good chance of securing well paid work along with a cottage to rent."

"Well that's good news then isn't it?" Said Edna

Annie sighed, "I'm not sure how Francis would feel about leaving her family and I'd miss Freddy very much."

"For Heaven's sake, anybody'd think it wer' t'other side o' world to hear you talk. It's time you went to the seaside. All the years Ivy's been askin' you to visit an' yer never 'ave, well now's your chance. Wi' a grandchild to spoil an' make a fuss of you'd be sure to go. People do get on coaches an' trains yer know, it don't just 'appen in films an' books. When ave' you ever been away from this city?" Edna looked stern, "You 'aven't 'ave yer. It could be the makin' of Freddy, out from under

William's shadow an' you might get to see summat different to the inside o' that soddin' shop."

Annie let out a long breath of apprehension. "We'll see, perhaps."

"Mam," George's voice called out urgently, "Mam," he ran across the grass, a big grin on his face. First kissing Annie, then Edna, he glowed from happiness, "Come on you two, meet my wife." He laughed, "My wife Mam, my beautiful wife." Edna glanced across at Annie, tears welled once more in the eyes of both.

Charles had stayed long enough to spend appropriate time with Fred Pearson and to eat a sandwich before slipping away. The hall was filled with animated chatter, John had held up his harmonica and called out, 'you've ten minutes to eat up then it's dancing'. Annie had kept an eye on Francis, Freddy typically hid his own anxieties so as not to deny George every happy memory of the day but Francis was quiet and Annie felt concerned. The baby wasn't due until around the 25th of June but the young woman looked tired and she carried very low. Her own legs ached from weariness, Annie sat down by Davina.

"My dear, I'm so enjoying myself, the cake is beautifully moist, you put ground almonds in the mix didn't you, I can tell, it's quite delicious." Davina squeezed Annie's fingers. "I have lived too long."

Annie instantly rebuked her, "That's a dreadful thing to say Davina."

"At my age it's perfectly natural to think that I take up a space which might be more usefully occupied. Ah, the music begins, well done John, I shall observe only, but you Annie dear should dance."

Annie kissed Davina's cheek but before she had chance to speak further, Billy stood before her.

"Come on Mrs.Eddowes," he said, "me poor ear needs a rest, it's been Ednarised!" He pulled Annie to her feet with his arm, that one arm made strong by its increased workload. As Billy led her about the hall, his hand firmly at her back, Annie remembered the letter, Catherine Appleyards words to her, 'dance my dear Annie, order your spirit to dance'.

"You'd think George and Alice had lived in that house for years rather than three weeks, they seem so settled there," said Freddy. "George put up shelves in their scullery last week and just as you'd expect, they're all as smooth as silk, he's sanded and varnished them and Alice has everything neatly stored."

"What are you and Francis going to do Freddy?" Annie secured the thread at the base of a button on John's shirt as she spoke. "Something has been preying on my mind since you told me what Mr.Rothero said. It's difficult because I need to break a promise but I feel I must. Before I do will you give me your word that you will never divulge the name of the person who gave me the information?"

"Whatever is it Mam? If you need me to promise then I will but don't worry yourself so, Francis has remarked how troubled you look."

Annie related the events of New Years Eve. Since she'd learned of James Rothero's regret at Freddy not going to see him when he'd first been made aware of the council's intentions, the fact that she'd not told Freddy of Joyce's visit and as it turned out, being unable to speak with Smithfield, had inwardly hoped it would come to nought, now tormented her thoughts day and night. Freddy listened, kissed her cheek and smiled.

"It would have made no difference Mam if you had told me back then, none of us could have foreseen the outcome. I would have sat tight, waiting for the council to make their approach so the stubborn Freddy Eddowes could have proudly told them that Bobbers Mill was nor for sale. I'm anxious only for Arthur to be paid a rightful sum, beyond that it's all too late. We've decided to go to Lincolnshire, Harold says I can work at Huttoft and there's a small cottage not far from Ivy and Reggie at Skendleby, it's unfurnished and a sensible rent. That will suit us nicely for the time, we shall take the furniture from Bobbers Mill. Francis's old boss at the seed merchants has very generously offered us the use of a lorry and David, her brother drives for the coal-yard in the week so he's used to handling a lorry and he'll help us load and drive us to Skendleby on the day."

Annie's eyes filled with wateriness.

"Don't get upset Mam, I know you worry for Francis, going away from her family, but Ivy's sure to make a fuss of her and Molly's there as well, can you imagine those two around a new baby? It's no real distance from here Mam, even Edna's been to Skegness. You and Hilda could come and stay a weekend, dad would manage, he's not as helpless as he makes out, John's there to help out anyway. Cheer up, I'll start again, you'll see, give me a year or two and there'll be an Eddowes dairy herd, standing in a field, somewhere in Lincolnshire with wheat growing tall the other side of the hedge."

"I do love you Freddy," said Annie tearfully.

"I know you do Mam and it's knowing that keeps me strong. Besides, we need to look forward to Mathew's christening, he deserves a day free of distraction. At least you can sit back on this occasion as Mrs.Tozer is overseeing it all. Celia reckons that her mam will have reduced the vicar to a nervous wreck by the time Mathew receives that splash of Holy water." Freddy chuckled. "I can tell that William is actually feeling nervous at the prospect. Gwendolyn Tozer does have that formidable air of authority. I'm glad Celia asked Rosie and Tommy to be Godparents. I think William favoured Edmund and Caroline, you know what he's like, probably convinced himself that they'd bring a bigger silver spoon. Rosie and Tommy are salt o' the earth and Celia spends a lot more time with Rosie and the twins than she does with Caroline."

The back door opened, it was Charles, he hung his jacket over the hook. Often on a Sunday, after the shop closed he'd spend an hour at The Standard. A pint to accompany the picking of bones, gossip and intrigue in long held tradition. It ever lured Charles and those of similar bent.

"There's been an almighty bust up between Stanford and Henry Wicks. They're sayin that Wicks refused to carry out Stanford's order to cut pay yet again. Apparently Wicks let Stanford have it, the verbal exchange between the two of them was that loud if the men had paused in their hammering they would have heard every word, even at the bottom of the shaft. It'll be interesting to see what happens, Wicks has kept the peace these last four years but if Stanford doesn't relent they're predicting big trouble again. I expect Steve Wainwright will be embroiled in it, you'd think he'd have given up by now wouldn't you?" Charles looked across at Freddy. "Whether a man works on it or under it, seems to me land is nothing but a source of grief."

He sat at the end of the table, Annie put down her mending, crossed to the range and took Charles' plate of dinner from where it kept hot in the oven. Freddy caught her eye they didn't need to speak, each knew the other's thoughts.

"Mathew was so good, our grandson is charming Annie," said Gwendolyn Tozer between sipping a glass of sweet sherry. The sitting room in which they gathered was becoming uncomfortably warm, outside the sun shone and the air was mild but a fire nevertheless burned in the grate. The men folk looked particularly awkward, dressed as they were in Sunday best and feeling ill at ease in such ordered surroundings. Even Davina's house, altogether larger and finer, ever displayed evidence of comfortable use, but Gwendolyn maintained a pristine household. If everyday items and general paraphernalia did exist, then they were secreted away. Jessie Tozer cast his genuine smile around the room but spoke little, as if years of competing with his wife's forceful enquiry of everyone and everything now relieved him of the need to utter. Edmund chatted animatedly with William while Tommy and Rosie were stoic in trying to hide their feelings of discomfort. They were used to the chaos created by Thomas and Samuel. Annie had detected a reticence between Rosie and William, remembering Tommy's remark that William now moved in a different circle, she imagined, as Tommy's wife, Rosie might frown upon William's remoteness from his oldest friend.

"Your daughter looks very pretty Annie, does she have an admirer as yet?" Asked Gwendolyn.

"I don't believe there is a young man occupying Hilda's thoughts, she enjoys her work at the library and time spent with her friend Laura, she's only seventeen," said Annie.

"I'm sure when the time comes she'll choose well. It's so important for a husband to have a solid background, good bloodstock. I do believe the prosperity of any marriage depends upon it. Jessie's father was a professional you know, the law, it almost certainly encouraged Edmund in that direction, but Jessie is far too modest, too mild at times. I've tried to persuade him to be more outgoing, socialise, attend functions. He prefers to spend his days making fine shoes in which other men might parade, I don't suppose he'll change now," Gwendolyn sighed. "Given his age he should retire and spend more time with me."

Annie was relieved when Celia came over and sat Mathew in Gwendolyn's lap. "Come and say hello to Caroline, I've told her she should watch you make pastry one day. Mrs.Stanford is very good with cakes but doesn't have your touch with pastry."

"I'm sure that's not true Celia," said Annie, " Mrs.Stanford's a very capable lady." Annie felt the need to defend Florence, remembering that day at the shop, their conversation, Florence's description of herself as unremarkably average.

A further twenty minutes or so had passed and Annie thought she could no longer ignore Tommy's unease, she returned to Celia's mother.

"Thank-you so much Gwendolyn, it has been a lovely time, everything was perfect. Because Charles has been alone with the shop all morning I think I really should be going now."

"If you think so dear, I'm sure you know best, shall Jessie walk you home?"

Before Annie could respond Tommy stood right along side her. "It's alright Mrs.Tozer, Rosie an' me should be on our way, her mam's had the boys all this time, they're a handful sure enough, I reckon she'll be glad to give them back. We'll say goodbye to the others and of course our thanks to you for such a good spread. We'll keep Mrs.Eddowes company for much of the way."

"You're very quiet Rosie," said Annie as they walked together.

"Do you really think I'm a fit person to be all those things to Mathew that the vicar spoke about? I wer' never that bright at school and I'm not sure if I even qualify for the ways o' righteousness."

Annie thread her arm through Rosie's. "Do you think you can always love Mathew? She asked.

"Oh that's easy, I can do that bit no bother," said Rosie, "it's all the other stuff."

"Mathew, if he had to could manage without all 'the other stuff' Rosie, but love, now that is something he will always need, all you have to do is give Mathew love."

Freddy had begun the evening milking. He'd spoken with the auctioneers and provisionally booked the 28th of May to sell the live and dead farm stock. His work was automated now, he denied himself those periods of deep thought when in the past he'd planned, dreamed of the future for himself and his family. Francis carried their unborn child, he couldn't afford to dwell on his disappointment and in so doing bring melancholy to her days.

He'd told Annie he would begin again, the residue of money he'd be paid by the council should be eighty pounds and the auction, while impossible to be entirely accurate, should bring in the region of one hundred and forty pounds, minus commission. He had a small running balance in his account at Barclays, before leaving he would meet with Rothero and request that his account be transferred to their branch at Skegness.

A tap came at the cows house door, Freddy was surprised to see Toby Hillier. "Don't let me hinder you, I can talk while you milk, I know cows are routine creatures."

"What brings you here Toby?" Asked a curious Freddy, he'd not seen Maggie's husband since George's wedding, and other than family gatherings for Christmas and birthdays, seldom did the two ever meet.

"Use what I'm about to tell you if you want to Freddy, I've had enough of it all, the money I take home to Maggie I need to know as honest, well earned. I can't satisfy my mind anymore. Three years ago the council paid for colliery land almost double per acre what they are paying you for Bobbers Mill. Can I ask what name the official gave the day he handed you notice?"

"Bradshaw, he said his name was Bradshaw, is he significant?" Asked Freddy.

"Anthony Bradshaw is married to Basil Stanford's eldest daughter, he has three, there's another between her and Caroline. The colliery land was bought from Stanford. Bradshaw is perhaps significant in another way, he's the youngest brother of Cynthia Woolascroft. I doubt many people are aware of that, the family are not originally from these parts, I believe Fred Woolascroft met his wife whilst working in Hull."

Freddy paused from milking. "If I use any of this, your work would end Toby, they'd guess it was you who told me."

"To hell with them Freddy. I understand Isaac Jacobson is looking for someone, since Edwin Garbett died he's been struggling along on his own but he can't cope anymore. Whilst I'm sure it will grieve him to pay out wages again, he hasn't any choice. Maggie will simply accept that I seek change, I shan't say more than that, it is kindest not to trouble her head with such things. I've written a letter giving them the required notice and I shall hand it in tomorrow. I'm sorry Freddy I wish I could change things."

Freddy rubbed his hand over the cow's rump, as if acknowledging her effort. "I owe it to Francis, all the things I promised that now seem so far away. I even owe it to these animals, they've provided me with a good living Toby. Thank-you for making me aware, I know what it's cost you." He shook Toby Hillier's hand, then laughed. Sorry Toby, I'm so used to the smell of the cows on my hands, I gave no thought to covering you with it."

"It's an honest smell Freddy, there's nothing offensive about it, nothing at all offensive."

Freddy's mind had turned the information over and over, it lay heavily and he resolved not to burden Francis with it. However it granted him some leverage, it was too late to reverse his own situation but he could yet help secure a just outcome for Arthur and Dorothy Cropley.

The next morning, after the yard work was done, Freddy casually mentioned to Francis his need to go into town. Busy with the laundry she didn't question why.

Two women were inside the shop, Freddy waited patiently outside until both had left before entering. Closing the door behind him he released the catch to lock it.

"Mr.Cheetham," he said, "I hoped I might catch you in the shop, are you serving on your own today?"

Robert Cheetham looked puzzled. "Yes, for a while, Gordon's out delivering, why do you ask?"

"I have something to say to you that I prefer to say in private. It will take but a minute or two, any customer I'm sure will be patient for a little while, seeing you inside they'd know you'd open the door to them eventually. What butcher ever turns away trade?" Freddy paused, thinking carefully. "I've always been mild mannered in the past, I see that now, but there are times when a man needs to stand up for what's right, if only to shame that which is wrong. I'm leaving Nottingham and do you know, I'm glad. I no longer wish to abide in a place where those who take it upon themselves to govern its citizens turn a blind eye to wrong. I know for a fact Mr.Cheetham that Woolascrofts were preparing a tender for the contract to develop Bobbers Mill, before last Christmas, yet I only learned of the council's intention to buy the land at the end of January. It wasn't common knowledge until February. The official who came to my door that day gave his name as Bradshaw, from the legal department. You and I are both aware that it's no coincidence that Anthony Bradshaw is Fred Woolascroft's brother in law and how convenient that who should he be married to but Basil Stanford's daughter. I am reliably informed Mr.Mayor, that three years ago the council bought up colliery land, that land was then owned by Basil Stanford and the local authority paid him per acre, almost double the rate they are paying me for Bobbers Mill.

Arthur Cropley shall receive for the sale of his title, the current market value, which allowing for these recessionary times, is two hundred and thirty pounds. If he does not receive that sum, I shall go to The Evening Post and open up the biggest can of worms imaginable. I shall stir up the mightiest, foulest stench, and you can be sure of that. The council wouldn't want a bad smell would it Mr.Cheetham. Just as the lids on the vats at your slaughter yard must always be tight shut, thoroughly sealed, everything contained, so must affairs of the council be! One day Mr.Mayor, one day the good Lord tells us, the meek shall inherit the earth. Remember that when next you gather in the council chamber, as I understand, every meeting there over which you preside, begins with a prayer. Two hundred and thirty pounds to Arthur Cropley or the lids come off."

Freddy gave the Mayor long enough to respond but Cheetham said nothing, he looked afraid and that fear bound his tongue. Freddy took two half crowns from his pocket and placed them on the counter.

"I'll take five bob's worth of best beef if you please." Cheetham wrapped the joint and handed it to Freddy. "Thank-you," said Freddy, "a fair exchange."

This place was becoming familiar, again Freddy sat outside James Rothero's office. Unlike the last time he could hear voices, faint, impossible to recognise but they confirmed a client was with Rothero. Freddy was anxious to do the necessary business and leave, hopefully whomever it was would soon appear at the door and clear the way for him to request Rothero arrange the transfer of his account to the branch at Skegness. Contracts were due to be exchanged and signed on June 6th. Arthur Cropley had been offered two hundred and thirty pounds for his one third share of Bobbers Mill and would sign on the same day.

The door catch rattled, Rothero shook the hand of the departing client.

"Good day Mr.Smithfield, I shall be in touch." Then on seeing Freddy, "Ah, come in Mr.Eddowes, you and your wife are well I trust."

Freddy and Andrew Smithfield briefly exchanged glances, then Freddy found himself sitting before Rothero, the seat of the chair still warm from the previous occupant.

Outside in the street, Smithfield waited, it could surely be none other than William's brother Freddy. He'd lost count of the number of times he'd been about to drive to Bobbers Mill, to speak with Freddy, to explain that he'd had no knowledge of Freddy's connection with the land there, but fearing that it might make matters worse, he'd stayed away. A feeble apology, an attempt at mitigating his own involvement, how pathetic it would seem to this young man whose efforts had been completely destroyed by the council's plans, by Smithfield's own call for more housing. He could not walk away today, not having seen Freddy, having passed inches from him by Rothero's office door. After twenty minutes or so Freddy appeared on the pavement, Smithfield approached him at once.

"It is Freddy, Freddy Eddowes isn't it?"

"That's right Mr.Smithfield, William's younger brother who likes to waste his time working on 'the land'." Freddy put emphasis on the last two words, applying William's sarcastic tone as he uttered them. Smithfield offered his hand.
"You called for more housing councillor," said Freddy, "I can't condemn you for that, I've see how some folk have to live, in this day and age it's a disgrace. But you'll pardon my caution, I would willingly shake the hand of any decent man, however, I don't know you Mr.Smithfield. Something inside me wants to believe you are a decent man, but today I must decline the courtesy." Freddy nodded his head to acknowledge Smithfield's approach, then turned to walk away.

Smithfield stood at the spot for several seconds, as if willing Freddy Eddowes to have a change of heart. For the young man to return, if only to challenge his integrity. Not until Freddy was out of sight did Andrew Smithfield urge his feet to take him from the moment, from this feeling of desolation. Mrs.Charles Eddowes could never more have regard for him. All that he'd won through his efforts with William, he'd now lost through Freddy. It was as painful to him as bereavement,

Annie Eddowes would consider him less than a friend. She was gone, Annie was surely gone.

CHAPTER THIRTEEN

Alice fingered the locket, since their wedding night when George had given her the small burgundy box and she had first put the love token around his neck 'My Alice', then the other 'Your George', about herself, so often in a quiet moment alone, she had lifted the fine gold chain from beneath her blouse and turned her half of the heart between her fingers.

George had a gentleness in his nature, a simple, contented outlook on the world, which filled Alice with a complete sense of security.

When her mother died Alice was too young to fully understand the circumstances. She remembered the doctor calling at the house a number of times but on those occasions she would be sent next door to Mrs.Phillpot who seemed always to be mangling. 'Turn the handle deary, mind you keep your fingers out o' the cogs'. Alice had heard those same words each time she'd been dispatched to the kindly neighbour and only when Mrs.Phillpot had one day thrust her own fingers into a pot of thick, yellow lubricating grease and applied it to the wheels on the side of the mangle declaring 'The only time fingers need go near the cogs , is when they need a bit o' greasin',' did Alice have any notion of what a 'cog' actually was. The afternoon Mrs.Phillpot had caught hold Alice's hand, looking at her with tears in her eyes, saying over and over, God help us, God help us', and led her back home, Alice would never forget. Her father sat at the end of the living room table, his head bowed over a sheet of paper. When he'd raised his face to look at her, even though she was a mere child with no experience of grief, instinctively Alice knew her mother was dead. He'd lifted her on to his knee and rested his head on hers, she could recall the strange sensation of moisture from his tears being spread through her hair, as he gently moved his chin from side to side, the stubble from days of self neglect prickling her scalp. He'd whispered a name, not Alice but Candace, again and again he'd whispered her mam's name.

Candace May Pearson was laid to rest in Witford Hill Cemetery, Alice was distanced from the proceedings, spared the sorrow, but as she'd turned the handle of the mangle she'd felt afraid. Not until Alice reached the age of twelve was she considered old enough to cope with death. Her grandmother had come to the house, taken Alice's best camel coat from the hallstand, held it out whilst Alice put her arms down the sleeves, turned her round to fasten the buttons as though she were still an infant, and said, 'We're goin' to visit your mam'.

Grandma carried a bunch of flowers. The rows and rows of headstones and memorials, rather than alarm Alice, instead intrigued her. They walked for several minutes, grandma leading Alice by the hand, not so much to guide her Alice sensed, but more to ensure a steady progress. It was not every day that a twelve year old girl walked between marble angels and stone crosses inscribed with lines of most morbid verse, to an enquiring mind they warranted closer study. Grandma found them much less engaging. They'd reached the graveside, put the flowers in a vase with nothing more than the rainwater, already collected by the dark green urn, which rested on a bed of curious small stones that reminded Alice of Mrs.Phillpot's soda crystals. Grandma stood without speaking for a minute or more, Alice too, had observed what appeared to be a ritual for the dead. Then grandma broke the silence, addressing not Alice but someone under the ground, beneath the soda crystals. 'Tell your dad I'm gettin' a gas stove'. As Alice grew older and questioned more, she'd wished that her grandma's words might have been. 'Give your dad my love'. Now married to George, Alice was sure beyond all doubt that whatever happened in the years to come, only messages of love would ever pass between them. Alice let the locket slip back beneath her blouse, took her coat from the hook and left the house to go to her dad's.

Every Monday and Thursday she went back to the small house where she'd grown up. Although Fred Pearson had done his best to give his daughter a natural childhood, the absence of a mother within the home inevitably led to young Alice growing up quickly. When only in her early teens she'd been more than capable of keeping house for her father and herself, much to the relief of her aunt, the only relative dwelling reasonably close by, whom while offering help, ever did so with a lack of real intent. The compassionate Mrs.Phillpot from next door, popped in between her frequent sessions of mangling to impart advice, to oversee the process of meal making and perhaps most importantly of all, to plant a kiss on Alice's forehead with the words, 'that's right deary, you'll make somebody a grand little wife'.

Alice was nineteen when Mrs.Phillpot passed away one night, in her sleep. Sometimes in the days immediately afterwards, Alice imagined she could hear the mangle turning in the yard next door and the voice of her old friend. 'Mind you keep your fingers out o' the cogs deary'. Alice had been so young when her mother died and so removed from her mam's bedside through her dad's belief that a child should not be aware of sickness and death, that her intense feeling of grief at losing Mrs.Phillpot caused her to harbour guilt, she hurt inside and the hurt felt to be greater than any she could recall from that time, years ago when her own mother died. Alice's only grandma lived in Buxton, while Derbyshire was not beyond sensible reach, it was a distance too far to be undertaken often. Fred Pearson worked at the tannery, it was a hard job and at a day's end he sought only rest, at home with his daughter. His parents were dead, his father through an accident at the pit and his mother from influenza.

Grandma Elliot was an intimidating figure, tall and full chested with a head of hair that grew thick and wiry even into old age, she wore it pinned back harshly at the sides with long Kirby grips but its robust nature caused it to bush out above the neckline of her clothes, like the cape of feathers on a cockerel. Just above the bridge of her nose she had a large, deep pink mole from which grew one whisker. In latter years when Alice went with her dad to Buxton, she was given the task of snipping the length of whisker from the mole with a pair of baby's nail scissors. They fascinated Alice, the blades formed a beak, the shaft a body, and the handles the wings of a stork, that long legged bird portrayed in books as being the carrier of newborn babies. Those same scissors now lay in a box of trinkets, given to Alice by her dad, following the emptying of grandma's house after her death.

Coming towards her along Connaught Street was a familiar figure. "Hello Mrs.Boucher and how are you today?"

The tone of his voice was mischievous. Alice laughed, she liked her cousin Kenneth, he was not a bit like his mother, aunt Freda, she was so very sober and rarely showed affection. Alice supposed Kenneth favoured his father. Sadly uncle Eddie had been killed at Ypres and Alice had only a vague memory of him. Kenneth was four years older than herself but his personality was youthful and his sense of humour had brought a welcome interlude of cheer to some of the darker times in Alice's life.

"I'm well thank-you, very well, made all the better for seeing you." Alice smiled warmly. "Where is Nottingham's intrepid reporter off to today, what revelations are you about to launch on the unsuspecting readership?"

"Every week when I'm handed the list I hope to find some novel misdemeanour, an offence inspired by ingenuity or eccentricity but perpetrated by a champion of the people. Just as always the list is routine, no modern day Robin Hood. Before the magistrates today are , three drunk and disorderly, two cases of poaching, a motoring offence and old Ted Shipside's been accosting folk at the embankment again, wearing only his long johns and professing to be John the Baptist. Apparently this time, two people visiting from the Antipodes were up to their ankles on the bottom step before Sergeant Beasley arrived on the scene. He explained Ted's senility and led the poor old sod away. Now Ted's little aberrations have reached the wider world he'll probably be committed to the asylum, a shame I call it."

"I would have thought that qualified as an offence inspired by eccentricity," said Alice.

"Oh yes it does, but it occurs so frequently it's no longer newsworthy and so the court column will be as predictable as ever. The police have had no luck in catching the cat burglar, as they call him, I purposefully go out late at night sometimes, what a scoop that would be if I could spot him, alert the police and be at the scene to report events."

Alice chuckled. "I think I'd rather enter the Trent with John the Baptist than I'd wait at the foot of a drainpipe to apprehend a thief. Poor Mr.Shipside, he wouldn't hurt a fly. Anyway I must get on, I don't want to be late home from dad's, I always make George a suet pudding for his tea on a Monday."

Kenneth kissed her cheek. "Give George my best, tell him I shall be in The Nelson for an hour tonight if he feels like a pint, Wrenshaw's have launched a new ale, you never know, it might lead to something newsworthy."

"You are incorrigible," declared Alice with a tut-tut of fake reprimand. With a wave of his hand and a roguish grin, Kenneth was gone and Alice hurried along.

On leaving school, cousin Kenneth had begun work as a general dogsbody at the newspaper office. His outgoing personality and good command of English had impressed the bosses and they'd offered him the chance to report the Magistrates Court Sessions. He'd comfortably met the requirement, continuing to write the column each week.

The week before Alice and George were to be married, an announcement appeared in The Post. It was Kenneth's doing, his gesture of affection. Alice had carefully cut the entry from the page and placed it in the trinket box for safekeeping. Just as she fingered the locket about her neck, so too did she regularly unfold the small piece of newspaper and read the words upon it.

Alice stopped by the entry to take the key of the back door from her bag, a sudden "Hello", made her jump. Since Mrs.Phillpot's death, the property next door had been occupied by a young couple with three children, the father now stood at the threshold of the entry, holding the hand of his youngest, a girl.

"Tell Alice it's your birthday and we're goin' to Lovatt's to buy an iced bun." The child was shy and buried her face in her dad's trousers.

"How old are you today Millie?" Asked Alice, "let me guess, are you four?" Her dad laughed and the little girl wriggled even closer to him.

"The cat's got her tongue today Alice. You won't need your key, your dad's at home, I spoke with him not many minutes ago. Come on then Millie, let's fetch that bun."

Alice felt anxious, she hurried across the yard, calling 'Dad' before she'd scarcely entered the scullery.

"It's alright love, I'm not poorly or owt like that, the kettles on I thought you'd be here soon, we'll have a cuppa and I'll tell you all about it."

"What will you do Dad, you've been at the tannery for years."

"It's not just me, Sid Strickland's got the push an'all. We're the two oldest, chances are we'd slowed up a bit but didn't realise it. Boss said he'd got to cut back on somethin', what else could he cut back but his wage bill. It's happenin' everywhere, the young ens'll have to work harder an' faster an' we older men must manage best way we can. Thank God you have your George, from what I hear Raleigh are bearin' up, with a bit o' luck, the men naturally finishin' through age anyway should protect the jobs o' the young ones. I've only meself to bother about an' I reckon Fred Pearson won't be idle for long. I shall go to the labour exchange later, at dinnertime when it's likely to be quiet. Havin' to stand in a queue, listenin' to all the aggravation don't suit me, I'd rather chew on the same crust for days than get drawn into one o' then rowdy episodes. I know you'll want to change me bed but there's no need for you to do anythin' else, I've already put the duster round and I've been over the floors with the mop. I'll walk with you to the end of Connaught Street in a bit. I can put me own meal on, shan't have anythin' else to do this afternoon shall I. They aren't likely to find me work that quick."

They sat at the table dipping gingernuts into their tea, the aging oil cloth had worn so thin on one side that Alice had turned it round in an attempt to prolong its life.

"Have another biscuit love, you need to keep your strength up, what with your own house an' husband to do for an' your old dad an'all, you allus look so pale." He realised the irony of his words and his expression changed instantly. Candace had faded in front of him despite every effort to restore her strength. "You are eating enough aren't you Alice?" He noticed her surprise at his tone and feeling guilty gave her a fond kiss, squeezed her hand and said, "Your dad's a silly old fool, take no notice love."

Alice changed the bedding and parcelled it up to take home with her. Downstairs Fred washed up the cups and forced himself to sing a cheerful song loud

231

enough for his daughter to hear. The day was pleasantly warm and as they walked along Connaught Street, the distraction of a child playing whip and top lightened the mood. A lady approaching, walking an unusual dog, looked mortally embarrassed when the perfectly coiffured creature insisted on squatting in their path. Fred smiled, inwardly thinking such a refined deposit should be reserved for only the very finest kid leather.

As they neared The Nelson, agitated voices could be heard. They reached the spot on the other side of the street where it was possible to see inside the open pub door. A group of men appeared to be in deep debate.

"Let's hurry along Alice, the more that are gathered in there, the less will be waitin' at the exchange." Fred Pearson shied away from trouble and the tone of voice inside the pub suggested unrest.

They parted company at the end of the street, Alice taking the parcel of laundry from her dad. She turned to wave back but he was already several yards away and intent on securing work of any honest discription before the crippling sense of defeat he'd witnessed in others, reduced his own mind to that treacherous mire, so soft and malleable it absorbed influences of bad as readily as it received notions of good.

He could remember clearly an alarming scene, which had unfolded before his eyes when only a lad of ten. He'd been walking a short distance behind a lean, shabbily dressed man who in turn was walking behind another, but of tidy appearance. The man at the front walked with two sticks, his progress was slow and his gait confirmed a stiffness of his legs, a rigidity of his ankles. Fred had seen this man fall to the ground, when from behind, the other man had grabbed the sticks hurling them over the railings, then with both hands delved into the pockets of the helpless individual at his mercy, before running away with whatever his villainous desperation had driven him to steal. The young Fred had felt frightened by what he'd witnessed but instinctively went to the aid of the victim on the ground. Both lower legs of this man were encased in heavy metal callipers that fitted to the bottoms of his boots. Fred had never before seen such a thing, but it was the face, not an old face but that of a young man, despair overwhelmed the features of a man no more than twenty. Fred had somehow found the strength to help him stand, where he could then hold on to the railings. Running to the end of the wall, Fred managed with the aid of a tree branch to carefully climb over the railings and gather the walking sticks from where they had landed on some grass. He'd passed them back one at a time, to the unfortunate young man, still clutching the wrought iron, then asked. 'Are you alright, shall I fetch a policeman'?

It was the young man's answer that Fred could never forget. 'Not even a policeman could free my legs of these shackles or that man's mind of his crippling poverty, we are both defeated'.

There was no one waiting outside the exchange and just two men at the counter within. Fred couldn't help overhearing the conversation between them and the clerk. The groundwork was to begin at Bobbers Mill, while all places requiring a trade were met through Woolascroft's existing workforce, temporary labour, shovelling and barrowing was on offer to a number of physically strong men for a period of several weeks. The pay was minimal and the hours long but no other work was currently available. The two men made their opinions known forcefully, only when the long suffering clerk said, "Do yer want the bloody work or not?" Did they grudgingly take the sheet of paper from his hand and leave, making a point of pausing in the doorway to propel their spit into the gutter.

It was Fred's turn. The clerk peered over his spectacles.

"Name", he said.

"Frederick John Pearson."

"Date of birth."

"March the seventeenth 1879."

"Previous experience?"

"I've been working at the tannery for the past twenty six years, a man can't survive that without puttin' a might o' strength in his arms an' perseverance in his head. The smell alone could drive any faint hearted man straight back out through the gates. I'll take one o' them places at Bobbers Mill if you please, a shovel'd be a good substitute for the paddle I've been stirring tanks o' dogs' mess with all these years."

It was a truth few people would want to believe but a vital element of the tanning process did indeed involve the use of dog excrement. Bernard Higgins, one of Fred's workmates, had once remarked, 'London's streets are supposed to be paved wi' gold, yer can't make boots out o' gold so it's as well Nottingham's are paved wi' dog shit'.

The clerk looked at Fred with disbelief. "Is that true they use dog mess."

"Gospel," said Fred, "you can take my word for it. Folk have been tryin' not to tread in the stuff an' all same time they've got it on their feet anyroad."

The clerk thought for a moment, "So it has a value then, the dog mess. Does the tannery have its own collectors or does it buy it off anybody?"

It was easy to see which way the man's mind was heading and Fred felt like a bit of harmless fun. "In your position of trust I'm sure you'll understand the need of confidentiality. Now have you ever had on your list of availability , the job of dog excrement collector?" Asked Fred.

"No I haven't, I'd remember if I had."

"Well that should tell you somethin'. Can you imagine the competition to bag up the most, folk'd be fightin' over it an' the potential to dictate an ever increasing cost of that vital raw material would surely lead to anythin' made o' leather doublin' in price overnight." Fred tapped the side of his nose with his finger. "It has to be 'hush hush', protected, like a mineral right or medicinal water, its commercial licence. Excretion with discretion, that's how the tannery refers to it."

"You learn something every day," said the gullible clerk. He handed a sheet of paper to Fred. "Present this with yourself next Monday mornin', 7o/clock start. If you're answerable to the courts then you're obliged to declare the nature of the offence. Consider yourself lucky, the next man to come through that door I can't offer anything to, not even hope.

Fred thanked him, folded the paper and put it in his pocket. As he walked away he felt relieved that his nature kept him from those gatherings such as he and

Alice had observed to be taking place in The Nelson. His innocent mischief had raised his spirits and next Monday morning held a purpose. Things could be worse, much worse, Fred Pearson was a long way from defeat.

The arrival in the early hours of June 30th of a healthy baby girl, at the cottage in Skendleby filled the family with delight and immense relief. Annie especially had been worried, leaving Bobbers Mill by lorry to travel to Lincolnshire only three weeks before the baby was due Annie had felt was unfair on Francis. However, when she'd voiced her concerns it was Francis who'd replied firmly. 'Our baby will wait for its new home and we shall make it a good home'.

Freddy and David Ripley had promised Annie that they would take the greatest care of Francis and travel at only a sensible and appropriate speed, given her condition. In the event, contented Miss Faith Eddowes proved to be in no hurry to enter the world, going over time by several days and weighing eight pounds ten ounces on arrival.

Mrs.Ripley had understandably gone at once to visit and on her return, called at Gregory Street to bring news of the situation at Skendleby. The baby was a joy, Francis was well, Freddy was proud and busy and their dwelling was charming in a Lincolnshire sort of way!

Annie had given Charles every opportunity, she would manage quite well enough if he chose to travel alone during the week but if he preferred then Hilda or John would go with him at a weekend, either way, she would cope with the shop in his absence. Annie acknowledged it was not possible for Charles and herself to be away at the same time. Hilda was too young to be left with the responsibility and whilst John finished work at midday on a Saturday, giving him a mainly free weekend, to ask for any time off in the week, other than in an emergency could prove unwise, jobs were precious, his work must take priority.

Charles was adamant, he would rather visit Skendleby later when the child had grown a little and so it was agreed that this Saturday July 12th, Annie and Hilda would catch the 12-20 train, that way the busy morning period would be covered before they needed to leave for the station and John would be home to help with the Saturday afternoon and Sunday morning trade. The return train would bring Annie and Hilda back at 7-30 on Sunday evening.

Annie weighed up a pound of dark, muskavado sugar and placed it in a box behind the counter. She looked again at the list, just one more item, eight ounces of crystallized ginger then Florence Stanford's order would be complete. Rex Madden often collected it around three in the afternoon, seldom did he make conversation and his duty was normally completed in no more than a minute or two with a mere nod of the head. The previous week Annie had been surprised when, about to give him the change he'd enquired after Freddy, asking if he'd found accommodation and work. She'd been so taken aback that after he left, she'd felt anxious, for surely her surprise would have been obvious to him, Annie could hear aunt Bella's disapproval, her stern rebuke at Annie's lack of politeness. She'd somewhat awkwardly explained the connection with Harold at Huttoft, the small rented cottage and the birth of the baby, but she'd been aware of the strain in her voice and could find no real cause of it. Rex Madden's response had been equally curious, a timid smile, a quietly spoken, 'that's good', and a marked trembling of his hand as he took the few coins of change. Annie would likely have pondered longer upon it, but for Mrs.Pagett's urgent need of a quarter of Ceylon tea and Garibaldi biscuits, to take to women's fellowship. Mrs.Pagett had entered as Rex Madden left and the good lady's enthusiastic mix of piety and domestic humdrum was enough to temporarily disengage even Annie's concentration. Not until preparing Florence Stanford's order today did her thoughts return to Rex Madden's uncustomary approach the last time.

The shop had been busy, the warm weather necessitated frequent custom to purchase the more perishable items. Some of the women were already planning that summer ritual of shopping, one item at a time through the continual toing and froing of children with no school to occupy them, getting them out from underfoot in the process. For Annie, serving in the shop, it meant a constant clanging of the doorbell. Last summer she'd ventured to prop the door open, to relieve her aching head, but an inquisitive Bull Terrier had nipped inside, cocked its leg up a sack of potatoes and helped itself to a copy of 'The Manchester Guardian' from the bottom of the paper rack on its way out. The newspaper Annie could overlook but having to transfer a half hundredweight of King Edwards from the piddly hessian to a sweeter smelling sack before the regal potatoes became contaminated proved tiresome.

When to Edna, Annie had voiced her observations on the matter, the response had been truly enlightening. 'Aunt Win 'ad a dog, years ago, the damn thing used to cock its leg over everythin'. She got that mad, it drove 'er to distraction, until one day she 'ad a brainwave. She bound its two back legs together wi' strong knicker elastic. Now you'd think it could 'ave chewed through that wi' no bother but the more the poor bugger tried, the more its teeth got caught up in the rubber, them long teeth in the front wer' the problem. Aunt Win reckoned that by the time it freed itself, its bladder must 'ave been fit to burst, it shot out through the back door an' didn't come back in for days. It worked anyroad, the dog never piddled indoors again but it must 'ave upset its nerves or summat, 'cause it took to chewin' a table leg, only the one an' aunt Win didn't seem to mind that, she just 'ad to be careful o' gettin' splinters when she wer' dustin'.'

Annie looked at the clock, ten past four, Hilda was usually home by five. They had their overnight bag to pack but Hilda would make sure that everything was ready long before they were due to leave. She was so looking forward to the train journey, to being with the family, not only Freddy's but Ivy's too. Not since the wedding in May last year had they seen 'the Lincolnshire Boucher', as George now referred to cousin Harold. Ivy and family had been unable to travel to Nottingham for George's wedding due to circumstances unforeseen. One of the men working the farm at Huttoft had been rushed to hospital with a burst appendix and Harold couldn't get time off as a result. Molly had already agreed to be bridesmaid at her friend's wedding on the same day, Reggie had been commissioned to make and erect a large stained glass panel in the lobby of The Four Winds Hotel at Cleethorpes, which had to be completed before the end of April and Ivy had admitted to being nervous at travelling alone following an incident on Skegness railway station, when a woman was robbed of her handbag. It was John's rendition of 'The Lincolnshire Poacher' during his happy episodes with the harmonica that inspired George's mischief. Annie knew that once the title was aired, cousin Harold would forever be referred to as such.

The afternoon continued with a steady flow of customers. Charles appeared at the same time as Hilda.

"Look Mam, isn't it lovely?" Hilda took from her bag a baby gown, soft winceyette, embroidered across the front panel in pink rabbits.

"Francis will love it Hilda," said Annie, "Alice popped in this morning with a present for Faith, I haven't had a peep yet, I thought I'd wait until you came home."

Charles 'huffed', as though the topic of conversation vexed him. Before his mood had chance to dull Hilda's eagerness, Annie suggested a cup of tea and a slice of Battenburg cake, now too dry to sell, would be welcome and she asked Hilda to put the kettle on. She turned to Charles, he'd pulled out the drawer of the till to see how busy she'd been. Annie was used to his unsubtle way of checking on her, it no longer irritated or even annoyed.

"Now you're here I shall make a start on the meal," said Annie. "I've never known Mr.Madden to be this late, it does seem unusual but he's not yet called to collect Mrs.Stanford's order so I can only imagine something has occurred to delay him."

"I met Bill Rashleigh earlier, he was talking about a meeting to be held at the pit. He may not work there anymore but he seems to be in the know. Apparently Stanford is to be at Birchdale when the men come off day shift and the others clock on for the night, some sort of negotiation according to Rashleigh. It would explain why Madden hasn't been, he drives Stanford everywhere, besides 'no show without punch' is there?"

"Oh dear," said Annie. "Mr.Stanford isn't known for his willingness to negotiate, I always worry for Gertie at times like this. Steve is a good man, over the years he's championed the miners' cause firmly but without inciting violence. I once heard someone remark that Steve Wainwright could articulate pain in such a way, that even those with no affliction felt a cramp. But he's not a young man, you may be a couple of years his senior but that's all."

"And I don't articulate very much of anything, is that what your implying, you should have married a man with a more able mouthpiece."

"That's not what I meant at all. Why don't you go with Hilda tomorrow, the change would do you good, I can go another time. Freddy would be proud to show you your granddaughter."

Charles stared back at Annie with cold eyes. "The work is to begin at Bobbers Mill next week. Articulate that to Freddy."

The day shift had come up but there'd been no exodus of men through the gates, instead they'd congregated in the yard with those due to commence the night shift. Over the past few weeks, Steve Wainwright and Henry Wicks had taken every opportunity to speak with each man, surface worker, face worker and foreman alike. Not with the intention of bringing unrest, but to discuss and deliberate on this evenings action, to impress upon every individual the importance of a united but respectable front. To achieve total agreement, unanimous accord for their plan. Steve had won their support, on what to him was a crucial element of negotiation. He would choose his words carefully when addressing Stanford, he'd speak for them, all of them the only way he knew how, boldly but not wildly, with tact, with craft. If his attempt failed there would be no sounds of contempt towards Stanford, nor ebullient cries of triumph if he succeeded. Like any other business deal it would be done in the appropriate manner. Miners were men of industry, they may not push the pen across the balance sheet but it was them who created the figures, without them the collieries would have nothing to balance.

Wicks had defied Stanford's order to yet again cut pay, it was inevitable that the situation would come to a head but Wicks had stood his ground and challenged Basil Stanford to meet with the workforce, his employees, to speak to them. In the past it was something Stanford had never done, he considered them so easily dismissed but not once had Henry Wicks known the 'mighty Stanford' to look his workforce in the eye.

Steve's conviction that purposeful dialogue carried greater weight than disorganised protest had been accepted by the men, even those with vitriolic tongues, all he could now do was trust in his own belief and their assurances of a maintained calm.

Stanford had arrived, clearly feeling beleaguered, for Rex Madden stood at his side, rather than sitting in the car as was usually the case. By now the night shift should be below ground but the winches stood idle. A sea of faces, close on two hundred and fifty, looking for all the world like a windswept mass of water, dark and deep where stood the coal black men just off day shift, but white, like breaking surface swell where those faces, as yet ungrubbied, mingled amongst the rest.

Henry Wicks stood to one side, Steve Wainwright, a pace in front of the gathering and the foremen, at intervals along the first row of men. A distance of no more than five yards separated them and Stanford and him looking down at his feet, twitchy and nervous.

Steve spoke. "Two and a half years Mr.Stanford, it's been two and a half years since we asked you for an answer. In all that time you've done nothin' but squeeze more an' more breath from our bodies.
We can't take any cut in pay, 'can't' Mr.Stanford not won't. We have wives and children, we'd be less than men if we didn't stand up for them. You have a family too an' I'm tellin' you, that down there." Steve pointed to the ground. "Down there is coal, rich seams of that black fortune, more than enough to keep you, your family an' your bank account well nourished far beyond your lifetime. But that's the crux of it, down there, it's deep down below Mr.Stanford an' to retrieve it you need lungs of steel an' a back that can stand the pain of twisted sinews, so taut, that every single movement stabs like a knife. It can take a man to the edge of endurance. Down below us lies your bounty, black gold I've heard some call it, but there is no gold, yet sometimes, when the coal falls at our feet, a piece will split, clean as a whistle, it'll catch the light from the lamps and glint, just for a second. If you didn't know, it would

240

be easy to think of gold, but we do know, we spend our days in that other world. When we see that glint, we shiver, the Devil's eye, that's what we call it. Up there," Steve pointed to the sky, "up there Mr.Stanford is God in his Heaven. A man rises to Heaven. Down below is Hell and The Devil. A man sinks into Hell. When we see that glint, that flash in the blackness, down there amidst the chokin' dust an' noise, we glimpse the Devil's beady eye, like he was watchin', waitin', tormentin', an' every strike o' the pick, each thrust o' the drill, takes us closer to him, fills our minds with visions of destroyin' our own salvation an' sinkin' into eternal Hellfire. We need your answer now Mr.Stanford, we've waited long enough. Tell these men that their pay will not be cut. That conditions of safety will not be compromised. Until you do, not a man will go down, not tonight, nor tomorrow. Tell them what they need to hear an' they'll fetch up that fortune, your fortune Mr.Stanford, they'll do that for you but you must acknowledge your need of them, because you do need them. Manager, foreman, men on the surface, at the coalface, without them that black gold stays with The Devil."

Stanford's chest expanded by several inches, looking across the tops of the men to the pithead beyond, as though addressing those cold steel structures that towered in importance over the mere flesh and bone so easily replaced that stood in their shadows. He bellowed like a madman.

"Mr.Madden shall fetch the police, if your not going to work then the law can escort you off my premises." Madden looked tense but remained on the spot.

Steve Wainwright responded. "If you want us gone Mr.Stanford then there's no need to waste police time, we'll walk away, but every man will walk, all that will remain is you and Mr.Madden, and what could he tell the police was our offence. Not a single voice has been raised in anger, nor a fist in aggression. No one is standin' in your way, if you want to go down in the cage Mr.Stanford, there isn't a man here would present any obstacle. The police are not empowered to force the men to work their shift, only to act where a law has been broken, no one here has broken any law, neither do they intend to. Yes, you can order us all off and send word to the labour exchange, 250 men wanted at the mine. But those men are the same as us, they need to eat, to pay rent, and support their families. How long do you suppose it would be before they all stood facing you just as we do now? Are you going to send every man away until none are left and then what would you do, call for the women? That coal won't grow, it won't sprout up through the ground like that cussed blade o' grass, which pushes its way through the cobbles of the backyard. It's dead, it lies there in black layers between the rock, waitin' to be gouged out. Are you goin' to do it Mr.Stanford, I mean no disrespect of you or Mr.Madden, but that mean, unyieldin' rock face would defy the both of you. An answer, the right answer will send the men with clean faces to their work an' we black faced buggers to our homes."

Steve Wainwright stood, looking directly at Basil Stanford. He awaited a reply. Henry Wicks walked across to Stanford and in a low voice said.

"For God's sake man, look at them. It's as much an insult to them as the pay, the way you cast your eyes to your feet, you look feeble, be a man Stanford, look them in the eye and tell them what they need to hear."

Rex Madden did show his eyes and they revealed much to Henry Wicks. What did Stanford have on the poor devil. All the miners felt used by Stanford, owned like chattels, but Madden, 'Stanford's man'. Surely to carry that title must be the least desirable of all.

"The pay will stay the same." Stanford spoke with venom in his voice, expecting to have to endure a roar of jubilant triumph from the throng. Not a sound, total calm, only Steve Wainwright spoke.

"It's customary for gentlemen to shake hands on an agreement. He extended his hand to Stanford."

"You've got your answer and witnesses to it, what more do you want?" He turned to walk away, muttering under his breath.

As Rex Madden was about to follow he caught the gaze of Henry Wicks. The smile that came so readily to Wicks, in that instant, passed to Madden, and was acknowledged.

Hilda stretched up to the rack above their heads to stow their bag, they'd expected the train to be very busy but perhaps a greater number had travelled on the earlier service, to make the most of the weekend. For a few minutes they were on their own in the compartment, then a woman and a girl of about eight joined them. Annie smiled but the woman seemed not to notice.

"Sit down there an' behave yerself or I'll tell the porter to put you in the guards van wi' 'is big dog as eats little children that don't keep quiet."

Hilda glanced at Annie then ventured to say, "Hello" to the child, who responded with a sigh and an unexpected declaration.

"I don't wet the bed anymore 'cause I'm a big girl."

The woman presumably her mother, took a small bag of sweets from her pocket, thrust a toffee into the child's mouth, with the caution. "Chew it properly or you'll choke to death."

The girl wore a white ribbon tied in a bow on top of her head, at either side her hair fell in ringlets. Her frock was floral patterned and over the top, a pink knitted bolero. White socks, not quite a pair, one having a lacy top the other plain and plimsolls, recently whitened with Blanco, those telltale streaks of grey peeping through.

"It's a nice day for the seaside, are you going to Skegness, that's where we're going," said Annie.

The woman sniffed, "Spalding, to me dad's, 'e's got emphysema." Her answer was short and in a curious way it felt to be final. At least Annie had tried to make conversation, if the woman sought quietness then Annie would respect her wish. Several minutes passed.

"When are we goin' Mam?" The little girl let out a long breath of impatience but was ignored by her mother. A guard walked by on the platform, his cap of authority caught the child's notice, as it is for the very young, a minute can seem like ten, if nothing is happening. The girl tugged at her mother's sleeve. "Tell the man to put a shillin' in the meter."

"You be quiet, play wi' your doll."

243

At last the whistle blew and that sudden surge of movement sent the doll tumbling to the floor. The child jumped to her feet, gathered it up and as if she'd been waiting for confirmation, some evidence of an actual journey, she carefully removed the dolly's coat and bonnet, put it to sit on the seat and clambered back up beside it. Hilda was amused by the activity but the face of the woman was set in an expression of irritability. The train left the station behind, picking up speed as it passed the sidings, eventually taking them through deep embankments of heliotrope and campions.

The girl began to sing in that endearing infant fashion.

Mary, Mary, quite contrary,

How could your mother know,

If no one tells and nothing swells………..

The woman's hand came down hard on the child's leg, Annie winced at the sound of the slap.

"How many times have I told you not to listen to that barmy lad."

Tears flowed and the poor child's crying became pitiful. A red welt spread across her skin bearing an impression of her mam's fingers. Looking across to Annie and Hilda the woman snapped justification, as she saw it. "That daft lad, I'll swing for the so an' so, next door are real rough pups, dragged up the kids are, dragged up. She's got a mouth on 'er like a sewer an' the father, well, if you was to see 'im first thing in the mornin', you'd think 'e'd just stepped out o' clink. When me dad snuffs it, I've told my Percy that me an' 'er are goin' to live in Spalding an' 'e can please 'isself." The woman wiped the girl's face with a hanky, none too gently. "You'd like to live in grandad's house wouldn't yer, 'e's got a clock as plays a tune an' 'e can't take that wi' 'im not where 'e's goin'. Though I reckon 'e'll 'ave a damn good try. Mam used to say 'e wer' too mean to give 'er the droppin's from 'is nose end."

The compartment eventually found a welcome silence. Annie, Hilda and the woman observed the passing countryside and the girl, having succumbed to weariness, slept in the crook of her mother's arm.

When the train stopped at Deeping they were joined by two youths in scout uniform and an elderly gentleman. The latter was well dressed, he carried a small, black attaché case and the cordial 'good afternoon' followed immediately by a smile so broad cast that it revealed an absence of teeth, did much to mitigate the overwhelming smell of camphor that he he'd brought to the compartment. The ticket inspector obviously knew him.

"Hello Mr.Sheedy, are you on beach patrol again? I reckon you must 'ave rescued more souls in Skeggy than all o' them African missionaries put together."

The affable Mr.Sheedy simply displayed his receding gums through a genuinely accommodating smile and said in a somewhat lispy tone due to his lack of dentures. "Indeed my son, indeed."

The two youths temporarily put down the Boys Own comic, which they'd been sharing, to hand their tickets to the inspector.

"What sort o' mission are you on then lads? I don't suppose there's much singin' o' Sankey an' Moody around the old campfire."

The boys responded with a chuckle that seemed to wake the little girl. She rubbed her eyes, viewed the compartment now bearing three male travellers who'd appeared from nowhere as her infant mind perceived it, and immediately gathered up her doll from the seat beside her, put its coat back on and turning to her mother asked.

"Are we nearly there, my knickers are wet."

When the train finally pulled into the station at Skegness, Annie was more than ready to alight and stretch her legs. People bustled about, all ages, all kinds but the familiar sound of Freddy's voice and the sight of him waving from the turnstile rendered everyone else invisible. Tight hugs of love and eager excited chatter, soon propelled them to a van parked just inside the station concourse.

"Come on," said Freddy, "we best be quick or I shall have the taxi drivers telling me off." Annie and Hilda both squeezed into the front with Freddy, giggling from the fun of such a hasty departure.

"I feel like we're being pursued by the Keystone Cops," said Hilda. "You're the villain Freddy, mam is the gangster's moll and I must be your sidekick."

Annie laughed out loud. "I can't wait to tell Davina that I became a gangster's moll at my age. I shall need to be saved by Mr.Sheedy."

"Who's Mr.Sheedy?" Asked a puzzled Freddy. Annie let Hilda explain, by now so many new sights intrigued Annie that her concentration was solely for the Lincolnshire countryside, the scattered population, a house here, a row of cottages there, a small church and a village school. So different to the densely populated city she had left earlier in the day. The road took them within yards of a working windmill, the vast sails paddling the air with impressive speed. Finally Freddy turned into a narrow lane and pulled up by a wooden gate, painted in white on the top bar, the name 'Bufton Cott'. "This is the terminus," he said, "Francis will be in there hopping from foot to foot, she's told Mrs.Mollard all about you, you'll like Agnes, we're the middle cottage of three, she lives on one side and Harry and his family occupy the other. Good man is Harry, he's the chap that had the burst appendix, doing alright now, his wife puts his recovery down to stout, Nora reckons it worked like magic. They've two children, both boys, only eleven months between them and according to Harry, 'that wer' down to stout an'all'. Mrs.Mollard is remarkable, she's never revealed her age but from some of the things I've heard her recall she must be in her eighties. Her husband died years ago, he was a chimney sweep in Skegness, like grandad Samuel, apparently he cobbled everybody's shoes as well and cut the hair of most of the men, in a wooden shed at the back of where they lived on the edge of town. They moved here when he retired. Even now folk around these parts seem to do more than one job, I suppose that with the population being so scattered, one line of trade only might not be enough to survive on. Skegness has grown a lot over the past ten years, more housing is being developed now but Mr.Shipman at Huttoft reckons it'll be many years before the landscape around the farm changes. Here at Skendleby it can be that quiet, if it weren't for the rooks giving out, a man could believe he'd gone deaf."

Freddy led them inside through a rear porch, a jug of honeysuckle sat on the window ledge, fragrant and cheerful. Work boots, a basket of logs and a wooden box containing all manner of freshly gathered vegetables stood at one side of the stone floor. Before he had chance to open the inner door, Francis appeared, her face beaming with pleasure. Motherhood suited her, she looked well, despite all the worries and disappointments of Bobbers Mill, the arrival of their baby daughter, a fresh start in this gloriously peaceful place, had restored Francis's spirit, her contentment was plain to see, Annie was instantly reassured. In the corner of the cosy living room, Faith slept in a Moses basket, a light dusting of hair, full face and hands that seemed to define her as female. The fingers long and slender, resting casually against a pretty covering edged with pink ribbon.

"She's beautiful," whispered Hilda.

Annie fought the emotion that welled inside her, this was not the time for tears. Bending low over the sleeping baby, hiding her face from the others whilst she gathered her composure, Annie drank up that smell of newborn, sweet, innocent, powerfully intoxicating to every maternally minded woman.

Freddy put his arm around Annie's shoulders and spoke softly in her ear.

"Your first grandaughter, for all those years you've had faith in me." He knew Annie's emotion and with kindness said. "Hilda shall make us all a cup of tea to have with a slice of the chocolate cake Francis baked especially.

The farm at Huttoft is a grand spot Mam, rich pasture, grows everything from flowers to leeks. From the top fields a man can look at the sea as he works, I couldn't do that at Bobbers Mill now could I?" Annie felt she must tell Freddy that work was due to commence, he listened, smiled, kissed her cheek and said. "It's difficult to explain Mam but I feel a strange affinity with this place. You know how some folk believe we all tread the earth more than once, reincarnation or whatever the terminology is. Well if such notions bear any truth, then I reckon I've passed this way before. Freddy Eddowes is at home here and you only have to look at Francis to know that Skendleby makes her happy too. Ivy and the family have been good as gold, we couldn't feel more welcome anywhere. She insists we all go for dinner tomorrow, she's getting it ready for midday sharp so you and Hilda will have plenty of time left to look around before you need to catch your train. It was no use arguing Mam, Ivy wasn't going to be denied this chance of a get together. You'll be amazed to see Molly, since our wedding last year she's blossomed into a really confident young woman. No wonder the village post office is busy, every unattached man for miles around must find a reason to buy stamps, it's a shame Hilda is only here until tomorrow, the male population definitely outnumbers the female in these parts. The migration of young men to work the land creates the situation. Hark at me Mam, I sound like William don't I, referring to 'The Land'. How is he anyway?"

"Celia called with Mathew one day in the week, he was in Leicester on business of Mr.Smithfield." Before Annie could speak further, Francis and Hilda came through from the scullery with a tray of tea and cake, the subject of William and Andrew Smithfield was lost at once to Hilda's revelation.

"Harold has a girlfriend, she's called Elizabeth and she works at a tearoom in Skegness."

"You women are all the same." Said Freddy, "a man can't as much as ask a woman what time it is without folk making out he's smitten."

Francis gave her husband a kiss and teased him. "I can't recall you even asking me the time, your mind had imagined me in a pinafore and Wellington boots before you even asked me out!"

Freddy relished the fun, "Poor Harold," he said, "hooked like a herring us fellas don't stand a chance."

The tea was welcome and the cake was good. Faith stirred and needed to be fed so Freddy decided the time was appropriate for Hilda and himself to go into the village. The box of vegetables in the porch was destined for Ivy.

"We'll be a threshing set tomorrow," said Freddy, using farming language, to liken their number around Ivy's dinner table to the hands working the combine harvester.

Hilda was charmed by the village of Skendleby, the modest cottages to no degree belittled by the larger and more elaborate properties. It was as if all stood in harmony and those dwelling within observed a mutual respect.

Ivy's house was down a leafy lane that ran behind the vicarage. An area of lawn and shrubbery to the front and at the rear, a cobbled yard with the usual privy and coal store but with an additional shed and an area of rough grass fenced around, a

248

number of chickens busily scrabbling behind the wire netting. An excited Jack Russell ran down the path to greet them, a bitch as it turned out, the proud mother of three pups, an unplanned litter as a result of the determined advances made by an opportunist Beagle hound. Ivy's home was just as Hilda had imagined, a glorious array of family photographs, hand crocheted chair covers in bright coloured yarns, books and jigsaw puzzles, a gramophone and an ingrained smell of baking, all of which filled the place with a sense of contentment.

"Where's Annie?" Ivy stood with a look of expectation, her hair pinned neatly, a crisp white pinafore over her flowery summer frock and in her hands a jug of vivid red dahlias, which she placed in the middle of a large table, already extended in preparation for their meal the next day.

"She wanted to spend some time with Francis and Faith but she sends her love and said to tell you she can hardly wait for tomorrow, to see you all again."

Freddy's reply Ivy accepted as only natural, if it had been her grandaughter she would have wanted to hold the baby as much as she could, while she could.

"You'll have to pop into the shop to see Molly." Said Ivy, "she doesn't finish until six and Harold is working, with you off this weekend Freddy he was needed at Huttoft."

Freddy grinned roguishly. "I'll have to make it up to him, you tell Harold, when he gets in, that next weekend he shall have all the Elizabeth time he wants."

"Now don't you go pullin' his leg, Reggie does more than enough o' that. I like the lass Harold could do a lot worse than marry a girl like Elizabeth. You'll likely meet Reggie on his way home, he had to go to the forge at Winthorpe."

Something within Hilda was envious of Molly. The shop sold all the staple items, bread, milk, potatoes and so on. The post office counter offered the usual stationery and wrapping paper but it was so different to Gregory Street, it felt almost like stepping inside someone's living room.

"You must go with us to Skegness this evening Hilda, only for an hour. Harold will drive us in dad's van," said the eager Molly. "Aunty Annie will want to stay with you and Francis, Freddy. There's sure to be lots she needs to ask about.

Tomorrow after we've had dinner, then aunty Annie can go to see the sights, but tonight, when it gets dark, the lights reflected on the water are so pretty, we can paddle our feet and buy a hot chocolate."

Annie took such joy from watching Francis feed her daughter. Freddy was downstairs reading the paper. They'd eaten a lovely meal of pork pie and chutney with a pudding of fresh raspberries and blancmange.

As planned by Molly, Harold had called for Hilda and the three young people had gone to Skegness for, 'a bit of fun aunty Annie', as the Lincolnshire Boucher had mischievously described their jaunt into town. Annie had noticed John's drawing of Bobbers Mill, hanging on the wall at the top of the stairs. Francis observed Annie looking at it.

"Freddy put it there, he said it reminds him of John more than it does of Bobbers Mill. I know he misses John and George, their names are spoken often but strangely, he seldom mentions William." Francis covered herself and fastened her buttons, Faith slept in her arms.

"I sometimes feel sorry for William," said Annie. "He has much of his mother in his nature. Enid was an enigma, she could wound with her tongue yet she crept under the skin, it was impossible not to feel affection for her. Enid wanted people to feel sure of her strength, even to be intimidated by it, it was her way of protecting herself. Underneath all that, I am convinced she was insecure, afraid of hurting, of experiencing pain. Byron, a dog we once had, would bark loudly, like a warning if a knock came at the door when we all sat together, yet if he'd been on his own and we returned, not until we were inside and he recognised us would he make a sound. It's just a show of bravado and William, like his mother is nowhere near as tough as he would have us believe."

"Let's go downstairs to Freddy, she'll sleep for a few hours now she's been fed," said Francis. "Before you leave tomorrow I want you to meet Agnes Mollard. She's a delightful cross between grandma Sarah and Davina. Freddy describes her as his 'homely hybrid'. She's taken a great shine to him, last week it was a bag of caramel whirls and this week she insisted on giving him a large bar of nutty chocolate, all because he repaired the lid of her coal bunker."

An hour or so passed before the sound of a vehicle outside alerted them to the return of the revellers. Hilda's face held evidence of her enjoyment, Harold and Molly stayed but briefly declaring, 'see you tomorrow, don't eat too much breakfast, mam has killed the fatted calf'.

"You look tired Mam," said Freddy, "I suppose you were up before light and busy in the shop all morning, we'll go to bed, all of us, tomorrow is going to be a full day of activity, I want to show you the farm, Mr.Shipman says I must bring you to the house to say hello. They're a good, honest family, proud of their achievements and rightly so. There'll be time to go to Huttoft in the morning before our 'feast' at Ivy's."

Hilda's chatter was incessant, the beach, the diversity of people, the shops filled with novelties, frothy hot chocolate at the café, street vendors selling balloons and crinoline dolls made from paper. Annie's eyelids began to droop. In the bedroom across the landing, a vague sound of Faith crying but not even that could keep Annie from sleep. Skendleby wrapped her about with warmth, it had been a good day, Annie was content.

Reggie's embrace on her arrival had been so fortified with affection that Annie's ribs ached still.

"That was a wonderful meal Ivy, the brisket melted in the mouth and your Queen of Puddings was so light." Annie took another plate from the draining board to dry with the tea towel.

"It must sound selfish Annie," said Ivy as she scoured the heavy roasting pan, "but I'm so glad that Freddy came to Skendleby. We were shocked when he wrote to us about Bobbers Mill and I knew how upset you would be but Harold has been like a dog with two tails since Freddy decided to take work at Huttoft. As for Molly and me, having Francis and the baby close by is a source of real joy, Reggie is the biggest softy, he gathers them up like one happy family, pullin' their legs, tellin' them yarns, he's like a big kid himself. I often wonder how he manages to create such things of beauty, the glass panel he did for the hotel at Cleethorpes took my breath away. He took me there, bought me a sweet sherry, just so I could see it. I felt that proud, then he comes home an' plays 'Harry daft', men, shall we ever get to the bottom of 'em. We all agreed that if it means we shall see more of you, then fate got it right. 'Annie could do with a good bit of sea air' that's what Reggie thinks anyway. Do you ever wonder if Harold and Frank can see us, I do."

Annie squeezed Ivy's arm. "If they can, then I believe they'd approve, we've kept the children safe and ever living in their memory. Charles doesn't have Reggie's easy manner, I'm sure it makes things difficult for George at times, but thankfully George is so like Harold in his ways and Charles did like Harold, they became friends, especially after Enid's death, so it works. I'd like to visit again Ivy, I really would but it is awkward with the shop, even on a Sunday the papers dictate that we open until midday. Charles will come soon, perhaps John will travel with him, as Hilda has been this weekend with me. I know George and Alice will want to see Faith and not one of us would come to see Freddy without calling on you too. By the end of the summer you'll be weary of us."

Just then Hilda's voice called out from the back yard. "Come and see the puppies Mam, one looks just like Miss Apps, the head librarian."

Outside in the shed, Molly and Hilda played with the pups, a ball in an old sock being the source of fun. The bitch, named Vera after Ivy's mother, took full advantage of the interlude and stretched out on the cobbles in full sunshine, teats swollen from her offspring's feeding frenzy, panting from the heat but loath to move. Annie watched from the doorway, laughing at the antics of both dogs and girls.

A sudden movement beside her and Harold's voice asking, "What do you think of the farm aunty Annie?" Made her jump. Harold's face had matured and now bore a strong resemblance to Frank, there was no mistaking George and Harold as first cousins.

"I was impressed, not only by the farm, the well kept pasture, the healthy looking stock but by Mr.Shipman and his family, they came across as genuinely decent people, not unlike Arthur and Dorothy Cropley. Freddy hides his disappointment well, Bobbers Mill meant a great deal to him and the financial loss was a big set back. He stubbornly refuses help in that regard." Annie let out a long sigh, it made Harold chuckle. "You and mam are just the same, cluck,cluck,cluck."

"Cup of tea," Ivy's voice called from the cottage door.

"Come on aunty Annie, I know Reggie has something planned," Harold put his face close to Annie's and whispered in her ear. "I think it involves the gramophone and two left feet."

Within minutes the strains of a waltz drifted across the front garden. Annie was given no chance to decline as Reggie led her about the lawn, just as he'd done at Robert Appleyard's dance afternoons. Francis stood with Faith in her arms, watching with amusement as Freddy twirled Hilda around the Hydrangea bush and Harold, definitely the owner of two left feet, reduced Hilda to tears of laughter through his attempts to master the simple rhythm of one, two, three, one, two, three.

Ivy had slipped off to put together a parcel for Annie to take back for Davina's birthday next month. "It's a few bits and bobs that I think will bring her pleasure. I haven't enclosed a greetings card, I shall post one nearer the time."

When they'd finally arrived back at Bufton Cott, having said their goodbyes, Francis lay Faith down in her Moses basket, told Freddy that they'd be no more than ten minutes, then took Annie's arm saying. "I promised Agnes that I would pop round and bring you to say a very quick hello, you too Hilda, I think meeting her will make your image of Skendleby complete."

A round faced, white haired old lady sat by a window, reading a book, a magnifying glass in one hand and a fat ginger cat curled up at her feet.

"No please don't get up," said Annie, planting a kiss on the old lady's cheek, it felt the most natural thing to do, Agnes Mollard epitomised the grandmother figure, yet sadly she had no family of her own. Her eyes displayed genuine pleasure and when she took Annie's hand, the squeeze of her fingers confirmed the loving nature over which Francis had so enthused. It was indeed true, a hybrid, a mix of Sarah and Davina bearing the name Agnes.

"Do sit my dears, I can see your faces more clearly if you sit down." The conversation flowed freely, her hearing was remarkably good for her age, which she'd proudly declared to be nearer eighty seven than eighty six. It was the whispered aside that touched Annie's heart the most. "Don't tell Freddy he thinks I'm much younger."

Annie had noticed, hanging on the wall behind where Agnes sat, a framed picture of Newstead Abbey. She commented on it.

"I used to do some cleaning for a couple from Nottingham, I think they moved to Skegness for her health. She suffered badly from depression, very weepy a lot of the time. When I was dusting their sitting room, I'd run my cloth over that picture and say, I'm glad I don't have to clean all of that grand place! Well one day she took the picture down from it's hook and said, 'you make me smile Agnes, I'd like you to have the picture, as a thank-you'. It really upset me when she died. It was a stroke that took her, first a minor one, then two days later, another more serious. She didn't recover. Constance was kind to me, very kind." The clock on the mantel struck the quarter past three. "You'll come again, I hope, I like it when someone calls, the days can be too long." It was no hardship to promise that they would.

Freddy was anxious for Annie to see the beach before going to the station. "You can't come to Skeggy and not at least pick up a handful of sand to take back for dad. Tell him it's only a loan and he must return it to the beach in person."

It was a tearful farewell, Francis shook from emotion, it tugged at Annie's heartstrings but they had to go. By the time they'd found a place to park the van, walked to the shore and put some sand in a jam jar to satisfy Freddy's plan and Hilda had purchased six sticks of rock and a 'kiss me quick hat' for her friend Laura, it was time to make their way to the station, their train was due to depart at 5-30.

"Don't forget to give our love and thank-you's to Celia and Alice for Faith's presents," said Freddy. His voice seemed thinner and Annie sensed that like herself, he was doing his very best to keep emotion at bay.

Annie bought a magazine from the newsagent's stand, it would help the journey pass more quickly for Hilda. A number of people appeared to be waiting for the train and only a few minutes passed before it came into view.

"Take care of yourself Mam," said Freddy. His arms encircled her and she could feel him trembling, then it was Hilda's turn, brother and sister embraced so tightly, Hilda's feet left the ground. The noisy engine pulled up alongside the platform with that hiss of steam that seemed designed to draw everyone's attention. Annie and Hilda stepped on board, moving along the corridor to a place where they could wave to Freddy. Tears were close by but Annie resolved not to leave Freddy with sadness. The whistle blew and the wheels began to respond to the mighty engine. Waving, blowing kisses until Freddy was no longer in sight, they turned to enter the compartment behind them. Putting their bag and Davina's parcel carefully on the luggage rack, they sank onto their seats with heavy hearts.

Seated in the opposite corner was none other than Mr.Sheedy, The Holy Bible, resting in his lap. Its worn cover gave testament to many years of devoted use. That all revealing smile came instantly to his face, it must surely confirm his mission a success.

Annie glanced at Hilda, already intent on her magazine. A wholesome tiredness washed over Annie, she leaned back, all tensions now retreated to another place, another time, they would doubtless rush her mind when she was least prepared, never did they surrender entirely to a good day, but merely re-form and recover discipline. Closing her eyes, Annie let visions of Bufton Cott, of Ivy in her home, of Francis cradling Faith, all drift past, behind her closed eyelids. Annie was happy to believe that the souls of Skegness were regularly ministered to. All would be well.

CHAPTER FOURTEEN

Late November

  Jack stuffed the ragged end of his scarf into his mouth as the urgent need to cough convulsed his chest, leaning back against the chimneystack, he inwardly cursed at his own weakness. He'd been watching the property for days, it had remained unoccupied. A large double fronted house at the edge of The Park, particularly well endowed with lead flashing at the base of each stack, of which there were three. Horace Clegg stood below, desperately trying to take some comfort from an aniseed flavoured winter mixture, which he rolled around his tongue, his hands he thrust into his pockets whenever he could and his feet did a dance on the spot in an attempt to keep circulation going. The nearest street lamp was several yards away and the moon had waned to a sliver. The sky was clear and the air razor sharp with frost. The truck they'd free wheeled into position round the back. Clegg felt nervous, not of the law, of their possible arrest, but for the condition of Jack. Something ailed Sulley, his frame held so much less flesh and his strength was dependant entirely upon his cussedness, as muscle and sinew seemed resolved to abandon him. Their night-time activities must surely cease. They'd not made enough to transform their lives but each had a nest egg, which enabled them some measure of hope.

  Jack pulled the bolster from between his shirt and pullover, of necessity he now tucked both into his trousers and even then he failed to fill the latter. His jacket hampered the process, yet to unfasten the lower button and let the cold air assault him even more would be unbearable.

  He'd lowered down to Clegg the lead from the two main stacks and after pausing for breath, Jack began to prise the lead from the smaller chimney at the back. This should be the easiest one, closer to the truck and on the side of the property least prominent, he felt relief, just a few more minutes and he could seek the shelter of the cab, take a gulp of brandy from the bottle beneath the seat. Brandy comforted, while it stung his throat like iodine on a deep cut, it instantly took away the taste of blood and for a little while he dared to feel restored. When the effect wore off Jack acknowledged to himself that it was merely the magic of alcohol that achieved to dull his senses. That was why he resisted taking as much as a sip from the bottle before beginning his climb. The scarf sucked the moisture from within his mouth and stifled the sound of his coughing but the frost hanging on the air, suddenly found his nostrils, rushing inside them, denying him breath. He spat the scarf from his mouth and the cough erupted, like a mighty retching of Jack Sulley's soul. The sound carried on the stillness, so sinister in its nature that on the ground below, Clegg shook from dread. Another sound, very different, overtook Jack's fading convulsion, now reduced to spasms of exhausted, bitter gasping. Footsteps, urgent, running, drawing ever closer. Horace Clegg panicked, he was on the same level as the approaching feet, nowhere to hide, in his desperation he convinced himself that Jack could get away with it, up there, concealed behind a chimney stack. He'd drive away as fast as he could, chances being if it was the law, they'd presume whom they sought was in the truck. By the time they got transport to follow, he'd be half way to Swinscoe and Jack would be safe to come down.

The breathless constable watched the lights of a vehicle disappear into the darkness, his chest tight from the effort of running in the chilly frostiness, he stood still to recover. Then a noise, a rush of movement and a thud alarmed him. Following his instinct he crept slowly, cautiously towards the area from where the sound had come. He shone his torch along the path, the beam caught the tiny crystals of frost forming at his feet, a man, a body, lay in a heap. Not knowing whether he'd come upon life or death, he trembled as he stooped over the figure. The man was breathing, the rise and fall of his chest was shallow, he was alive but barely, Jack had been unconscious even before he fell. The constable was shaken by what had happened, to apprehend a burglar was one thing, to be alone with someone he feared was close to death was another thing entirely. He felt sticky moisture on his hands from where he'd lain his fingers over the man's chest when feeling for a heartbeat, the light from his torch revealed a bloodiness, it was horrible, the whole incident was sickening.

Horace Clegg drove somehow towards Swinscoe, battling the tears. His panic now receding, guilt replaced it, deep, painful guilt. In his rush he'd not even covered the lead already on the back of the truck, if he was stopped there'd be no denying his wrongdoing, yet his desertion of Jack, his mate, now felt the much greater sin. All he could do was drive, reach Swinscoe, stash the lead and in the morning, go to Winchester Street, to make sure Jack had got home all right.

Sergeant Beasley reached the hospital soon after the ambulance, his presence in uniform could not be ignored. A nurse led him into a side room where a doctor worked on the subject of his inquiries.

"I'm afraid he's in a poor state," said the doctor, passing only a brief glance to Beasley before returning his attention to the man on the bed. "His injuries we cannot immediately determine but the blood appears to come from within, which would suggest internal damage. If you come back in the morning we should know more by then. You'll appreciate officer, that my job is to keep him alive and wherever possible, ultimately to heal him. Your duties require you to enforce the law, to apprehend the offender, I can understand your frustration, but I assure you, whatever this man's crime, he is confined here at the hospital just as surely as he would be at the police station. His own inability to propel himself beyond this bed renders it so. Here, he is no threat to anyone but himself, now you should leave and permit me to do my work, which in turn might hopefully allow you officer, to do yours."

Beasley reluctantly agreed to return in the morning, indeed it was morning, just after 2am. It had been difficult to see very much of the man, so bedraggled, crumpled, like something of no worth, discarded waste. The face, the features, gaunt though they were, retreating behind a growth of stubble and before him but briefly, nevertheless confirmed the man's identity, Jack Sulley, husband, father, no good idler. Might have guessed, thought Beasley, Jack Sulley, might have bloody well guessed. When daylight broke he would establish just what had gone on at the property in The

Park. He'd wager there'd be a marked absence of lead on the roof and who was Sulley's accomplice? Beasley needed Sulley to survive, to spit out the name of the other 'no good', he'd relish the task of forcing that out of him.

The undeniable human element found sufficient gap in Beasley's thinking to halt, for a moment, his self satisfied scheming. Sulley's young wife and child, his mam and dad, all had in due course, to be told either of Jack's crime or of his demise. Would any decent individual ever want to hear of one or the other? Jim and Elsie Sulley were good people and Lillian, she was just another of those cowed, naïve young women forever at the mercy of a disenamoured ego.

Billy cupped his hand about his mouth and breathed over his fingers as he walked home from his work at the telephone exchange. The pavements were icy in places, even the milkman's fingerless gloves had failed in their purpose this morning. The crash of breaking glass, a volley of blasphemies and a fast increasing flow of milk from the doorstep confirmed the poor man's lack of feeling in his digits. His tongue however, was undiminished by the wintry elements.

"It's sods bloody law, it couldn't be the last place could it, oh no, they only 'ave ordinary but 'ere, nowt but the best, gold top, channel soddin' island!"

Billy moved along quickly, thoughts of porridge and a warm bed for an hour or two did wonders to encourage his cold feet. He turned into Winchester Street and startled a dog having a piddle up the lamppost. That same misty vapour hovering over Billy's outgoing breath, lingered about the patch of urine.

"You're brave to take it out ol' fella, I reckon a chap could be excused for peein' in his bed on a mornin' like this. Aye up, what's a copper doin' on the street." A policeman was walking towards Billy from the opposite direction, Billy drew level with No.24 on the other side of the cobbles, he crossed over. Before he turned into the entry he looked up the street, it was natural to be curious after all, or bleedin' nosey, as his mam would often describe Mildred Tomlinson, a neighbour who seemed permanently affixed to her front room window. The policeman stopped outside a door, checked the number then rapped with his knuckles, it was Jack Sulley's door. Billy sighed, it had to mean trouble, coppers seldom delivered good news and Jack Sulley's door almost certainly held trouble within.

Edna was clearing her bowl and a cup from the table. Each morning she caught the bus to Brassington at half past seven. Expecting the pavement to be treacherous, she would leave in good time today to walk the length of Sherwood Road to the bus stop.

Billy kissed her cheek, "Dress up warm love it'll get into your bones else." He wrapped his hand around the teapot, it was hot. Edna always managed to time it just right, he'd once made comment on it, she'd looked at him in disbelief and said, 'How many years 'ave you been workin' the night shift Billy Dodds? Fourteen, fourteen soddin' years all the same, so if I couldn't work out by now what time you'd get 'ome for your breakfast I'd be dafter than a wagon load of arseholes'.

Edna seemed frustrated over something. "I've told Myra to stay home from school, 'er throat's like a rasp an' she wer' coughin' in the night. Make sure she takes a spoonful o' cherry menthol linctus, it's on the drainin' board. Liza'll be up in a minute. Remind 'er to bring home a new bottle from Hastilow's an' a tin o' Zubes." Edna raked the grate of the range and put on a shovel of coal.

"There's a copper outside Sulley's, must be summat up, as early as this, an' knockin' on the door," said Billy as he poured himself some tea.

"Just so long as they keep their troubles over there I don't care," said Edna, putting the coal bucket down on the hearth with a grunt of backache.

"Yer don't need to worry about Myra," said Billy, sensing Edna's concern, "I'll keep the fire well stoked an' she can stay in this room where it's warm. Didn't your Ada give her a jigsaw for 'er birthday, I 'aven't seen 'er doin' it yet. We can both 'ave a go. I thought it looked like a hard one, all them trees in the background, that's likely what's put 'er off." Just then a knock came to the back door.
"Whatever it is, I'll see to it," said Billy. "You get yourself ready for work."

Lillian Sulley stood in the yard, a cardigan around her shoulders, looking blue from the cold. "What's up lass, come inside afore yer freeze to death."

"I can't stop, Norma's on her own, she's still asleep." Lillian hesitated. "Jack's in hospital, he fell off a roof, last night, in The Park, he wer' up to no good. The policeman said he's knocked up bad." Tears started to roll down Lillian's face.

"Edna's off to work in a minute but if yer bring Norma over 'ere, I'll keep an eye on 'er while you go to the hospital." Softhearted Billy tried to reassure the young woman as best he could but she was frightened, he could see fear in her eyes.

"Will you ask your Liza to do me a favour? Miss Turpin's shop isn't far away from Melton Road, No.6, if Liza tells Jack's dad, he'll know what to do. I shan't go to the hospital yet, I'll wait to see what Jim says. Jack can be difficult, yer know how he is, can't help hisself." Before Billy could respond, Lillian was gone.

"Just how did yer suppose yer wer' goin' to look after Norma, you've been at the exchange all night, it's bad enough that I've got to leave you with Myra to see to." Edna had been listening from the living room.

Billy put the pan of porridge over the heat. "Its not the lasses fault Edna, God forbid any of our girls should 'ave such trouble but life's a lottery, some 'ave it good an' some bad, who decides these things I don't know but if a daughter o' mine wer' as frightened as Lillian Sulley is right now an' I weren't with 'er, I'd hope somebody took pity afore they took judgement."

Edna pulled on her coat and hat. "Promise me Billy, that you won't get involved in anythin' more than keepin' an eye on Norma. I've allus said that Jack wer' trouble, it's a mercy that Lillian didn't conceive another by 'im 'e's not fit to be a father. May poor Ted and Winnie forgive me for sayin' such a thing of their grandson but Jack Sulley should never 'ave been born."

Edna pulled the back door closed behind herself, leaving Billy to dwell on her words, 'should never have been born'. Florrie Haynes had once told him that she'd overheard two neighbours talking about Victor, years ago when he'd been but an infant. One had remarked, ' he don't look right, never will'. The other had replied with words that had cut Florrie's heart, 'should never have been born'.

Little had presented itself to give him any satisfaction but this morning Andrew Smithfield sat at his desk indulging his thoughts in the events of the previous afternoon, when he'd left Gerald Birkett to ponder upon Andrew's total withdrawal from Braithwaites. Being far too polite to offend Birkett with an unrestrained explanation for his action, he'd simply told the pompous manager that his financial affairs, both business and personal, would be better served in an atmosphere of mutual respect. Birkett had predictably expressed concern and regret, his bowing and fawning turned Andrew all the more, he'd left Birkett's office with a great deal of satisfaction, a feeling of liberation and a sense of aunt Alicia's approval.

His aunt's estate had gone through probate and been finally proved. Following a meeting with the solicitor, Smithfield had resolved to inform Birkett that he would be closing his account and taking his business elsewhere. Alicia Plowright had banked with Barclays, her account now having been closed, her estate in its entirety passed to Smithfield. The smug, self opinionated Birkett irritated Andrew immensely. His aunt had been an honest, upstanding woman all her days, he would not allow her memory to fall into the clutches of Birkett. All his finances were now lodged with Barclays Bank.

James Rothero came across as genuine, a man not disinclined to walk and talk with rich and poor alike. Patrons of the orphanage, both Rothero and his wife spent time at Snenton, first and foremost it identified them as public spirited, charitable in thought and most significantly, in deed also. Andrew compared theirs to the cold hearted, insular approach of Birkett and was convinced that aunt Alicia could abide in peace, only under the sympathetic authority of Rothero.

William's head appeared around the door, considering his boss to be less than busy he entered at once, launching into his latest round of gossip.

"The police have got him, the burglar, in The Park last night. They're saying he was taken away in an ambulance so something drastic must have happened. I suppose a truncheon can inflict serious harm if an offender resists and the copper's determined. I dare say we shall know who it is by dinner time," he laughed,

"Christmas in clink on bread and water, all those roof top exploits, how are the mighty fallen now." Andrew could hear William laughing still as he walked back to his work.

William Eddowes had become a thorn in Andrew's side. Since that day outside Barclays when he'd watched Freddy walk away, the shallow, selfish William had achieved through his presence, to remind Andrew of his unwitting but undeniable part in the development of Bobbers Mill and the resultant misery for William's brother, Freddy Eddowes. Late one afternoon, Andrew had steeled himself to go to Gregory Street, to Eddowes' shop, in the hope of seeing Annie and explaining himself but he'd found Charles behind the counter. Their exchange had been cordial but brief and he'd left with no more than The Evening Post and a packet of mints.

Alicia's estate had proved to be considerably more than Andrew could have expected. Shares and bonds made up the majority, there was a sum of money and the house. Andrew had not ever in his mind converted the home they'd shared into a monetary value, it was simply aunt Alicia, but as the solicitor had pointed out, the property was large, well constructed and desirable to many which in turn attached considerable value. To Andrew it was home and nothing beyond that. It afforded refuge, which he sought more and more.

Edna could overhear William talking amongst the others, his speculation over the burglar's identity began to annoy her. Despite her opinion of Jack Sulley, Edna had sat feeding the Vyella through her machine, remembering Winnie and Ted Bacon, all their many struggles. Winnie's unique philosophy on life, which could leave any individual who received it, believing they'd accidentally strayed into uncharted territory, treading ground where no man had gone before! Edna could have enlightened William, sated his ravenous curiosity but she found no actual satisfaction in the knowledge of Jack Sulley's criminal activities and his come-uppance the previous night. Instead she let her mind drift to her eldest daughter Annie, so similar in age to Lillian Sulley.

Last Sunday, when Annie and Alec had come for dinner, Edna had noticed reluctance on Annie's part to eat very much, she'd looked pale and seemed fidgety. Edna had commented on it to Alec, the old fashioned look which he'd given her and his reply, 'nothing to worry about', with a wink in his eye, had tormented her thoughts ever since. Edna knew her daughter only too well, Annie would say nothing until it was confirmed but Edna dared to hope for a grandchild sooner rather than later.

Poor Lillian, Billy was right, it wasn't her fault. At least Jim Sulley was back from Barrow, he'd spare Lillian and Elsie all he could. Norma was barely old enough to have any real understanding, she would know only that her dad wouldn't be coming home for a while. Edna let out a deep sigh.

"Who do you think will turn out to be the villain then Edna?" William stood at her side, with the sound from her machine as she'd treadled faster, trying to shut out the chatter that grated on her nerves, she'd not heard him approaching, William had a silly grin on his face.

"Do yer remember that stuffed cockatoo you 'ad as a child, yer wouldn't be parted from it, took it with yer everywhere, even to bed. It was your comforter, wi' that dead parrot under your arm, yer wer' content. I sometimes wish yer still 'ad it." Edna put her foot down hard on the treadle, propelling the cloth through the machine as if it fled the company. Her tolerance today would not extend to William Eddowes.

Horace Clegg stood behind a group of men who'd gathered in a bus shelter to share a cigarette. Their conversation had told him of Jack's fate, he'd nodded and thrown his own casual, 'yea and nay' into the mix. It relieved him of the need to go to Winchester Street but if Jack was taken to hospital, as the men had said, then how bad was he? He dare not go there, the police would be watching for sure. He'd driven the truck, and the lead in it, away from The Park, they'd know Jack couldn't have done that. Clegg felt sick and inadequate, without Jack everything seemed to threaten him. Suddenly the men grew larger before his eyes and his nerve shrank through their menace. Whilst they continued to theorise on what drove the criminal mind and whether or not the class divide should be held accountable, Clegg moved away. Out on the street he was vulnerable, too exposed, he should retreat to Swinscoe until it all blew over. Jack was tough, he'd always been tough but the notion did nothing to stem the nausea welling in Cleggs' stomach or the tears stinging his cheeks.

"If you would wait here officer, I shall fetch the doctor." The nurse hurried away leaving Sergeant Beasley to his mood of impatience. It had been the task of one young constable, to climb a ladder and determine the extent of Jack's activities on the roof in The Park. The bolster was found in a gutter where it had become lodged, when Jack, sinking into unconsciousness had released his grip. The lead from two chimneystacks had been removed, not just from the roof but from the entire scene. A coil of rope was wrapped around the smaller chimney but Jack had fallen before barely making a start on the lead flashing at its base. Beasley's determination was fired up, he'd make Sulley spill the name of his accomplice, another out an' out no good who needed to be put away. If Sulley had survived the night then he couldn't be that bad, a few broken bones wouldn't disable his tongue and the sooner the wretch was in custody the better.

"Good morning officer," said the doctor, himself looking weary from lack of sleep. "I imagine the past few hours have been busy for both of us. The man whom your officers escorted into the hospital was unfortunate enough to have arrived at the same time as another emergency, however he is being dealt with but will need to remain here for a while yet." Beasley considered his own official capacity to be equal to that of the doctor.

"Nothin' could be unfortunate enough for the thievin' no good. I'm here to speak with Sulley. My concern is for the well being of the wider community, another man is still at large, it's my duty to bring this second offender to justice an'all. Sulley needs to cough up the name of his stooge."

The doctor openly cringed at Beasley's words.

"The patient has a broken ankle and a dislocated shoulder, both these injuries have been treated, however the blood over his scarf and about his mouth suggested internal damage. You may speak with him for a few minutes but we need to run some tests with a degree of urgency, so five minutes, no more I'm afraid officer."

Beasley looked down at Jack Sulley, laying on the bed, his face pale, a nurse having recently washed and shaved her patient. His eye's were closed but Jack felt the presence and spoke.

"Made it easy for yer didn't I? Fell right into yer lap, don't s'pose many give the'selves up wi'out a fight." His eyes opened and he smiled.

"A name Jack, you know why I'm here. It'll be a day or two before I get the pleasure of escortin' you to the nick an' in the meantime I want your accomplice. Who is it helped yer Jack? Tell me an' it might help you when the judge deliberates, the law acknowledges co-operation, a gesture of remorse."

Jack's breathing was laboured, he replied slowly, his words fighting his need to cough. "Nobody 'elps Jack Sulley, nobody, they never did, I'm me own man Sergeant, me own man."

Beasley's temper flared. "You're a rotten bastard Sulley, rotten to the core, your family deserve better, help yourself an' them an'all, give me the name o' the bugger that drove away wi' the lead, he didn't care about you did he, why should you give a monkeys about him." Beasley leant over Jack menacingly.

"You're a bully Beasley, a big bully, but yer don't scare me." Jack's eyelids came down once more.

"I'm afraid you must leave now officer," said sister, "we need to take the patient for some tests." Her smile was genuine but Beasley in his frustration returned an ill humour.

"I need to run some tests an'all, to establish if the patient has a brain."

Sister made no comment and faced with her charge over the situation, Sergeant Beasley nodded to acknowledge protocol and left with his determination to get Sulley and his accomplice even more intent.

Lillian sat with Norma on her knee, the child sang a nursery rhyme as they waited for the milk to heat in the pan over the fire. Two basins sat on the table, each with pieces of bread and some sugar. There was cheese on the slab and a few eggs but

Lillian needed comfort food today and hot, sweet bread and milk delivered soothing for the nerves.

Jack had been in hospital for two days. Jim and Elsie had been to see their son but as yet, Lillian had stayed away. Frightened and protective of Norma, she clung to the house, not even venturing out to the shop, this meal would be the last of their bread. Today her hand was forced, word had come from the hospital. As Jack Sulley's wife she was requested to attend Dr.Speakman's clinic and to bring with her their daughter Norma. The appointment was for 3-45pm. The milk began to bubble around the rim, Lillian poured it over the bread stirring gently to dissolve the sugar.

"When we've eaten, we must have a wash and put on your nice warm frock that grandma gave you." The little girl sat at the table blowing over the basin. "I know it's hot but we need somethin' hot inside us before we go out." Lillian sat beside her daughter. "Shall we go to see your dad this afternoon, you'd like that wouldn't you?"

Norma reached for her mother's hand, ceased blowing and said. "Shall we have to stop long, that frock makes me itchy."

"We'll put a petticoat underneath, then it can't make you itch, afterwards we'll go to the shop to get a loaf and you can pick some sweets from the jar." The notion satisfied the child and the bread and milk began its comfort.

"It won't be long now, we must be next." Lillian and Norma sat in a small waiting area, no one else, just them.

Eventually the door alongside them opened and a kindly voice said, "If you'd like to come in now Mrs.Sulley."

Dr.Speakman was a man in his fifties, his manner was calm and gentle, he smiled at Norma. "I have a granddaughter not a lot older than you, we play dominoes together, do you like dominoes?"

Norma was relaxed by the soft tone of his voice and his easy friendliness.

"We play cats cradle, I don't drop the thread now do I Mam?" She looked up at Lillian but her mother was so tense her lips trembled ahead of her words and a nod of the head followed by a faint, "Yes" was all Lillian could manage.

"Please take a seat Mrs.Sulley while I explain my reason for calling you and Norma here. Your husband has been coughing badly my dear, is that not so?"

"Yes, gettin' worse," said Lillian. "I hear him spittin' in the privy, I've tried tellin' him he should take somethin' for it," she hesitated, "but he don't like bein' told." Lillian lowered her face and fumbled with her coat button.

"I'm afraid your husband has tuberculosis Mrs.Sulley, he's obviously been ill for some considerable time. The condition is advanced, I wish he'd sought help and relief when he first felt unwell."

Dr.Speakman rubbed his hand across Norma's hair. "We need to take some samples from both you and your daughter but you mustn't be alarmed, it is a simple procedure. As Jack's family, living in close proximity to one another, there is the possibility that you too might be infected. As neither of you appear to be troubled by a cough I am hopeful that all is well. Try not to worry Mrs.Sulley, we are duty bound to run the tests, to establish either that you are clear or that we need to begin treatment. If in the early stages, tuberculosis can respond well to medication and therapy. Afterwards I shall take you to see your husband, that I'm sure will be the best medicine for him."

Lillian led Norma by the hand as they followed the kindly doctor, to where and to what she hardly dare think. Each month she'd thanked God in her prayers for keeping her body free of Jack's will, another baby would bind her to him beyond the endurance of her strength. When Norma started school Lillian planned to find work, to leave Jack, to remove them from his moods, his ill temper. Now the possibility that something else of Jack grew within her, threatened Norma, filled Lillian's mind with such anguish, she wanted to run away from all of it, away, far away, but she could not. 'You made your bed now you must lie in it'. Those words of her father echoed about the hospital corridor. Lillian squeezed Norma's hand tightly as Dr.Speakman held open the heavy swing doors for them to pass through.

"We'll attend first to your daughter, cat's cradle eh, and without dropping the thread, my word you are a clever little girl, I bet your dad's proud of you."

CHAPTER FIFTEEN

Annie looked up at the dresser, the jam jar of sand still awaiting a response from Charles. Each time she'd written to Francis and Freddy she'd made an excuse for him. John had gone with George and Alice, twice, so taken had they been with Skendleby but Charles no longer even bothered to offer a reason for not visiting Freddy, Annie felt it was more than unfortunate, it was tragic. She was writing back to Francis having received a letter just the day before, if it was alright with everyone and provided the weather allowed them to travel, then Freddy, Francis and Faith would come in the van on Christmas Eve and stay until Boxing Day afternoon. Annie felt so pleased at the prospect, indeed the whole family would be delighted, so tonight she was writing a reply for Hilda to post on her way to the library in the morning.

The year seemed to have flown by, Davina had remarked, 'wait 'til you reach my age, half a day is gone before I manage to pull on my stockings'. Dear Davina, her arthritis grew worse but her spirit remained stoic as always. Sarah too struggled her way through the months, especially the colder ones. Maggie went to Mitchell Street every day, if only for a few minutes. Annie called on both Sarah and Davina as often as she could but Charles' behaviour became more and more unpredictable, it was virtually impossible for Annie to plan any activity beyond the shop. He'd taken to staying in bed, often until midday, then, after having something to eat, he'd disappear for hours. It was as if he viewed the situation now to be so changed due to their children having been married or engaged in work, that Annie had nothing but the shop with which to fill her time.

Last Sunday however, she'd locked the shop door on the stroke of noon, left a note for Charles on the table and with Hilda and John, gone to Ainsley Road to have dinner with George and Alice. It had been the interlude Annie needed, her son George, so obviously happy. The atmosphere within that small house as warm and welcoming as the lively fire that burned in the grate, casting its heat over a row of chestnuts, which George had declared, 'a prelude to Christmas', adding that his mate Ron had given him a bagful in return for manning his barrow the previous afternoon while he got a tattoo of two lovebirds, a surprise for his intended. 'How could I stand in the way of romance?' George had said, casting a fond look at his wife. Their own love heart, shared as it was every day, concealed from others but ever present, just as |Alice would finger her locket, so George would feel those words 'My Alice' gently move against his skin while he worked.

Fred Pearson had so impressed the foreman at Bobbers Mill that he'd been taken on full time. Resentful of the low pay and disillusioned by predictions of worse to come, most had laboured grudgingly but Alice's dad embraced the work ethic, it gave him self-respect, however humble the task might be. He'd worked with a will and shown interest and ability beyond his obligation. Now on the books at Woolascrofts as a labourer to the masons and recognising his daughter's obvious happiness, Fred Pearson whistled his way to work and returned home each day free of those troublesome notions, which stirred others to kick back against the traces.

Charles had one day walked past Bobbers Mill, curious to see the extent of progress. To the layman's eye it appeared a confusion of trenches and rising above them were various elevations of brickwork, random, in need of concentrated expertise to bring a structured orderliness. Very different to the scene before Freddy's eyes only a few months before.

Charles had almost succeeded in persuading himself that Skegness could present nothing untoward. It was 1930, he was forty-nine years of age, yet always an inexplicable doubt crept inside his head. He held a vague recollection of travelling as a child with his mother, to Skegness, to visit an elderly couple he imagined could only have been his grandparents. For whatever reason the event had not been repeated, he'd have surely remembered a later visit. The image of his mother Hilda, had ever been of a gentle woman, young in face, for her death had come when Charles was but eighteen. Enid haunted still his pensive moments and regrets over the way he'd treated his father, even now after so many years, could achieve to torment him. Skegness felt like a distant passage of history, not raising its head to challenge him, peaceable, undemanding. That niggle of doubt at the back of his mind when he'd contemplated going to see Freddy, Francis and his granddaughter, had been enough to convince Charles that whatever lay sleeping in Lincolnshire was best left undisturbed. The jar of sand had failed to compel him, it was after all only sand, the same could be found on any beach. If thrown over the back yard it would simply disappear into the cracks between the cobbles, so it remained on the shelf of the dresser. Freddy's hope and Charles' dismay contained in a jam jar.

Annie looked up from her writing, now addressing the envelope. Charles stepped inside the back door, glanced across the scullery to where she sat at the kitchen table and said.

"The shops in town have put up decorations, you should ask John to gather some holly from The Meadows on Saturday afternoon. Hilda will help you make the place look seasonal and festive, it might encourage them to part with a bit more." He sat down in the chair by the range and fell silent.

Annie folded the letter and sealed the envelope. "I've replied to Francis," she said, " we can manage for two nights, John and Hilda won't mind sharing and Mrs.Tozer has insisted on Celia, William and Mathew joining them on Christmas day along with Edmund and Caroline. George and Alice will come for tea but naturally Alice wants to be with her dad. Sarah will be at Maggie's but Davina must come here, Freddy will fetch her."

"Why there has to be so much fuss I can never understand," muttered Charles.

"You have just said the shop must be made festive," Annie felt perplexed.

"That's commercial good sense, a bit of glitter works wonders, they forget all about the rentman when they see a strand of tinsel," said Charles, pulling off his shoes, "I'm going up."

Annie listened to his tread on the stairs and the sound of their bedroom door. Most nights she was the last to bed, sitting quietly on her own, turning over events in her mind. She propped the letter in its envelope against the clock, made safe the fire and entirely without premeditation found herself saying aloud, "Put out the lamp and bolt the door." It caused her to smile, she would decorate the shop as Charles wished with a sprig or two of mistletoe amongst the holly. Even aunt Bella had softened under a Christmas kiss. It was a slender hope, but hope was all that Annie had.

Florence eased the sleeve of her cardigan over a bruise, it had reached that dark, murky purple stage and spread across her forearm like a map of Australia. She'd finished the floor at last, as she grew older the flags on the kitchen floor seemed to multiply, each week demanded just that bit more effort. Basil would inspect them as though he were checking a scalp for lice. Once he found a raisin adhered to the floor and made her do it all over again. At least breakfast was easier these days, since the doctor had advised him to cut down a little, his weight having increased to fifteen stone, the morning routine consisted of a bowl containing eight prunes, the number must not vary, and two slices of bread spread with butter and whisky marmalade. For weeks his mood had been sullen, Florence tried to move about the house as discreetly as the church mouse, breathing relief when Rex drove him away to wherever Basil's various meetings and activities required him to be. Three days ago he'd returned home, dismissed Rex Madden until the morning and first locking away in his bureau a long brown envelope, he'd then turned his malign at Florence, the tone of his voice filled her with dread. Over the years she'd come to recognise the signs, his daily sarcasm and deliberate attempts to undermine her spirit were usual and no longer threatening but when his voice held that power of command which caused her to shrink from its savagery she knew that unlike the church mouse, there was nowhere for her to hide.

'You stupid woman, not even enough sense to guard your tongue, you wouldn't last five minutes in a man's world'. He'd bellowed the words at her, grabbed her by the arm and pushed her down onto a chair, where she could do no other than endure his tirade as he stood over her like a jailer. 'Surely you don't think that I sent you to Eddowes' shop each week just to socialise with her, it's the son, the eldest who interests me, hungry for success I've heard, not weakened by sentimentality.

Purchasing a few items each week establishes a connection with the family, a foot in the door. It's the way of business, thinking ahead, but what do you do? Give her our family pedigree, tell her that Patricia is married to Woolascroft's brother-in-law. I suppose that you couldn't wait to tell her that Bradshaw works for the council. Haven't you any savvy woman'? His angry outburst fell upon her so harshly that she wept from the sheer deluge of it. She'd responded as best she could.

'I might have mentioned in passing the name of Patricia's husband, we only ever spoke in a natural manner about our children. Caroline is married to William Eddowes' brother-in-law that should be connection enough. Why does business require such a contrived approach? I'm quite sure that I did not speak of Anthony's work, I had no reason to. Why is it so crucial anyway'?

He'd lowered his face to hers and as he fired back his answer, droplets of his spittle transferred to Florence. 'But for me you'd starve, you've not the sense you were born with'.

For an hour she'd sat alone in the room, afraid to stir for fear of attracting yet another of Basil's assaults. A bruised arm was minor, once he'd locked her inside a wardrobe for almost two hours, releasing her just before Caroline was due home from school. Both Patricia and Julia had attended private school, it was almost immediately after Basil's father died that things changed. The early years of their marriage had been reasonably happy, Basil had left the house to go to his work with a pleasant demeanour. Their two young daughters enjoyed his attention when he returned home and the house ran smoothly. Mrs.Tucker came in four mornings a week, to do some cleaning work but Florence had always undertaken to cook for her family. The day after Claude Stanford's funeral, Basil had stood by the hearth in the sitting room and ordered Florence to sit before him. It was as if his being had been taken over by another, a stranger with no feeling for her. Mrs.Tucker would come no more, charwomen were prone to tittle-tattle. He had automatically taken over the reins from his father and would be committed solely to running the pits, Colver and Birchdale. She, Florence, was to be thankful for her privileged situation as a mine owner's wife, it commanded a certain respect among the community, a status.

Florence very soon learned that respect certainly came from no other source, his moods, his outbursts constantly belittled her. Only after his 'meetings' when his ego was inflated by the toadying brotherhood did he pay her any regard as a wife and then to sicken her with such hypocrisy and false sentiment, she flinched from his advances.

Caroline was conceived not through love but from Basil Stanford's undeniable will, his determination to have his way. Whether it was that fact which influenced his mind or his fast developing meanness Florence couldn't tell but Caroline was to attend the local authority school and Florence was to obey, obey and further obey, whatever his command!

Patricia grew to worship her father's arrogance, she seemed to embrace it for herself and he responded by lavishing gifts upon her, taunting Julia for being so withdrawn. Florence recognised her second daughter's difficulty, toe the line without question or put up with being on the outside. At the first opportunity Julia left home, putting the distance of a continent between her father and herself. While Florence missed Julia terribly and cried herself to sleep many nights, in truth she was relieved that Basil could not impose his will from such a distance.

Caroline was a bright child, perhaps more perceptive than either of her sisters. Despite Florence trying to shield their youngest daughter from Basil's temper, for the child's sake ever offering some excuse for his behaviour, Caroline nevertheless grew to judge him, using the evidence of her own eyes and ears. She loved her mother but had no regard for her father and Florence had said and done nothing to influence the verdict. At least today she had time spent with Caroline to look forward to. They were to meet in town, Christmas shopping an hour or so either side of a simple lunch at Griffin's café. Were it not for an account in her own name, which Florence had kept since the death of her mother, when a modest sum of money and the rent each month from a property on Denman Street had been bequeathed her, she would be virtually penniless. Rex Madden, under Basil's instruction, collected and paid for orders from Burton's and Eddowes'. Household utilities Basil himself settled, he deemed his wife's needs to be fully met through this arrangement. She wore clothes from so many years back that adjustments of length had been necessary in order to blend with the present. This she'd achieved mainly through her own ingenuity, stitching engaged her mind, periods of inactivity were more challenging.

A knock came at the door, the postman, a package from Italy. Julia in her letters often told her mother that she should come to visit, explore the ways of another country. Florence wished she could but it was the thought of returning to Basil's wrath if she defied him, he'd made it quite clear her place was nowhere other than this house, she was afraid. If Caroline could go with her and if they could both escape, then Italy sounded like their ideal refuge. But Caroline now had a husband, her life was in Nottingham. Florence sighed, she would make herself a cup of tea and read news of Julia. The words on the paper brought her second daughter very close for those few precious minutes. At that moment her mind travelled to Annie Eddowes, Lincolnshire was a far cry from Rome but Annie had told her of the pleasure she took from reading letters sent by her daughter in law Francis, the feeling of hope when their content revealed happiness. It was strange they barely knew one another save for those brief conversations Annie and herself exchanged at the shop, yet Florence, if she ever truly needed a friend, would likely turn to Annie Eddowes before anyone else.

'Dear Mother,

I hope all is well, I have exciting news, which I hope will be equally so for you. A young man whom I have been seeing for some months has asked me to marry him. There was a time when I thought I never would, but Mother I do believe that I have learned at last the language of love'.

Florence wiped tears from the corner of her eye, her hands shook as she picked up the sheet of notepaper from her lap to read on. Like Annie, a feeling of hope warmed her and lessened the bruising.

Annie had arranged the items in the window using the cake as a centrepiece. Trade had been brisk, especially for those ingredients needed to make the cake. While Burtons displayed the most elegant iced confections and all manner of festive food, which met the needs and desires of the better off, Annie's simple approach had achieved to inspire the faint hearted and swell the shop's takings as a result. She had used a recipe from a book that aunt Bella had kept on a shelf in the front room at Winchester Street. 'The economy fruit cake'. Annie had baked it a number of times over the years and found it successful. Writing out the recipe in bold print on a large piece of card and adjusting the title to 'The economy Christmas cake', Annie placed it at one side of the window with the additional words 'all ingredients on sale within'. The other window she'd filled with baskets of nuts and oranges, sprinkled finely with mixed spice to release that rich fruity smell of Christmastime. Boxes of chocolates and colourful tins of toffees, one particularly attractive box of assorted chocolates to be raffled, the draw would take place on Monday the 22nd of December, the first customer of that day would pull from the large sweet jar, the winning ticket.

A tap-tap came at the window, Annie looked up to see Edna, her nose pressed to the glass, a roguish grin on her face.

"Our Annie's expectin'." The doorbell had barely ceased to 'clang' before Edna delivered her news. "Early next summer, I dare say all o' Nottingham knows by now, Billy's that excited he told everybody who called the exchange last night, I told him 'e ought to 'ave put a notice over the entry, like the King does at palace gates when there's a royal announcement, soppy sod." Edna flopped down on the chair by the counter.

"I'm so pleased for you all Edna," said Annie, "Billy's a proud dad and now he's looking forward to being a proud grandad." Edna let out a deep sigh. "Whatever's the matter, Annie's well isn't she, Alec must surely be pleased." Annie knew her best friend well, something was taking the edge off Edna's usual enthusiasm, for any new baby, and a sigh after declaring she was to be a grandma had to mean a problem.

"Our Annie's as fit as a flea an' over the moon wi' joy, Alec an'all. It's Lillian Sulley, I know the doctor told 'er that they'd caught it early but the poor kid's sick wi' worry. Thank God Norma's clear. Elsie's tried to persuade Lillian to move in wi' 'er an' Jim, what with the rent an' everythin' but she's convinced that she'd give it to them an' no amount o' tellin' can change 'er mind. She's takin' in washin' an' ironin'. Elsie helps out as much as she can wi' bits o' food but Jim's not earnin' anythin' like as much as 'e did at Barrow. What Jack did wi' his ill-gotten gains nobody knows, smoke an' booze most likely, Jim wer' allowed to visit him, 'e told me it made him cry, the sight o' Jack in that sanatorium. The place they've put him in is no better than a workhouse, e'll die in there wi' the sound o' coughin' an' chokin' all around him. Jack'll never see Norma again, its not likely e'll see Lillian neither. Jim's thankful that she's been advised not to visit, given 'er own condition. How they'll manage to keep Elsie from goin' God knows but I reckon it wer' the thought of his mother seein' Jack in such a place that upset Jim, yer could tell the poor man 'ad been cryin', his eyes wer' swollen an' sore. I'm that happy at our news, a grandchild, summat good to look forward to but what 'ave Elsie, Jim an' Lillian got to anchor their minds to, nowt, nowt at all."

Annie rubbed Edna's hand sensing how close her dearest friend was to tears. "When Harold was killed at the yard George was so young he didn't understand what had happened. I had to go back to work and leave him with aunt Bella. He loved Bella and she loved him. Looking back I do believe aunt Bella found great comfort in George's company. She'd grown fond of Harold, now his young son filled her days, spared her those hours of dwelling in grief. Aunt Bella wasn't a young woman and she did look and feel very weary. Winnie Bacon would pop her head over the wall and say, 'I'm having Jack for a bit today, you bring your George round and the two of them can play together, give Bella a break'. Elsie would be doing something with the others or attending the dentist, chiropodist or whatever demanded her time and so Jack would be in the care of his grandma until his mother collected him. Even then, still an infant, he'd climb like a monkey with no fear, onto the roof of the privy, and the coal shed, it was as if he preferred to be off the ground, contrary to most everyone else Jack felt safest when he was above the 'day to day'. I don't think he's more than four years older than George, Ted would get cross and slipper the boy's backside but it made no difference. Now when I think of how life for Jack has become, it saddens me. I know he's done wrong but I can't think of him now without remembering those times when he and George played together. It's the most cruel hurt for Elsie and Jim, but if they lose Jack it will be the rest of their family, their other children who'll bring them comfort. I shall call on Lillian, after Christmas when things have settled.

Customers are still preoccupied with Jack's arrest, forever talking about the burglaries and their condemnation can be savage, I cringe at it. Lillian will want to be alone with Norma and I can understand why but soon folk will move on to another topic of conversation and Lillian will feel more able to face the world beyond her door. She's done no wrong but that won't stop her feeling soiled."

At that moment the shop door opened and in came Mrs.Rashleigh. Seeing Edna at the counter her question was immediate. "Have the coppers found owt yet? I heard they've been searchin' Sulley's house."

Edna passed a piece of paper to Annie, "That's me Christmas order, I'll be off now." She turned to Mrs.Rashleigh, "Lillian an' Norma are copin' best they can, thank yer for askin'."

"It's no use us goin' door to door on the streets round 'ere, everybody's hard up, we need to go where there's brass, Langley Drive, The Ropewalk, knock on a few doors there an' we might rake in a bit. If we're goin' to sing then we've got to do it proper, they won't put as much as a farthin' in the tin if we don't sing in tune. What are you like? Give us a few bars o' Silent Night," said Jack Wainwright to his mate Charlie Jones.

"I can sing," said an indignant Charlie, besides I'm two months older than you so if anybody's goin' to do the judgin' then it should be me."

"Well I'm not goin' to sing to you on me own, we'll just do our best an' hope the women answer the door, if we give 'em a smile 'an wish 'em a happy Christmas I reckon they'll be a soft touch. Shepherds Watched, O come All Ye Faithful an' Silent Night. I know most o' the words for them, if we forget any then we'll make out we've got a cough an' carry on, might make 'em feel sorry for us, give a bit extra." Jack pulled the knots tight at either side of the tin, he'd made a handle from string with which to carry the empty malt tin. A small piece of tinsel he'd stuck to one side with sealing wax and put two thruppeny bits and a sixpence in the tin himself. "They're sure to look in, if posh folk see a tanner they won't want to put in less, they're like that, the nobs, got to keep up wi' the neighbours an' they'll think we got this money from the folk next door to 'em."

Charlie could see the logic but couldn't stop himself from asking where Jack had got two thruppeny bits and a tanner.

Borrowed 'em from me dad," said Jack, "I've told him I'll pay him back wi' interest, instead o' getting' a bob he'll have 1/6d. We shook on it, fair dues an' all that."

Charlie was impressed, it was the next part of Jack's plan that inspired him very much less.

"You should be the one to hold out the tin, when they see that you've not got all your fingers that's sure to make 'em feel sorry for yer, prick their conscience, they'll likely drop nowt but silver in the tin then." Charlie was about to object when the sound of St.Andrew's church clock struck six. "Come on, afore it gets too late," said Jack, "mam'll 'ave me tarred an' feathered if I'm not 'ome by nine."

It took them a good half an hour to reach Langley Drive, it looked hopeful, every house appeared to be lit so folk were at home. "We'll try Wicks, he's not got a missus, she died, but me dad reckons Wicks is decent enough, it's Stanford as never breaths out, sucks in, allus sucks in but don't part wi' as much as a breath of air."

"Which door are we supposed to go to, back or front?" Asked a hesitant Charlie.

"Front," replied Jack boldly, "we're not hawkin' owt, we're providin' a service." They walked up the path to the front door of Henry Wicks' house, Jack knew which house was Henry's from scrumping apples off the tree at the back. "Right, are yer ready? We'll do O Come All Ye Faithful, two verses then knock on the door."

"I only know the first verse," said Charlie.

"That's all I know an'all so we'll sing first verse twice," said Jack, "you get ready to hold out the tin when I knock."

A little nervously the two began to sing, but it was Charlie who found his confidence and the sound he made caused Jack to look on his friend with amazement. The shadow of a figure approached the door but for a minute or so the door remained closed and whoever stood on the inside waited until the voices faded on the last note before reaching for the latch. Henry Wicks opened the door wide, he looked upon the two lads and smiled. Charlie's hand, minus two fingers, held out the old malt tin, as close as he could to the light from inside the house, enabling Henry to see the coins resting at the bottom.

"Do you know any other Carols? He asked.

"Silent Night, we can do Silent Night," replied Jack. Apart from a cough of necessity during the second verse when the words of the fourth line escaped their memory, their rendition of the popular Carol was as pleasing to Henry Wicks as might have been a performance of The Hallelujah Chorus by the entire Huddersfield Choral Society.

"What's your name?" Henry directed his question at Charlie.

"Jones sir, Charlie Jones."

"Well young man, it was a pleasure to listen to such a fine piece of singing and you so ably supported by your friend, who is?" Henry now directed his question at Jack.

"Wainwright Mr.Wicks, Jack Wainwright, you know me dad Steve, works at pit."

"Ah yes, I know your father very well, I like to think that he and I are old friends." Henry reached into his pocket, Charlie quick as a flash, dangled the tin in front of Henry who observed the missing fingers. He made no comment but let two coins fall from his hand into the tin. Jack noted the clatter, bit o' weight in them he thought to himself.

"Merry Christmas Mr.Wicks an' ta very much." Jack doffed his cap, a gesture so old for his years. Henry watched the two boys walk away, a smile spread across his face, Charlie Jones sang like a lark, a lark with a damaged wing. One thing Henry felt sure of, many hearts would soften at the sound of the boy soprano, and Jack, not so musically gifted but possessing a charm which raised the spirits, could sell their doorstep Carols effortlessly with his bold approach. Good luck to them thought Henry as he closed the door, humming the tune of Silent Night.

It was almost half past eight, their enterprise could not continue without severe consequences when reaching home so sitting in the porch of St.Andrew's, they divided their takings.

"Don't drop it Charlie," said Jack as he counted out the coins, his own into his cap, plus his dad's dues, Charlie's into his cupped hands. "One pound three shillings and sixpence each, blimey we could do this for a livin'."

"It'd be a poor livin', we'd only work at Christmas," observed Charlie, carefully depositing his earnings into his jacket pocket before any slipped from his deficient hand.

"Wi' your voice an' my nous I reckon we'd make a killin'. That bloke at The Ropewalk wer' really impressed an' if he teaches music at Blackmore's like 'e said, then he must know a good voice when he hears one. Me dad says that if God gives yer an ability to do summat a bit special then yer shouldn't throw it back in his face. We'll go again on Monday night, do The Park an' the posh 'arf o' Castle Road. You an' me are pure genius Charlie, that's what we are, pure soddin' genius."

Annie now dared to hope that the weather would hold and no snow would fall to prevent Freddy travelling from Lincolnshire. While everyone bustled about clad in warm hats and scarves, the roads were clear and predicted to remain so. She'd taken up a mug of tea to Charles, some would condemn his apparent idleness but Annie found it easier simply to get on with her work and not allow the situation to overtake her thinking, too many other challenges demanded her attention. The papers were sorted, she'd swallow her last few gulps of tea then open up. John had left for work only Hilda shared with Charles the comparative luxury of a later start. The library opened at 9-30, Hilda was required to be there by nine. Banking up the fire in the range, Annie then scrubbed her hands free of the coal dust and newsprint. Always after handling the papers her hands were black, several chaps tormented her fingers but they came with winter and left with spring, all part of the yearly cycle.

The first customer on his way to Player's, after purchasing a paper and a quarter of barley sugars, happily obliged Annie in drawing the winning raffle ticket.

Rex Madden was the name written on the back, curiously as Annie perceived it, she felt a degree of pleasure at this result. The box of chocolates was indeed splendid, bearing a colourful printed lid of flowers arranged in a fine china bowl and of dimensions that would enable the box, once the contents had been consumed, to serve many a useful purpose. Annie herself kept sewing needles and cottons in one similar. Mrs.Madden would surely be delighted and Rex would derive great satisfaction from securing the prize for his wife. Over the months Annie had come to view him as an unworthy recipient of the title 'Cratchet'. Rex Madden had a softer side she felt sure, but just as Florence Stanford lived under the domineering authority of her husband, so too did the unfortunate mortal who was Stanford's man. The thought of happiness within the Madden household when the box of chocolates graced the table there, brought a genuine smile to Annie's face.

The morning passed quickly when an altercation between two men outside on the street, thrust the shop into the path of the furore. Requiring a constable to restore order, it served to entice those of a nosey nature to the scene and then to the shop where Annie must endure their animated gossip between cutting bacon and cheese, weighing tea and sugar and declaring as forcefully as she could, her total lack of knowledge concerning the extra marital affairs pursued by Walter Waverley, one of the two offenders escorted away by constable Peak.

The arrival of Celia and Mathew early in the afternoon brought a welcome interlude. Charles had eaten and gone out to wherever his mood had taken him. The shop very often experienced a lull at about this time of day, Annie imagined it was ordained that mankind should pause in his activities, a greater influence deeming it necessary to allow drained minds, halfway through the day, to regain substance. She'd not ever thought of it until the inspired Mr.Pagett had one early afternoon remarked, 'God's toppin' up time Mrs.Eddowes, they're all indoors bein' refilled'. Mathew was not yet walking, Celia lifted him from the pushchair and handed him to his grandma. A naturally friendly child he planted a kiss on Annie's lips and chuckled with delight at the notion of sweeties. Their visits to the shop ever resulted in some small treat being given Mathew and today his eyes took in the array of colourful goods on display, the Christmas decorations especially caught his attention. A small wooden reindeer that Annie had placed by the till drew him like a magnet.

"Here you are then," said Annie, "you can take it home and show your dad, be careful not to break it." She was amused by the little boy's dexterity, the wooden figurine was immediately tucked inside his coat pocket giving Celia no chance to take it from him. The women laughed. "Could you do something for me Celia?" Asked Annie. "The raffle has been won by the Maddens, their address is, 72, Glover Street, not far from you, if you could carry it on the ledge of the pushchair and deliver it to them, that would be a big help. I doubt if Rex Madden will come to the shop between now and Christmas Eve."

Celia went through to the back to make a pot of tea and to find a shortcake biscuit for Mathew. Between customers Annie managed to spend some time with her daughter-in –law and Celia promised they would call in on Christmas day to see Freddy and the family after leaving the Tozers'.

"William seems surprisingly keen to spend time at mothers," said Celia. "I can't imagine his enthusiasm is for her usual inquisition, I rather think he enjoys chatting to Edmund and Caroline, gleaning any information he can on the affairs of Mr.Stanford. Though he would never admit to it, I do believe that William is just as inquisitive as mother and equally selective over whom he considers to be appropriate society."

Celia checked the number, worn faint from weathering it nevertheless confirmed that she stood outside the Maddens, No.72. a house like most others on the street, its only distinguishing feature was a globe of the world positioned inside the window of the front room. Celia had observed it many times as she'd walked by. With no nets to obscure the interior, the large orb bearing its map of the continents and oceans proved difficult to ignore. It appeared incongruous, an item to aid learning, to deliver knowledge, residing on Glover Street where the great wide world seemed far removed from the ordinary folk leading mundane, unadventurous lives. Celia smiled down at Mathew as if to reassure him that her knocking at this door would only delay them for a moment. After a minute and her repeated knock, the door was slowly opened and the face of a middle-aged woman peered cautiously around it. Her eyes held alarm and Celia felt compelled to explain herself with urgency.

"It is Mrs.Madden isn't it?" A brief nod answered Celia's enquiry. "Your husband had the winning ticket in the raffle Mrs.Madden. I'm Celia Eddowes, Mrs.Eddowes' daughter in law." The woman's expression was vague. "The shop on Gregory Street, they held a raffle, Mr.Madden bought a ticket." Celia lifted the bag containing the box of chocolates from the pushchair but Doris Madden had opened the door wider and almost as though oblivious to Celia's explanation, she'd stooped to hold out her hand to Mathew, he readily clutched her fingers and chuckled in his usual friendly way. "He'll stand any amount of attention, a typical male," said Celia humorously. Doris Madden straightened her back and turned to Celia.

"What's his name?" She said timidly.

"Mathew, he had his first birthday last month," replied Celia, handing over the chocolates.

"Thank you, thank your mother at the shop."

While she couldn't be sure, so quickly did Doris Madden withdraw into the house, Celia thought she'd seen tears welling in the eyes of this quiet woman and suspected not even a splendid box of chocolates would remedy the cause of them.

"That's the house where Jack Sulley come off the roof," said Charlie pointing across the road.

"How do you know it's that one?" Said Jack, pulling his collar about his neck, tonight there was a biting wind chill.

"Me dad wer' cleanin' windows here the day after it happened, the coppers wer' all over the place, askin' folk if they'd seen owt, sniffed around me dad for days, 'cause of his ladders I reckon. They had Sulley but not the bloke as helped him, whoever he is drove away wi' the lead. A copper even come to our house, put the wind up me mam, looked in the privy, searched the shed. Grandad thought 'e wer' from Sally Army, come collectin' so 'e give the copper a tanner an' asked him to bring the band to play outside our house. Grandma loved the Sally Army band, she knew all the hymns, every word."

"It's a pity you don't know all the soddin' words," said Jack, "I've heard the first verse of 'O Come All Ye' that many times I could recite the words in me sleep, next year we'll get a book wi' Carols in so we can learn all the verses an' sing 'em proper."

The fact that a group of singers had been door to door in The Park only a short time before them, had resulted in less generous offerings and their malt tin wasn't holding enough to satisfy Jack. "We'll do one more here then move on to Castle Road. Apart from Davina, this lot's been miserly, I knew we'd do alright at Mrs.Wright's, she's a good friend o' me grandma Sarah's, allus been generous, we used to go to her house at Christmas but the family's gone too big now an' she's too old to cope wi' us all."

They stood outside an imposing property, bay windows either side of the front door. "This'll do, we'll make this the last one here." Jack led Charlie up the path, light shone through a glass panel above the door and from an upstairs window. On the wall beside the brass knocker a plaque, that too was of brass, it bore a name, Jack ever curious, squinted in the dim light but achieved to read the letters, Dr. Hugh Bennett, F.I.C. Both knocker and nameplate were badly tarnished. The boot scraper by the step sat amid an accumulation of leaves and general debris, including a dead blackbird. "Come on, sing up Charlie, this one's our last hope of makin' the tin rattle with a bit more lucre."

They sang 'Silent Night', knocked on the door and waited. About to knock again Jack had raised his arm but heard movement. The door was opened by a very elderly gentleman, he peered over his spectacles at the boys.

"Is it just the two of you?" He asked in a soft voice and with a kindly expression.

"Yes sir, happy Christmas doctor," Jack prompted Charlie to hold out the tin.

"There were too many of the others, my wife couldn't stand to be surrounded by so many, she's not well you see. Would you be good enough to come in and sing to her, I would be grateful."

Jack passed a quick glance to Charlie and whispered. "Wipe your feet. Be our pleasure doctor, you lead the way." Expecting to follow the old man through the hallway to a sitting room the boys were surprised when he led them to the foot of the stairs.

"My wife's in bed, only two short flights, come this way if you will." Charlie felt nervous, the house was so very quiet, not even a clock ticked to break the silence. "In here." Dr.Bennett crossed the floor to the bedside and spoke gently to a woman lying in the large, four-poster bed. "Two young men have come to sing a Carol for you Agnes." He stepped back and beckoned Jack and Charlie forward with his hand. The lamp on a small cabinet by the head of the bed, burned with a soft light and the elderly woman's face appeared ivory like under its beam. A neatly folded man's nightshirt lay on the pillow beside her. 'Silent Night' seemed most appropriate so the boys sang it again, two verses, nervousness brought a tremor to Charlie's voice, adding to that boy soprano innocence. "That was just right, Agnes really enjoyed your singing, could you do it again, just while I refill her bottle, it will only take me a minute or two, her feet get so cold you know." He reached under the covers at the foot of the bed and pulled out a hot water bottle. "I shall be back very quickly, just sing to Agnes she'll be no bother." He left the room with the heavy stone bottle under his arm.

Again the strains of 'Silent Night' fell on the air, but two lines in Jack reached forward and touched the woman's face. Charlie gave him a quizzical look but reluctant to disrupt their rendition Jack sang out confidently, inwardly considering Charlie's nervous disposition too fragile to bear his discovery, at least until they were once more outside on the street. Hugh Bennett returned to the bedroom, carefully lifted the bedcover and put the bottle against his wife's feet. He turned to face the boys, reached into his pocket and took out two half crowns.

"May I wish you both the very best of the Season, Agnes and I are so very grateful to you, indeed you do sing very well." He dropped the coins into the malt tin, smiled and led them downstairs.

Jack waited until they'd walked half a dozen yards down the pavement.

"Bloody Hell Charlie, his missus is dead, dead as a stone."

Charlie's hand shook, sending the malt tin from side to side on the ends of the string. "Can't be, how can yer be so sure?"

"She's dead I'm tellin' yer, Agnes is lyin' in that bed as cold as a codfish."

"What are we goin' to do? We should tell somebody," said Charlie, "the poor old bloke's goin' off his head."

"Uhm," said Jack, deep in thought, "he give us a shillin' a verse, what we'll do is come back tomorrow night an' see what happens. If he asks us to come in an' sing to his missus again we'll give 'em two verses o' 'While Shepherds Watched', then go straight to Tommy Spooner to tell him, afore she starts to smell."

"I'm not singin' to a corpse, besides what if she's already started to smell?" Charlie was in a state of disbelief.

"Then we'll only do one verse. Yer don't need to be afraid o' the dead, they won't hurt yer." Said Jack.

"It gives me the soddin' creeps, dead bodies, I want to go home."

"Only one body, what's up wi' yer." Scoffed Jack.

"Two, that dead bird an'all."

"Yer big sissy, come on, Castle Road to do, Stanford lives there, now that will be like getting' blood from a stone as me mam'd say. Five bob from the dead wer' a cinch compared to prisin' a penny from that tight fisted old bugger."

"Well you can carry the bloody tin then, my fingers are freezin'." Charlie passed the string handle to Jack and thrust his hands inside his pockets. "Another arf hour an' I'm off home, you can do as yer like"

Jack grinned, "Trouble wi' you Jones is you've no nous."

Henry Wicks raised his glass, "To you Andrew, and may it be a peaceful Christmas for us all."

Andrew Smithfield smiled. "Four days, four days of silent machines, that in itself is a welcome peace."

Henry took a sip of the whisky. "Thank you for coming, there's something about Christmas Eve spent alone that weighs down a man's spirit, a woman's too I shouldn't wonder. You are several years younger than me Andrew, find yourself a wife, one with a mind to challenge your own, with strength that every day surprises you and with a heart that beats with the very same rhythm as yours. Leonora is dead, I am to the world outside, a widower, yet in here," Henry pressed his clenched fist to his chest, " in here Andrew I have a wife still. At such times as the Eve of Christmas, it's not being able to feel her warmth that's so disheartening, it creates the inability to feel a part of that big celebration going on out there." Henry cast his eyes to the window where he'd drawn the curtain across all but for a gap of a few inches, just enough to allow him not to feel a total isolation. "Did you here the tragic account of Hugh Bennett? A brilliant mind, he's been retired for many years but as a younger man he lectured at The Royal Society, worked on groundbreaking projects. He maintained it was his wife who enabled him, herself a bright woman, she kept his mind constantly vibrant. Apparently she died some days ago, but he'd carried on as if she were still alive, though she lay dead in their bed. It's hard to imagine the despair in that house, a man, his wife of many years, now the realisation of mortality, so final, is it really so shocking that in Bennett's great mind she lives still. We are fortunate, Hugh Bennett and myself, what we have inside, nothing and no one can take away, but you my friend, I worry for you. Since your aunt died I have detected a deep loneliness, in this coming year Andrew you must seek to change that, if only to dispel my concern as your friend."

"I am not so very much younger than you Henry," said Andrew, "and set in my ways by now I'm sure, what woman could find any attraction, I can't imagine that I shake the ground beneath their feet," he hesitated, "besides, I have a flaw in my character. There have been only two women to whom I've ever felt drawn, neither was free to return even a fondness. I admired aunt Alicia for her honesty, her entirely decent nature, if she'd known of my weakness, my desire for something, someone already attached, she would have lashed me with her tongue and she'd have been right to do so, wouldn't she?" Andrew looked into Henry's eyes expecting to see a shocked disapproval, instead a smile came to Henry's face.

"I am saddened to hear of your dilemma Andrew. In such matters of the heart I am not wise enough to be judge. I was lucky in love, not everyone is so blessed, I would find it easier by far to advise on affairs of business, where the 'fors and againsts' are more clearly defined. The complexities of 'man and woman' require someone with far greater experience. Having said, I'm quite certain some relationships, even marriages, are not what they appear to be. May God forgive me for voicing such a belief but if ever a woman needed rescuing, then it is surely Florence Stanford. I dread to think what that gentle lady has to endure. Basil is a bully, a tyrant. What a confusion life is Andrew, an utter confusion."

"Stanford approached the council with a view to selling more of his land, an acreage at the old Colver site. As I understand it, Cheetham informed him of the current financial situation, I'm nothing to do with the finance department of the council but we've all been made aware that the coffers are seriously depleted, it came as no surprise. Stanford will have to hang on to his land until matters improve but with the economy so sluggish, I can't imagine that will happen very soon. Bobbers Mill is a large commitment, meeting all the costs of that will prove difficult." Andrew was relieved to have steered the conversation in another direction.

Henry was pensive, he sighed. "That will do nothing to lighten Stanford's mood, I'm tired of doing battle with him."

"That was very telling Henry, are you thinking of retiring?"

"I've always wanted to visit Europe, Leonora held no desire to travel abroad, she maintained that our island offered every sight enlightening to man. Since the war and all that happened, I feel duty bound to see with my own eyes, those lands where our young men fell."

"Who would Stanford put in your place?" Andrew was genuinely curious, men like Henry Wicks came along rarely.

"I know who he should make manager but Stanford is too ridden with hypocrisy, too obsessed by power to recognise true leadership. Steve Wainwright could run that pit and make a fine job of it, he's nobody's fool. The office Eddie Wills knows as well as I, with his experience of the admin' and Steve's ability to calm and encourage the men, they'd be a winning formula. Stanford would reap the gain but it's him who's the fool, too blinded by snobbery to see. They're related through marriage, Steve and Eddie married sisters from a family of several offspring, sadly the only two sons are both dead, the eldest was killed in a tragic accident at the slaughter yard, before ever Cheetham had it. In fact the eldest was Mrs.Eddowes first husband, it must have been a dreadful time for her, I believe their child was but an infant when the accident occurred. Then the other son was killed in the war, I think there are four or five daughters, Steve is married to Gertie and Eddie to Mavis, I've got to know them over the years, solid, sound people. When I go Stanford will likely poach someone from another pit, someone he considers useful to his competitor. He'll dangle a carrot in front of them, rub his hands with satisfaction at the deal done, but it won't take the poor devil he lures very long to realise that the carrot is only sweet at it's tip, the rest is a bitter chew."

A sudden sound in the hallway caused both men to pause in their conversation.

"What was that," said Henry, getting to his feet. He crossed the room and peered around the door, an envelope lay on the mat, just inside the front door. He went to pick it up then returned to his companion. "A card I imagine, delivered by hand." Henry opened the envelope to reveal a greetings card, inside the words. 'With every good wish for the Season, from Steve Wainwright and family'. He handed it to Andrew to read for himself the strange coincidence.

"We shall take another dram of fortitude my friend." Henry poured whisky into each glass. "This time we shall raise our glasses in a toast to the solid and the sound."

The two chinked their glasses together in full accord declaring.

"To the Wainwrights of this world."

CHAPTER SIXTEEN

LATE MARCH 1931

When Sergeant Beasley came to the vicarage, Reverend Hockley anticipated bad news of some sort. Not since the blessing of the war memorial had they exchanged conversation, a handful of customary good mornings, or good afternoons had been the extent of their address. So when the uniformed officer had stood at his door, Mathew Hockley felt no rush of pleasure at the sight, no expectation of anything other than an official account of some poor mortal's adversity. Why then did Beasley's word so confound him, Jack Sulley, defiant offender, was asking to see the Reverend Hockley of St.Andrew's.

'While you're about it vicar, get Sulley to spill a name, if he thinks it'll buy him salvation he'll likely tell you who's the other arf of his lawless partnership, you'd be surprised how many so called tough men squeal like infants when they think their time's up'.

Beasley was a lucky man, he had the ability to detach himself from human weakness, to treat it as being outside his remit and therefore of little consequence. The Reverend Hockley, a man of God, he must deal with such irritations.

With an unsettling nervousness, Mathew Hockley made his way to the sanatorium at Ilkeston. He'd heard of its grim interior, no funds wasted on that phenol spattered holding pen for TB ridden villains, who'd never known dignity and thus required none. But nothing could have prepared him for what he now witnessed. Death hung on the air, even through the mask he'd been given to cover his nose and mouth, death's overwhelming presence found his breath and made heavy his lungs. He'd sat by many a bedside offering comfort to the sick, the dying, but there death had waited quietly, patiently. At this place death refused to tarry somewhere out of sight, instead it gripped the slender life in its vice, slowly but deliberately tightening its hold, here was to be no release.

The warder sniffed, "In there, you'll not get much out of him, nor likely put much in him, too far gone."

His words were careless, cast randomly as though he considered the vicar's attendance a complete waste of time, an unnecessary interruption to the well ordered routine of institutionalised demise. Despair reached the pit of Mathew's stomach as he looked upon the frailty, the empty, retreating features of the once defiant Jack, now so reduced in flesh he appeared no more than a pasty, impoverished youth, not long for this world, yet unclaimed by the next.

"Hello Jack." Mathew's voice was muffled by the cloth across his mouth but Jack's eyes opened and a smile, a courageous smile as Mathew deemed it to be, touched this long experienced Reverend, sending a hurt deep into his heart.

"Ta for comin' Rev, I knew yer would." Jack's voice was faint, his chest sunken, his breathing laboured, Mathew cautioned him.

"Don't try to speak Jack, I'll sit with you a while, you keep your strength."

Jack smiled again. "What strength I have left I must use to tell yer summat."

Mathew tried to dissuade him from the effort at this moment feelin no concern over the identity of Jack's accomplice. Sergeant Beasley might consider it crucial but he didn't look into the face of a man drowning in his own blood, surely knowing there was nothing he could do to spare the man's suffering. But it was not on revealing the name of his helper that Jack chose to spend his failing strength.

"I'm sorry Rev, I stole from your boss, took lead from the roofs of his houses." Listening to Jack as he struggled to make himself heard pained Mathew greatly, it was an ordeal that passed so slowly, each word fighting for enough breath to grant it relevance. "Go to our house, see Lillian an' our Norma, look at 'em, really look at 'em, like yer wer' s'posed to remember every detail, then you decide. In the scullery, under the sink, a loose flag', lift it up wi' the claw hammer I keep on the shelf o' the coal shed. A baccy tin, wi' all the money in I got from sellin' the lead." Jack's eyes held no light, they stared up at Mathew veiled in acceptance of the inevitable. "It's all there, what I stole from your boss, I didn't use any, yer can give it back to him, or yer can give it to Lillian for our Norma. You decide, whatever yer do I respect your decision, 'cause you won Rev, you took the ground, fair an' square."

Mathew swallowed hard and shook his head. "No Jack, there is no winner."

Jack was determined, he reached for Mathew's hand. "You're still standin' Rev I'm flat on me back, a man has to recognise when he's beat, it's only sportin'. Now I need yer to do one more thing, count me out, a ten second count."

Mathew made to protest but Jack became stressed. Pulling the mask from his face Reverend Hockley said. "It doesn't work like that Jack, only the Lord can decide when."

Jack gave his brave smile and spoke again. "Do it anyroad, a proper count, stand wi' your arm raised over me, it's only ten seconds, that's all Rev, just ten seconds." When Mathew's faltering voice uttered the number ten, Jack's features suddenly found a curious peace, his tortured chest for a moment paused in its convulsion. "Ta Rev, you go now, tell Lillian I'm sorry, an' give our Norma her dad's love."

Mathew walked away from the gates of the sanatorium with an anguish inside him that would not be quelled, perhaps if he asked God for guidance he would find calm, but something undeniable prevented him from sending up a plea for help when his dilemma was so bound in 'earth', too shocking for the delicate tenderness of heaven's counsel. If he gave in to weakness and went straight home, would courage leave him altogether, would he ever force his steps towards Winchester Street, could he there compel his hand to knock at the door, order his eyes to look into Lillian Sulley's eyes and remain composed before the child. He sat for a moment on a wall, no particular wall, just one solid enough to bear the weight he carried about himself, not unlike the one outside the Mechanics Institute where he'd sat with Jack that day their minds had sparred a friendly round, shaking hands at the result. If St.Jude should come by this spot then surely he would recognise the lost cause trembling at the wall, waiting to be found. Only busy people, ordinary, everyday people passed by, St.Jude was not among them. Resigned to his task, the Reverend Hockley made his way to the home of Jack Sulley, to look upon Jack's wife Lillian and their little girl, to decide.

His gentle tap-tap at the back door was answered by Lillian, in the midst of ironing, her face was flushed from the activity. The last person she'd expected to see was the vicar, taken aback, she remained silent.

"May I come in Lillian, don't be alarmed, nothing has happened that need call you from your work."

She opened wide the door and stood to one side for him to enter. A child, naturally pretty, played on the floor of the living room, nervous from numerous visits by policemen, she gave only a brief glance to Mathew before returning her concentration to a set of wooden blocks which she turned from side to side, trying to match the pieces of a picture. An old blanket covered the tabletop on which Lillian ironed, two large baskets of laundry awaited her attention. The young woman looked tired and drawn, the apron tied about her waist emphasised her slight frame, a man could have easily spanned her middle with his hands. A fire burned in the grate, the flat iron sat over its heat on a solid trivet. The tension in the room could not be borne by either of them, Mathew must do what he had come to do as quickly as he could and leave them in peace.

"I've come from the sanatorium, I spent a little time with Jack. He is sorry Lillian, I believe he is truly sorry and he sends, through me, his love." Mathew reached down and smoothed his hand over Norma's hair, still Lillian didn't speak. "Jack has asked me to do something, it requires me to find a hammer in the coal shed, and with it raise a loose flagstone beneath the sink."

Lillian looked bewildered but calmly took the iron from the trivet and continued her work. Under the flag, in a hollow of the ground lay a tobacco tin, just as Jack had described. Mathew prised open the lid, a few one pound and ten shilling notes, a scattering of silver, this was Jack's hoard. He could no longer hold back tears, it was a pathetic sum over which to condemn a life. Mathew replaced the flagstone, returned the hammer to the coal shed and desperately trying to control his shaking, he crossed the room to where Lillian worked.

"Take it, you need have no fear, you've done nothing wrong Lillian, I've handed this to you." He smiled to offer reassurance. "If the vicar himself has passed this tin to you then how could you possibly be at fault. Use its contents for your daughter, only ever a little at a time, keep yourselves warm and fed. It may sound strange when I tell you Lillian, that the money is God given, but it's the truth, the money is for you and Norma, from God."

As Reverend Hockley walked away from that small house on Winchester Street he pondered upon Lillian's silence. Mute throughout his time there, not questioning, nor crying, without a single utterance, the unfortunate young woman bore her adversity with no complaint. But Mathew's inner voice spoke, to that absent individual who so occupied his mind, his challenger, who had looked beyond 'the cloth' and seen 'the man'. 'The decision was flawed Jack, you won, you took it on points, there is no doubt, Jack Sulley took it on points, fair and square'!

That evening, as light faded and dusk led day across the divide to night, so Jack's life went too. Quietly, just as time itself, barely noticed.

CHAPTER SEVENTEEN

George lay with his head on his hands looking up at the sky where high above them a pair of buzzards soared on the thermals, not making a sound the two birds appeared to fly effortlessly in wide arcs, crossing one another's path in a synchronized display of unity, of understanding, a partnership that without the need of voice, graced the heavens with its perfection.

He turned to look at Alice lying beside him, her gaze was concentrated on the dozens of delicate seed heads, floating on the air like a distant, passing angel host. Again she blew softly over the spent dandelion, releasing more of the dainty seraphs of nature.

George laughed. "They'll likely come down in some manicured cottage garden, there to produce defiant clumps of weed among the hollyhocks and delphiniums."

Alice cast the dandelion stalk over the grass and turned her face to George. Her kiss was warm and lingering, a feeling of himself being airborne, George soared like the buzzards in great arcs of delirium. But a sudden clamour of animated voices brought him back to the firmness of earth.

Below them, further down the slope of the grass bank, a group of young people had been watching the ford, the water splash, as it was commonly referred to by the villagers of Tissington, waiting for the unsuspecting driver of a low vehicle to become marooned when the water at its height, stifled the exhaust and disabled the engine. Cries of delight now fell upon the unfortunate driver, but well used to this event and followers only of harmless fun, the able young men of the group pulled off their socks, rolled up their trousers and ran down the grass bank to redeem the situation. Within minutes the car was high and dry and a truly grateful driver was energetically shaking hands with his rescuers. George grinned, by now both he and Alice were observing the scene. The place had a charm about it, a sense of well being.

"Come on, let's walk back, our landlady will have scones and Bakewell tarts out of the oven by now." George jumped to his feet and held out his hand to Alice. They had visited each of the five wells at Tissington, Yew Tree well being especially beautiful. The flower petals, seedpods and other materials gathered by the village folk courtesy of nature's goodwill, decorated the ancient wells magnificently. Prepared for Ascension Day the previous Thursday, a few of the more flimsy petals had faded slightly by the time George and Alice viewed them this Saturday but still they created an unforgettable spectacle. As Alice had remarked 'they were great works of art but unlike those of the masters, hanging in secured stately homes and musty galleries, these were free for any man to gaze upon and their splendour glorified the spring of life'.

When the Black Death had taken the lives of countless numbers up and down the country, the water that flowed through the wells at Tissington remained pure and kept safe all those people who drank from them. As they walked hand in hand, George indulged in a feeling of pride. Here they were, he and his wife, enjoying the Derbyshire countryside on a day so clear that from high ground the views extended for miles without a factory chimney or pithead in sight.

When Percy Pollard had called him into the office early in April, shook his hand and said, 'George me boy you've made foreman, from next week you'll be overseein' your section, every cog, spoke an' bloody chain along wi' every gripe, ache an' soddin' excuse the soft buggers come up with, you deserve it lad, the responsibility an' the eight bob a week extra. Be firm, be fair an' may God help yer'.

George's first thought had been Alice, of being able to surprise her with a treat. Since their wedding they had made their home a place of pure happiness. At the end of each working day, a simple contentment allowed them to speak, eat, sleep and make their own harmony, it bound their lives in threads of gold. George considered himself a very lucky man, now he could show his wife just how much he cared, he would take her away for a long weekend to a place where memories could be made, special, long abiding memories, which would weave rich colour into their past.

He'd listened many times to grandma Sarah when she'd let her thoughts drift from the black and white of the present to those of early years when she and Samuel lived in the happiness of each other's company. The image her words created in his mind was ever in richest colour, never a drab grey or a solemn black but vibrant rich tones that made those long gone days seem much less distant. When one day he and Alice would sit talking to their grandchildren they too must have colourful stories to tell, while their future was exciting and George embraced it with every fibre of his being, so too must he provide them with a past. He'd read of the charm and peace of the Derbyshire villages, especially Tissington where the well dressing each Whitsuntide created a spectacle not to be missed. First confirming with Percy that he could take the Friday off, George had made enquiries about coach times and availability of lodgings. When he'd achieved to book them into a small bed and breakfast at Ashbourne and arranged their departure by coach from Nottingham he'd delighted in telling Alice of his plan.

Satisfied at all times by the simplest of activities, her excitement at the prospect of a weekend away, staying in a boarding house and being entirely free of routine for four days, transported her from diligent duty to carefree abandon. George had chuckled at her childlike enthusiasm and impatience, she must wait two weeks for this treat. Her kisses each morning as he left for Raleigh and each evening on his return had bathed him in innocent devotion, he rejoiced in a sense of deep satisfaction, his Alice, his wife, was completely happy. Such knowledge enabled a man, George Boucher, foreman at Raleigh, wouldn't call the King his uncle!

"Look over there, a fox." Alice pointed at the far hedgerow where upright ears and alert eyes studied their approach. For several seconds the animal stood motionless, every muscle taut as a spring, then, deciding it had observed them for long enough, it sped across the field and out of sight. "It's beautiful wild and free." Alice ran ahead several yards, her arms outstretched like wings, buzzards' wings, Angels' wings, George watched her flight, his heart followed her, an understanding without the need of voice. Breathless, she stopped, turned to look back and called out, "Come on slow coach, scones and Bakewell tarts, and who knows what else may tempt you."

She blew kisses and laughed with a gloriously liberated mischievousness. They were making memories, together they would create those colourful stories to relate to their grandchildren, Ashbourne, Whitsuntide, 1931.

"You can't take on everybody's worries, you'll kill yourself tryin' an' they won't lay awake at night grievin' for yer', it'll be me an' our two lads as does that, let it go Steve, you've stood up to the bosses long enough, it's time a young blood took over."

Gertie skewered the breast of mutton in place around the stuffing, anxious and frustrated at the sight of her husband seated at the kitchen table, cradling his head in his hands.

Henry Wicks had been gone no more than a fortnight and already Stafford Hinds, Wicks successor, had shown his colours. Firmly in the pocket of Basil Stanford he paraded his allegiance with the zeal of a convert. Jack Haynes had summed him up in just two words 'arse licker', not a dignified eloquence perhaps but nonetheless accurate.

The back door suddenly opened with a rush of air. "What a carry on, one o' Wrenshaw's 'osses collapsed comin' down Monsall Street, dead, just dropped dead, nearly strangled the other poor 'oss as it fell. Driver sent somebody to fetch help an' the police come, then the fire brigade turned up but neither could do owt. Woolascroft's got liftin' gear on site at Bobbers Mill so they've got to wait for the bloke as can drive it to come an' hoist the poor old 'oss on to a flat bed lorry." Jack stood panting from the exertion of running home to deliver the news.

"Where's Henry?" asked Gertie with a sigh of exasperation, "You surely haven't left him at Monsall Street, they'll be out in their droves by now, nothin' draw a crowd quicker than summat dead or dyin', he'll be lost in the crush."

"Henry's alright, we bumped into aunty Maggie an' the girls, they were on their way to The Theatre Royal to a matinee, one o' them singin' an' dancin' shows by that Novello bloke, all a bit poncy if you ask me. Anyroad, aunty Maggie said Henry could go an'all an that I was to tell you that she'd bring him home after."

Steve looked at Gertie and winked. The last thing he'd want for either of his sons would be to work at the pit, yet in Jack he saw that spark, that glimpse of vital energy, which fired a man's courage and kept him alight where others faded at the slightest deviation of draught. Steve had seen it in Jack Haynes too, a fearless conviction that remained unbowed from pressure, never one to use three words where two would do but a deep thinking individual with well considered opinions.

"Are yer comin' then Dad, it's not every day a dead waggon 'oss gets lifted off the street an' there'll be a right scramble for the manure. It must 'ave been the pressure when it hit the ground 'cause it shoved it out like cannon fire, an' I reckon it wer' shock as made the other shed a load. Bill Rashleigh says there's nowt better for rhubarb than 'oss shit, I could likely make a bob if we make haste."

"There's no such thing as an 'oss," said Gertie, "it's just as easy to say horse as it is to say 'oss."

"It's written on the board outside the wheelwright's at Radford," said Jack, "a rollin' stone gathers no moss an' a broken wagon idles the 'oss. How are you goin' to make horse rhyme wi' moss?" Jack gathered up the bucket and shovel from beneath the sink. "Waste not, want not, I'll wash 'em after."

Steve pulled on his jacket and chuckled. Planting a kiss on his wife's cheek he whispered roguishly. "I think my love you could be floggin' a dead 'oss!"

"Give me strength," said Gertie, "you're worse than me dad, mam wer' forever tryin' to improve his P's an' Q's but Davina would always laugh an' plead with him to recite, 'how now brown cow' in broad Yorkshire."

"Won't be long, I wanted to call on Eddie for a few minutes anyway." Steve turned to look at young Jack, on his way through the back door with the bucket. "He'll do love, our lad'll do."

"Do you want middle or streaky this week Edna?" Asked Annie as she worked her way down Edna's list.

Edna let out a huff of breath as she pondered. "Better 'ave middle, Billy likes the rinds crisped up, 'e nearly 'as a fit when 'e sees Nellie Draper hang 'er's up for the birds. I told him, one o' these days I shall see him take off from the wall wi' his neck outstretched an' his beak wide open, folk 'ould think I never fed him. Our Myra's as bad, she's got the appetite of a donkey, she's into same size knickers as me an' she's only twelve. Poor Annie's fed up wi' bein' so big, only a couple more weeks to go. She's not sleepin' much, can't get comfortable whichever side she's on." Edna picked up the bacon from the counter and put it into her bag with the other items. "I heard a bit o' news yesterday, if it's true then I expect somebody'll bring it into the shop. If I'd seen our Susie she'd know but her an' Joe aren't comin' round 'till tomorrow teatime. Joyce Spooner an' William Haynes have got engaged while he was home on leave."

"Well I'm pleased," said Annie, as she weighed up sugar. "The girl deserves some happiness and William is the steady sort, he'll look after Joyce, I believe Pat has a young man too, Hilda saw them together in the arboretum. I keep thinking about George and Alice, they've gone away for the weekend, a treat to celebrate. George has had a pay rise and promotion to foreman of his section."

"Your George was always goin' to do well. Bella might have been a sober mortal but she filled you wi' learnin' an' George could recite the alphabet afore most his age could pick up a spoon. Billy has allus believed that if Harold had lived, 'e'd be somebody famous one day, like Brunel or that Stephenson fella, wasn't 'e a George an'all? Billy reckons Nottingham 'ould 'ave a monument to history named after your Harold, the Boucher viaduct or the Boucher locomotive. It's down to George now, 'e's got to be the one." Edna paused and sniffed as she put the bag of sugar with the rest of her shopping, "mind you, 'e could be in the process o' creatin' as we speak. Mark it on the calendar an' nine months from now we might be gettin' the first peep at his accomplishment."

"They're walking the Derbyshire countryside taking in some clean air," said Annie, taking a packet of cornflour from the shelf.

"Oh aye," said Edna, "I'll take a quarter o' sherbet lemons an'all, I could do wi' summat fizzy." Her raised eyebrows made Annie smile, she was about to reply when the shop doorbell rang and in came Mona Dallymore. It was a curious fact that although Mona had been married for years everyone seemed to refer to her by her maiden name. Being a woman of such large stature and ample flesh Annie imagined it was the unlikely surname of Mona's husband that brought about the anomaly. 'Little', Mona had married Gordon Little, to speak of Mona and little in the same breath apparently defied everyone. If it bothered her then she certainly didn't show it.

"I must sit down here a minute," Mona lowered herself onto the chair by the counter, not surprisingly, it creaked under the weight of this outsized occupant. "I've come over all strange, I can feel the sweat runnin' down the front o' me brassiere." She picked up the piece of card from the counter on which Annie had displayed the price of this week's 'special', custard creams and fanned herself with it. "I went to collect the mantel clock from the menders, it stopped workin' when Gordon shifted it to paper the wall with anaglypta, they do say you shouldn't move a clock, anyroad, I wer' walkin' out the shop door into the street just as a lorry went by with a dead horse draped over it. I'd swear its eyes wer' fixed on me an' its tongue wer' hangin' out the side of its mouth. Wouldn't you think that somebody would have had the decency to shut the poor things eyes and tuck its tongue back in. I haven't stopped tremblin' yet, in fact I don't know if I'm tremblin' or havin' a palpitation. Gordon's mam gets palpitations."

"Shall I make you some sweet tea Mona?" Said Annie.

"I think I could do with somethin' stronger, have you got a drop o' brandy?"

Edna gave Annie an old fashioned look. "Is that all my stuff now?" She asked.

"Yes Edna I've done everything that you had on the list plus the sherbet lemons. Give my love to Annie and Alec."

Edna took her bag from the counter, "Cheerio then Mona, I dare say you'll feel better very soon."

"I'm not usually this sensitive," Mona placed the piece of card back by the till, "but I cried last week when next door's lad caught ringworm, he works at Cheetham's yard an' he's such a good lookin' lad. Me mother thinks I'm enterin' an early change, I have been 'any old how' lately but I'm not forty 'till next November.

Brandy's supposed to be a restorative so I've taken to drinkin' a small 'nip' just now an' again."

Edna sighed, "Me mam wer' still regular at fifty six, God 'elp me." The bell clanged as she opened the door to leave, sending Annie hastily through to the back to pour the withering Mrs.Little a small restorative.

"I see your Hilda's got an admirer then," said Mona as she took the glass from Annie's hand, already displaying a return to strength.

Annie was puzzled. "Hilda has friends but I don't think there is anyone in particular."

"Well he looked like he was a particular to me, they were smilin' an' chattin', I've noticed him waitin' outside the library a few times. He must work the early shift 'cause he's allus scrubbed up an' clean whenever I see him with your Hilda."

Annie couldn't but ask who this mystery admirer might be.

"Haynes, Jack Haynes, I bought a Tilly lamp off him once for Gordon to go froggin', them chemists in the laboratories pay good money for a bag o' frogs, for their experiments an' that, but Gordon soon got fed up wi' creepin' around the banks o' The Trent all night so he give it up. I knew he would, that's why I didn't want to shell out for a new Tilly, Gordon's done that many different things since we got married. He were attendant at swimmin' baths for a year, he mucked out police stables, did a bit o' grave diggin' at cemetery, now he's drivin' a steamroller with the work gang on the ring road."

Annie took the empty glass from Mona. "Was there anything you needed from the shop?"

"I'll take a bit o' cheese while I'm here, about half a pound o' cheddar, packin' him up every day takes a lot o' cheese but Gordon don't care for bloater paste and he's not so fond o' luncheon meat neither." Mona stooped to pick up her bag, placing it on the counter she took from it the clock. "Twenty to four, it's still workin' an' it's right by yours," she said, looking intently at the clock on the wall of the shop. The cheese paid for and thanks extended for the brandy, Mona took her leave.

Annie was pensive, Jack, Victor's brother, if Hilda was spending time with Jack then why hadn't she said something. He must be several years older than Hilda but not so many as to make it awkward and Florrie's family was so familiar to them through Billy and Victor. Hilda would likely declare it simply to be Mona's imagination, yet Annie had noticed her daughter's far away look at times, as though her thoughts were elsewhere and she did seem to take more effort over her hair these days. At a weekend, her absence Annie had presumed was due to her spending more time with Laura, young women could chat and window-shop for hours. Tactfully, after supper, if Charles and John were out, Annie would mention Mona's observation, dropping it into their own conversation along with general events, casually, without it seeming to Hilda to be nosiness on her mam's part.

Earlier in the day the postman had delivered a number of envelopes which Annie had put on the dresser in the kitchen until she had time to look at them. Charles would probably have opened any he considered important before he went out. It was in the evening when Annie finally had chance to sit down that she read any letters. Seeing Francis's hand or Catherine Appleyard's writing on an envelope was always a genuine pleasure, which Annie relished at these rare quiet moments. Hilda would often sit with her and share the news of family and friends. Annie had noticed an envelope amongst today's post that looked unlike a bill, yet it bore no familiar handwriting. Mrs.Glasson entered the shop at that moment, seeking potatoes and onions, she was followed by a steady stream of customers that diverted Annie's thoughts and the rest of the afternoon was lost to their demands. It was almost 5o'clock when Charles returned, at least his time had been spent usefully and not on pursuits which furthered no one, including himself. Davina was fretting over some boxes of old papers that had sat in the attic at The Park for years. When Annie had last called there Davina's anxiety had been too intense to ignore. Annie was perceptive enough to realise that her old friend was trying to put her house in order, should her health fall victim to that often cruel natured and persistent ageing process. Alice Hemsley's decline had preyed on Davina's mind. Initially, Annie scolded her for being pessimistic but latterly, when Annie sat alone in the solitude of the late evenings, she'd acknowledged to herself the natural desire that old age must bring, to somehow organise that untidy jumble of life's collectables, which to the individual responsible for there accumulation had ever been of importance but to any other, merely represented tiresome effort in sorting and disposing of.

Charles had received nothing but kindness from Davina, if he couldn't show his gratitude by spending a couple of hours fetching boxes down from her attic then it was shameful on his part. Surprisingly he'd not protested over much, a token, 'I thought she had a young cousin somewhere', had been his only regrettable response, other than that he'd declared the task, 'as good a time as any to disturb the moths'.

"Is Davina happier now?" Asked Annie when Charles came through to relieve her.

"It must all be rubbish, I dare say Mrs.Pooley will end up burning it in the grate. It was the same with father, old bill, invoices, why do they keep it all? Going through it will occupy her for a day or two. I've opened the post, you have a letter, Sheffield postmark but typewritten envelope."

Annie felt amused by his obvious curiosity, seemingly indifferent most of the time, his scrutiny of the postmark on this typed envelope confirmed if nothing else, her husband's interest in the source of his wife's correspondence. Annie had often wondered if Charles would even notice should she seek a passionate interlude outside of their entirely correct, housetrained marriage. It would have to be pursued behind the shop counter or around the back of the vegetable stand of course, she was never away from either long enough for even the slightest urge to develop a first breath. The thought of him peering at the stamp on the envelope with a determination to establish from where it came, in a strange way, heartened her. She would make an apple pie for pudding, Charles especially liked apple pie, if any was left he would eat it before going to bed, along with a piece of cheese. He had obliged her in helping Davina after all, she could have asked John to go instead but one day the inevitable would happen, it would be Davina's seventy ninth birthday this coming August. It was past time Charles returned some measure of kindness, Annie sincerely hoped that Davina would live to reach a ripe old age but who could possibly tell. Anyway, the deed was done and Davina could now sort and satisfy and be free of those wearying anxieties that led to her state of unrest.

John had been roped into a game of darts with some of the other men from Raleigh, at The Nelson. Charles had finished his meal in a good humour and gone to The Standard, to play a hand of cards. Annie knew by now that 'a hand' in fact meant several. Hilda had helped her clear away the dishes and wash up. Annie had casually enquired if she was going out.

"Not tonight Mam, I shall keep you company instead."

Hilda made a pot of tea and Annie settled in the easy chair to open her letter. It did seem unusual, apart from the Hemsleys she could think of no one who would be writing to her from Sheffield and Walter's last communication had been written and addressed in his own hand.

'Dear Mrs.Eddowes, Annie, at first it seemed improper for me to address you by your first name, but then the alternative felt even less correct so I am entering both, along with my genuine regard and fondness.

So many years have passed since 'your' aunt Bella, 'our' Miss Pownall, came to the house in The Park at Nottingham to teach my sister and me our lessons. I confess my recollection of that time is vague but my awareness of the affection in which my mother and father held both you and your aunt is quite clear. This is a difficult letter to write and so I do hope you will forgive any error I might make in conveying to you the sadness of the past months.

It was Christmas Eve when we received a call from the hospital, asylum actually, but we thought of it as a hospital, it made the situation more bearable somehow. Mother had died in her sleep, towards the end she did little else but sleep, perhaps in their wisdom they administered a sedative, her mind had become very confused, at times the confusion led to distressing episodes that took so much of mother's strength. We tried our very best to rally father's spirit but never have I seen anyone, man or woman, fail so quickly, the decline was alarming and despite the efforts of family, of doctors and nurses, nothing halted his fall. On March 19th last,

307

father left us to join mother. All of their married life had been a total devotion and I am convinced in my mind that just as nothing could separate them in life, so it was in death. Therefore we consider his passing so soon after mother to be a blessing and while we miss them very much, we have determined ourselves not to grieve but rather to be thankful for the mercy that it was.

I have written also to Davina Wright. Bearing in mind her age and the fact that she lives alone but for her housekeeper, I have endeavoured to impart the news as gently as possible. It is a strange coincidence that my work requires me to travel to Nottingham at some time before the onset of autumn, if it is not inconvenient I would like to call on you, for just a brief visit. The links with the past that so connect us may be gone but I believe Miss Pownall, mother and father would be sad if they knew we had not continued the friendship..

Perhaps you will let me know of Mrs. Wright's health, for I shall surely visit her as soon as I can if you assure me it would be appropriate. Margaret sends her finest regards.

Yours truly.

Anthony Hemsley.

"What is it Mam?" Asked Hilda.

Annie passed the letter to her daughter, it was one of great sadness but Hilda was eighteen, she had never known the Hemsleys, other than through Annie's memories. It shouldn't distress her and now a young woman, gradual awareness of pain and loss was favourable to being constantly wrapped against the chill, only to be one day caught in such a storm that her protection was woefully inadequate. Hilda read in silence, Annie observed the young face, the simple prettiness. She remembered Edna's remarks at George's wedding when Jack Haynes had been watching through the railings, 'he's smitten, you mark my words'.

"I shall go to Davina's tomorrow afternoon," said Annie, "if she received her letter today she'll be upset. Alice Hemsley was her dearest friend and Walter had continued to write when Alice lost her mind and could no longer compose a rational letter. Davina is strong in spirit but nevertheless such news is bound to affect her.

Your dad went there today to fetch down some boxes from the attic. I shall ask him if he noticed any change in her demeanour.

Hilda folded the letter and placed it back in the envelope. "Do you think that dad's demeanour might change if I told him that I was seeing a young man?" Hilda hesitated just for a instant, "It's Jack Haynes, we walk together sometimes, mostly when I leave the library or on a Sunday afternoon when we listen to the band in the arboretum."

Annie was relieved that Hilda had spoken of her attraction to Jack without the need of prompting but concerned that she should fear Charles' reaction. Most fathers were especially protective of their daughters but Hilda's apprehension seemed to be for something beyond the regular 'vetting' undertaken by dads reacting to the sudden realisation that their 'little girl' had become a 'grown woman'.

"Why ever do you suppose that your dad would be disapproving, Jack is some years older than you but that can be a good thing, a man has a greater sense of what he wants and in which direction his life should go when he's already experienced a number of working years. I don't think your dad will worry over the difference in age, besides, Victor is twenty four and so Jack can't be more than twenty seven that's not really such a big difference is it?"

"It's not that," said Hilda. "You must have noticed how tensed dad becomes whenever Billy and Victor come up in conversation. I saw his expression turn instantly stern when George brought home the news that Raymond Haynes had been made manager at Players. What has Florrie's family ever done to make him dislike them, but he does, I can tell that he does and when he finds out that I'm seeing Jack he'll go into one of his moods, then everyone will suffer."

Annie took the envelope from Hilda's fingers and held her hand. "Charles isn't like Billy, he can't simply accept people as they are and Victor is even more of a challenge than most, he behaves a little differently, has a look that sets him apart. Billy hasn't the slightest care about such things, to him they are unimportant, Billy sees simply Victor, innocent, gentle, inoffensive Victor. Your dad is afraid of what he doesn't understand, that's all it is really."

"Do we have to tell him?" Said Hilda, as yet not convinced.

"He's sure to find out sooner or later, he'll probably see you together," said Annie.

"Dad's activities never take him anywhere near the library or the arboretum, neither has drink or cards."

"That's too harsh Hilda," Annie sighed as she crossed the room to put Anthony Hemsley's letter on the shelf of the dresser.

"I'm sorry Mam," Hilda was close to tears.

"George and Alice are calling here for tea on Monday, before they go home. They'll no doubt have a lot to tell us about their weekend, let your news slip into the conversation, that way it will be a part of the happy account and your dad won't have chance to dwell on it. Pour us another cuppa and fetch a bar of Fry's Mint Cream from the shop, we'll indulge ourselves."

The house was quiet, John and Hilda had gone up to bed more than an hour ago. Charles had eaten the last piece of apple pie before taking himself upstairs and Annie had quickly tided the sink, locked up and followed him. He lay on his back, the profile of his face outlined by the light from the street lamp that now managed to penetrate the curtains, so thin had they become through age and the rigours of being laundered each spring.

"I keep thinking of George and Alice," said Annie, "I hope they're enjoying themselves."

"At their age, if they're not then there must be something wrong with them."

So age is the defining factor thought Annie but she kept her voice light and cheerful. "Edna came in for her usual bits this afternoon, only a couple of weeks to go now before Annie's baby, it will be such a happy event for all of them. I can picture Billy's big grin, not to mention Victor, he's always liked babies, he was so good with Myra." Charles was silent, Annie tried again to initiate some response. "Edna told me that Joyce Spooner has got engaged to William Haynes. I'm really pleased for Joyce,

William is the steady, dependable sort, in fact all Florrie's sons have turned out well, don't you think?"

"Have you come to bed to sleep or to give me a news bulletin. How could I have any idea, I've never had anything to do with Florrie Haynes or her sons. I can't imagine Joyce Spooner being fussy so I'm sure this chap will do nicely. He's in the army isn't he, well there you are then, I bet he's been about a bit as well, an ideal match."

Annie overlooked Charles' unnecessary sarcasm. "The letter from Sheffield was from Alice Hemsley's son. It's so sad, Alice died last Christmas Eve and Walter a bare three months later. I can only just remember Anthony, the family left Nottingham to move to Sheffield when I was ten. He has a sister, Margaret, they're both older than me of course, aunt Bella had been teaching them before I was born. He said he'd written to Davina, did she mention anything to you this afternoon?"

"No, but it would make sense. She seemed agitated, uneasy. I think she was surprised when I turned up, I dare say she expected to see John, not me. It was only when I was about to leave that she appeared to calm. If she'd read such a letter in the morning it would explain why she was troubled, probably wanted rid of me so she could have a weep in peace. Mrs.Pooley comes across as a sensible woman, I'm sure she'll keep an eye on Davina if she's aware of the situation." Charles turned away to face the window. Annie lay wakeful, envious of the ease with which Charles drifted into sleep. A mix of emotions occupied her mind, doubts, hopes, silly fears, 'please God let George and Alice be happy wherever they lay their heads, grant William patience, bring reality to Freddy's dreams and help John to progress. Allow Hilda and Jack to follow their hearts, regardless of age'. Annie made her plea to the Almighty and eventually found sleep.

Mrs.Pooley was frustrated, it was evident in her manner, sighs and numerous flustered 'deary mes', escaped her lips between the front door and the sitting room.

"She's in there Annie, you'll have to excuse the mess, it looks as though I spend my time here doing very little, papers, God help us there are papers everywhere. I've bundled them through the range 'til it got that hot, I boiled dry the potatoes, I'm surprised you can't smell them. I opened the back door and put the pan outside to soak but that burned smell is up my nose for the rest of the day now an' still she keeps givin' me more. I've told her it would be easier to have a bonfire outside but she's adamant that there's too much breeze and they'd be blown all over the garden and beyond."

Davina sat at the table, spectacles perched on the end of her nose, a box beside her on the floor, another by her elbow on the table. "Annie my dear, what a lovely surprise, I shall take a break from my sorting, if only to relieve my sinuses of the dust. Come and sit down in an easy chair and tell me what's happening with the family. You know what men are like, I asked Charles but he is the typical male, they know every cricket score, the price of a pint, the current phase of the moon but absolutely nothing about anything that matters."

Annie was puzzled, Davina displayed no distress, nothing to suggest Anthony Hemsley's letter had arrived. "Let me help you with the sorting," said Annie.

"No, no my dear, I won't hear of it, this long overdue activity gives me something to help pass the time. I am truly grateful to Charles for going up into that dreary old attic and bringing down the boxes. I confess I was surprised to see him, I don't know why but I imagined you would send John. I shall write a note to Charles, to thank him properly, not only did he put up with all the dust, he also tolerated my silly chatter over Mrs.Pooley's tray of tea and ginger cake and I swear he uttered not a single complaint, not as much as a sigh."

"Charles would expect no thanks, he merely returned to some small degree, the kindness you have always shown him." Annie paused for a moment while she considered what best to do. "In fact Charles thought you were not yourself, anxious over something possibly." Annie tried tactfully to prompt Davina to share her sadness over Alice and not to hide it. Davina had indeed been anxious, finding Charles was to be her helper had thrown her into a state of considerable agitation. The boxes

312

contained all manner of papers, old letters and documents from the bank dating back many years. She had gone through each and every drawer in the house and was satisfied no item remained that could cause any upset to Annie and her family, but those boxes high up in the attic presented a threat, which until Davina sorted through them and disposed of their contents, dominated the days and denied her peace of mind. John was far too young to be remotely interested in an old lady's dusty past but should Charles have given in to curiosity what might he have discovered. His manner had reassured her, Davina felt confident that Charles had discharged the duty as swiftly as possible and left with nothing more than dust to take away with him.

"I am ashamed of myself Annie, I was so preoccupied with my thorough 'spring clean' that I came across to Charles as being troubled, not so my dear, just determined that this year I shall make a better effort. Mrs.Pooley is forever telling me that I hoard far too much. Do you know there were twenty five Kilner jars on the pantry shelf, the clips on every one completely rusty from lack of use and in the understairs cupboard our purge resulted in thirty eight copies of The Lady seeing light of day after being incarcerated for more than ten years."

Annie smiled. "If you move much more you'll suffer from the draught their vacated space creates."

Davina chuckled and picked up a dish of butterscotch from the side table. "Pop one in your mouth Annie dear, I shan't feel so guilty if you have one too. Boredom is my enemy, at least when I'm busy the temptation to stuff myself with comforting sweets doesn't arise."

Annie was content to believe that Davina's letter had not yet arrived. While she worried for her friend's distress on reading the news, which would almost certainly be delivered on Tuesday, it did seem only correct that whichever words Anthony Hemsley had chosen to use, they should be allowed to reach Davina before Annie spoke of the sadness.

After an hour or so chatting easily about George and his weekend away with Alice, of Edna and Billy's excitement at the prospect of becoming grandparents and Mona Dallymore's alarming near collision with a dead horse, Annie said her goodbyes to Davina and Mrs.Pooley, leaving the house with a bagful of The Lady magazine, having been instructed by Davina to pass them on to Celia and Alice so the young women might enjoy some of the articles, one in particular being relevant to Celia. 'How to complement the aspiring husband and yet remain demure'!

"Nice trifle Mam," said George. Mrs.Maguire gave us a huge breakfast each morning so we didn't really need a lot more to eat but there was a pub not far from the B&B called The Plover and a couple of evenings we went in there to have a pie, speciality of the house. We tried the beef last Friday and the rabbit last night, I think the landlord must have taken a shine to Alice because he sent over the waitress with Alice's plate and her helping was larger than mine. He gave the biggest wink from behind the bar and the waitress whispered to Alice so none of the other customers could hear, 'Mr.Doyle says you're lookin' too pale for these parts, Ashbourne women know how to trough' poor Alice was afraid to leave any and daren't pass any to me either 'cause Mr.Doyle was watching every mouthful, she was still full up this morning so I had to eat her bacon." They all chuckled as they scraped the last bit of sweet custard from their dishes.

"Did you do much walking?" Asked John, "or was it all belated anniversary canoodling?"

"Really John!" Annie tried to sound shocked but inwardly she smiled.

"Miles of it," said George, with a grin on his face from ear to ear. "We walked through Dovedale to Hope, it's so lovely there it makes you feel compelled to go further, so as not to miss any of the scenery. At Tissington the well dressing was remarkable, so much effort had gone into making the village look special, in fact it was so striking that we decided to go to the church service there yesterday morning."

"The vicar is a lovely man," declared Alice, taking up the story. "I think he guessed we were visiting and he asked where we came from. It's the strangest coincidence, we'd been undecided over whether to attend a morning service at the village or go to Ashbourne church last night. It sounds soft but everything was just perfect, we'd enjoyed ourselves that much it felt only proper to give thanks for it all.

314

Would you believe the vicar at Tissington knows the Reverend Hockley here at St.Andrew's, they were at Ridley College together, in Cambridge. When we told him it was the Reverend Hockley who'd married us he was delighted, so much so we felt like frauds, we had to confess that we didn't attend church regularly. Then he asked us if we'd walked through the beautiful countryside, if we'd paused to actually hear the cheerful birdsong, stooped to smell the cornflowers and scabious and listened to the constant rhythm of the water over the falls. We said 'yes' and it was true, we had and relished every moment of it. It was his next remark that I'm sure I'll never forget, words of wisdom, from a vicar who perhaps understands more than most, he shook our hands with real warmth and said, 'we should all of us remember, that God has a garden as well as a house'.

Annie was heartened by Alice's account of their weekend away and for those few minutes had forgotten the conversation she and Hilda had exchanged on Saturday night.

"Jack said that one day soon he'll take me to Papplewick and from there we'll walk to Newstead, to see the abbey, it was the home of Lord Byron and there's a statue to the memory of his dog, Bosun. There's a pond with water lilies and azaleas. A footpath goes through the estate and Jack says at the far boundary there are some caves and rumour has it that someone or something inhabits them, people have heard sounds coming from inside, strange sounds no one can identify but Jack's promised we won't go that far. I don't suppose caves would bother Jack but they'd frighten me."

Hilda smiled nervously, but it was George who spoke first. "How come aunt Gertie's Jack knows so much about Newstead, I can't imagine he's ever been there, I didn't know about the statue or the caves, he is a cough drop that lad, grandma Sarah reckons he's got the head of a thirty year old on a boy's body."

John laughed, "I suppose you heard it was Jack and his mate Charlie Jones who told Tommy Spooner that Dr.Bennett's wife had died. Tommy said that Jack related the circumstances with all the gravity of a seasoned undertaker."

"Not Jack Wainwright," said Hilda, "Jack Haynes, I've been spending some time with Jack Haynes."

Charles' eyes immediately fixed upon Annie. "You knew didn't you," he stood up, sending the legs of his chair noisily across the flags. "You already knew." He strode across the room to the back door and grabbed his jacket from the hook.

"Where are you going Charles?" Annie felt despairing of his thoughtless pique, the chatter and atmosphere around the table had been so happy.

He fired back the one word, "Out," and slammed the door behind him. Annie turned to look at her daughter, the misery in Hilda's expression told Annie what the tormented young woman was thinking, 'it was too harsh, it was all too harsh'.

CHAPTER EIGHTEEN

Late August

"Folk must look at us an' think we're from a different tribe, Billy wi' all his disfigurement from the war, Victor the way 'e is an' now our Annie's pushin' around a baby with a hair lip an' cleft palate. Karno's soddin' army, that's what we are."

Annie sat by the open window enjoying the movement of air on her face as she looked across the street towards aunt Bella's, as she would forever think of that house.

"You were right Edna, about last Whitsuntide." Annie smiled at her friend who folded the last few items of laundry picked down from the clothesline before the heat of the sun dried them beyond easy ironing. "Alice is pregnant, George called in last night, I thought he'd burst his skin from excitement."

"Must 'ave been all that fresh air," said Edna, giving Annie a roguish look. Both women gave in to laughter.

"The doctors have told Annie they can rectify the cleft palate, it'll mean operations, poor mite'll be in an' out of hospital, but they can't do owt 'til she's comin' up to twelve months. They try to make Annie feel better. 'It's a little girl', they say, "when she's grown up she'll wear make-up like other young women, the hair lip'll be easily disguised'. Well some things yer can't hide, a bit o' face powder couldn't disguise Billy's mangled ear nor put the spark back in his injured eye. No amount o' face paint'll ever make Victor look like everybody else, so why should we believe that a dab from a powder compact'll one day make our Janet look normal."

Annie sighed. "I see such diversity of humankind come in and out of the shop. You would probably look at them and say that only the manner in which they dress, the style of hair, their state of wealth distinguished one from another. That stripped of their chosen disguise they would appear the same. But skin is all that really disguises us Edna, beneath the skin are so many differences, hidden away. Some truly beautiful should we glimpse them, others alarmingly ugly. Your family is thoroughly beautiful Edna."

Edna sniffed. "I wish I knew what had got under Smithfield's skin, 'e gets worse, I'm sure 'e does. He's empty, no heart for anythin', I don't think Henry Wicks bein' away helps. He told me that sometimes of an evenin' he an' Wicks would have a drink together, talk about things, 'like minded', that wer' the term 'e used. After Wicks' wife died they reckon the poor man went down wi' a sort o' depression, loneliness I suppose. Smithfield's not been 'isself since Mrs.Plowright passed on. It drives William to distraction, not blessed wi' a lot o' patience is 'e, your William an' even less compassion. I know you'd tell me off if I didn't refer to 'im as 'yours', but the blood that flows through his veins has got none o' your goodness in it. That Enid wer' a fiery, self-centred piece o' work, dyin' like she did wer' tragic, you'd never hear me say other, but William's blood comes from 'er an' Charles an' his nature is theirs an'all, your William is 'their' prodigy, no two ways about it."

Annie couldn't bring herself to deny it. The past weeks had been difficult enough, but William's encouragement of Charles' unreasonable dislike for Jack Haynes had produced an unbearable atmosphere. Annie had wanted to slap William when he declared Jack to be a chancer with a big mouth and a small brain. Most disturbing of all had been Charles' barbed pronouncement the night of Hilda's revelation, he'd waited for Annie to come to bed and without discussion said. 'Young women are fickle, give it six months and she'll likely tire of him, someone will come along with more appeal but not until Hilda is twenty one can she do as she likes and if she persists in seeing Haynes, then she must abide under someone else's roof and not mine'.

Annie had made no reply, afraid that anything she might say would further antagonize him. She had known first love, the elation of new found emotion, a real love, it was very many years ago but the memory enabled her to recognise it in Hilda. Her daughter's fondness for Jack Haynes was undiminished and Annie ached from dread.

Just then the back door opened and Victor entered Edna's scullery carrying a bunch of carrots and a string of onions, followed by Billy bearing a basket of potatoes and kidney beans, both looking hot and bothered from their efforts at the allotment.

It was automatic, that smile of Victor's which achieved in an instant to light up his entire face, the beam could come from nowhere but within. "Hello Mrs.Eddowes," he said. Dropping the onions and carrots on the kitchen table he crossed to where Annie sat by the window and put his hand to the collar of his shirt.

"Liza, Liza give it to me, an' Miss Turpin give it to me an'all." Victor's finger pointed to a small pin brooch in the shape of a crown, the word 'Corona' spelled in letters, one on each pinnacle of the coronet.

"It's lovely Victor," said Annie, "it looks very smart."

"Corona, fizzy," Victor's tongue travelled along his lips, turning to look directly at Edna, he gave his usual repetition, "Corona, fizzy."

"Alright Victor you shall have a drink o' pop," said Edna.

"He deserves one, you pulled up all the onions didn't yer Victor, put 'em to dry in the shed an' then dug the potatoes. All I did wer' pick beans an' sit down on the bench wi' me paper." Billy rested his hand on Victor's shoulder, Annie noticed his fingers flex as he squeezed him, a gesture of affection. Edna took a bottle of orangeade from the bucket of water keeping cold the pop and the milk, she poured a large glass and handed it to the thirsty young man.

"Don't drink it too fast or it'll go up your nose an' take your breath away." Edna took the vegetables from the table and put them into a wooden crate by the dolly tub, shaking her head as she moved about between her tasks. Annie observed the scene and envied its simplicity, beautiful on the inside. Annie at that moment longed to be of the same tribe as Edna and her extended family.

"Something's happening," said Celia. "I can hear voices and it looks as though a group of people have gathered outside one of the houses further along." She peered through the window, Mathew's curiosity was aroused and he tried in vain to see over the sill.

"For heaven's sake, it's probably a domestic brought on by the heat." William sat reading yesterday's Evening Post. Removing his shirt and sitting with only a singlet vest on his upper body, something he would never normally do, William considered it to portray an image of aimless mentality, did little to relieve the oppressive heat. The day had got gradually warmer until by mid-afternoon, back doors were propped open, semi naked children were given buckets of cold water in which to play, dogs searched for shady places and the streets became virtually bare of people as they sought that cooler air inside the houses, which perversely, at other times drove folk onto the streets to escape if only briefly, the damp that caused 'winter wheezing', a doctor's adopted title for that seasonal complaint common to tenants of sub-standard housing and unscrupulous landlords.

Celia lifted Mathew 'til his feet found the window sill, holding him tightly she observed the scene, a vehicle, at first obscured by the gathering, now moved away from the pavement.

"It's an ambulance," said Celia, "oh dear someone must be very poorly." She lifted Mathew down and came away from the window. "I'll fetch us some cold lemonade, I stood it in the bucket more than an hour ago, it should be nice and cold by now."

William looked up from his paper, "I didn't know Steve Wainwright had stood down as union representative, there's an article in The Post. His successor is Jack Haynes, voted in unanimously, it'll be interesting to see how somebody like Haynes stands up to Stafford Hinds. According to Basil, Hinds never loses sight of his goal. Wicks was too soft, the men manipulated him like putty but Jack Haynes has bitten off more than he can chew this time." William laughed sarcastically.

Celia passed him a glass of lemonade. "Isn't Basil perhaps a little too familiar William, you've worked for Mr.Smithfield since you were eighteen but I'm sure you don't address him as Andrew. From what I've heard Jack Haynes will represent the miners just as forcefully as did Steve Wainwright."

Celia wished now she'd gone to Rosie's this afternoon, for Mathew to play with the twins. When Rosie had asked her, foolishly as it now seemed, Celia had thought it unkind to take their young son away from his dad on a Sunday, the only free day William had to spend with Mathew. In the event, just like Charles, William sat behind the newspaper ignoring the child, grunting and muttering at whatever he read that didn't coincide with his own opinions.

"I shall take him for a walk, we've had a cold drink and under the trees at the arboretum it will be shady and pleasant. Would you like to come with us?" She felt it a complete waste of breath but Celia asked anyway.

"I don't share your curiosity but I'm sure you'll manage to satisfy your nosiness if you ask enough people, someone's bound to know who's gone off in an ambulance, I prefer to read about more enlightening events."

His manner and tone vexed Celia, taking Mathew by the hand they set off in the direction of the arboretum, relieved to be free of the mirthless William. By the time they reached the end of Forest Road Celia could tell that Mathew's legs needed a rest. The pavement was bone dry so they simply sat down where they were. The paving slabs were warm, almost too warm and it wasn't long before Mathew began to fidget.

"Come on then, not far now." Celia brushed her hand over the seat of his pants. It was unusually quiet, since leaving the house no more than a dozen people had passed them. Celia thought she heard a distant rumble of thunder. "Let's be quick in case there's a storm coming." Carrying Mathew for much of the way they reached the arboretum gates just as a bright flash confirmed it. Celia hastened her pace, panting and soaked from sweat she coaxed Mathew up the steps and into the bandstand, where several people had already taken shelter, including Jack and Hilda. At once Mathew sought his aunty Hilda and clambered onto her knee. Celia sat down beside them with a long sigh of relief.

"Just in time I reckon," said Jack, "we shall have a bit o' music in a minute even without the band, more percussion than anythin' melodious but when the rain starts it will cool everythin' down." He wore a lilywhite collarless shirt, open at the front, sleeves rolled up to the elbows, the simplest mode of dress for any man. His hair sat on his head as nature intended it, no affectation of hair cream or style. Pronounced veins travelled down his arms like tramlines, his hands appeared almost cured, like leather but not in any way suggesting roughness. The light in his eyes seemed unguarded as though anyone looking directly into them would find nothing obscuring their vision of his soul. Celia could understand why Hilda was drawn to Jack, why she would feel in his company, in those arms, entirely safe from all harm. Annie had confided in Celia her dread of Charles' threat if Hilda continued to see Jack Haynes and Celia was in no doubt over William's opinion on the subject, but like Annie, Celia understood Hilda's emotion, love for such a man would surely be greater than any threat, even one made by Hilda's own father. There was on this earth 'man' and less prolific there were 'men', Jack Haynes was definitely of the latter.

Another vivid flash of lightning was followed almost at once by an almighty crack of thunder. Mathew's eyes opened wide, he displayed no fear, again lightning and that sound of a furious bombardment from all sides and above. At last the first drops of rain, they fell gently, almost cautiously, as though instructed to assess the land, like a vanguard, then they gathered in strength, not delicate drops of moisture bringing nourishment to the plants and grass but big, noisy deposits of water, descending ever harder onto the roof of the bandstand, bouncing on the path outside so high and so fast they became a blur, another flash of light and crack of thunder, the storm was overhead. Mathew sat on Hilda's knee transfixed, not making a single whimper. The sound of rain drumming on the roof above was painful to the ears. It began to ease.

"Goin' over now." One man ventured to remark. The woman at his side trembled, she wore a charm bracelet about her wrist, Celia sometimes wore one very similar, a gift from Caroline last Christmas, she would watch as the charms quivered with the slightest movement, especially if she travelled on the tram or a bus.

Now the rain returned, again pelting the bandstand and the ground outside, a deluge, a solid wall of water before their eyes, for five minutes or more it was relentless, then in an unearthly instant, it stopped. The air was cooler, it smelled different, fresher, washed of city dust and grime. A faint, now distant rumble of thunder restored the nervous woman. She reached inside the pocket of her skirt, took out a hanky and blew her nose. It was as if that common, everyday sound made by humankind, now signified a return to normality. Folk stood up and began to walk away down the waterlogged path, all except Jack, Hilda, Celia and Mathew.

"You're a tough little chap." Said Jack, casting a wide smile over the child, "I've seen grown men shake like a jelly at rumbles less violent than that. It thunders regular down pit but that's from man's doin'. I reckon every now an' again, the Gods make a point o' remindin' us who's in charge."

"We decided to leave William to his newspaper and brave the heat to come to the arboretum, you like the birds don't you?" Celia prompted Mathew to speak. The boy slid down from Hilda's knee and clambered onto Jack's lap instead. He wriggled himself into a comfortable position, leaned back and sighed. Hilda and Celia looked at each other and laughed. Jack was completely unfazed by the antics of the child.

"We none of us knew when Victor might suddenly decide to climb into bed with us. He allus slept in mam and dad's room but sometimes he'd take a fit in his head to leave his own room an' come into ours. We wer' never less than three to a bed so when Victor climbed in to make the fourth we'd be cheek by jowl. I can remember the feelin' of another's breath waftin' over me face in the dark an' sometimes when I woke in the mornin' Victor would have his hand down inside the front o' me nightshirt, it wer' allus wet wi' spittle 'cause he sucked his thumb but he wer' like a hot water bottle, that much warmth come from him. It wer' lovely wintertime but in the summer we'd wake up stuck together, like toffee that had been in a pocket for days. Don't William care much for walkin' then?" Jack directed his question at Celia, it was asked with no hint of antipathy and so Celia answered truthfully.

"Some days William doesn't care much for anything, perhaps the storm will have stirred him, if only to put the old towel on the window ledge in the scullery. It gets wet in hard rain, there's a patch of rot in the wooden frame. We'd best be getting back, a certain little person will want to jump into every puddle on the way so it will take us a bit longer than it did to get here. Give aunty Hilda a kiss Mathew and say goodbye to Jack."

Once outside the bandstand the full effects of such a downpour were evident. The grass held vast accumulations of water, the trees dripped their soaking from every branch and twig and the pathway, in places had disappeared. Celia wondered how long it would be before Hilda and Jack, now alone in the bandstand, made their way too. It was a sobering truth that the company Celia had just left felt so much more inviting than the muttering sarcasm of her husband to whom she must now return.

While every puddle did indeed prove irresistible to Mathew, they nevertheless covered the distance in reasonable time, there progress was no longer hampered by the stifling heat of earlier. A surprising number of people now filtered through to the streets, the scene so different from just an hour or so ago. The gutters ran with water, in places so fast all manner of debris had been dislodged, from the cracks between the cobbles, from chinks in the walls where children pushed chocolate bar wrappers to see how long they could remain there. Empty cigarette packets which normally awaited the road sweepers broom, bobbed up and down in the torrent when their journey was halted by the queue of similar items traveling in advance of them, now only seconds away from disappearing through the grille over the storm drain. Pigeons had re-emerged from places of shelter and waded through the puddles, picking at anything that floated just in case it proved edible. A drainpipe, cracked at the top where the cast iron had corroded through sent a spout of water over the pavement and two small children, clad in nothing but underpants, held a mongrel dog under its flow, rubbing it over at the same time with a bar of Sunlight soap. Eventually they reached the end of Forest road where it joined with Glover Street. Mrs.Talbot, a friendly woman from No.65 was approaching from the opposite direction.

"My dear Celia, and young Mathew, did you ever know such a storm as that? I had to sit with our Rover on me knee an' his feet wer' shakin' that much he managed to rip one o' me suspenders off even through me top skirt an' me underslip. Edgar said he'd not heard thunder an' lightnin' like that since 'e wer' in the

Dardanelles, his lot thought they were bein' bombarded, fired eight rounds o' mortars afore somebody felt rain spots an' realised it wer' a storm. Then it didn't know how to stop, it rained an' rained like the end o' the world was nigh, 'til they wer' in more danger o' drownin' than they were from Ataturk. I suppose you've heard about Doris, I do feel sorry for Rex Madden, he allus looks like a man weighed down wi' worry an' now they've rushed Doris into hospital. Her nerves are awful you know, funny thing the mind, can't stick a bandage on it an' kiss it better can yer? She collapsed, that's what I heard, she wer' standin' at the sink one minute an' in a heap on the floor the next. God help us, what an afternoon. Apparently there's a flood at Bobbers Mill, Fred Woolascroft won't be very happy. The drains they've just laid couldn't cope with so much water, it wer' comin' off the roofs faster than the drainpipes could contain it. Like Edgar says, if yer cover a field in concrete, stands to sense the rain's got to go somewhere, it can't soak in no more, so it backed up an' wer' lappin' the walls on the bottom row of houses. Makes yer begin to realise what problems poor old Noah must have had. It'll be an end to the summer now, first day o' September next Tuesday."

Mrs. Talbot hurried on her way. So the ambulance was for Doris Madden. Celia decided to say nothing to William on the subject, she wouldn't grant him the satisfaction of smugly reminding her of his prediction. Besides, it would only turn his thoughts to the possible inconvenience Rex Madden's troubles might bring to 'Basil'.

Annie had the kettle simmering on the range and a plate of marble cake sitting under a teacloth on the table, along with the best cups and saucers she'd taken from the 'rarely used shelf' of the dresser. It was almost 3 o/clock. Charles had grudgingly agreed to come back to mind the shop, it was unlikely to be for more than an hour, Anthony Hemsley must travel back to Sheffield. His letter had arrived early the previous week, advising Annie of his intention to call on her and Charles, God willing, on Wednesday September 2nd if convenient to them. It would be mid afternoon, after he'd completed his work at Mapperley. It felt strange the prospect of seeing again someone from childhood. So many years had passed and during that time the events and happenings had been too numerous to relate at this brief meeting, yet they'd fashioned life into the shape it now was and Annie could only hope Anthony would not be disappointed by what he found here. In any unforeseen situation they would pass by without a thought, for neither could possibly recognise the other after such a span of years. Charles had no acquaintance with the Hemsleys, for him it would be even more awkward.

Anthony had not revealed the nature of his work and other than a brief mention of his sister Margaret in that first letter, he'd written nothing of family. It seemed strange that he'd not included his wife when sending his regards, Annie remembered, albeit vaguely, aunt Bella receiving a letter from Alice in which she'd excitedly announced that her son was to be married.

The clock struck a quarter past, Annie willed a knock to come at the door, she'd replied by return of post assuring Anthony that Charles and herself would be pleased to welcome him, to catch up on all the lost years. She could hardly write the truth, Charles had been anything but pleased and not until last night had he actually responded to Annie's request that he be around to at least share the duties of the shop, keeping her in a state of unease as long as he could before muttering a resentful agreement. Anthony needed to arrive, to chat, have tea and leave.

She could hear an unfamiliar voice coming from the shop, a man's voice, the dialogue grew clearer as they approached. Why she'd presumed Anthony would come to the back and not through the shop she had no idea, in fact it felt foolish now as Charles stood by the passage door bidding Anthony enter the room where Annie had prepared for his arrival. A man much taller than Annie had imagined cast a smile across the kitchen.

"Annie how good it is to see you, and to meet Charles. Normally such a day as this would be nothing but tedious routine but I have really looked forward to this afternoon." He took her hand and kissed her cheek.

"I'll get back to the shop," said Charles, "we all have our tedious routine."

"To call midst your hours of work is thoughtless of me, you should have written to tell me so. It's just that I must drive back very soon so a brief visit before leaving Nottingham was all that I could manage and I do intend calling on Mrs. Wright too. I have discovered from sorting with Margaret all the old letters and papers, how very close mother was to her friend and neighbour of old."

Anthony Hemsley looked intently at Charles, standing a good four inches taller and considerably broader across the shoulder, from where Annie stood Charles appeared to shrink from the domination of this stranger before him.

"It's my wife you've come to see naturally. I understand that so I'll leave you to catch up with one another." Charles fled to the shop where the counter stood between him and any unknown.

"Please, sit down Anthony, I've made some tea. How is Margaret and her family, your father was kind in writing to me when it became too difficult for your mother, but he wrote little about family, so I must enquire after you all, is your wife well?" Annie poured the tea and uncovered the cake. "Please help yourself you have a long way to drive before having a chance to eat again."

"Margaret is in good health, indeed her family is prospering, her son Archie is a lawyer and her daughter Emma is married to a dentist, or to give him his correct title an orthodontist. Her husband as I'm sure you'll know from mother's letters of many years ago is an accountant, like father. Dear mum was probably more delighted by Margaret's marriage to an accountant than by any other event. I suppose she believed that nothing untoward could possibly happen to the wife of an accountant, mother had a very sheltered life in many ways, father did his best to shield her from anxieties, such an irony that towards the end he could do nothing to relieve them. She no longer recognised him, became distressed when, 'the strange man' came," Anthony sighed. "All Margaret's family is based in Manchester. You kindly ask after my wife," he hesitated and took a drink of tea. "We drifted apart somehow, Gloria is a strong minded woman, my work often takes me away from home, sometimes the distances I have to travel render it necessary for me to overnight in lodgings. We didn't have children, not from any decision, it simply didn't happen. If we had they might have strengthened the ties, who knows. Anyway, we live apart, 'separated' I believe is the term used. It's not recent, I moved out of the house many years ago. Mother and father were in every way inseparable, poor mum, she never understood how such a situation

327

could come about. Margaret blames me for mother's decline, I don't think father ever did but Margaret is vehement, apparently I turned mum's brain with my selfishness. Wedded bliss should have been all that I ever displayed to mother, all that I ever created for Gloria, in essence I am the cause of mother's madness, me, her son." He took another drink of tea and continued. "Margaret has barely spoken to me since. Sorting the house following father's death has been like some kind of penance, in my head as I sifted through drawer after drawer I could hear Margaret's voice demanding my punishment, 'you shall suffer, you should suffer'. In fact we worked almost in total silence but she was granted her wish, handling all those personal things, reminders of childhood, of happy times, caused suffering, inflicted pain." Again he put the cup to his lips.

Annie felt she must speak. "I'm sure Margaret will regret any harsh words, in time when she can reflect with less emotion she will realise that your mother became ill but not an illness that can be transmitted from one to another, not even by son to mother. Margaret's hurt must be intense, to lose your father too, so quickly after Alice. Margaret's own mind will be struggling to cope, be patient."

"You are a remarkable listener Annie and I am a most ungracious visitor. I have come to see you after a period of more than thirty years only to pour out my woes and to ask nothing of your family. Tell me about your children, grown now as they are I shall listen while you describe them to me, I promise not to utter a word and the piece of delicious looking cake, which I am about to take from that plate will guarantee it."

Annie chatted freely, Freddy at Lincolnshire, William at Brassington, George and John at Raleigh, Hilda busy with her duties at the library. It was easy to relate to Anthony the endeavours of her children and furthermore, satisfying. Not often did Annie have occasion to speak about the progress of her family in such a way. She found herself with a warm sense of pride.

"I haven't asked the nature of your work Anthony, what actually brings you to Nottingham?" Annie had begun to think of Charles, he'd be getting impatient, she should tactfully remind Anthony of his need to call at The Park. "I know Davina will be curious over your work, she is always interested in the boys' activities. I think it helps her to feel involved, a part of things still, at her age she must feel at times as though she's no longer relevant."

"I am a mineralogist Annie. There is a theory being considered, that a different type of mining might be possible on a site at Mapperley, 'open cast' extraction. I have been there today to take a series of core samples from the strata, at varying levels. I can't imagine Mrs.Wright will find my work all that interesting, most people see it as no more than a study of old, inanimate matter fit only to be trodden upon, but I shall do my best to make it sound suitably important." He chuckled. "I should take my leave of you now but we mustn't permit another thirty years to pass before seeing one another again Annie."

A wry smile came to her face. "Indeed we should not Anthony, we may well find our meeting rather too 'spiritual' if we do."

Charles was handing a customer their change.

"It is a pleasure to meet you Charles," said Anthony, as the shop door closed behind Mrs.Glasson. He held out his hand, Charles took it responding with.

"Likewise, I dare say you will call again when business brings you in our direction."

"I do hope so. Now I must seek Mrs.Wright, spend a few moments with the lady whom it seems considered my mother to be her true friend and confidante."

Annie felt Anthony's gaze linger on Charles curiously, she could tell it made Charles uneasy. Anthony's choice of words too puzzled even herself. 'Confidante'. People favoured certain words in their vocabulary, Stanley Pagett was always calculating, 'I calculate this' or 'I calculate that'. Mrs.Glasson ended her account of any event with 'Glory be' and the elderly Mr.Freeman, on receiving his change would invariably say 'capital my dear, capital'. The bell clanged as their visitor finally left through the shop door.

"Thank God for that, he's not short of a word is he?" Said Charles. "I'm going to have a cup of tea and some cake, if there's any left."

Annie had little opportunity to dwell on either Anthony's conversation or Charles' lack of it as Mabel Rashleigh entered the shop at that moment looking purposeful.

"I've not seen 'im afore, that fella as just left, on business is 'e, got that look, yer can usually tell when they're after summat."

"I believe he's in Nottingham to call on old friends," said Annie.

"Aye, well, I best take a pound o' pearl barley for me broth an' I'll have a packet o' semolina an'all."

Annie began to weigh out the barley.

"You've heard the latest on Madden's wife I suppose, she's in City hospital, 'er heart, summat wrong with 'er heart. She's had trouble with 'er nerves for years, lives in a world of 'er own most o' time. Makes yer wonder don't it, which is worse, heart trouble or head trouble?"

Annie reached the semolina from the shelf saying nothing but inwardly questioning if it was possible to have one without the other.

CHAPTER NINETEEN

Late November

Jack always waited, he'd say 'let the dust settle', but twelve months had passed since they'd done the job in The Park, Jack would expect him to shift the lead, to make some money of it, especially this last lot, all Jack had gone through would be for nothing if he didn't see the job to its end.

Horace Clegg sat behind the wheel of the truck where he'd pulled up a dozen yards from the entrance to Bobbers Mill. The flood following the storm last August had proved the drainage installed at the site to be inadequate, it had been necessary to undertake considerable alteration and improvement. It was common knowledge that Fred Woolascroft had raged like a bull at his men, not so commonly known was the fact that on his own instruction, short cuts, some deviation from the plans had been applied, all money saving of course. Re-laying and further trench work to ensure no repeat of the flooding had cost and that cost took a slice of Woolascroft's profits. The man vent' his anger and frustration on those least accountable, the labourers on site, cutting their pay and ordering off any who made a stand. Fred Pearson had observed the regular 'tete a tete' held by the foreman in overall charge of construction and Woolascroft, the lowered voices and nods of agreement between the two. The expression 'smell a rat' was entirely justified when indeed there was a stench, when it offended the senses and when what created it was so furtive, so 'underground' it was virtually impossible to catch sight of it, yet its presence, that 'smell' was undeniable.

Without Jack, Horace Clegg was weakened by nervousness, his fingers wrapped and unwrapped the steering wheel as his confidence flowed then ebbed away. When his head found courage his legs lacked it. Trying to co-ordinate mind and body took time but he couldn't sit here forever. At last a surge of strength held long enough to enable him to open the cab door and step outside the truck. He pulled his

331

cap over that bald spot where the old wound revealed his scalp, like a patch of mange on those untamed creatures, which scoured bins of rubbish for any morsel that might sustain life.

If Woolascroft had lost money over the flooding then he'd be receptive to any deal that saved him a quid or two, there couldn't be a better time to make approach.

Clegg walked on to the site, giving the briefest nod to any man who glanced his way. It happened to be Fred Pearson, pushing a wheelbarrow across the track in front of Clegg, to whom he directed his enquiry.

"Can yer tell me where I'll find Mr. Woolascroft?"

"Which one?" Said Pearson, "The son Dick or the big noise, Fred Woolascroft himself?"

"Big noise I reckon," replied Clegg, trying his best to sound calm and controlled, while within he shook like a leaf.

"Well it makes no difference 'cause neither one is here today, see that hut over there," Fred pointed to a small wooden shed, "the site foreman's in there, he'll likely talk to yer, his name's Briggs, round these parts it's bastard Briggs, although I prefer to call him Mister."

"Ta." Clegg gave a feeble smile and forced his feet to take him to the hut, to bastard Briggs!

"Come in." A harsh, rasping voice responded to Clegg's knock. A man sat at a makeshift desk, the floor about his booted feet held ridges of caked on mud, butt ends were strewn between them along with spent matches and sweet wrappers. A few inches away from the leg of the desk, a dead frog, almost completely flat but for its head, from which the tongue, swollen and crimson with dried blood protruded with gruesome proof of the poor creature having been either trodden on or squashed by a movement of the desk. A heavy jacket over the back of his chair was the most likely source of the overwhelming smell of stale body odour and the cap sitting on top his head appeared vulcanized along its rim, like rubber, so heavily coated had it become in dirt and grease, lifted from his fingers at each putting on and taking off.

"What do you want, if it's work then you'll 'ave to prove you're up to it, I've seen more muscle on a dead man."

Clegg swallowed hard. "I'm 'ere to do business, I've got summat I reckon you'll be interested in."

The foreman swivelled his backside about on the chair so as to face Clegg.

"Oh aye, business yer say, an' just what would be the nature o' this business then?"

"Lead, I've got some lead to sell, good stuff, I can let yer 'ave it at a decent price an'all."

Briggs proceeded to pick between his teeth with a sharpened matchstick, presumably achieving to dislodge the troublesome piece of nut that had escaped the half eaten bar of nougat by his elbow on the desk, as he then did a sweep of his upper and lower jaw with his tongue. It felt to Clegg like the tough bastard Briggs was savouring the moment, already tasting blood but the foreman's response delivered relief and Clegg's chest lost its tightness.

"We can always use a bit o' lead, whereabouts is it?"

"I've got a truck parked outside, it's on the back o' that," said Clegg.

Briggs stood up, nudged the dead frog into position, in line with the open door and before Clegg had chance to stand aside, booted it with such force, the scrap of dead amphibian flew past Clegg's shoulder and onto a mound of sand where it stayed momentarily before tumbling down the side, leaving a perfect imprint where it first landed.

"Yer best drive your truck onto the site, a man can't do business out on the street can 'e, I need to look at this lead."

Clegg nodded, hastily walking past the masons and labourers, aware of their interest in him. Within minutes he'd driven the truck to a clear area only a couple of yards from the side of the hut. Briggs stood in the doorway, first spitting at the ground he crossed to where Clegg now stood by the back of the truck, his hand lifting a piece of old canvas floor covering, which he'd used to conceal the lead.

"What do yer want for it?" Briggs' voice could have hammered copper with every intonation.

Clegg sniffed. "Three quid an' that's cheap."

"Thirty bob an' that's all you're gettin'."

By now Clegg wanted only to be rid of it, to drive away from Bobbers Mill and leave the past behind.

"Put it over there in that crate." Briggs watched while Clegg carried the lead from the truck to the crate and satisfied himself that none remained beneath the canvas. "Come in the office, I'll get your money." A one pound note and a ten shilling note Briggs took from a cash box, locking it immediately afterwards and placing it back in a drawer, the key he deposited in his trouser pocket. Then he took a sheet of paper from a note pad, a pen from a jam jar still bearing the label 'Duerrs Ginger Conserve' and writing the date at the top of the paper he passed it along the desk to Clegg. "It's a cash transaction, I can't risk you comin' back an' makin' out I never paid yer so put your name on there, I presume yer can write."

Clegg was indignant. "Cause I can bloody write, there." He pushed the paper back to Briggs. "Me mam wer only nine when she finished schoolin' but she could read an' write, what do yer take me for, some kind o' soddin' idiot."

Thrusting the money into his pocket Clegg left the hut, climbed inside the cab of his truck and drove once more past the curious workforce and out onto the road.

"There you go Jack, finished, all bloody finished." He felt strange, thirty bob sat in his pocket yet it brought Clegg no satisfaction. He looked over at the empty seat beside him, pulled off his cap, lay it down where Jack would have sat and taking the two notes from his pocket, placed them inside the cap, rolling it around them. "The cap wer' yours Jack, yer dropped it on that last job. I'll do right by yer, just like yer did by me all them years ago." He started the engine, feeling the tears welling he forced himself to whistle a tune and drove resolutely towards Sherwood.

334

Briggs sat in his so called office grinning to himself, the receipt in his hand. "Horace Clegg." He shook his head, folded the piece of paper, placed it in the inside pocket of his jacket, laughed out loud and took another bite from the nougat.

Winchester Street was quiet, before nosy parkers could peer through their nets Clegg pushed the flattened cap with its lining of thirty bob through Lillian Sulley's letterbox. As he drove away, whistling a tune became very much easier and the seat beside him, now strangely felt much less empty.

"All done Jack, it's all done."

"I am grateful to you Mr. Woolascroft," said sergeant Beasley, "very grateful indeed."

The 'reformed' Dick Woolascroft rose to his feet, casting his eyes down to the piece of paper now before the police officer, he gave a shallow smile, insidious to anyone knowing of the hypocrisy that lay behind his toadying pretence.

"My father runs a tight operation sergeant, he would countenance no disreputable dealings, this city, its progress and development are what drives him, he keeps society's best interests always at his heart."

"Commendable, highly commendable. I shall inform him on our success in apprehending Clegg, it will give me a great deal of satisfaction to hold that reprobate by the collar." Beasley offered his hand to Dick Woolascroft, both men acknowledged the courtesy.

"What's he likely to get for his crimes? A hefty custodial sentence surely," said Woolascroft, "in these times of recession the lame brained will surely turn to theft more and more if this wastrel isn't held up as an example of law enforcement and justice, a deterrent to all those of similar ilk."

"I only nab the blighters, it's for the magistrates to decide their fate but Clegg won't be hangin' up his stockin' for his Christmas orange at home this year, I'll safely predict that."

Woolascroft left, chuckling as he closed the door behind him. Beasley sat back in his chair, now alone he studied the name on the receipt. "Horace Clegg, why Sulley didn't spit you out God knows but I've got yer now." He spoke aloud, satisfying his need to feel convinced of success. "I hope your watchin' Sulley, from above or below I hope you're bloody well watchin'."

"I'm sure it won't come to that Hilda, if your dad hasn't said anythin' more then 'e'll likely be regrettin' his words an' feelin' miserable," said Sarah prodding at the fire to encourage more flame. "You can stop here at any time, you know that, it's your mam I worry for. Annie knows nothin' but work, hard work an' stress, she's not a young woman anymore, all that business with Freddy took a lot out of 'er." Happy with the heat now coming from the grate, Sarah pushed the damper in a notch and hung the poker back on the 'companion'. "All the years I've managed with just a poker an' the old coal shovel, now Maggie's given me this fancy stand with a brush, a poker an' a shovel, all with matchin' barley twist handles, I don't know meself, if I forget to hang 'em up she'll say 'Mam, that's what a fireside companion set is for, to keep stuff out the way of your feet so you can't trip over'. She's had this fixation ever since old Mrs.Truscott caught her foot on the poker and fell onto the mantelpiece, you've never seen such a state as what her face was in, eye's black an' blue an' a gash over the bridge of her nose that took two weeks to heal. But I'm not daft, nor so blind that I can't see where I've left the poker."

Hilda smiled but refrained from pointing out that Mrs.Truscott would almost certainly have made the same claim.

"George come to see me the other evenin', he didn't stop long an' he made me promise that I wouldn't say anythin' to your mam but he's concerned about Alice. He says she gets so tired, she just can't seem to shake off her weariness. She's three more months to go yet, you do get tired in the later stages but George was anxious I could tell. Not havin' a mam of her own must make it hard for 'er. I know Fred Pearson allus did his best an' George will an'all but there's a limit to what a man can do, even a good 'en doesn't have that instinct God give to a woman," Sarah sighed.

Hilda sat back from the fire, the flames now leaping the back of the grate.

"I shouldn't get too warm or I'll feel chilled when I go out. On Saturday I'll spend some time with Alice, take her some malt, Mrs.Haynes swears by malt, she reckons if it weren't for malt she'd have lost her strength long ago. Jack's good to his mam, he's a lot like George in his ways, I think they would always get on, George gets on with everybody." Hilda was silent for a moment then with a tremble in her voice said. "If dad declares I must leave then I shall come straight here Grandma but everyday I will go to the shop, to make sure mam's alright, he can't banish me from the shop can he, it's a public place. I can't stop seeing Jack Grandma, I just can't."

Sarah's heart went out to Hilda, many times over the years Charles' behaviour had made Sarah want to smack him like she would a tempestuous child, for his own good. It was difficult, only George was her true grandson, Sarah loved them all but to interfere when she had no actual claim of authority she feared might only incite Charles to further ill temper and moodiness.

"I best get off home," said Hilda, "no matter what he decides, it no longer feels like home, the tension affects us all, even John's afraid to speak. He used to come back from Raleigh with stories to tell us that were so amusing we looked forward to the laughter. Now John eats his meal and barely utters a word, we all eat in silence, we could be monks and nuns of a silent order, anyone observing us would think we were making earnest preparation to enter such a covenant of peace, but it isn't peace at all, it's a trial, a torment. Mam and John would probably be better off if I did move out, perhaps then they could relax, knowing that the source of dad's anger was removed from the table."

Sarah squeezed Hilda's hand but could think of no words to reassure the young woman.

"Jack is the easiest man in the world to love," said Hilda, "dad must surely be the hardest."

Sarah made no reply but inwardly recalled episodes in the past when she'd felt Annie's despair, there was no denying, Charles Eddowes was a hard man to love.

It had not taken sergeant Beasley very long to track down Horace Clegg, now sitting opposite this impoverished individual, he was intent on securing a confession that would finally close the chapter on Jack Sulley.

"Not the brightest button in the box are yer, I suppose Sulley was the brains o' the outfit, shame 'e didn't point them in another direction. Lead you into a life o' crime did 'e, you're a sight smaller than 'e was, you 'ad to do as yer wer' told didn't yer. You weren't his mate 'e had you for a lackey."

Beasley's words ignited fire in Horace Clegg. "Jack Sulley wer' the best friend I ever 'ad an' I'll not deny him. 'E didn't lead me into crime, it wer' this place, this soddin' city an' them as govern it drove us both to defy the bloody rules, rules made by men who take pleasure from grindin' ordinary folk into the ground. Jack led me away from trouble, even carried me when others wer' set on kickin' me head in. 'E allus stood up for me, well 'e can't stand up for 'isself now an' I'm not goin' to sit 'ere while you run 'im down, sergeant or no sergeant." Clegg jumped to his feet. "Lock me up on bread an' water, do yer think there's not been times when our house wer' bare o' food, I've been hungry afore an' guts ache is a bloody sight better than the gripin' pain a man gets if he betrays his mate." Clegg shook from emotion, the sincerity of it surprised Beasley.

"Jack's six foot under, defiance didn't get 'im far did it? Anyroad, before I do anything else I've got to send you to a doctor." Beasley folded his arms and sat back in his chair, as though anticipating Clegg's response.

"There's nowt wrong wi' me, yer can't make out I'm daft an' put me in a loony bin, I've heard what you do to them wi' faces as don't fit, locked up for darin' to open their mouths. Well I'm sane I tell yer, sane as you are sergeant so you can forget about a doctor, prison's one thing, rottin' in the mad house is another."

"Sit down!" Beasley raised his voice to show authority. "You must know that Jack was sick, tuberculosis. For the welfare of others I need it confirmed by the medics, if you've got T.B. an'all I can't mix yer with other men, workin' wi' Jack as you were, the infection could easily have passed to you."

"I don't cough, Jack wer' forever coughin', coughed 'is guts up at times I've seen 'im sweat from the effort, then shake like his chest wer' about to cave in, but me, I never as much as clear me throat, there's nowt wrong wi' me Beasley."

"Sergeant Beasley to you, an' it makes no difference if you only ever spit lavender water, you're still goin' to be checked by a doctor. Tell me one thing Clegg, how did yer manage to hide the lead when yer drove it away. My constables were searchin' lorries an' trucks day an' night."

Clegg smiled. "Me an' Jack, we did what this place done to us, we shat on the lead, all over it an' do yer know sergeant, once that's happened to yer, no one sees yer anymore, yer become invisible, like yer don't exist. If your constables had looked underneath they'd 'ave found the valuables, but who wants to touch shit sergeant?"

Beasley hesitated, then as if he thought better of what he'd been about to say he stood, walked around the desk, tapped Clegg's shoulder and spoke simply to say, "Follow me."

Annie stirred the saucepan of stew, a sinking feeling in the pit of her stomach had intensified with the hours. Charles had uttered only one remark the entire day. 'Six months I said, six months'. It was the last day of November, it was like waiting for the axe to fall. Hilda was upstairs, John would be home any minute and Charles stood behind the shop counter like a judge waiting to pronounce sentence. Hilda loved her Jack, perhaps she would be altogether happier living somewhere else. William, Charles' first born couldn't wait to leave, he'd preferred to call The Park his home and live with Davina. Freddy had followed soon after, moving in with the Cropleys. George had relished the prospect of living in that small house on Ainsley Road with his dear Alice, only John and Hilda endured the unpredictable atmosphere at Gregory Street, never knowing whether their dad would tolerate some degree of happiness or if the sound of laughter would prove too much for him to bear. Annie could hear footsteps outside in the yard, the back door opened and John came in carrying a bag.

"From George, it's apples, his pal Ron gave them to him, but Alice gets so tired these days, he thought they might not get used in time, they're not keepers so he sent them for you to make a pie for dad."

Annie peeped inside the bag. "There'll be enough for more than one pie, I shall bake one for George and Alice and take it to them on Sunday. I'm about to serve up now, give your sister a call and I'll relieve Charles while he eats."

John sensed his mother's nervousness, the date had not escaped his mind either. "Hilda's a young woman now Mam, a bright one, she knows her own mind and I reckon she's sure of her heart as well. I know you worry about her and she worries about you but it's strange how fate so often gets things right, in spite of our misgivings. Grandma Sarah gets lonely, aunty Maggie goes to Mitchell Street every day to see her, if Hilda was living at grandma's, how much easier would it make life for Maggie. Jennifer and Amy are still so young, it must be a struggle for her. Hilda's chatter wouldn't allow grandma Sarah to feel lonely would it? We both know that house with the smiley face on the front door would welcome Jack Haynes, when has anyone not been welcome at grandma's? It may not happen Mam but if it does it will solve some problems and you can't honestly believe that Hilda won't seek you out at some point every day, besides, you still have me!" John kissed his mother's cheek. "Percy Pollard's mother died last night, her name was Dorothy. He told me that the family called her 'Duchess' because their dad used to sing the old music hall song to her, 'Me Dear Old Dutch'. We've got a new woman's bike coming into production, the men took a vote and every hand went up in favour of calling it 'The Raleigh Duchess', I think it pleased Percy." John crossed the passageway to the foot of the stairs and called up to Hilda, "Tea's ready."

Annie was serving up Charles' meal when he appeared, Hilda's eyes looked at Annie, John stared at the table.

"Before the damn shop doorbell goes and your mam runs off I've something to say. If you tell me Hilda that you'll not see Haynes again I shall say no more on the matter but if you cannot assure me of that then it will be the last night you spend under this roof."

"Charles, please, why are you being so vindictive?" Annie's expression pleaded with him to relent and cruel tears filled her eyes with abject misery.

"Me, Charles Eddowes, I'm a man too and for once my opinion shall count for something." His voice was raised to an alarming pitch, his face was flushed with temper. "I shall be heeded in my own house do you hear, this is my house and I have spoken." He pulled out his chair, sat at the table and waited for Annie to put his plate in front of him.

"Very well Dad, if that's what you want," said Hilda, moving away from the table. "I have already packed a bag, I shall go to grandma's, John will bring the rest of my things at the weekend." She looked into Annie's eyes as she continued. "In all these months Jack has not once spoken a single disrespectful word about you or anyone else of this family, in my company he has been every bit a gentleman. We cannot choose with whom we fall in love, it simply happens, we can however choose whom we respect and trust and whom we honour with all our heart and soul. Hilda walked across to Annie, "I do love you Mam." She held her mother so tight it hurt, then Hilda went upstairs for her things.

The shop doorbell clanged, Charles proceeded to eat his meal. Annie threw some cold water over her face and went through to the shop. John stood up from the table, carried his plate to the scullery and went out through the back door.

Mrs.Glasson gave Annie a quizzical look, "Are you alright Mrs.Eddowes, you do look pale."

"It must be that time of year Mrs.Glasson," said Annie, "the days are so short of sunlight there's little to put colour into anyone's complexion unless we resort to a pot of rouge."

"I need some butter an' a quarter of Ceylon, the caddy's nearly empty. I better take a pound of puddin' rice an' some porridge oats an'all, I allus breathe a sigh of relief when spring comes, the cold weather drives the appetites in our house, what wi' that an' the need for more fire I sometimes wonder where the next penny's comin' from. But I try to count me blessin's , I go to bed of a night in me own place, you've heard about Doris Madden I suppose, she's been taken into city hospital again, the ambulance wer' called for this afternoon, I've never been in hospital an' I've allus prayed that I'd die in me own bed. It'll be her heart I dare say, same as last time. Them doctors are very clever though, my neighbour's 'ad an ulcer on her leg for years but they've managed to heal it at last. She's only wearin' a light bandage now, just to stop her knockin' it on somethin'. Would yer believe they took skin from her thigh an' grafted it over the ulcer, that's how they done it. Makes yer wonder what you'll hear next, Glory be!"

Charles had eaten and gone straight out so Annie worked the shop until closing time and cashed up. When she went through to the back she found John in the scullery washing up the pots.

"I waited at the corner Mam, for Hilda, I walked with her to Mitchell Street and promised to take the rest of her things there in the morning, early, before work. I shan't leave you on your own in the evenings until he gets over his mood. You should eat something Mam, grandma had already had her tea when we got there and Hilda said she wasn't hungry but grandma said she must have something so she made Hilda eat a basin of Oxo with bread in it. What shall I get for you, would you like some toast and a mug of hot milk?"

"That would be nice, did you finish your meal?"

"Yes, I wasn't going to waste it after you'd cooked it, lovely bit o' stew Mam. You've not read your letter yet." John crossed to the dresser and took the envelope from the shelf. "It's Francis's writing isn't it?" he handed it to Annie.

"With all the upset I'd forgotten about the post."

Annie sat by the range and opened her letter. John busied himself pouring milk into a pan over the hob and cutting a thick slice of bread which he pushed onto the toasting fork then held over the fire.

"What's happening at Skendleby Mam, are they planning to come for Christmas?"

Annie looked at John with tears in her eyes. "Freddy is going to be a dad again, Francis is four months pregnant." She could hold back emotion no longer. John lay the toasting fork down and held her in his arms.

"It'll be alright Mam, you'll see, everything will be alright."

Annie found calm, kissed John's forehead and smiled. "Where's that toast and milk?" As she forced herself to eat for John's sake he suddenly began to chuckle.

"You know what this means don't you Mam, for once Freddy will be ahead of William, father of two." Even Annie could not resist to share in John's amusement, for an hour they enjoyed one another's company.

John looked at the clock. "Let's go up before dad gets back, we've all had enough for one day."

"You go to bed," said Annie, "I'll fill a bottle and follow you."

She watched as he crossed the passageway and climbed the stairs. Dear John, he'd always been the gentle one, he'd been tender hearted as a child. She poured what was left in the kettle into the stone bottle, left a low light on for Charles and wearily took herself to their bedroom. The feeling of desolation was too great, Annie took her nightie from beneath the pillow and her hairbrush from the chest of drawers, she needed to feel Hilda's presence, to close her eyes and see her daughter looking happy.

On the chair in the corner of Hilda's room sat the bag containing the rest of Hilda's things, Annie could hardly bear to look on it. One day Hilda would marry Jack and make a home away from Gregory Street, but the pain had come earlier than Annie had expected. John too would doubtless lose his heart to a young woman, he was twenty after all. Just Charles and herself, drifting through the days and nights, clinging to hope, which the children created as the next generation entered this world. Annie laid her head on her daughter's pillow and longed for a time so far back it must surely have been in a previous life.

'May every window open to the sun

and life for you be full of pleasant ways,

343

so that you may, as the seasons run,

look out upon a world of happy days'.

Annie thought of Doris Madden, lying in a hospital bed, everything strange to her. Mrs.Glasson was right it was a blessing to lay in a familiar place. Annie pulled the pillow around her face, it smelled of Hilda, of Palmolive soap. The hot water bottle began to warm her feet and the love of her children soothed her to sleep.

"It is good to see you back Henry and looking so well." Andrew Smithfield's sentiment was genuine. It had been a long summer, problems at the factory were ever present and always at the root of them was money. People were slow in paying their bills, two accounts had closed altogether, customers were cautious, no one wanted more stock than they were confident of retailing quickly. Banks squeezed and clients felt the pinch.

Henry Wicks did indeed look well, the evidence of warm summer sunshine visible still on his skin, those weary features of earlier in the year seemed revitalized, his conversation was lively, filled with descriptive passages, his travels, people he'd met, foods he'd eaten, all were now laid before Andrew's imagination with such eagerness. Henry made comparisons with industry, taking the way of management on the continent and putting it alongside the British approach to job creation and the production line. Andrew listened, absorbed, and recognised in Henry an enthusiasm which the years at Birchdale must have drained from him as not before had Andrew felt such energy coming from his friend, a vitality that persisted in raising his own languid spirits from the doldrums where they had lain for so long.

"I sensed the determination Andrew and questioned why our own dithers behind that presumed certainty of a better tomorrow. 'Today' is all any man can possess. I stood on ground in France and smelled the bloodshed, there was nothing of man's evil in my sight, empty space. No noise to assault my ears, absolute peace, but the magnitude of destruction, the scale of waste aroused my determination too. In Belgium, I met a man of similar age to myself, he spoke sufficient English for us to converse. I told him that for many years I had wanted to see Europe, he patted my arm and said, 'My friend, you have waited until there is less of Europe to see, but very much more to feel'. I knew exactly what he meant, at that spot, not far from Ypres, it became personal, it felt immense, I could find no words to describe the feeling inside me, all I knew was that I owed them, all those young men. A memorial of stone isn't enough, it's nothing like enough. I owe them my determination, to strive while ever I live and breathe to ensure that their children and grandchildren know a better life, but I can't presume a certainty of that better tomorrow, I must employ today. I sat opposite a man on the train, an interesting chap to talk to. He told me of plans being considered to mine at Mapperley but 'open cast', a very different method to deep seam production. Tests will either prove or disprove the feasibility but first signs look promising. It would bring competition to the established collieries, to Basil Stanford and his ilk, give the men more bargaining power. Open cast extraction requires less set up cost and in principle, enables higher and quicker returns.

"You know that Steve Wainwright has stepped down as union rep?" Said Andrew.

"Steve came to see me before I left last May, he told me then that it was his intention to move over, to give voice to a younger man. He said he would nominate Jack Haynes, I wasn't surprised by that, like Steve I have observed Jack's character strengthening year on year. He's level headed, tough when he needs to be but not allowing his mind to be swayed by populist opinion. He questions, in the same vein as Steve he's not afraid to challenge if the broader picture demands further debate."

"You don't think competition would actually threaten the existing pits?" Asked Andrew, in his mind applying such a situation to his own industry.

"The world needs coal Andrew and it's possibly one of the most difficult commodities to produce, difficult and dangerous. Stanford could ill afford to have the winches idle, a strike could cost him dear if an open cast operation at Mapperley is successfully mining what this more modern world demands. Stanford could no longer hold that degree of power over the men, which in the past has achieved to contain their argument. No industry is able to concede to unreasonable, unworkable demands, someone like Jack Haynes has sense enough to understand that fact and logic to realise it applies equally to employer and employee. A development of this nature at Mapperley I do believe would rationalise attitudes, effectively bring about a more measured system, less divisive and therefore more inclined to overall success."

Andrew suddenly raised his hand listening for a repeat of the sound his ears had detected over Henry's dialogue. "I think someone is knocking at your door Henry."

A quick glance at the clock confirmed it to be a little after nine. "That's odd, I never have callers at this hour, I won't be a minute Andrew." Henry left the room and speaking more to himself than Andrew, on reaching the hallway said. "At the back door, someone's at the back door."

Andrew could hear voices, muffled at first but becoming more defined as they drew closer. It was a man, Henry was definitely returning to the room with a man but Andrew couldn't identify the voice.

Henry stepped into the sitting room and at once cast a look at Andrew that suggested he should stay.

"Rex has need of a quiet corner, I certainly can appreciate that and I feel sure that you too Andrew have sought an interlude when circumstances would overwhelm. Come inside Rex and sit down, I shall pour us all a drink."

Andrew had heard of Rex Madden, 'Stanford's man', but no occasion had caused them to meet until now. The man appeared beaten, reduced to a shadow. Henry put a glass in Madden's hand and passed another to Andrew.

"Rex's wife has been unwell for some time, sadly she died this evening, in the hospital and while that place can be a comfort through its attempts to maintain life, its waiting rooms and corridors serve only to intensify pain when those best efforts fail."

Rex took a drink from the glass. "I couldn't face home, for just a little while I needed another place, in a few minutes it will pass, I shall be alright, then I'll go. I've been to see Tommy Spooner, Handley's will do the funeral, he said about a week, it should be about a week." He took another gulp from the glass, Henry was about to stand, to pour him another. "No, thank you Mr.Wicks, I'm not a drinking man, I'm grateful for the fortitude the whisky delivered but I should call upon my own strength at this time." Neither Henry, nor Andrew spoke and the quietness of the room seemed to grant Rex Madden a real sense of neutrality.

"We'd been married fifteen months when Doris conceived for the first time, we were delighted like any other young couple, but at the three month stage she miscarried." Rex paused, sat forward in the chair and rubbed his palms over his knees, as if feeling again a rush of pain, pain for the past, pain for the present. "We rallied our spirits, after all it was early days, these things happened. Doris conceived again, twelve months later, she was nervous, tense, she tried not to show it but I could tell. Three months passed and her confidence began to return, the house held a lighter air, Doris allowed herself to smile, even to laugh. It was at four months that she bled, miscarried again, she was very poorly, I could see alarm in the doctor's expression. Doris recovered but for a time her nervousness almost consumed her. It's difficult to comfort a wife when simply laying close causes her to shake from fear. Eventually she found some peace, a calm and what is natural to man and wife she allowed again to happen. We'd been married five years when she conceived again. Claude Stanford was a good man, he recognised my dilemma, one day at the end of shift he took me to one side and said, 'Rex I need a man, a patient man to drive me, my eyesight is not good and will become even less reliable, my blood pressure and humour suffer as a result'. Claude pulled me from working underground, where for hours at a time I could do nothing for Doris. In my new position I could call at home, only briefly at odd times of the day, check that she was coping, her state of agitation had returned, I needed to cast a smile over her, distract her with simple chatter, bring a sense of normality to the days so they passed with the least stress possible. It seemed to work, the months went by, each one a relief, an achievement. The progress lightened her mind, at the eighth month she allowed herself to believe, to buy things for the baby, to knit, to prepare. She went full term, it was a boy, the delivery was normal, we called him John. Doris wanted him to have a biblical name, I'm sure she considered his birth a miracle. Everything was good, Doris was so happy. I remember Claude's response when I told him, he put his hand on my shoulder and said, 'A son Rex, now we both have a son'. I'd swear he was close to tears. Five weeks later we held John's funeral, he died of congenital heart disease, there was nothing the doctors could do to save him, or to spare his mother." Rex took a deep breath and continued. "Her nerves were shot to pieces, so were mine, I didn't know how to help her, we couldn't help each other, Doris entered a world of her own. Three years went by, Claude Stanford's health was deteriorating. I couldn't confide in him, even if his health had been sound, how does a man speak of such things, I was lonely. One night I was on my way home, after driving Claude to a meeting. It was late, I stopped outside a house on Forest Road, the house where other men stopped. I remember looking up and down the road, it was empty of people. I went up to the door and knocked. She said nothing, just stood aside for me to enter. There was no one else in that house, I'm certain of that. I paid her for sex. When breath came back to my body I felt a shame so great it propelled me from that place with all the urgency of a retching sickness. Even then my guilt made me look up and down the road, no one, there was no one.

It was not long afterwards that Claude Stanford died. I didn't know what to expect, he'd created that job for me and I imagined his son would see no need of it. I was wrong and surprised when Basil informed me I was to remain in my current job. It soon became clear I was now, in every way 'Stanford's man'. Basil knew of my weakness, my one fall from grace. He confronted me with it, declared his knowledge of it like a triumph. There is only one way he could have possibly come to know, the Downing woman must have told him. He manipulated me like a puppet, if I didn't dance to his tune, move to his design when he pulled the string, he would have told Doris. I couldn't risk that, her state of nervous tension was so extreme I couldn't countenance what she might do to herself.

When that scandal broke surrounding councillor Rathbone and Estelle Downing I saw fear in Basil Stanford, I knew that he and Rathbone were drinking partners. It was at that time Stanford sold the first parcel of land at the Colver site, to the local authority, soon after he sold another. Rathbone did time and I'd guarantee that he took the rap for Basil and that it cost Basil a lot of money. I'd paid for one disgusting session of sex, Basil paid for Rathbone's silence. You must remember Mr.Wicks how some folk speculated at the time, that more than councillor Rathbone had been behind Downing's successful business! It was possibly before your arrival in Nottingham Mr.Smithfield, before you would have been aware of our city elite. I've always been wary of gossip but such a theory was not so unlikely. I found it very hard to believe that Hannibal Burton was involved. I'd only ever heard him spoken of with sincere regard. He was successful in business but his own intelligence and gift for the skills of retailing made him so. Furthermore he was most generous to the bereaved during the war years, donating foodstuffs to families that might otherwise have experienced hunger as well as grief. That is not the nature of a corrupt mind. Blackmore too, pompous though he can be, is far too stiff upper lip British to surrender his self respect for monetary gain. Cheetham and Birkett, who knows?"

Andrew had listened intently, feeling compassion for Rex, such an account of life, and death, but this revelation, how could Andrew's curiosity not be aroused. "What happened to Rathbone?" He felt compelled to ask.

"He served his sentence and disappeared with his earnings. It was by a strange coincidence that I learned of his fate. I'd driven Stanford to Derbyshire, he had a meeting with someone at the Blue John mine. Whatever his business there might have been it obviously came to nought, he never went there again but I had an hour to kill while he was engaged with the manager. I felt hungry so I bought myself faggot and chips. I was about to screw up the newspaper when I finished eating but my eye was taken by the word 'Rathbone'. The outer sheet of newspaper was the obituaries page of The Stoke Post. It was him alright, I later discovered that councillor Rathbone, to give him the title he'd worn in his heyday, died as a result of a perforated stomach ulcer, which poisoned his system. Ironic don't you think, a poisoned system." Rex attempted to laugh at the irony but his head bowed from the weight of emotion, years of pent up misery now overwhelmed the man and he wept.

"You are among friends Rex," said Henry, "here no one stands in judgement or doubts your integrity."

Andrew Smithfield rose to his feet. "I shall drive you home Mr.Madden, you must let me know the date and time of your wife's funeral."

"Yes indeed," said Henry. "Events can demand of us a greater determination, not to act for our own sake but to honour the life of another. Don't give up Rex, you must not let it beat you now." He walked them to the front door, Andrew stood outside, Madden turned and spoke quietly.

"Thank you Mr.Wicks." The two men shook hands.

"Henry, please Rex, it is your friend Henry."

Andrew drove to Glover Street, glancing towards William's house as they travelled slowly towards No.72. "Do you know William Eddowes? He's a foreman at Brassington, he lives here on Glover Street with his wife Celia and their infant son."

"I've heard of him but to say that I know him would be untrue. I see his mother, Mrs.Eddowes at the shop on Gregory Street, a very decent woman, kindly, always pleasant."

"What you say Rex is entirely my experience also. Annie Eddowes I have always found to be the most decent of women but her eldest son William, despite the fact that he has worked at my factory for eleven years, I still cannot in all truth say that I know him. I believe this is home." Andrew pulled up outside the house with the globe, the street lamp shedding its light over the window behind which lay Rex Madden's world!

"Goodnight, and thank you Mr.Smithfield."

Andrew watched until Rex turned the key in his door and disappeared inside. It had been an evening of unusual developments, so much conversation to fill his mind, why then were his thoughts unable to move beyond Annie, to find a way through the impasse that kept him forever at the same place. A light, only dim, was now showing, somewhere inside No72. It was time for Andrew to seek home, that empty, silent place, just like Henry's abode and now like Rex Madden's too. How different it must be at Gregory Street, family in and out with all their news, young life, happy chatter, bound together by that most decent of women, kindly, pleasant Annie, Mrs. Charles Eddowes.

CHAPTER TWENTY

"Next year will see both the ring road completed and the development at Bobbers Mill. I've been keeping an eye on progress, if I can write up a good comprehensive report the Ed. might let me loose on something more challenging than the notices and the court sessions," said Kenneth as his hand hovered over the plate of assorted biscuits, finally homing in on a fig roll. "At least I can write an article for the column about the cat burglar's accomplice. I thought they'd be a lot more forthcoming at the police station but they seemed a bit cagey, not desperate to fill me in on their successful capture and arrest, normally they can't wait to sing their own praises. Horace Clegg is the name of the elusive villain and apparently he made no attempt to deny his crimes. His downfall was trying to sell some lead to Woolascroft. I went to Bobbers Mill, the foreman, one Bill Briggs who took great pains to establish his name firmly in my mind was only too happy to tell me 'for the record', exactly what happened. He bought it off Clegg with the sole intention of getting a signed receipt then he handed that vital piece of paper to Woolascroft who passed it on to the police. Feathers in the caps of 'Woolascrofts all' and no doubt noted in the echelons of power, shrewd mover is that Mr. Woolascroft. I waved to uncle Fred, he was busy mixing concrete, I wonder if anyone at the building's completion will remember to put a date in the mortar before it sets. That's what they did at Bestwood, like a royal seal I suppose. I read in a library book that when Queen Victoria and Prince Albert visited St. Michael's Mount in Cornwall, on stepping from the boat that carried them across the stretch of water from the mainland, they each put their foot onto some soft mortar, to mark the uniqueness of the occasion. Folk visit that place especially to see the imprints, which in theory should remain for centuries." Kenneth's chatter was comfortable and Alice sat back in the chair letting his voice simply wash over her until she heard him say with rather more urgency. "Are you alright?"

She managed a smile, though she felt heavy with tiredness. "I didn't realise that carrying a baby for nine months would prove so demanding of strength, I do get weary. Poor George has had nothing but bought cake for weeks, I just can't muster the energy to bake. His mam gave us a big slab of homemade Madeira cake last week, I saw George seize upon it with relish. I shall make it up to him after the baby is born, I'll see that he has homemade cake in his pack up every day. He worries about me but I managed to persuade him not to bother the doctor, it is the depths of winter after all and I've not succumbed to a single cough or sniffle so I can't be that feeble can I?"

Kenneth stood, leant over her and kissed her cheek. "I shall rinse up these cups, no arguing if you please, then I must get back to the office and type up my article. Bear up cousin, only a couple more months and I shall be putting the announcement in The Post, the birth of baby Boucher. You must give him or her at least two middle names. I'm quite convinced that to a large extent life is decreed by a name. Last week I entered in the notices the announcement of the arrival at Sedgley Hall of, Christopher Meredith, Montague, to Horton and Arabella Boller-Flint. It sounds so undeniably splendid it's impossible to consider anything less than success in one of the professions, or notoriety among high society for such an impressively and colourfully named individual, how could a sepia Bert Bloggs ever hope to compete!"

Alice giggled. "You are funny Kenneth. Thank you for coming to visit me, even if it was only seeing dad at Bobbers Mill that reminded you of my existence." She taunted him mischievously.

You know you are my favourite." He took a small paper bag from his jacket pocket. "Pear drops for Alice," he said with a big grin on his face. "Something sweet for my sweetest cousin."

The churchyard was unable to offer any shelter from the searching wind, it blew from the northeast. Andrew Smithfield's own feeling of chill had prompted him to look up at the weathervane as the procession of mourners followed the coffin along the path, if indeed they could be deemed a procession. Inside the church, a handful of neighbours, mostly women had sat quietly, the presence of Basil Stanford and his wife seemed to impose a hush, they sat alone, towards the front, Andrew imagined few of Doris Madden's neighbours would feel comfortable seated alongside Stanford. His demeanour achieved to distance him from those folk possessed of humility. The congregation stood and Rex endured the service as best he could. He cut such a lonely, bereft figure both Andrew and Henry Wicks were unable to leave him to walk behind his wife's coffin without the comfort of friends. Everyone else had drifted away, including the Stanfords. Now at a spot among the gravestones and most poignantly, alongside the small, weathered granite memorial dedicated to John Madden, aged just five weeks, Henry and Andrew flanked Rex as the Reverend Hockley committed Doris Madden to the ground. So grey was Rex from cold and grief that his face bore no more colour than the ghostly marble that seemed to observe almost stealthily, from here and there, leaning to peer at them from behind erect, less curious gravestones. At last it was done. The vicar lay a comforting hand on Rex's shoulder and smiled but spoke no more, understanding that words held little meaning at this moment. Tommy Spooner stood discreetly a few yards away, nodding his acknowledgement of Henry and Andrew's attendance. Despite the numerous funerals over which Tommy had presided, the death of a child never failed to touch him, to remind him of William's brother, Daniel Eddowes, Tommy's first encounter with infant mortality. He'd read the name, John Madden, the tender age, and no amount of professionalism could stem the emotion within, his own two small boys so deeply rooted in his heart.

Andrew had parked his vehicle a few yards away from St Andrew's. He'd called for Henry and the two had travelled together. Now it was Henry's concern for Rex that bound him to suggest they all go back to Langley Drive.

"It's very kind of you Mr.Wicks, Henry, but I have things to which I must attend and I shall find them all the more daunting if I allow my mind to delay. I am truly grateful to you both, for your support," he held out his hand, "and for the friendship."

"I shall drive you home Henry, then take Rex to Glover Street, I'll not agree to anything other Rex, you must allow me to see you home." Inside the car they all felt a relief from the searching wind.

Henry stood by the gate, watching them until the car was gone from view, with a sigh he turned his face to his house, studying its façade, its desirability, its likely value. He knew what Leonora would say, 'don't dither, do it'. She was right he would speak with an agent today!

"What will you do?" Asked Andrew as he drove towards Glover Street. Henry has returned from his travels with so many thoughts and ideas and I sense, a great impatience to implement them, but you, will you stay with Stanford?"

Rex took a handkerchief from his pocket and wiped his nose of the wateriness induced by the cold air. "It is his deception I so abhor, his presence at the service, that veneer of decency, which I know to be tissue thin, yet others fail to see through it. I have been informed already that I am obsolete, no longer of use. Whether or not that means the actual job is obsolete I wouldn't care to say but now Stanford has lost his power over me it was to be expected that my services would no longer be required, may heaven help any replacement his appetite might seize upon. It makes little difference, I had no intention of continuing in the post, even 'Cratchet' was worthy of some respite." Rex smiled, "I found it amusing that folk should liken me to the doggedly servile clerk of fiction. I'm sure they thought that I had no idea of what was said behind my back but in fact it was they who had no idea of just how loudly they spoke."

"Surely now that Stanford can no longer threaten the well being of your wife and knowing of his somewhat lurid past, you might expose him for what he really is," said Andrew.

"Have you ever met Florence Stanford Mr.Smithfield?"

"I saw her in church earlier but other than that I've not at any time been introduced or had occasion to as much as pass the time of day I'm afraid."

Rex felt in his jacket pocket to check for his house key. "Florence Stanford, Basil's long suffering wife is a fine woman, a good woman, as innocent as was Doris."

Andrew nodded. "Of course, I understand."

"I am free, liberated," said Rex, he opened the car door and thanked Andrew. Stepping out on to the pavement he lowered his face and before closing the door said, "Tell me Mr.Smithfield, if you will, if you can, after all these years and now at my time of life, what am I supposed to do with all this freedom?" Not waiting for a reply he knew Andrew would find difficult to give, Rex walked to his front door, turned to look back, pointed to the window, to the globe beyond. He called out. "In here my world stands still."

Andrew sat for a minute or more, he felt an affinity with Rex Madden. One period of weakness, many years ago had dominated his life and now, despite the freedom granted by the passage of time, Andrew Smithfield's world stood still.

Sergeant Beasley read again the letter from the hospital, what those doctors could find out from a drop o' blood an' spittle beggared belief, but here it was in black and white, Horace Clegg, while displaying no symptoms of tuberculosis nevertheless carried the disease. That was the all-crucial word, 'carrier', able to infect others whilst himself remaining free of the cough, to all appearances not affected by the gradual consumption of the lungs, which so often in others led to a merciless lingering death. Like that of Jack Sulley, in Clegg's own words, the best friend he ever had! Beasley took the letter from his desk and was about to put it in the drawer, but its content explained much and was, after all relevant to a man in his charge. Criminal or otherwise, Clegg was entitled to read it.

Beasley unlocked the cell door, Clegg sat on his bunk, a pathetic figure as the sergeant now considered him. 'You're a bully Beasley, you're nowt but a bully'. Jack Sulley's words came back to him like a sudden haunting, they'd held no potency when Jack defied him with that response, refusing to give him a name, protecting to the very last this scrap of humankind. Now Jack's words were powerful and it was a subdued sergeant Beasley who took the letter from his pocket and handed it to Horace Clegg. He watched Clegg's eyes follow the lines of type, slowly and in silence. Eventually he looked up at Beasley.

"Can yer understand what it says?" Beasley felt compelled to ask, the expression on Clegg's face, pain, such crushing pain, how would he ever erase from his memory the look on Clegg's face.

"It says that I killed Jack, it wer' me as done for 'im." Clegg's voice trembled, his slight shoulders shook as he slumped forward and tears fell over the letter in a tide of despair.

Beasley took the paper from Clegg's hand, all the self important gloating that he'd planned to inflict on this one time source of torment now lost its appeal. Instead sergeant Beasley did his duty, as an officer of the law and as a human being.

"You will serve your time in solitary confinement Horace Clegg, where a man must do little else but think. I can do nothing to keep you from your own mind, but I can at least tell you that in solitary no one will bother you, no bully may enter there."

Annie would be relieved when Charles came back from wherever his afternoon activity had taken him. A headache had persisted over the last two or three hours and she longed for a few minutes of quietness. The doorbell with each customer activated hammers behind her brow, beating remorselessly as though they were determined to pound their way through her very flesh and bone. So many things troubled her mind, the situation with Hilda and her dad, the letter from Francis revealing the happy news of another baby but also bringing disappointment, they would not be coming to Nottingham for Christmas. This year it was Freddy's turn to work the holiday, the farm at Huttoft demanded labour even on Christmas day, it was understandable of course but it felt like yet again Annie's home was to be denied laughter, some happiness if only for John's sake. Most disturbing of all was Alice's state of health. After calling on Alice and George, with an apple pie, Annie had taken him aside and told him he should ask the doctor to visit, to examine Alice. Her continuing tiredness and lethargy was extreme even in her condition, she was after all a young woman at the ideal age for bearing a child. Dr. Casley had called at Ainsley Road and before leaving, had taken a small sample of Alice's blood, telling her she should not be alarmed, many mothers to be developed a degree of anaemia. His words were thoughtful but they did nothing to ease the tension Annie had felt since, they must await the results of the blood tests. With all these things distracting her, the shop drained away even more of her usual resolve and when at around half past two, the doorbell clanged and she'd looked up to see Anthony Hemsley, Annie had felt less than accommodating, she was too anxious, too preoccupied for an interval of pleasantries.

'I would offer you tea Anthony but Charles is not here at the moment so there is no one else to man the shop'. 'My dear Annie, I have no need of tea but finding myself again in Nottingham I couldn't pass up the chance of seeing you, I purposefully didn't write in advance, I knew you would feel obliged to make some preparation for my visit, for Charles to tolerate my chatter when I felt sure he would prefer not to be hindered'.

Annie had sensed Anthony to be almost pleased at Charles' absence, at first she put it down to her own feeling of relief when Charles disappeared for a while, imagining it somehow coloured her perception of Anthony's reaction at being told that Charles was out. It was that 'top up time' referred to by Emily Pagett and for a good ten minutes or more no customers came. They conversed but on this occasion it seemed strangely more difficult. Anthony's constant scrutiny of her face filled her with unease. Then footsteps approaching the shop drove him to kiss her cheek and place his hand over hers, holding it there until the customer entered, only then easing it away, so slowly. 'Thank you Mrs.Eddowes', he'd said and turned to the elderly Mr.Freeman, tipped his hat with a cordial 'good afternoon', and left.

What had been a mild discomfort somewhere at the back of her brow, from that moment progressed swiftly to a full-blown headache. Mabel Rashleigh's pearl of wisdom danced along the rows of hammers as they pounded. 'Yer can usually tell when they're after summat'. Annie earnestly hoped that Anthony Hemsley would not come again.

Finally Charles returned, he came through to the shop. "I've put the kettle on and I've brought you something, it's on the table." He spoke without at any point looking into her face, the very opposite of Anthony's unsettling attention.

A package sat on the kitchen table. First warming the pot and putting some tea to brew, Annie then unfolded the end of the pastel striped bag and with curiously timid fingers, slid out a woman's blouse. Making sure there was nothing on the table top that could mark the cloth she laid it out. Paisley patterned Vyella, so soft to the touch, delicate pale blue buttons up to the small, rounded collar, almost certainly a product of the factory at Brassington. She lowered herself onto the chair by the range and closed her eyes, for just a few moments, Annie needed peace.

CHAPTER TWENTY-ONE

Late January 1932

They'd agreed to meet at the bus stop on Sherwood Road, Kathleen with Beth, Rosie with the twins and Celia with Mathew. Susie and Joe with Liza and her fiancé Harry had been to an evening performance in the week.

Billy and Edna were happy to see Liza engaged to Harry Ollerton. He was a hard working young man, well thought of at Clark & Brown's. When Edna one day had gazed at the worn, sunken seat of Billy's chair, already granted an extension of life through the two flock cushions, wrapped around in an old cot blanket and shoved down into the hollow, Liza had declared, 'Harry can fix that'. Indeed Harry did fix it, with a tin of tacks, some horse hair and a remnant of heavy curtain material he gave the ailing chair a new lease of life. The only down side, as Billy saw it was that prior to this grand refurbishment he'd been permitted to sink his weary bones into the 'pit of antiquity' as he liked to refer to his chair, without first having to divest himself of the trousers set aside for allotment days. Now before he could take his ease he must first render himself spotless. 'It's as bad as poor old Bert Eathorne, his missus never let him anywhere near their front room', observed Billy, 'she reckoned he'd make it smell o' the knacker yard where he worked. But when the poor sod died, all of a sudden over a binful o' bones, she told the undertaker she wanted Bert laid out in their front room until day o' funeral, after he'd been scrubbed wi' carbolic and she'd smelled every inch of him afore they dressed him in his chapel suit an' put him in his box. It must have been the most intimate moment Bert an' his missus ever had, but he made it to the front room an' for the best part of a week an'all'.

Celia and Kathleen had been at the stop for several minutes before Rosie came into view. Thomas and Samuel being held by the hand and approaching at an urgent pace. The pantomime started at 2o/clock, it was the Saturday matinee and the main attraction for the enthusiastic group was Kathleen's Ernie, playing one of the ugly sisters. Joe had declared Ernie's performance to be, 'bloody marvellous, he should tread the boards for a livin' '. Kathleen wondered if Beth would recognise her dad but apparently his costume transformed him and in Susie's words, Ernie looked like a mongrel of Elizabeth the first and an Irish navvy! All the children were in a state of excitement, so much so that Thomas had wet himself just as Rosie had been about to leave home.

"He's not had wet pants for more than twelve months," said Rosie, between gasps of breathlessness, " and right through his best trousers an'all."

Thomas looked suitably sheepish as his 'accident' was related to aunty Kathleen and Celia, not to mention Beth and Mathew who seemed to be staring at his nether regions for any remaining evidence.

The bus was in sight, the women gathered the children together with the caution. "The nice man is before us in the queue, don't push."

A middle-aged man carrying what appeared to be a new gardening implement of some sort had been waiting quietly, only the long wooden handle was visible, the other end had been carefully wrapped around in strips of brown paper, then tied fast with a length of string. Rosie had looked at it and thought at once of grandad's gout. When she'd been taken by her mam to visit him, the heavily bandaged foot, rested on grandma's hatbox, had kept her rigid with fear. 'Don't you go near an' knock it our Rosie or grandad'll 'ave yer locked in the coal shed'. The thought of being incarcerated in that musty smelling, pitch black place, with the spiders and uncle Ronnie's gin traps that hung behind the door along with a fox pelt, a trophy from one of his poaching expeditions, filled the young Rosie with dread. The memory now fresh in her mind, she held on to Thomas and Samuel until the man with the bandaged implement was too far ahead of them for either of her young sons to 'knock it'.

"Hello," said the conductor who had been told to watch out for them by Joyce, "pantomime is it? Well don't you forget to shout at the dame, 'it's behind you', and when he," the conductor quickly corrected himself, "when she says, 'oh no it isn't', you have to shout as loud as you can, 'oh yes it is'. The children were overcome by a bout of shyness and stood mute. The friendly conductor laughed and rang his bell, sending the bus on its way to the city centre.

For a number of years the amateur dramatic society had staged a 'panto', in its early days they had performed in the church hall but so popular had the event become that for the past few years they had been permitted to occupy the Theatre Royal for three nights, with a Saturday matinee. Ernie Searle had often helped with scenery and props, when the previous year the dame had broken his ankle falling from a ladder just two days before the opening night, Ernie had been persuaded to save the situation. Not only could he remember much of the part from being present at rehearsals but he could ad lib so successfully he'd performed to rapturous applause. His workmates at Player's had learned of Ernie's fetching performance as Dick Whittington's landlady and flocked to the theatre pushing up revenue from ticket sales to such a degree the management of the Theatre Royal, on a percentage, practically insisted on Ernie again playing the dame.

Celia had a bag of Tom Thumb drops in her pocket to dispense during the show, Mathew's favourite. Whenever they went to Gregory Street his grandma would produce a cone shaped bag of these little sweets, knowing of the planned trip to the pantomime Annie had given Celia sufficient for all of the children and a quarter of chocolate éclairs for the mothers.

Sometimes Celia hardly knew what to say to her mother in law, so many troubles seemed to surround Annie. Alice's health had become even more distressing. The blood tests had shown a condition the doctor called Leukaemia. It was almost certainly present in Alice before she was pregnant but the development of the baby had advanced this serious disorder of Alice's blood. The week before Christmas, Hilda had gone to stay with George and Alice so she could help, preparing George's dinner box before going to the library, making a meal each evening and generally busying herself with the household chores, but by mid January it became apparent that Alice needed to be where someone could check on her at regular intervals throughout the day. Annie was fearful for the baby and desperate to help relieve George's mind, how he was managing to concentrate at his work she couldn't imagine. After talking together, as Annie and Alice did openly and sensibly, they agreed it would be best all round if the young couple came to stay at Gregory Street, it would make life less fraught. Hilda would return to grandma Sarah's, John would move into Hilda's old room and George with Alice could occupy the larger bedroom where there was plenty of space for a crib.

Annie had discussed the arrangement with Charles before saying anything to the rest of the family, she'd expected a less than helpful response, he'd been very quiet of late. Charles had surprised her, perhaps after all, his quietness was partly due to concern for Alice. His expression bore genuine regret when he'd said, 'George must be beside himself with worry, to know that Alice is here with you while he's at work will help him more than anything. I can do more in the shop until the baby comes'.

So George and Alice had travelled from Ainsley Road in a taxi, along with some clothes and personal bits and pieces, plus the all important 'baby bag' and Moses basket. George had turned the key in the door of their little house until his wife's health improved.

Dr.Casley had been gentle in his explanation of the illness, radiation treatment had been tried some years earlier but in many cases it proved more damaging than beneficial. Until the baby was born and Alice had recovered from the strain of labour, he could not sensibly decide the best way forward. Meanwhile bed rest and nutritious meals, taken regularly could do nothing but help the situation.

The routine at Gregory Street had changed quite naturally without discourse. Annie kept a fire burning steadily in the bedroom, Hilda had chosen some good reading from the library, to help Alice pass the time and the young woman obliged Annie in eating her meals, so vital if the baby was to thrive to a healthy weight when he or she entered the world. Charles had been true to his word, rising earlier to help with the newspapers and spending less time away from the shop. John still prickled from his dad's treatment of his sister, he viewed Charles' sudden, amenable approach to be the measure of satisfaction Charles gained from believing the present arrangement mitigated his decision over Hilda. No room would have been available if she lived still at Gregory Street. It seemed to escape Charles' reasoning that had the problem of accommodation arisen, then John would simply have gone to stay with grandma Sarah, enabling Hilda to be present, especially in the evenings, to help Annie. Annie was just grateful, and sympathetic of Charles' own anxieties in a way she could not expect John to be. Alice's poor health frightened Charles, ever more so as the date for the baby drew closer. How could he remove from his memory the loss of Enid. Circumstances here were entirely different but Annie could understand Charles' dread, she recognised it in his eyes.

Celia had done her best to be helpful, baking a cake, some buns, boiling a piece of ham. She'd felt almost guilty at going to the pantomime where there would be merriment. Annie had hugged Celia, cast her eyes to Mathew and said, 'take him to a happy place, I shall look forward to a full account of Cinderella, indeed we all will'

Only two more stops and they would be getting off the bus. Town was busy, Saturday afternoons found a number of barrow boys on the streets and 'stretched' households took advantage of the bargains in slightly damaged or over-ripe fruit and vegetables. By the later part of the afternoon the bread shop reduced any items that would be unfit by Monday, the very fortunate might even secure a cake, on the dry side but visually appealing to children who would rarely see anything sweet beyond a crust spread with jam.

The women made sure all coats were fastened on the children and no hankies had been left on seats. It was uncle Joe's fault, he'd shown Beth how to make a rabbit from a handkerchief, the rolling, folding and tying of knots certainly resulted in a creature with long ears but no self respecting bunny would have given it the time of day. Nevertheless it had inspired Beth to show the others and seldom had a hanky been used for any other purpose since. Even Mathew's little fingers did their best to follow Beth's instructions. "Now when I see you again I shall want to know all about it," said the conductor as he helped the little ones down from the footplate to join their mams on the pavement.

Kathleen couldn't resist a bit of fun, "It's behind you," she sang out the words roguishly. The conductor hadn't noticed the man with the bandaged implement standing at his rear, waiting to alight. Celia and Rosie chuckled but the sober gent didn't crack his face to smile as the conductor stood aside to let him by. When the man had gone enough yards to be out of earshot the friendly conductor leaned out of the bus and whispered.

"That's Lucifer you know, he's been shopping for a new fork to stir his fires."

"Shame on you," said Celia, pretending to be shocked, "putting such devilish notions into these innocent heads. She looked over at the children.

He rang the bell. "Don't forget, 'Oh yes it is', as loud as you can shout it."

They waved as the bus pulled away, the friendly banter had put them in a happy frame of mind and they made their way to the theatre with a spring in their step. Inside the foyer the children were agog. The colourful posters about the walls, the deep red carpet at their feet, showing signs of wear but still proclaiming elegance. An exotic fern in an enormous, decorative pot, although as yet unnoticed by theatre staff, a rolled up programme with a nob of chewing gum in the top had been pushed down into the soil at the fern's base. At the ticket office a young woman with a heavy application of make up, leaned forward and peered over the ledge in front of her, as if checking that the number of children tallied with the number of lower priced tickets Celia had requested. Apparently satisfied that all was in order she passed the tickets to Celia with the question.

"How many programmes?"

"Just the one please," Celia cast a glance at Rosie who was clearly bursting to say something. Finally they were ready to move along and Rosie contained her desire to challenge the manner of the young woman ticket seller. An usher stood at the entrance to the auditorium, a man, vaguely familiar but the light was shadowy and Celia couldn't identify him. He took the tickets from her and read the numbers. "Row nine, seats eleven to seventeen," he led them to the end of their row, smiled and returned to his station where the next group of people awaited his assistance. Already there were very many seats occupied, a lot of children, as would be expected at the matinee. The low drone of mothers and grandmas trying to cap the ever rising level of excitement, was matched and at times overtaken by youngsters too wound up to be stilled. Everything was spellbinding, the huge curtains concealing the stage not like any curtains these children had at home, these drapes were as tall as a house and woven in gold at the hem. The wall lights shone upwards from giant scallop shells, these too were gilded. It was like a picture from a storybook, even the smells were nothing like home. No smokiness from damp slack that promised heat but took an age to deliver it. No lingering evidence of liver and cabbage having been cooked for tea. A marked absence of that curious smell, neither pleasant nor unpleasant, which rose from damp flannelette underwear, airing in front of the hearth and perhaps most noticeable of all, no odour of embrocation, ever prevalent in the homes of miners from the devoted efforts of wives and mothers as they strived to relieve the relentless ache in muscles so strained, that even a loving caress could prove almost too painful to bear. Here the upholstered seats, over the course of years, had acted like blotting paper, absorbing the residues from people's efforts to look and smell good. A subtle hint of ladies' perfume, of gentlemen's cologne, the faint but detectable spiciness of pomander that hung in wardrobes beside best suits and dresses.

Movement at the front of the auditorium proved to be a group of musicians taking up their position, adding to the anticipation the lights were suddenly lowered. Every child's gaze now fixed on the grand curtains, the percussionist struck his cymbal and through the middle of the curtains appeared a player, all eyes were riveted on the figure of a young man, dressed in uniform, smiling over the audience in an expression of warmest welcome.

"My name is Buttons," he announced in a confident, most cheerful voice, "and I am about to tell you a story, but this story is not read from a book, this story is real. There are no pages, but people, colourful, dancing, singing people. It is the story of my friend, the lovely Cinderella, I call her Cinders. Soon she will be your friend too and you will love her, like I do."

A big 'aah' came from somewhere behind him. "So sit back, open wide your eyes and minds, for now the story shall begin."

Buttons waved his hand with a flourish and disappeared into the wings, the musicians struck up a lively tune and the curtain went back to reveal a brightly lit stage filled with feasting for the eyes. The scenery depicted the scullery where poor Cinderella toiled day after day. As the characters entered, the delight of the audience reached such a height the atmosphere was magical, such pace and energy filled every moment, but it was the first appearance of Griselda, the elder of the two ugly sisters that brought to all those present, young and old alike, a display of pure genius. Kathleen laughed until tears streamed down her face, a combined response to the irresistible fun and overwhelming emotion at the knowledge that it was Ernie, her very own Ernie who transformed not just himself but for a couple of hours changed all those mundane, routined, un-lustrous lives into brilliance. Beth could have no way of knowing that Griselda, in her striped red and yellow frock, bright orange stockings and purple shoes, boasting a glorious bosom, so bountiful it could give sanctuary to legions, hair of corn coloured ringlets framing a face with rosy red cheeks, scarlet lips like cupid's bow and jet black eye lashes that curled like ocean waves, was none other than her dad, who came home each day from Player's looking just like all the other men who poured through the factory gates at 5o/clock. Beth had not the slightest suspicion when Griselda leapt from the stage to run up and down the sides of the auditorium, throwing toffees to the children, the hoops of her skirts rising and falling like voluminous bellows as she bounded up the stairs, that at bedtime, this very same person would give her a goodnight kiss and whisper, 'be a good girl for your dad'.

They had been captivated, singing along with the cast, shouting, just as the bus conductor predicted, laughing and clapping 'til even those of senior years who had attended pantomimes in the past were completely caught up in the exhilaration. Standing to sing the National Anthem, a sense of that enduring British spirit made every back just that bit more upright and folk began to walk to the exits with wide smiles of pleasure. As they streamed out of the foyer and back onto the street it felt as though they'd briefly glimpsed another world.

"Now catch hold hands while we walk to the stop," said Rosie, anxious that the children's state of wonder might distract them. "I wish that Tommy could see the panto but he says he must be on call. Joe would be alright I'm sure but you know Tommy, always the responsible one."

Celia held on tight to Mathew while the pavement was so busy with people. The exodus of theatregoers, now seeking their bus stop, headed off in all directions. Kathleen sailed along on a wave of pride and rightly so, Ernie Searle, the irrepressible Griselda, was a storming success. The last few Tom Thumb drops were dispensed on the bus and alighting at Sherwood Road, Celia and Rosie said goodbye to Kathleen and Beth who walked through the arboretum to reach home, while they could keep one another company for some of the way.

"How's William?" Asked Rosie.

Celia sighed, "In all honesty, I don't know. He seems strangely quiet, not a sullen quietness, more a 'deep in thought' sort of quiet. All the worry at Gregory Street must affect him. It affects the whole family but I sense there's something else. I've learned it's best not to press William, whatever it is he'll declare it when he's ready."

"I bumped into Mr.Pearson the other day, he looked anxious, surely after the baby's come the doctor will give Alice something to make her better." Rosie's simple belief was too comforting to question but inwardly Celia was less confident. Although Annie had conveyed to her nothing more than the doctor's kindly words, the serious nature of the illness was never far from Annie's mind Celia could tell. George seemed to be in denial but even that Celia suspected was for his mam's sake, he was protective of his mother. George had been taught to show respect to his elders, Charles was his elder, but not his natural father, out of loyalty to Annie he showed respect to Charles but Celia sensed there was little love.

"Say goodbye to aunty Celia and Mathew." Rosie prompted the twins who obliged with vigorous waving and unified cries of 'ta-ta'.

It had been a joyful afternoon and Celia was determined not to allow more melancholy thoughts to invade what was left of it. When they reached home she would make something nice for their tea and listen while their son told his dad all about the pantomime.

William waited until everyone had left the factory, Celia was taking Mathew to the pantomime so there'd be no one at home wondering why he was late. Andrew Smithfield was putting away the ledgers in the filing cabinet when a 'tap' came at his office door.

"Yes William, what is it?"

"I need to talk to you for a moment." William turned his head as though making doubly sure no stray worker remained to overhear. His manner was awkward, causing Andrew to speculate that William might be about to ask for a rise in pay. He had after all taken on extra responsibility for a month while Robert Armistead had a hernia repaired and William had never been one to give generously of his time. "Regrettably Mr.Smithfield I must give you a week's notice of my intention to leave your employ," said William, rather too formally. Andrew said nothing at this point but awaited further explanation. "I shall be thirty later this year and I feel that my life is not going in the direction I would choose," he hesitated, "a man must take charge of his destiny if he's not to leave it too late for change." William spoke the last few words with some air of authority and it obviously satisfied him, a smile had begun to creep from the corners of his mouth but Andrew's continued silence unsettled him and now with a hint of nervousness he asked in a less confident tone. "That will be alright then will it?"

"A week's notice is all that you are required to give under the terms of your employment. You are entitled to pursue whichever course your mind dictates William but if the circumstances are regrettable then I feel some concern."

Why wasn't Smithfield asking him more, surely he must be curious to know where William would be working after leaving Brassington? William was perplexed and Smithfield's apparent indifference riled him. Well sobeit, he'd told the man. William was almost through the door when the sound of the filing cabinet drawer going home and that 'clump' of closure prompted him to turn back and announce the nature of his future employment, let Smithfield stew on it all weekend.

"I'm going to work for Basil Stanford. He's been waiting for Rex Madden to decide whether or not he wished to return to work following his wife's death. It now seems Madden has chosen to retire from his job as Mr.Stanford's driver and so he's asked me if I would be interested, along with some additional duties as was often the case with Rex Madden as I understand it. I've given it a good deal of thought and arrived at the conclusion that the time is right for me to pursue change and working for Mr.Stanford, being a part of colliery activity will correspond more with my interests and aims in the long term."

Andrew felt sickened. What a devious, unsavoury man Basil Stanford was, but William had clearly set his mind on serving the purposes of Stanford, no doubt believing his loyalties would propel him forward to greater things. The way William had delivered the information, almost proudly, convinced Andrew that his young foreman was not about to reconsider.

Since that day outside the bank, when Andrew had spoken with Freddy Eddowes, William had pulled at Andrew's emotions, a constant reminder of his involvement, however innocent, in the miserable situation that overtook the sincere, hard working Freddy. Yet William's presence at Brassington kept a slender thread of association between Andrew and Annie. But now came a new torment to his conscience.

"I would say to you William, be very cautious, all that glistens is not necessarily gold. Beyond that I wish you only well."

Andrew heard the heavy outside door close with its usual thud, the original door of the munitions factory still greeted them all when they arrived for work, Andrew had resisted replacing it with a less formidable looking entrance, the war, the terrible suffering, the humbling bravery should not be so easily removed from man's vision or from his sense of gratitude. To stand and pay tribute at the war memorial was only correct but Henry Wicks had been right when he said, 'it's not enough, it's nowhere near enough'.

The sound of the van starting up, of William driving across the yard and then silence, sent Andrew to his chair where he leaned back and sighed. Should he tell Annie what he knew of Stanford's character, inform Charles Eddowes of the ways in which Basil Stanford used people for his own ends? William had chosen to leave Andrew's employment after eleven years, they would likely consider any comment made by himself to be nothing but sour grapes on his part. What happened at Bobbers Mill would deny both Annie and Charles any confidence in his judgement and if William were made aware of Andrew's approach then he would certainly take umbrage. What could Basil Stanford possible have on William anyway, since he was eighteen William had worked at Brassington, Andrew had known him from youth. Stanford obviously conversed with William when they met at their Lodge, so many times Andrew had heard William mention Basil's name but imagined it to be simply William's unfortunate tendency to imply his importance among the 'names' of industry. Perhaps Stanford genuinely liked the young man, saw something of himself in the ambitious William Eddowes. Andrew pondered the whys and wherefores everything seemed to be changing. Henry Wicks was seeking a buyer for his house with the intention of investing in the planned operations at Mapperley.

These days Andrew would sit at council meetings staring at the members, trying to decide which of them were beyond reproach and which sat within that chamber for the purpose of self-perpetuation only. If Henry Wicks had not pointed out, that from outside a closed door not even the most diligent and honourable man could influence the business being conducted within, Andrew would have resigned from the council immediately after Rex Maddens revelations. He locked the drawer of his desk, checked that all was shut down on the factory floor, took his coat from the hook and sought home. The weekend, that long period of thinking time, the prospect held no encouragement and Andrew's tread across the yard to his car was laboured and slow.

"We're home." Celia called out as she and Mathew took off their coats. "Go tell daddy about Cinderella." The child ran to the living room where William sat by the fire. He scrambled onto his dad's knee and began his account of the afternoon's events.

"It sounds as though you had a good time," said William as Celia stood before the fire warming her hands.

"It was wonderful I wish you had finished early enough to come with us. Perhaps you and Tommy could go tonight, he's reluctant because of being on call, should there be a death, but as Rosie said, Joe would be able to see to things. She's tried to persuade Tommy, he must relax sometimes, he might go if you ask him."

William stared at Celia as if she'd spoken words of utter madness. "You expect me to ask Tommy Spooner if he'd like to join me in attending a performance of Cinderella?"

"Now you're just being silly, I didn't suggest you ask him like it were a date. If you were to put it to Tommy that it's the last showing tonight and everyone else has enjoyed it, including most of Player's workforce, he might agree to go, it would do him good to have some simple fun, it wouldn't do you any harm either. Ernie Searle is marvellous as the ugly sister Griselda, you'd both benefit from a good laugh, God knows William, life is serious enough."

"Well Tommy can please himself but I can do without Ernie Searle prancing about in his mam's frock playing silly buggers. Besides, after tea I want to tell you something."

William took Mathew's feet in his hands and lifted the child's legs as he leaned back on his dad's chest. "Good strong pins haven't you son? It's about time we thought of a brother or sister for him."

Celia had been about to leave the room but stopped in the doorway. "At least on that we agree William, in complete accord." She smiled, "I shall make some chips to go with cousin Robert's finest sausages, then after I've settled Mathew, you can tell me your news, whatever it may be." Celia crossed to the kitchen humming one of the tunes the musicians had played at the theatre and feeling particularly happy.

Mathew was fast asleep in his bed, Celia had cleared away the dishes and now sat by her husband in anticipation of some good news, something significant at the factory, further responsibility, a small increase in his wage, or perhaps it was not so good news, a need for him to travel greater distances to gain more orders, she was always anxious when Mr.Smithfield required William to be away overnight and although she tried not to show it, even the insensitive William might recognise her dismay each time she packed his 'away' bag.

He leaned forward in his chair and cast his gaze about the room, as if trying to spot a fly that had left its place of winter hibernation to occupy, long before time, William's own space. Without reason he suddenly declared. "I've never liked this house." Celia looked at him in bewilderment but before she could respond, William began his statement his 'not to be questioned' decision on the future. "I've given Smithfield notice, I shall finish there at the end of next week. I'm going to work for Basil Stanford, he needs someone he can rely on, a good driver to replace Rex Madden."

But Celia did question, she'd listened in disbelief. "Why William, why ever would you leave the good job you hold at Brassington, working for the decent Mr.Smithfield, to become of all things 'Stanford's man'. That's how people refer to Mr.Madden you know, Stanford's man, like he was merely a chattel, nothing more than a lackey."

William stood. "You don't know what you are talking about, you listen to the foolish, weak minded prattle of people with no aim in life and accept their opinions without as much as challenging them. Basil needs someone he can trust, a right hand man, that's how Madden would have originally earned his title, but years of familiarity, and I daresay domestic problems, by all accounts his wife was one of those nervy, depressed women, diverted Rex Madden's mind from his position. I was going nowhere with Smithfield, the man has been like a ship without a sail since the old aunt snuffed it. I'm thirty this year, I need to make my mark, and with Stanford I can. His is an industry with thrust, you don't suppose I intend being his driver forever and a day. Basil told me himself that Stafford Hinds is an 'interim', though I don't think Hinds knows that, the man is in his sixties for goodness sake, no younger than Wicks. There's opportunity to be had and I don't plan on missing it."

Celia couldn't share William's vision. When visiting Edmund and Caroline, she'd many times noticed her sister in law's less than fond regard for her father Basil, she bristled at the mention of his name. It was not Celia's imagination, Edmund had questioned Caroline's reactions but always she avoided answering with any real explanation, little asides, words with traces of sarcasm but never giving actual reason for her attitude toward him. William was entering the unknown in more ways than one.

"You know nothing about mining, you talk as though it's so simple, like you could sell Vyella one week and anthracite the next. I don't know what to think anymore William, you defy all logic."

"Management is about making a profit, whatever the product. Mining is about creating a bloody great hole in the ground and sending men down into it to dig the coal out, then management turn it into money."

Celia was defensive. "Sending men down into it, sending, you sound like a gang master William, will Stanford supply the whip or must you purchase that yourself?" After the happy afternoon Celia had shared with Rose and Kathleen, she felt despairing of William's unfailing ability to destroy any sense of well-being. "Becoming Stanford's man is nothing but a backward step I tell you." She spoke forcefully to William.

"Oh no it isn't," he replied, equally determined.

At that moment Celia's longing to hold on to a happy memory drove her to respond in raucous, pantomime fashion, "Oh yes it is!"

They'd wrapped a length of stiff wire with green raffia and made the bloom from some red flannel begged off Florrie Haynes, dear Florrie was convinced that a pad of red flannel worn over the kidneys in cold weather, did more than any fortifying tonic to keep a mortal free of winter ailments. The 'romantic' red rose now stood in a milk bottle and propped up beside it, a piece of card with the words. 'Will you marry me Griselda'. It awaited Ernie Searle's arrival at his workstation.

No man could expect to create such a wealth of laughter for his workmates and not receive some gesture of their appreciation! Ernie however, walked through the factory gates this Monday morning, oblivious to the mischief planned for him. It seemed to be the desire of Player's workforce, on this day in particular, to be at their post before the modest and unsuspecting Ernie made his way to their source of fun.

"Yer daft buggers, wait 'til I tell my Kathleen." The place erupted to laughter and great applause. Ernie puckered up his lips and blew a kiss.

One bright spark called out. "What 'appened to yer tits?" another shouted. " 'E's been playin' wi' 'em all weekend, they've wore away."

Raymond Haynes watched the proceedings smiling. They were a good bunch of men, one or two of the younger ones would feel their feet every so often but he considered himself fortunate, guided by the knowledge Reg Yeats had passed on to him, most days found a contented and productive atmosphere under his management. 'Never forget to greet 'em with a good mornin' an' send 'em home wi' a goodnight, at least listen to their excuse afore yer wallop 'em an' let 'em laugh as much as they want, do that an' they'll love yer like their mam'. Reg's philosophy when dealing with the working man.

The day passed cheerfully, the mood had been buoyant. Just before clocking off time Raymond walked from the office to where Ernie was about to finish. He carried what could only be a bottle, wrapped in brown paper.

"Thanks Ernie, from all of us, yer did Player's proud. If we could only bottle the spirit of Griselda it'd be the finest pick me up ever created." Raymond handed the half bottle of whisky to Ernie and everyone cheered.

Then Ernie spoke. "Yer know lads, I learned a lot, up there on that stage, lookin' out on all them folk waitin' to be carried away by a fairy tale." He paused, the men fell silent, Ernie's demeanour had taken on a serious side. "Sometimes if a man is lucky, 'e discovers summat that changes his life in a way he could never 'ave dreamed. I can tell yer, it's a revelation to me," again he paused and sighed, creating a sense of something profound. "Puttin' on a pair o' soft satin bloomers over 'is three piece suite is summat every man should do at Christmas, there can be no better way o' wrappin' nuts!"

When the banter was finally over and Raymond had said 'goodnight' to them all, he sat at his desk letting the peace settle about him. He'd bumped into Reg Yeats the previous day, they'd sat for a while on the wall outside The Institute. Raymond had often observed it as curious, that while women ever exchanged conversation and chatted away quite happily standing up, men invariably chose a wall on which to sit when talking together. He couldn't recall at any time, seeing the female of the species lower their frame onto The Institute wall, despite its ideal height. Reg was not well, prostate trouble. 'Can't bloody pee lad'. Raymond could hear the weariness in Reg's voice, he'd sensed the anxiety behind his words.

Time to go home, Raymond did truly wish there was such a preparation as 'Griselda tonic', to be taken once a day, twice if the situation demanded a stronger dose, not just for Reg to find a measure of strength but for his mam too, whenever Raymond called these days, Florrie looked so old and tired. Ernie's rose now stood on a window ledge where it would doubtless remain until the red flannel was faded and lay under a film of dust. Satin wrapped nuts indeed! Raymond chuckled as he turned his key in the lock on the factory gates, for a Monday it had been alright.

CHAPTER TWENTY-TWO

"How is your daughter in law Annie, and of course I must ask about the baby, he's three weeks old now surely." Florence Stanford had come to the shop with a list of items to be collected by William on Monday. Since Rex had left and William had replaced him Florence had agonised over whether or not to confide in Annie her concern for the young man. Basil had been adamant, the arrangement of a few groceries, purchased each week at Eddowes' shop should continue as before. Florence would have happily made all her purchases at Annie's, she'd come to think of that shop as a place of friendship, but always Basil had some ulterior motive, a design to suit himself and that knowledge denied Florence peace of mind. She had however said to Annie that William must not feel any obligation to his new employer. If in the event the post proved not to be what he'd imagined, then he should make no delay in seeking something more suitable elsewhere. When Annie had returned an anxious look Florence had quickly added that William had impressed Mr.Stanford over a period of many months, she had no doubt over his ability to meet the demands made of him but her husband was a business man, as he ever reminded her, not prone to sentimentality and for a young man such as William, Basil's rigid approach might render some days too uncomfortable, too bare of any light heartedness to consider a working life in that vein.

Annie had herself been dismayed by William's decision to leave the factory at Brassington. It had afforded him security and advancement, enabled him to start a family without all the pressures endured by so many his age.

Annie, despite all the disappointments of Bobbers Mill, had never really doubted the integrity of Andrew Smithfield. He'd not known of Freddy's involvement, in fact when Edna had revealed just how troubled and despondent he'd been on learning of it, Annie had actually felt a degree of sympathy for the man. William could have prospered under Mr.Smithfield, Basil Stanford was much less sincere, a character all together different Annie felt sure. Florence had always appeared timid, even when removed from her husband's domineering presence his shadow cast far enough to keep her within its bounds. Rex Madden too came across as a man firmly under Stanford's thumb. Yet William literally celebrated Stanford. It was Edna's remark that perhaps came closest to the truth. 'Like attracts like'. It saddened Annie to hear it and even more to recognise the accuracy it conveyed.

"Hilda is with Alice and the baby, they're all in the kitchen, why don't you go through to them, I'll go with you before the next customer comes," said Annie.

"Oh I would love to, if you think Alice won't mind," said Florence eagerly.

Annie laughed, "Alice is looking forward to going home. George has arranged for them to go back to Ainsley Road tomorrow. I worry that she might get too tired but I can understand why that little home of theirs attracts her so, their infant son, all the joy he brings, here they must share the emotion with the extended family when it should be reserved for man and wife, concentrated between the two of them, not diluted by well meaning but un-entitled brothers, sister, mam, dad, in laws and outlaws! It can't feel quite right here can it?

Dr.Casley has consulted with a specialist at the hospital, there is no known cure for Leukaemia, they briefly considered radiation but past use of such treatment proved more damaging to the patients' health than it was beneficial. They will monitor her condition and in the meantime Alice must take good nourishment and sensible periods of rest. I do know with all certainty that she will be delighted to show you her Samuel and with equal certainty I can predict that you will melt at the sight of his face. It's that sensation we mothers experience, beyond accurate description, the utter devotion to any infant regardless of kin."

Florence squeezed Annie's arm, "My dear I shall pray very hard."

Samuel Boucher was taking a feed, from a bottle, Alice's poor health had prevented her from breast-feeding beyond the first few days. The young mother greeted them with a broad smile and Hilda paused in her folding of laundry to offer

Mrs.Stanford some tea. Before the tear in the corner of Florence's eye had even been dabbed with her hanky, the shop doorbell clanged, causing Annie to sigh.

"Enjoy a little baby time Florence, our new grandson is to be recommended for lifting any low spirits, all we have to do is look on his face." Annie ran through to the shop, Saturday afternoon often produced a steady flow. John had gone with George to Ainsley Road, to light a fire, the house had been empty all these weeks of winter weather, it needed to be aired. They'd taken some food for the larder, the rest would go tomorrow, George had booked a taxi.

Although Hilda had not yet said anything to her sister in law, she'd told Annie that if the days ahead proved too arduous for Alice then she would explain the situation gently to grandma Sarah and go to stay at Ainsley Road, to offer help, as she'd done before.

Annie had called at Dr.Casley's surgery, to tell him of Alice's wish to return home, to seek his advice. He'd expressed his concern, but also encouraged Annie, 'contentment itself is a remarkable therapy', he'd said, 'I've witnessed its success many times. Leukaemia as yet defies our knowledge, there have been occasions when the body has defied our understanding. Alice is surrounded by love, a young woman with all that mysterious inner strength which men, including doctors, secretly admire. For now, I can do no more than entrust the situation to Alice's own body'. Annie felt he'd stopped short the sentence by omitting 'and to God'.

When the young couple had first come to stay at Gregory Street and Annie had sat one evening keeping Alice company, she'd noticed the locket, showing at the neck of her nightgown. When Alice had told her the story of its origin Annie had fought back tears. Ever since, although making no mention of it to George, Annie had imagined his half of the heart, tucked inside his shirt, with him every day. She had still the amber hatpin, Harold's gift to her that first Christmas. It was a nonsense but because no occasion ever presented itself for Annie to wear the elegant, droplet necklace that Charles had brought back from Egypt, she felt unable to wear the hatpin either. Whether Charles would even notice the small decorative pin she wasn't sure but it presented a dilemma and so she contented herself by fingering the amber coloured stone and remembering.

"Two tins of stewed steak did you say Mrs.Piper?"

"Yes dear, that's right, yours is cheaper than MissTurpin's."

Annie smiled to herself as she took the tins down from the shelf, Mrs.Piper had no such torment of loyalties, 'like it or lump it' as Edna would say.

"I best be off before dad gets back," said Hilda, she kissed her two fingers and with them touched Samuel's brow. "I shall call on Monday, after work."

Alice smiled, "I shall put on enough tea for the three of us, tell grandma Sarah."

Hilda was about to say goodbye to Mrs.Stanford but the lady rose to her feet and declared that she should also be going. "We can walk together for a little while Hilda." Her smile was warm and although Hilda felt somewhat awkward at the prospect of walking with the wife of Basil Stanford, just as her brothers had been taught always to respect their elders so too had Hilda. Jack never spoke of conflicts at the mine but she imagined he and this lady's husband were ever at odds.

They spoke briefly with Annie before leaving through the shop. Hilda had no wish to see her dad, on the couple of occasions they had overlapped the air had been strained, it only made things worse for her mam.

"Samuel is a beautiful baby, for his mother to be ill with such a serious condition is so unfair," said Florence. Hilda was silent for a few moments then she voiced her thoughts.

"I suppose I am some sort of opponent Mrs.Stanford, Jack Haynes, my young man is the union representative at Birchdale."

"Our middle daughter Julia is to be married," said Florence, "next month in Rome where she works. Julia left home many years ago, to escape, some fathers, for whatever reason, can be too controlling of their daughters. I miss her but this summer she promises to come over to England with her husband Luciano, to visit. They will stay with Caroline and Edmund, sometime during august. Mr.&Mrs.Luciano D'elia, doesn't that sound splendid. The Italians have the

380

reputation of being naturally romantic while the English male is renowned for his reserve. Is your Jack romantic my dear?"

Hilda was taken aback by the question. "Jack is a little older than me and because his father was badly injured and died shortly after the war, he shoulders more responsibility, as all his brothers do, except Victor. He's the youngest, he was born with a condition that sets him apart, people say he's mongoloid, whatever that means. Victor is like a little boy, but full grown and never rough or cruel like some boys can be. We've sort of grown up always knowing Victor. Jack has love in his heart, not just for his family but for others too. He always speaks to children, smiles at the elderly and despite my dad's unreasonable attitude, not once has Jack ever criticized him. With me he is gentle and kind, I'm not really sure what romance is, I do know that I feel completely happy when I'm with Jack, I could endure pain and poverty provided he was there."

Florence began to walk more slowly, almost stopping altogether at one point. "We are not opponents Hilda, we are women doing our best to understand all of life's complexities. I look upon your mother as a very good friend, we share many beliefs and some concerns. Your brother William now threads through both our lives, I didn't have a boy but in my experience, a mother is only too aware that she cannot control a son. In the same way that she endeavours to direct her daughter so she tries to direct the young man, for his own good. From what you have told me, it would seem that Mrs.Haynes has been the very best guide to Jack and his brothers. Please give him my regards, Mr.Wainwright, Jack's predecessor, I admire greatly, it takes courage to oppose Mr.Stanford's opinion, a great deal of courage but I believe your Jack will serve the miners well." Florence halted, "I must go in this direction now Hilda, I promised to call on Caroline. Be happy my dear. I also confess to not knowing the true meaning of romance but to have 'love in the heart' must surely be the first requirement. Goodbye."

Not quite sure of how to respond and feeling a rush of loyalty to her mam the young Hilda said. "William has a good heart too deep down, but like dad he thinks showing it makes a man soft. I shall give your regards to Jack, thank you." She waved as she walked away towards Mitchell Street and Florence to Purbeck Road.

"Rex came to see me yesterday," said Henry, "he has made up his mind to leave Nottingham. At first I thought he spoke of merely a possibility and wondered if the wrench of leaving the place where his wife and infant son are buried would in the end dissuade him. As he continued in his explanation however, I became convinced it was indeed his intention to go. It seems Rex lost his mother when he was sixteen, his father was devastated by her death and never really got over it. Two years later Alfred Madden determined himself to travel to South Africa, he'd read about the successful mining of diamonds in the Transvaal. Although he tried hard he failed to persuade Rex to go with him, by then Rex had met Doris and for the young man in love I suppose moving to the other side ot the world was much less tempting. Alfred Madden duly departed for South Africa and Rex stayed at the pit, Colver, working for Claude Stanford, by then at the coalface. His father journeyed safely and wrote immediately he got off the boat. In fact he corresponded regularly and his letters revealed that he'd secured work, not mining diamonds but gold for De Beers Consolidated, Cecil Rhodes in essence. The operations were established at an area called Witwatersrand. The letters continued with no less frequency, Rex said that looking back he believes it was his father's way of being still just that, a father. As a child Rex remembers only kindness ever being shown to his mother and himself, Alfred Madden was a caring man. Then a letter came, not from his father but from one of the men with whom Alfred worked, he was dead, not from any catastrophe at the mine, there'd been no accident, but from heart failure, he'd simply died, he was not even working at the time but playing cards with a group of men off shift. They'd buried him in a recognised graveyard and marked the place. Now Rex wants to find where his father's buried, to stand there before it's too late."

"I'm not sure I'd find the courage," said Andrew, "I admire him."

Henry smiled. "So do I, I went to Europe and while every foreign country is fascinating in its way I was aware that only a narrow band of water separated me from home but South Africa, that must surely be for a more adventurous nature than mine. Rex will sell the contents of the house, including that magnificent globe, which apparently he bought in a sale more than twenty years ago for the sole purpose of locating on the map that place where his father settled and ultimately died. 'I no longer need it Henry', he said. The lot will go to auction early next month, the proceeds he will put with what money he's managed to save over the years and then Rex Madden will bid us goodbye."

"There must be great satisfaction for the man who stands at the place where his father was laid to rest feeling pride and affection for his memory," said Andrew, "I have never held the slightest inclination to visit the spot where they put mine."

Henry stood and crossed to the bureau, took a letter from within and from the cupboard below, two glasses and the whisky. "The agent has lined up another viewing of the house, next Tuesday. That will be the ninth but as yet no acceptable offer. This couple however must find a property to suit them in Nottingham before too long, the husband is an eye surgeon, soon to take up a position here at the hospital."

"Where do you propose to live Henry?" Asked Andrew with genuine concern. "There is plenty of room at home, I rattle around in that house trying to converse with my own echo, you would be more than welcome."

Henry chuckled. "My dear friend I don't for one moment doubt your sincerity in offering me a place of abode, but I have not yet given up on the hope of seeing you married and living happily with a good woman. A rather 'tatty' and not altogether useful 'Henry Wicks' within your home I doubt would encourage the development of romance."

"You talk nonsense Henry, utter nonsense." Andrew took a drink from his glass. "Tell me in all seriousness, what is your plan?"

Henry put his glass down on the small side table. "I am a man of simple tastes and my needs are met in simple ways. I require only a small cottage, a bedroom, a living room, a small scullery, merely a place in which to sleep, eat and think. I have decided to invest along with a handful of others in the open cast project at Mapperley.

It is encouraging that the mineralogist who took the core samples has himself chosen to invest, that could only be a good sign. It seems he used to live in Nottingham as a boy but moved with his family to Sheffield. His father was an accountant here as I understand, although the name means nothing to me. Hemsley, there's no reason that it should, I'd worked very many years for Stanford before my affairs warranted the services of an accountant.

Do you know Andrew, I could eat a cold beef sandwich with a nice bit of mustard, Leonora maintained such a combination was essentially English, of course my dear wife was convinced that on the continent they ate only horseflesh, washed down by vast amounts of wine. It accounts for their unpredictable nature she'd say, just like the horse on which they fed could without warning, rear up and thrash the air wildly, so to could they and permanently intoxicated they were unable to offer any rational explanation for their behaviour." Henry chuckled. "Leonora would have made an excellent politician but could have isolated us as a nation through her 'unique' diplomacy. I shall make us a plate of essentially English supper and then you can tell me what is happening in the world of textiles. Last time we talked you were considering branching out, adding a new fabric to your production, 'Celanese' as I recall. Enough of mining, you must give me the low down on this latest Brassington enterprise, perhaps I shall invest in that too. Henry Wicks has his determined hat on."

Annie had lain awake listening to the rain, she'd not slept since Samuel had disturbed, she'd heard George tiptoe downstairs to heat some milk, that had been at around half past four, it was half past five now and the papers would be arriving very soon. Charles was fast asleep, sliding quietly from between the covers Annie dressed and pinned her hair. In the scullery she washed her face in cold water, pushed a handful of kindlers amongst the embers in the range and when they began to flame, lay a few nubs of coal over the top.

The rain had eased, she peered through the door of the shop, no papers yet. The outer wrapping that supposedly kept the papers clean and dry in their bundles would have little chance of success this morning, the pavement was saturated.

George had agreed to Annie's suggestion that a hot meal before they go would be sensible, she'd prepare their dinner for midday. When the taxi came Annie would go with them to help Alice make up the bed and organise everything for Samuel.

Annie sighed, the situation worried her, George needed to work, Percy Pollard had been understanding, giving George time off when the baby came, but with rent to pay and jobs too scarce to risk losing a good one, George was naturally anxious to keep his place at Raleigh. Annie's thoughts were interrupted by the arrival of the paper van. She unlocked the shop door and stepped outside. With any luck the driver might condescend to carry some beyond the pavement.

"Mornin' missus." He opened the back doors of the vehicle, the first bundle he passed to Annie, she hurried to put it inside the shop but before she had chance to take another he'd thrown two more down onto the ground by the door and was about to cast the fourth.

"I'll take the bundles from you," said Annie, "that way they won't get wet."

"Missus if I'm as much as ten minutes late my life wont be worth livin'. I've got nine more drops afore I can take the van back to warehouse an' if I'm not home in time for me Hail Marys at 8o/clock Mass my Nora'll be tellin' Father Docherty that I've been wi' another woman. Twenty minutes last month, twenty minutes I had to sit in that bloody cupboard convincing Father it wer' only 'cause I'd dropped Hyson Green's News o' the World at Alfreton Road an' I had to go back to sort it out that I wer' late home.

'My son', he said, 'your wife is at that delicate stage of life, when the blossom loses its abundance until eventually it fails to bloom at all. When for a woman, a trivial matter can take on epic proportions, but it is all part of that sacred union which God made for man and wife. Humour her my son, humour her'.

The bloody cheek o' the man, what could 'e know about it, bloody blossoms, 'e wouldn't recognise a menopausal woman if she baked a cake and spelled it out in letters across the soddin' icin'. That's just like it is, sweet an' sour at the same time, one minute everythin's lovely, then the next you're bein' called all the names under the sun." He passed the bundle of papers to Annie and as she carried them inside she heard the thud as two more were thrown onto the pavement. The van doors closed noisily and he drove off at speed.

She retrieved the remainder before the soggy wrapping transferred its dampness to the papers then locked the shop door. The activity beneath their bedroom window would surely have roused Charles. The papers now safe from possible damage she could have some breakfast, at her delicate stage of life the 'warming cup' and a bowl of porridge would humour her!

It was George who appeared in the kitchen first. "Are you alright Mam, I heard the van, Alice and Samuel are still asleep." Annie detected a tremor in his voice and when he lowered himself onto a chair by the table George could hold back emotion no longer.

Annie cradled his head as weeks of stifled stress, on this Sunday morning, finally surfaced. She smoothed his brow, passing her fingers gently over his hair, several times she repeated the comforting until his distress subsided. "Alice wants her own little home George, I can understand that. See how the days progress, Hilda will help again if needs be and I can come." Annie lowered her voice, "I know Charles frustrates you but if I need to be with you, Alice and Samuel, he wouldn't put any obstacle in the way. You have a beautiful son George and a lovely wife, be strong for both of them."

Movement on the stairs alerted them to Charles' approach, he was quiet, even the difficult Charles sensed the nervousness in George at leaving the safety of his mother, with a new born baby and a wife whom he knew had a frailty that challenged even the most learned doctors.

"Eat some porridge George," he said, pulling out a chair and sitting down beside his stepson. "An empty stomach is no use to you today and whatever your mam tells you, heed it, I've never known her to be wrong." Charles glanced at Annie, his face was as full of despair as George's had been, that same look of pleading in his eyes.

Annie poured the hot tea and spooned the strengthening porridge into their bowls. 'Every day the same, never two days alike'. Dear Winnie Bacon how right she was.

Samuel had taken his feed and now slept in his crib upstairs. The fire burned hot in the grate creating a comfortable feel to the house. Annie had covered the slab in the pantry with enough food for days and the shelves were stocked with packets and tins, the drawers were full of neatly pressed clothes, even a bowl of sweet smelling hyacinths stood on the living room window ledge.

Alice sat on the edge of their bed, fingering her locket, George had insisted on walking part of the way with his mam, despite Annie's protests. Gregory Street was not so very far away, yet both Annie and George felt their hearts stretch across the distance and it hurt with a pain that each recognised in the other. When they'd parted, Annie to walk on to the shop and George to return to Ainsley Road no words would come, just that deep thickening of the throat as emotions welled inside them and they held each other tight, for just those few seconds mother and son breathed as one.

On her lap Alice now held the trinket box containing all her little bits and pieces, she took out the two newspaper cuttings. First she read again the announcement of their marriage, she smiled, dear Kenneth, ever enthusiastic over his work, if there was any justice in this world then one day he would surely run his own newspaper. The second cutting was the announcement of Samuel's birth, on the 27th February 1932, to George and Alice Boucher, the gift of a son, Samuel, Fredrick, Harold. She saw the stork shaped baby's scissors that came from grandma Elliot's. Samuel's tiny fingernails were not requiring to be trimmed just yet but she took them from the box and laid them on top the chest of drawers. Grandma Sarah had been so pleased when George declared their son's name to be Samuel. Annie had seen a likeness to the Bouchers at the very first moment, even while that new face, unaccustomed to the light, wrinkled and puckered about the tiny mouth, crying from alarm at the big world into which birth now thrust Samuel Boucher. Annie had recognised it, felt it, in this child was something handed down by Harold, he would develop a liking for mints, be always whistling and singing and on good days when his happiness inspired pride, 'he wouldn't call the King his uncle'. But all these thoughts Annie had kept to herself saying only to Alice, 'now you are a mother and more love comes with your baby than you would ever have believed possible'.

Her son lay on his back, his blankets tucked in to keep him warm. Alice stood by his crib, looking at this wonder, she felt it, just as Annie had said, more love than she'd ever believed possible. Samuel, Frederick, Harold had completely taken over her life.

George was back, he put more coals on the fire and hurried to his wife. "Mam says she'll come for an hour on Tuesday, she'll be missing her grandson too much by then to stay away any longer."

Alice lay back on their bed gazing up at the ceiling. "Do you remember the buzzards that day in Derbyshire, now whenever I try to picture them all I see is a stork carrying a baby." She turned her face to George, smiled, then kissed him, long and lingering, the very same way she had kissed him when they lay on the grass bank at Tissington. Together they soared in great arcs across the heavens, glorious, carefree flight.

CHAPTER TWENTY-THREE

Late May 1932

Edna had not once asked for a day off, whatever event had taken place she had worked around it, Saturday afternoons and Sundays were the only times Edna felt it 'normal' to be away from the factory.

'He is deeply morose' had been the words used by Andrew Armistead to describe Andrew Smithfield. On the few occasions Edna saw him, when he walked the factory floor, he appeared remote from the present. Even allowing for the anxieties experienced by many businessmen his mood irritated Edna. Compared to the average man, working long hours for little pay, going home to a houseful of kids and a wife constantly making do and making mend, Andrew Smithfield had nobody but himself to bother about, he had no claim on misery.

She put the blouse on which she'd been working over a hanger on the rail, rubbed her hands down her skirt to pull out the creases from being so long seated at the machine, sighed and made her way to the office.

"Come in." He'd responded immediately to the knock at his door but his expression held surprise when on looking up it was Edna wishing to speak with him. "Is there a problem Edna?" He hadn't shaved and the collar of his shirt looked grubby, there was little evidence on the desk to suggest he kept his mind fully occupied, even the tea caddy of pens and pencils lay on its side where a ledger had obviously clipped it and knocked it over. Edna's patience snapped, she went back to the door, closed it firmly, returned to the desk gathering up the contents of the caddy as she spoke.

"Our granddaughter's havin' the first operation on 'er cleft palate at City Hospital next Wednesday, 'er mam'll be beside 'erself wi' worry, I know Billy could go with 'er but it aught to be me as sits wi' our Annie tryin' to keep 'er from heartache, that's a mam's job. It's difficult for 'er husband Alec, he works at Briggs

Engineerin' served his apprenticeship there, but yer know what it's like, if they think you're goin' to want time off for owt an' they need to shed somebody. I wondered if I could have that day off, I'll make it up somehow."

"That will be alright Edna." His voice was laden with gloom as if he carried the cares of the world.

Edna could tolerate it no longer. "Now you look 'ere Mr.Smithfield, you'll likely tell me to mind me own business but somebody needs to say summat afore yer drive us all round the bloody bend. Yer sit in this office day after day wi' a face like a fiddle, whatever's the matter wi' yer? Our Annie's got all the worry o' little Janet an' what them doctors are goin' to do to the poor mite but she still manages to smile. Alec's uncle Reg is goin' downhill fast, the lad's allus been close to his uncle, especially since his dad wer' killed in the war but Alec still gives us a smile. Annie Eddowes soldiers on in that shop, sick wi' worry over George's wife Alice an' their baby so young. Hilda's moved back to Ainsley Road again, so she can help but for how much longer will that be enough. The doctors can't do owt, Charles wanders round in a dream, he's never been any use in a crisis, they all lean on Annie, but when I went there last Saturday, first thing she said was, 'tell me if there's anythin' I can do when Janet goes into hospital' an' she smiled, Annie give me a smile 'cause she knew I needed that more than owt else. For God's sake Mr.Smithfield, count yer blessin's an' look around yer."

He got to his feet and crossed to the window, now her outburst was over Edna began to wonder if she'd gone too far, perhaps she'd have more than next Wednesday off, he might tell her to pack up her machine and go right away.

He spoke quietly, a hesitancy in his voice. "Do you suppose I wouldn't take all of Annie's worries from her if I could, give her a life of happiness and peace, protect her from the harshness of this world. I would gladly devote all my efforts to Annie, but she is Mrs.Charles Eddowes isn't she Edna?"

She was numbed by his confession, for surely that was what it was, a confession of love. Edna had teased Annie many times over Andrew Smithfield's obvious regard for her but it had simply been mischief, never had she imagined his feelings to be so intense, this man truly ached from longing. Edna crossed the room to stand beside him, her intolerance now replaced by compassion.

Annie has been my friend for so long, I know her better than anyone. Believe me, I wish I could say to you, win her away from Charles, free her from that treadmill, but I can't, she would never leave him.

Annie was raised by her aunt Bella, I used to think it was that strict upbringing that made Annie so correct, so stubbornly committed to a man whose irritable moods and irrational notions brought a degree of dread to every day. Now, all these years on, I think the decency was born in Annie, there right from the start. I love her that much I'd be frightened to contemplate life without her, to have a friend like Annie is more than wealth, I shall never have money beyond each week's need but I know how blessed I am. Be her friend Mr.Smithfield, God knows she needs friends."

"It's different for you Edna, you're another woman, but for a man to befriend a woman is just not permitted by society, he's expected to court a single female and stay away from all others, otherwise he's a cad." He turned his face from the window and smiled resignedly.

"Bugger society an' all that claptrap," said Edna, "go to the shop, buy your bread an' bacon or whatever else yer need, cast a smile over Annie, ask if yer can do anythin' to help, carry a bit o' strength there, every day saps more of hers away. Think o' George watchin' his wife grow weaker an' not knowin' what to do, even Charles could use a few words of encouragement. Forget about yourself for a while, although a shave an' a clean shirt wouldn't go amiss." Edna gave him a stern look afraid to weaken in her reproach of him, her own emotions were struggling to remain contained, here before her was an altogether decent man declaring his love for her best friend Annie, who had not known such devotion since Harold died at Josiah's yard. Yet it would change nothing, Annie was Charles' wife, mother of his children, including William and Freddy. To even be aware of Smithfield's feelings for her would only add to Annie's problems, for then she would despair over his misery.

"I do believe Edna that the spirit of Alicia Plowright, by some miracle, now lives in you." Andrew chuckled and in so doing seemed to surprise himself. "I

391

have indulged in self pity, it is misplaced, as you so rightly point out I should look about me and consider others more. I confess to being despondent over my good friend Henry Wicks leaving Langley Drive to live at Babbington. It isn't so far away and we both have transport, it felt like the onset of yet another void, an emptiness, again I was just feeling sorry for myself." He fell silent for a moment, then looking nervously at Edna said. "You won't give me away will you Edna, I promise I shall do better."

"I know what folk think o' me, mouthy old Edna Dodds, more yap than sense, even me mam used to say I had tongue enough for two. But I'm not so daft, I know when it's right to speak out an' when it's better to keep me mouth shut. Now if I'm not sacked I'll get back to me machine an' I'll tell me daughter it'll be alright for me to go with 'er an' the little 'en next Wednesday."

"Perhaps I could take you to the hospital Edna, your daughter too of course."

Edna was about to respond with 'we can get the bus', when her conscience pricked her, what was the use of telling him to consider others only then to reject his kindness. "That would be a great help Mr.Smithfield, thank you," was instead her reply and when they exchanged smiles, each understood the other completely.

"It would mean so much to Freddy, you've not seen his home, his surroundings. It's been two years all but, since Freddy took Francis to begin again at Skendleby, now they have Faith and Grace, our two granddaughters. At Bufton Cott that family wait, they wait too see you walk through their door Charles. I can't be absent from here while Alice is unwell and at least I have been to Skendleby, to see them all. I look forward to going again but at the moment difficulties here dictate that I stay close. If things deteriorate," Annie hesitated unwilling to even think about the possibility, "then it wouldn't be right for Hilda to remain at George's she's nineteen, too young to witness such suffering, I might have to go to Ainsley Road. At present, Hilda's help in the early mornings and after her work at night is enabling Alice to cope but only just, her tiredness crosses the line to weakness. Samuel is totally dependant and will be for some time yet. Go away for a weekend Charles, take a break from the shop, from the pressures of the situation while you can, if not for your own sake then for Freddy's."

Annie had tried her hardest to persuade Charles he really should go to Lincolnshire, Freddy's second child, another girl had been born on May 2nd. Going over time by several days, Grace Eddowes had weighed 8 pounds 14 ounces at birth but all was well. Annie had purposefully written little of Alice's illness in her letters to Francis, having one daughter in law so poorly was distressing enough, causing Francis anxiety in the later stages of her pregnancy would have been irresponsible and unkind. The young couple's excitement as a result had been freely expressed when Grace arrived and Annie was thankful for that. She remembered the concern George had felt over his wedding celebration, coming as it did so close to Freddy's departure from Bobbers Mill, his torment at showing such open happiness when his brother was experiencing dreadful times. Freddy had smiled bravely through the wedding and all its merriment, not wanting to deny George and Alice a single moment of pleasure. It was good that three weeks ago Freddy and Francis had been able to rejoice in the birth of their second child without the knowledge of just how seriously ill Alice was.

John had been stoic, helping his dad each evening to bring up stock from the cellar, working closely with George at Raleigh, watching constantly for any sign to suggest that his brother was not coping.

Only Percy Pollard had been told of the situation, a man with a good heart, he'd put John to work alongside George and told the younger brother, 'I'm here if you need to ask for anythin' lad, a bike's only a pair o' wheels when all's said an' done'. If any of their workmates had learned of Alice's condition then they'd said nothing but both young men were popular and sometimes it was what men didn't say that vouched most for their loyalty.

Charles drank the last of his tea, he'd managed to eat the potted beef sandwich Annie had made for his supper, his appetite had been poor of late. None of them ate with relish, it was only the need to keep strong that drove them to clear a plate of food. John had already gone to bed, a book Hilda chose for him at the library had achieved to capture his imagination and a few pages of reading helped him find sleep.

"I might go next weekend, we'll see." Charles' gaze was directed automatically to the jar of sand, still on the shelf of the dresser. "Anything you have for the baby get ready in case, I dare say Celia and Hilda will have bought a present for the child, even Alice will have likely asked Hilda to get something for her and George to send. If I do go John must help with the papers on the Sunday, it's Whitsuntide weekend, it could be busier than usual, I'll think about it." He rose to his feet. "Are you coming up now?"

Annie nodded, she would have been happier if Charles' mind was more positive but he'd not said 'no' and her better judgement convinced her it was sensible to say no more on the subject for now. Tomorrow would be Saturday, it granted her several days over which to apply gentle coaxing but each week became ever more crucial. Annie carried an intense heartache for George, she needed to know that Freddy was content, otherwise that little home at Bufton Cott pulled at her emotions too. If Charles went to visit it would allow her much relief. As Annie so often did, she offered up a silent prayer as she climbed the stairs, yet more and more she wondered if The Almighty heard and if in the confusion of so many pleadings he remembered the ones that came from a small, unimportant shop on Gregory Street.

Andrew sat looking at the globe, he couldn't explain sensibly to Henry just why he'd been so determined to buy it at the auction, but his was the successful bid and the orb bearing the world map, suspended on its heavy oak stand, now found residence at Andrew's abode.

He'd identified the Transvaal, running his fingers over the gently rotating globe until the site of Rex Madden's destination revealed itself. He should be there by now, Rex had promised to write, it was something both Andrew and Henry looked forward to with eagerness, the first letter containing news of South Africa. It had been a touching farewell, so many miles ahead of Rex and travelling alone, word of his safe arrival and progress in reaching that place most significant would be received with relief and some measure of satisfaction. Rex had escaped Stanford's clutches, not without the sorrow of losing his wife Doris but Rex Madden was overdue a life of his own. Perhaps Henry and Andrew, if they were entirely honest, envied the random nature of Rex's new life, he smiled to himself. Enough of such fantasies, it was Saturday afternoon, the factory was shut down until Monday, he could not ignore Edna's arresting remark. 'Go to the shop, take Annie some strength'. That he could do without evoking society's condemnation, what was it but claptrap anyway? Edna reminded him so much of aunt Alicia. He took his jacket from the hall stand, checked the money in his wallet and set off to make his purchases at Eddowes' on Gregory Street.

Henry Wicks had accepted the offer made by Dr. Gerrard Coots, the eye surgeon, anxious to move his family before taking up his post. The solicitor acting for Henry had predicted a completion of the conveyance by the end of May. It had been harder than Henry had expected, more than two years ago, he'd finally mustered the heart to sort out Leonora's clothes, donating them to the mission to be distributed among the most in need, yet still he found so many items when emptying drawers and cupboards, simple, personal things of no particular value but as they had lain in his hands every one had halted his progress, suspended his thoughts as memories carried him back in time. Alone as he was through the process, tears could fall freely, and they did.

Babbington Village was a sensible distance between the familiar place he'd known as home and Mapperley, where his future interests lay. A small cottage type property in a terrace of five offered everything Henry needed. There he could be warm in winter by the hearth of a cosy living room, appreciate the small but charming back garden overhung with orange blossom in summer, feed himself through the facility of a basic scullery, find rest in the quietness of a plain but adequate bedroom and perform his ablutions, as so many must do, over a wash stand. To relieve himself, a scrupulously scrubbed and lime washed privy, stood discreetly by the back door, hanging on the rear wall of which was a print in a frame bearing the reminder, 'cleanliness is next to Godliness'. 'I shall add a small bathroom at some stage', Henry had told Andrew, ' but for now I shall revert to the ways of my youth'!

Having far more furniture than he could possibly accommodate at No.2 Florence Cottages, Henry had anticipated having to arrange the removal of all surplus items to the auction rooms but Dr.Coots had agreed to buy, for an additional sum, any pieces of furniture Henry could identify as 'not going with him'. It was a mutually beneficial arrangement and relieved Henry of yet more taxing organisation.

Andrew had tried to share Henry's obvious enthusiasm but Babbington was not the convenient bolthole that Langley Drive had been. Now as he drove to Eddowes' shop he reproached himself, again Edna's words rang true, he'd thought only of his own disappointment at Henry's choice of situation and not of his good friend's future happiness in new surroundings, albeit a dramatic change of dwelling, it was Henry's chosen course and Andrew should embrace it without question as a loyal friend.

Annie was serving Emily Pagett when the bell clanged and Andrew Smithfield stepped inside the door, he smiled briefly and seeing Annie was busy with a customer he stood by the paper rack and read the headlines. The newspaper with the least alarming caption was The Mirror so he chose that. Most concentrated on the fluctuating exchange, the city jitters, Andrew had read all he could stomach on that subject over recent months, 'Unidentified object in the sky over Basildon', held some intrigue at least and captured the imagination rather than fixating the mind on advancing austerity, which many believed was 'ratcheted up' by the very same people who two facedly maintained its inevitability.

Mrs.Pagett appeared to inspect Andrew Smithfield as she was about to leave, pausing by the door and casting her eyes up and down his figure. Apparently satisfied of his respectability she said, "Good afternoon dear," and immediately began to hum the tune of 'all things bright and beautiful'. Ever polite, he opened and closed the door for the good lady, turning face to Annie he tried to hide his nervousness but the smile Annie instantly gave him sent a wave of relief to his stomach where tension had already taken hold.

"Mrs.Pagett is very well meaning," said Annie, "and long suffering, her husband Stanley is not the most congenial other half. Some would observe that his presence creates a heaviness in the air, which proves stubborn to disperse. In the shop it can be disturbing, a little fresh lemon juice squeezed onto a sponge, out of sight behind the till is our only remedy for what Charles, perhaps a little harshly refers to as 'the unholy stench', but given that Stanley constantly belittles his wife's commitment to the Women's Fellowship, Charles' description of Stanley's aftermath could be fitting." Annie chuckled and her easy manner calmed him further.

"How are you Annie? I've learned through Edna that illness in your family is causing you considerable worry. It seems totally inadequate to simply ask if there is anything I can do to help but I do ask, in all sincerity."

Annie put her hands together on the counter, as if entwining her fingers, as she now did, somehow summoned up sufficient strength to enable her to speak of her daughter in law Alice. He listened, moved by the sadness of Annie's account. She went on tell Andrew of Freddy's second child, there was no evidence of resentment in her voice as she spoke of Freddy. He felt immensely relieved.

"I've been trying to persuade Charles he should go to Skendleby, he's not visited there since Freddy and Francis left Bobbers Mill. On the dresser in the kitchen sits a jam jar filled with sand from the beach at Skegness that Freddy sent back with Hilda and me that first summer, a ploy to urge Charles to visit, to return the sand to its rightful place by the sea. Because of the shop we can't both be away at the same time. I feel too anxious to be absent from here as things are and Charles needs a change of scene. Freddy would be so proud to show his dad the area around their home and the farm at Huttoft. Always Charles presents some obstacle, last night I was feeling quite optimistic that he'd made up his mind to go next weekend, but this morning he declared that on second thoughts the train would likely be packed being Whitsuntide so his visit to Freddy would have to wait. Before too long I shall need to be with Alice and George far more than here. At present Hilda is staying there, she helps Alice before leaving for her work at the library and again in the evenings but I fear Alice will need someone to be there at all times, Samuel is just a baby, he naturally requires attention by day and night. Charles will be tied to the shop and though Freddy, when he learns of the seriousness of Alice's condition will have only concern for his brother, it bothers me that no one from the family will have seen Grace, our new granddaughter in Lincolnshire. This time it should be Charles who goes, Freddy's dad."

Andrew recognised the anguish behind Annie's words. "You know Annie, for some time now, since losing aunt Alicia really, I've felt the need of a distraction, a change of routine. Your dilemma has given me a wonderful opportunity, I've not seen a stretch of water since crossing from Ireland on the ferry. It's a daunting prospect, journeying alone but I would find a trip to Skegness, to the coast, altogether inviting if Charles were to travel with me for company. I could drive him to Skendleby and return there for him on the Sunday evening. My time would be spent enjoying the complete change Skegness offers and Charles could be relaxed knowing he didn't have to board a busy train for his return journey, mutually advantageous."

Annie didn't know what to think or say, it did indeed seem ideal but persuading Charles of the notion was another matter entirely. "Charles isn't here at the moment but he should be home within the half hour." Annie's frown revealed her apprehension.

"There are several items I need from the shop, perhaps by the time they are ready Charles will be back." The doorbell clanged and Mrs.Rashleigh with three of her grandchildren bustled inside. "Do serve this lady Mrs.Eddowes," said Andrew, "I'm in no hurry." His reluctance to leave without first speaking to Charles prompted him to seize the moment.

"Mabel Rashleigh gave him a quick, "Ta very much." Looked directly at Annie with a 'what's 'e doin' 'ere' expression, clipped the middle child round the ear for touching a jar of lollipops on the counter and declared, "Unsmoked bacon this week if yer please, all these years Bill's been eatin' smoked, now 'e reckons it's repeatin' to him. I bet it'll make not an iota o' difference, it's not the bacon as gives him heartburn an' indigestion, it's the age of his gut. Like I said to him, them poor old pipes of his 'ave been makin' music since 'e wer' a babe in arms, it used to be 'The Sun Has Got It's Hat On' but now they're playin' 'Auld Lang Syne'.

Annie had weighed up and taken from the shelf most of Andrew's list when Charles appeared, he looked surprised to see Annie's customer.

"Hello Charles, I'm glad I've caught you, it seems fate has favoured me. I need to go to Lincolnshire next weekend," said Andrew, it wasn't a lie, he did need to take himself away from yet another weekend of maudlin. Annie felt herself tremble. "Your wife tells me that you'd hoped to go there yourself, it wouldn't be sensible for you to contemplate catching a train on such a busy weekend when very many will be heading for the coast by rail and as a matter of fact I wanted to talk with you about a new enterprise I'm considering, you were in the trade, I would value your opinion."

Charles looked from Andrew to Annie, immediately suspecting some contrivance between them. "I suppose the two of you have hatched a plan to get me to Skendleby, what opinion could I express on your business Smithfield, Annie can be very persuasive but you don't have to go to such lengths."

"It is pure selfishness on my part," said Andrew, "to suppose you might make the drive more pleasurable by granting me some company, and furthermore listen while I voice my doubts over whether this new enterprise is feasible at such a time, or whether these economically squeezed conditions in which we operate might be crying out for fresh products to invigorate the market. I've spoken of it briefly to Henry Wicks but as I'm sure you're aware, Henry is moving house very soon so his mind is occupied with the demands of such an upheaval."

Still Charles needed to be convinced. "Do you know about this?" He fired the question at Annie sharply.

"I have no idea Charles and your response of Mr.Smithfield is less than polite."

He fell silent for a moment, gazing down at his own feet. "Very well, I shall travel to Lincolnshire with you Smithfield, sharing the cost of the petrol."

Before Andrew could reply Annie's eye's launched an appeal, he understood and shook Charles' hand. "Agreed Charles, a mutually advantageous decision."

Wrapping some cheese, the last item on Andrew's list, Annie's breathing became easier. Thank God, thank God for Mr.Smithfield's enterprise, whatever it may be, her thoughts were unspoken but entirely sincere.

They were clear of Nottingham and motoring through countryside. The day was pleasantly warm and Andrew had removed his jacket whilst they'd waited at a level crossing a few miles back. Charles sat in the passenger seat, genuinely drawn to the landscape as it rolled past the window like the scenery that young Hilda used to pull through the back of her cardboard theatre, a gift from Davina at one of those early birthdays. Charles saw very little beyond the sprawl of the city. Not since his travels through the course of the war had his eyes taken in a view so open, miles of green fields and scattered dwellings. It was strangely calming and while Andrew Smithfield could have no way of knowing it, Charles quietness came not from awkwardness but from a relaxing of his mind as he allowed the motion of the car and the sound the wheels made on the road's surface to lull his senses, rather like an infant responding to the gentle rocking of the crib in which he or she was cocooned. Ahead of them Andrew could see cattle, a farmer was moving his herd of cows to fresh grazing and drove them through a gateway onto the road.

Andrew stopped the car and smiled, "We mustn't hurry the ladies," he said with a chuckle.

Charles turned his face from the window at his side and now stared at the procession of black and white cows, ambling along, the farmer now closing the field gate to follow them. The man raised his stick in a friendly acknowledgement of their need for patience.

Charles' first remark seemed to come out of the blue Andrew hadn't expected it. "Did Edna send you?"

Andrew started up the engine and drove slowly forward, seeing the cows disappearing into another gateway on the opposite side of the road. "No Charles, Edna didn't send me. She came to me in the office and asked if she could take a day off, last Wednesday in fact, to go with her daughter and granddaughter to the hospital, for the first operation on the little girl's cleft palate. In talking she'd voiced her own worries over your daughter in law, Edna is concerned for you all. It occurred to me that it might be helpful to Edna if instead of using the bus, I drove them to the hospital. That thought led me to question if there might be something I could do to be useful to yourself and Annie. I live alone Charles, outside of the factory time is a commodity I have rather too much of. When I called at the shop to ask if I could assist in any way, the conversation Annie and I exchanged revealed the coincidence of my need to go to the coast and your need to visit Freddy. In that, my question was answered but I do feel the arrangement is lacking on my part, it would seem I am being useful but it requires no actual effort from me, in fact I am the one to gain. I have company as I travel and my petrol costs are being shared."

Charles made a vague, "Uhm."

"Have you heard of 'Celanese' Charles? It's a new semi-synthetic fabric, very lightweight, soft, and the nature of the fibre allows it a unique quality in that it 'breathes', effectively making it ideal for underwear garments, especially ladies and children's. I have the opportunity to adopt Celanese as one of our product lines, a completely new and attractive range. I like Vyella, always have and I shall continue to use it but in addition to what we already produce I think Celanese could be successful at invigorating the market, creating confidence. I have enough skilled women to work with the material, it will require that sense of 'feel' for a fabric, which comes with experience."

Charles smiled. "You have Edna, she began her work at father's. Edna may be an old gossip but you won't find a better seamstress."

Andrew felt amused by Charles' description of Edna, remembering her own recent words, 'even me mam used to say I had tongue enough for two'. "I don't know which way to jump Charles, the economy is fragile but a new, attractive line of

401

underwear, different in so many ways to the old stuff we've been churning out for years, might just prove a winner, what would you do?"

Charles looked at Andrew with a bland expression. "You'd be better off asking Annie than asking me."

"I wouldn't dream of asking Annie, don't you think Charles that she has already far too much to trouble about? Any illness in a family is a source of worry and very often cause of additional work, especially for the women, but a serious condition such as the one afflicting your daughter in law must drain the strength of all involved. You are a man Charles so I am asking you."

Charles took a deep breath and wound down the window by an inch or two. "If it were me I'd go ahead, it sounds like a good opportunity, but as it is unique, an entirely new fabric, I would be sure to attach to every garment, even one as simple as a child's vest, a striking label, embroidered with your trade name, 'A genuine product of Smithfield's' or words to that effect. Others are bound to imitate the range but it will be the original that most folk seek out. It would give you an edge."

"I'm sure you are right, thinking about it, that special identity should be stamped not just on the garment but on the market. My thanks to you Charles, it is often the way that confidence is bolstered through a shared belief. How is William? Is he happy at his work with Basil Stanford?"

"William is as happy as William ever is. He's like his mother, whatever Enid wanted by some means or other she got and then she moved on to the next want. It's curious, there's not a drop of Annie's blood in Freddy any more than there is in William, yet he's so like her, his nature, his character is almost identical to George, they may not look remotely similar but anyone knowing them could easily take them for true brothers. William surprises me with his ambition, father never really sought a position of importance and if I ever did, it's so long ago I can't remember."

"Some men I do believe are born to lead, to inspire," said Andrew, "others burn with an ambition to succeed, to acquire wealth but the vast majority simply seek contentment, how that contentment is measured of course is down to the attitude of each individual. My aunt Alicia would often use the quotation, 'Two men

402

looked through prison bars, one saw mud the other stars'. I try to look up at brightness rather than down to gloom but at times it proves hard, loneliness tends to cast a man's vision downward. What I need is that new enterprise, if Alicia were alive still she would admonish me for even hesitating. I think that is what enables Henry, his late wife Leonora was a very strong minded woman, quite fearless. When he first told me of his interest in a proposed open cast mining project at Mapperley and of his intention to study its merits his words were, 'Leonora would tell me to get on with it'."

"I heard about that," said Charles, "the fellow who came to take core samples at Mapperley called to see us, well, to see Annie really, I don't know the man and it's been that many years since he and Annie last saw each other, I don't think Annie would consider that she knew Anthony Hemsley. Her aunt Bella used to teach the Hemsley children, a boy and a girl, when the family lived at The Park. They are several years older than Annie and because their father moved them to Sheffield when Annie was no more than ten years of age, in all that time since it was only correspondence between Mrs.Hemsley and Bella, kept alive the acquaintance. After Bella Pownall died Mrs.Hemsley continued to write to Annie, the parents are both dead now apparently."

"What a strange coincidence that this Hemsley fellow should know, albeit loosely, Annie and yourself. I shall tell Henry," said Andrew.

"During your conversations with Henry Wicks I imagine colliery affairs come up as a topic much of the time," said Charles, "has he expressed any opinion on Jack Haynes who replaced Steve Wainwright as Union rep?"

"Yes as a matter of fact he has. Henry speaks well of Haynes, like Wainwright Henry believes Haynes is very responsible, measures a situation carefully and considers the wider picture, has his head screwed on the right way. I suppose you feel a greater interest in what might be occurring at the mine now William is with Stanford, I can understand why you would."

Charles sniffed and cleared his throat. "Jack Haynes is courting Hilda," he said.

"I didn't realise, well Charles, from what I have heard you need not to worry. Henry once described to me the Wainwright family as solid, sound people, he likened Jack Haynes to them."

Charles made no reply but leaned his head back in the seat and closed his eyes, conversation it seemed was for the time at an end so Andrew looked at his watch, a quarter past two, they had travelled together with less awkwardness than he had anticipated. For a Saturday afternoon Andrew's spirits were light.

The village of Skendleby was just as Annie had described and on this day in late spring, with a clear blue sky above and sunlight threading through the freshly clad trees it verily excelled itself.

"Where shall I drop you Charles?" Asked Andrew.

"You needn't feel anxious, Freddy would show you no malice if you were to come to the cottage, he's far too polite," said Charles.

"No I shan't intrude on your weekend, you have little enough time as it is. How about the church gate, if I drop you off there and we agree a time for tomorrow I'll collect you from the same place?"

"The church will be fine, I can't be too late getting back to Nottingham, would half past five be alright with you?"

"Ideal, I shall return at 5-30 tomorrow evening."

A comfortable atmosphere had developed between the two and Charles now found himself eager to see Freddy and the family. Andrew surprised himself by feeling almost excited at the prospect of seeing the coast again after so long. Henry Wicks was right, a man's needs were met in the most simple ways.

Andrew had found bed and board for the night at a small terraced house not too far from the seafront. The elderly lady who'd fed him with a delicious meal of steak and kidney pudding the previous evening and again with the most robust breakfast of egg, bacon, sausage and fried bread this morning, had proudly declared her age to be seventy-six. Her manner was charming, the room in which he'd slept could have soothed to rest the most resisting mind, behind the closed chintz curtains, underneath the soft eiderdown and perhaps for Andrew the most comforting element of all, a faint scent of lavender drifting around him in distant memories of childhood and aunt Alicia, he'd surrendered completely to the peace of it.

He'd spent the morning looking around the town, it fascinated him, a comparatively small place yet every corner of it seemed to be utilised for something. Traders made the most of the good weather offering all manner of beachwear, even the local dogs seemed more enthusiastic, wagging their tails at visiting people who walked about with ice cream cornets, ever hopeful of some small titbit their good natured approach might win them.

After a cup of tea in a busy little café aptly named 'Wavecrest' Andrew made his way to the beach. Such a diversity of humankind, every age, and on listening to their voices it was clear that the 'well to do', along with those who'd likely saved up all year for their day by the sea, mixed and mingled at this place without any thought of difference or divide. He watched with amusement the popular donkey rides, especially a boy of about seven who wore a splendid cowboy outfit and sat astride a dark brown donkey like a character from the wild west of America. His mother had paid for him to remain on the animal for three sessions up and down the beach. His urgent pleadings had achieved to send his mother's hand again into her purse for a fourth. Now another boy, a year or two older who'd waited patiently for a mount, pulled at the donkey handler's sleeve and shouted above the general noise of the gathering, 'make 'im get off mister'. It did indeed seem unfortunate for the ever-growing number waiting for a ride, there were only two donkeys working. The cowboy duly arrived back at the end of his fourth ride and threw a violent fit of temper at having to dismount. The image of a cowboy in full regalia, screaming and kicking as a burly donkey handler led him by the scruff of the neck to his mother made Andrew laugh out loud.

He couldn't come to the seaside and not paddle, Andrew took off his shoes and socks, rolled up his trousers and walked closer to the water, it felt cold but irresistible, he let it lap about his ankles. At the edge of the water the sand was firm, easier to walk on so he followed his gaze to the second beach, further along the shore. There the people were much fewer in number, he found a warm sunny spot at the foot of the dunes, sand martins were flying in and out of holes in the bank behind him, crossing in flight with a display of aerobatics right above his head.

Despite having slept well the night before he dozed, drifting in and out of awareness. The figures in the distance on the first beach, shimmered in the heat from the bright sunshine, it was almost unreal, a dream, yet he wiggled his toes and they responded, he laughed as he childishly tried to bury his feet in the loose sand. A family arrived with a kite, the impatience of the children as their dad prepared to launch it into the wind was entertaining in itself, their enthusiasm alone could have powered flight if the wind had proved insufficient. But it didn't and Andrew watched as the old box kite rose high above the beach, the canvas on its sides almost waving back to them as it flapped with each gust.

The afternoon passed so quickly. He must walk back to where he'd parked the car and drive to Skendleby. If Charles had found the pleasure in this weekend that Andrew himself had found then surely Annie would be relieved. Edna was not just a good seamstress, she was a pillar of wisdom, lucky indeed to have Annie for her friend but blessed too was Annie in having such a constant in her life. He would go ahead with the Celanese project, there were too many worthy people whom he could call friend for his spirit to fail him.

It was nearly 5-30 when Andrew pulled up by the church gate, on the notice board it gave the time of Evensong as 6pm. What a peaceful place at which to worship thought Andrew, as he sat quietly waiting for Charles. Within a couple of minutes two figures came into view, walking his way. It was Charles and with him, Freddy. Andrew took a deep breath, he got out of the car and stood by the door. Nervousness now crept over him.

"Hello Mr.Smithfield," said Freddy, "it's been great having dad with us, when we got mam's letter saying he was coming it threw us into a state of excitement, being able to show him around and of course to put his new

406

granddaughter in his lap. Thank you for giving dad a lift." Freddy extended his arm and offered his hand, smiling as he did so with warmth in his eyes.

Andrew grasped Freddy's hand like a vice.

"My pleasure Freddy, my very real pleasure."

CHAPTER TWENTY-FOUR

Early August 1932

It was towards the end of June that the situation at Ainsley Road took a turn for the worse, in the early hours Alice had been violently sick, Hilda had been stoic, reassuring George and helping Alice into a clean nightgown, cleaning up the evidence of her distress, settling Samuel when he roused, but it seemed to trigger a rapid deterioration in Alice and when Hilda had come to Gregory Street, one morning before work and cried her heart out, Annie knew she must go there, stay for as long as was necessary. The visit of an hour or so most days, which had been the pattern hitherto, was no longer enough.

Annie had wrestled with a nervous nausea throughout the day, but it had to be spoken of, so after the meal and while John was absent, she asked Charles to sit down for a moment before going out and to listen to what she must tell him. His compliance made her think that even he had no stomach for a scene, he sat by the table in silence, not uttering a single word as she explained, and pleaded with him to agree that Hilda must come back to live at Gregory Street, to be there to help in the shop, to cook for her dad and brother John, to keep house. For Charles to understand the young woman's emotions were raw and that he must accept Hilda's need of seeing Jack Haynes and not to cause his daughter any more despair than she already suffered.

Alice was not getting better, she was becoming more and more frail. Annie needed to be there. Hilda was nineteen, it was not right for someone of that age to be witnessing the decline of another young woman, especially in this circumstance where the relationship was so close and truly heartrending, Samuel was just a baby.

Charles had listened to Annie's words, not once interrupting, almost too quiet. Then he'd responded in such an unexpected way, Annie had cried from relief. 'It's Hilda's life she must do with it whatever she wants, it's not for me to interfere'. Perhaps the words he'd used revealed the reason for his change of heart, 'Hilda's life', how could Charles live with the dread of Alice's death and yet not allow happiness to flourish within the life of his own daughter.

It was now august 6th and Charles had been true to his word, all at Gregory Street was peaceful. Hilda had explained the situation to her employers at the library and they'd been kind, it was however difficult for them to hold open her job, not knowing when she might be able to return. Hilda had possibly looked further into the future than anyone else, thanking the chief librarian for all the instruction she had received since beginning her work there, she'd suggested it would be sensible for them to replace her without delay. In Hilda's mind she pictured George and Samuel rather than shelves of books, she heard the child's gurgles and cries over the sedate quietness of the panelled library. When the seemingly inevitable happened, her mam must return to her dad and she Hilda, must keep house for her brother George. She felt not the slightest resentment, Jack's first thought was always of 'family', he would understand and be patient. It was existing day on day with that crippling numbness, the inability to feel real hope, which reduced them all to a state of fragility. Tears fell at the least little thing, Hilda had cried, when pegging out the clothes she'd trodden on a snail and crushed it. Meals passed in a haze of indifference, no one savoured the smell of their favourite anymore or even consciously tasted it. Kindly sleep now grew fickle and contrary, often the night seemed to be twice the length of a day and an unrelenting tiredness muddled the senses 'til it was easy to see or hear something but in an instant forget what it was.

Annie had settled Samuel to his nap, George sat with his wife upstairs. All his hours outside of his work at Raleigh were spent at her bedside.

It was Edna's habit to call at Ainsley Road on a Saturday afternoon before going to the shop for her groceries. Annie filled the kettle and sat it over the heat, she'd baked some Parkin the week before, it had moistened nicely, so she cut a piece for each of them. Alice's appetite was pitiful, when her dad had called with a bag of iced buns from Lovatt's, which had been her favourite as a child, her attempt at eating one, to please him, had sent Annie to the yard under the guise of. 'It looks like a shower, I best pick in the clothes', she'd hidden herself in the privy and wept 'til her hanky was saturated and even the sleeves of her blouse were wet from blotting up the tears.

The back door catch rattled, it was Edna. "Only me," she said in a whisper. Annie gained more fortitude from a short time spent in Edna's company than from anything or anyone else. Davina and Sarah came together in a taxi each week, but Annie found those times draining as she tried desperately to appear composed and in control of everything, to spare them as much as she could. With Edna there was no need of pretence, they had been through so much together over the years, in one another's company their hearts were ever laid bare and the certain knowledge each had of their friend's constant love and understanding bound them in trust. Without Edna, Annie would doubt herself, with Edna she felt empowered, whatever lay ahead she would cope.

"How are Billy and the girls?" Asked Annie as she poured boiling water into the teapot.

Edna put her bag on the floor by her feet and sat down with a hefty sigh. "Doctor thinks Myra needs 'er adenoids seein' to. All the coughs an' sore throats she's had these past few winters, I thought 'e'd say it wer' 'er tonsils but no, 'e's sure its 'er adenoids, common problem 'e says, reckons havin' 'em done'll make all the difference. I can remember our Vera havin' summat wrong wi' 'er adenoids, she wer' right as rain after they'd done whatever it is they do, the times I've seen Myra wi' a finger up 'er nose I'm surprised she's got any adenoids left." Edna sipped her tea and took a bite from the Parkin. "That's lovely, I like a bit o' ginger. How is she then? I have to make meself ask, yer know what I mean. Billy sends his love an' Liza's put a package in me bag to give to yer, 'to let aunty Annie know I'm thinkin' about 'er', she said.

Annie rubbed her fingers across the back of Edna's hand. "We've got through another week," she smiled, "thanks to you Edna. I look forward so much to you coming." They chatted about little Janet's latest operation, about the factory and the new line in underwear soon to be in production. They spoke of Reg Yeats' failing health, of the happy news that Caroline and Edmund Tozer were expecting their first

410

child and of Lillian Sulley's improved health since she'd met a man who worked with the road gang. The ring road now completed, the men had moved their activities to Sherwood where sections of cobble were being replaced with asphalt.

Movement upstairs and the sound of Samuel stirring caused them to pause their conversation. All fell quiet again.

"George will have lifted him from his crib and taken him to see Alice," said Annie.

Edna got to her feet, took Liza's package from her bag, putting it on the table and said. "I best get off to the shop, Charles an' Hilda are alright yer know, no need to fret."

The two women hugged one another, then Annie felt her friend's arms tighten around her and Edna's voice tremble as she spoke. "For the first time our Annie wer' able to give Janet a spoonful o' food wi'out it comin' out of her nose." Edna's tears fell in a flood, tears for her own family and for Annie's too. For several seconds they comforted each other, now confined to sniffles, Edna's emotions subsided. "Send John if yer need me, yer know I'd come, day or night, Smithfield 'ould understand."

Annie waved from the doorstep when Edna looked back and blew a kiss. 'Please God let us all get through another week'. Annie whispered the words into the air, just in case He was listening.

William was again sitting in the car waiting for his boss. This morning he had driven him to Birchdale and been instructed to 'get out of the car today William, take a good look around'. Basil Stanford was meeting with Stafford Hinds, such 'pow wows' lasted about an hour so William set off to wander around the grubby site wishing he wore something on his feet other than his new shoes. Two maintenance men appeared to be rectifying a problem with some lifting gear.

"How do?" The one had said, while the other had given William a hard look, lifted the end of some heavy-duty chain, rattled it against the steel upright to beat off an accumulation of dirt and said.

"How do yer like bein' coupled up to Stanford then, take the strain can yer?"

William had sensed the man's animosity but rather than ignore it with simply a nod and an indifferent smile before moving along, in typical William fashion he'd chosen to aggravate. "You do your job and I shall do mine, in due course we shall see who best takes the strain."

Now William sat waiting for Stanford to come out from the offices of his solicitor, not as his foolishly, inquisitive mind had hoped might be Chaucer, Caffin and Holt, where his brother in law Edmund worked, but the firm of Neilson and Bradbury on London Road. It seemed to be a favoured address of the professions, no fewer than three solicitors were situated at intervals along the road's length, together with a chartered accountant, a dentist, an optician and somewhat incongruously, a massage and tattoo parlour, very respectably presented, so much so it could be taken for a funeral parlour, William imagined it was obliged to show the very 'correct' façade given the nature of its neighbours.

At last Stanford appeared and William got out of the car to open the door for him. Stanford eased himself into the passenger seat, despite his efforts to control it, his weight had continued to increase and once in his seat William had observed the man's lap disappear beneath the bulk of belly that travelled forward of the rest of him. He never sat in the back, preferring to be where his view was equal to that of his driver. He would speak quite readily of his family, especially his eldest daughter Patricia, a favourite William concluded. Today however, Basil's conversation centred on the visit in a couple of weeks' time of his middle daughter.

"You must meet Julia William, and her Italian husband of course. They are to stay with Caroline and your brother in law Edmund. I imagine Julia considers me far too lacking in sophistication to play host to her learned Romeo. Now that Caroline is 'with child', it might persuade her sister to produce a little cross breed, another one for Mrs.Stanford to drool over. I can't find much fascination for babies, I prefer them at a later stage, when they begin to display their natural traits, its possible to tell by then whether or not they are likely to excel in any way. What about you

William, do you and your wife intend having another child, even one sibling creates healthy competition?"

"As a matter of fact we took the decision to try for another earlier this year, although I would like to move from Glover Street before we add to the family. It was alright at the beginning but I've grown tired of the place, it does nothing to inspire me," said William, as he wound down the window to rid the car of a bluebottle.

Where would you choose to live?" Stanford's curiosity was aroused.

"I've always thought Wollaton to be a good area, Clifton is quite nice but a bit too far out, if I took Celia there her mother would need the services of a retainer, to undertake periods of surveillance, after which they would be required to report back in detail."

Stanford chuckled. "Your mother in law is like most women William, man has never achieved to maintain a big enough nest to satisfy the female, given her way the young would be hatched fully feathered and paired up, all within one almighty roost, an extension of the original nesting place! You don't want to fall into the rental trap again, money down the drain. You should at least aim to put a down payment on a property of your own. You're a young man in regular well paid work, the bank would surely consider a mortgage."

"We would need a bigger house than the one we live in now," said William, "a garden, a bathroom too, I doubt the bank would lend me sufficient to secure such accommodation," he sighed implying frustration, "I would like to present Celia with a home she could be proud of."

Stanford's belly rose and fell as he laughed. "My dear young friend, I have connections in all the right places, let me know if you'd like me to put in a good word. Grasp the nettle William, you should always grasp the nettle."

Annie had just come down from taking Alice a cup of hot, sweet milk, thankfully she would accept milk, her meals were now too small to deliver any real amount of nourishment. Samuel sat on the living room floor propped up with cushions, not yet able to crawl but strong in his back, he liked to be in a position where her could watch what was going on around him, he sucked on his teething ring as Annie began to peel potatoes. A knock came to the back door, it couldn't be Davina or Sarah, it was only yesterday they'd called.

"Hello Mrs.Eddowes, I thought it might be a good time to spend a few minutes with cousin Alice, I know she's too tired by evening."

"Come in Kenneth," said Annie, "Alice is awake, I've just given her a drink, I'll take you to see her, then if you'll be alright for a few minutes I'll make us a cup of tea."

Kenneth crossed the room and went down on his knees in front of Samuel. Without looking up at Annie he said. "How is she?"

"Doctor Casley has prescribed something to help her rest, she smiles a great deal, at all of us, but she is aware, I'm quite certain that she is fully aware. So we must smile back Kenneth," said Annie encouragingly.

"I understand Mrs.Eddowes. I promise I shan't be anything other than cheerful whilst in her company. I can't promise to show such a happy front to the world when I leave. Why Alice, wasn't aunt Candace enough? I don't know what to say to uncle Fred, I saw him earlier this afternoon, I told him I was coming here, the poor man was too choked to speak."

Annie picked up Samuel from the floor and put him in Kenneth's arms, she spoke quietly. "Play with him on Alice's bed, I do that as often as I can but the child needs fresh air and when I return from a short walk with Samuel in his pram I need to do some chores before George gets home. If I sat looking on her frailty for too long I'd likely crumble Kenneth, it's how I cope."

Annie led him upstairs. "You have a visitor Alice."

In the two weeks since Kenneth last called Alice's face had turned from white to grey, hollow cheeks aged her, even her lips had lost their pink colour, those too were that bloodless grey. Yet her eyes acknowledged him and Samuel with warmth and just as Annie had described, they were welcomed with a smile.

414

"I shall finish peeling the potatoes then make a cup of tea for Kenneth, I know he likes an Eccles cake."

Annie left them together, it would be hard for Kenneth, seeing Alice as she now was, but for George, who sat with her, lay with her, every moment he could, it was the worst kind of cruelty and Annie could do nothing to take the agony from him.

Alice patted the bed beside her. "Tell me all the latest, my very own intrepid reporter." Samuel gurgled his delight at finding himself on the counterpane with the sewn on fabric flowers. Over recent weeks he'd successfully achieved to loosen several and at once one of the thoroughly sucked, bedraggled blooms of linen was thrust into his mouth to deliver more soothing to his troublesome gums.

"Woolascroft today wrote in the mortar at Bobbers Mill, 'Work completed August 9th 1932'. I saw uncle Fred, he laid the small patch of concrete by the entrance to the estate and Dick Woolascroft performed the honours, inscribing the words using a piece of copper pipe. So there it is, recorded for all time, like Victoria and Albert's footprints in Cornwall. I shall write a fitting article and bring the first copy off the press to you, my favourite cousin."

"I want you to promise me something," said Alice. She smoothed her hand over Samuel's hair. "Don't be upset, please don't be upset."

Kenneth felt anxious and held out his hand for Samuel to clutch his fingers, even the feel of the little boy's grip helped to keep at bay his trembling.

"I so often take the notices from my trinket box and read them, slowly, over and over, remembering the moments, the happiness. Our marriage, Samuel's birth. When I go, I don't want you to put a notice of my death in the paper. Promise me Kenneth that you won't. I couldn't bear to think of George carefully cutting it out to save it, then for him to take it from the box and look at it over and over, remembering, not that Kenneth, please not that."

Kenneth took her hand, the fingers so slight but despite everything they gave him comfort. "If that's what you want then I promise, no notice in the paper." He leaned forward to kiss her forehead. He couldn't patronize her by making hollow remarks to suggest she would get better, that would have distressed her far too much. Instead he'd given his word to abide by her wish. "I shall visit uncle Fred each week, I promise that too."

Kenneth was hard pressed to keep the promise he'd given to Annie, tears were very close to breaking through but Annie's tread on the stairs saved him just in time. She carried a tray of tea and some biscuits, an Eccles cake for Kenneth and a bottle of milk for Samuel. The room held a perfect peace, amid a swirling, ever gathering storm cloud of despair, for a little while, Alice, her young son, cousin Kenneth and Annie, together shared the calm.

One day merged with the next until times and dates seemed irrelevant. Annie would try to define them by picturing in her mind the customers in the shop, the regulars so predictable she could nominate the days on which they bought their bacon, their butter and flour, the men their smokes. It was an exercise that kept a slim connection with normality. She'd been ironing, it was Thursday evening, Mr.Freeman would have called at the shop for his Gazette and almost certainly half a pound of arrowroot biscuits. Charles would have handed him his change, 'Capital Mr.Eddowes, capital', she could hear him in her head as she folded the old blanket and put the flat iron in the scullery. She was about to put away the pressed clothes when the back door opened and Hilda, along with Jack and John walked very quietly inside. Jack latched the door again, so cautiously, afraid to make a sound. It was curious how the situation seemed to compel them all to observe this unnatural, silent approach. Annie thought back to Catherine Appleyard when one day she had spoken of her daughter and the other sisters at the convent, so forthright in her opinions of their silent lives. 'Death is peaceful Annie, but we should at least have the patience to await it'.

"George is upstairs, go to them," said Annie, "Alice will manage a smile, she always does."

Hilda nodded but Jack turned to Annie and said. "I'll sit with you for a while Mrs.Eddowes, I reckon you could use a bit o' company."

Hilda and John understood, Jack didn't really know Alice, he would feel uneasy in the young woman's bedroom, so very poorly as she now was. Besides what he'd said was right, their mam did need someone too.

"Sit down Jack, tell me how is your family?"

"They're alright thank you Mrs.Eddowes. Mam gets tired but we all try to make things as easy as we can for 'er, even Victor'll sit down quiet for ten minutes these days, well, maybe seven or eight." Jack chuckled and Annie clutched at the sound. "When me dad wer' close to the end, I used to look at me mam an' it wer' not knowin' what to do for 'er that ripped at me innards. I couldn't do owt more for me dad, but mam, she wer' still able to respond, mam needed help to get through it. So I asked 'er, 'what can I do for yer Mam? I expected 'er to say summat ordinary, like bring in some coal or pick in the washin', stuff like that cause mam never asked for much at the best o' times. But she didn't, she looked at me same way you looked when we come through the door, an' she said, 'Sing to me Jack'. I didn't know what to sing. I shall never forget the way she smiled, 'Silver Threads Among The Gold', that wer' what she wanted."

Annie sat back in her chair. "It's been a long, long time since anyone sang to me Jack, I think like your mam, I'd like that too."

Jack began to sing, easily, with no more awkwardness than a mother singing to her infant.

> *"Darling I am growing old,*
> *Silver threads among the gold*
> *Shine upon my brow today,*
> *Life is fading fast away.*
> *But my darling, you will be*
> *Always young and fair to me.*
> *Yes, my darling, you will be,*
> *Always young and fair to me*
> *Love can never more grow old.*
> *Locks may lose their brown and gold.*

Cheeks may fade and hollow grow,
But the heart, still love will know.
Never, never, winter's frost and chill,
Summer warmth is in them still."

Behind her closed eyelids Annie now pictured Harold, the way he'd tell her stories, sing to her. Jack's soft voice and the memories it stirred strangely caused Annie not to cry, not to fight crippling emotion, but rather to drift carelessly through an interlude of kind relief. When his singing ended she opened her eyes, smiled from genuine happiness and said.

"I'm so glad that Hilda has you Jack."

They'd walked together, Hilda, John and Jack, reaching Gregory Street first and each harbouring their own thoughts Jack kissed Hilda and said.

"Find some sleep, I'll see you tomorrow," then to John, "stay strong for 'em." He gave John a hug, as if he knew just how badly he needed it. His mam ever put her arms about him but to feel the strength that passed from Jack to himself meant a great deal.

"Goodnight."

All three spoke the word together and Jack went on his way. As he walked along Glover Street he could see the figure of a man approaching from the other end, they met only a couple of yards from the front step of William's house.

"Hello William," said Jack.

William responded grudgingly with the one word only. "Haynes." He would have walked to his door without further acknowledgement but Jack spoke again.

"We should try to get on William, for everyone's sake."

William glared back at him. "You're right Haynes, we shall likely be seeing a lot more of one another by and by," he gave a self-satisfied smirk. William's thoughts were for the mine, for all the future times he would stand along side Basil Stanford, staring across the divide at the miners and their union representative.

"Indeed we shall William," said Jack, "for I intend to marry your sister." William muttered something under his breath. Again Jack spoke, he'd noticed William's smart attire. "The meeting you've just come from fills yer with notions of importance, of what makes a man. Well I can tell yer that it's not a puffed up chest, an' power over another, its not money in the bank, nor a big posh house. It's feelin' right in himself, try a bit o' humility William, go to your brother, sit with him, offer him your shoulder, give strength to your mam."

"Alice is a young woman, they're so full of maudlin, but she'll turn a corner soon, surprise them all." William's voice wavered and Jack could see the nervous twitching of William's hands.

She's dyin' William go there, or the day will come when you'll loathe your own weakness an' that's a judgment hard to bear."

Jack offered a smile, and unable to withstand the fearful dread, William looked back helplessly.

Annie could scarcely believe they'd got through another week. A tearful Edna had been and gone, Dr.Casley had called and spent time with George. Celia had taken Samuel out in his pram, along with a confused Mathew, he knew something was wrong, his young mind questioned the strange quietness, his senses detected anxiety. Annie had purposefully sent them for a walk, for Mathew's sake. Then Annie had taken a terrified William up to Alice's bedroom, Annie had been so surprised to see William standing in the scullery with Celia, he'd not called at the house for weeks, she was perceptive enough to realise why. William had lived with fear of death since, when a small child, his mother had gone from this earth leaving him troubled and frightened, his confusion had prompted him to ask so many questions at the time and no one had been able to answer that little boy with any real delivery of comfort.

William needed to see George and George needed to see him. Alice now drifted in and out of consciousness, she made no sounds of distress. Her father, Fred, had sat by her bed the previous evening with tears streaming down his face, uttering but one word, which Annie recognised as not mistaken but identifying the source of Fred Pearson's relief, just as the memory of Harold had relieved her when Jack sang. Fred spoke his wife's name.

"Candace."

It was almost half past four, Annie had begun to prepare a meal of sorts for George and herself. Samuel was taking a small amount of solids now, he favoured carrot and potato mashed into gravy followed by rice pudding. All was quiet upstairs, the child was with his mam and dad, and no doubt sucking the linen flowers on his 'beloved' counterpane as they lay together. A tap-tap came at the back door, Annie had started to wipe her hands on her pinafore when the door opened. She couldn't contain her joy at seeing Freddy. They held each other tight, neither spoke, for several seconds that was how they remained.

"I have to go back in the morning Mam but I couldn't not come, it's bad isn't it?" Annie nodded and squeezed his hand. Freddy pulled from the inside pocket of his jacket, an envelope. "Francis wanted you to have these, she said to tell you that she thinks of you all the time. It's photographs Mam, of Faith and Grace. His hand went into another pocket, this is for you to put on the dresser, Faith has drawn a picture, I don't know what it's supposed to be but she's put kisses on the bottom." Freddy's face unlike William's so full of fear, held nothing but compassion.

"I'll take you to them Freddy," said Annie. She had no need of further words, Freddy was in every way a man, he would quietly and calmly give to his brother all of that love, which Freddy ever carried in his heart.

He'd stayed with them for more than an hour, eventually they came down stairs together.

"She's asleep Mam," said George, "I think Samuel's getting hungry." He held the child in his arms as if he was reluctant to be parted from the comfort his son gave him.

"We shall eat now, put Samuel in his chair, Freddy must be hungry too, travelling from Lincolnshire. Francis has sent some lovely photographs of the girls," Annie tickled Samuel under the chin, "of your cousins young man."

"I shall go to Gregory Street later, see dad, John and Hilda. John won't mind me sharing with him tonight."

They ate, then while Annie cleared away the dishes the men kept Samuel occupied until the little boy's eyelids began to droop.

"I won't be long settling him Freddy," said Annie.

"Don't fret Mam, I shan't go anywhere before you come back."

The two brothers talked of many things, sad and happy, but their conversation flowed without obstacle of doubt, entirely comfortable. When Annie returned the atmosphere in the room where George and Freddy sat had taken on a more natural feel. George for a moment appeared freed of that gaunt, haunted expression. It was fleeting, Annie could tell he began to feel anxious at being away from Alice's bedside.

"It's alright George, Freddy understands," said Annie. The two young men embraced, Freddy ruffled George's hair with his hand and as he watched his brother walk away Annie saw Freddy's chest rise when he took that deep breath, the breath they all drew every time the pain struck, it struck with such determination and regularity.

"You don't have to go just yet do you?" Annie's appeal was touching.

"I'll sit with you for a little while Mam, bring you up to date with Skendleby news. The farm is doing really well, Mr.Shipman says it's been the heaviest yield of hay ever and the corn is looking very promising. Harold and Elizabeth are soon to be engaged, on her birthday next month. Molly is still fending off admirers although Walter Small, I do believe, is beginning to grow on her, you've got to admire his tenacity. Try and come when you can, I know it's difficult, but later on," Freddy hesitated as he struggled with his thoughts, "perhaps George and Samuel could come with you."

Annie took his hand in hers. "I think that would be a very good thing for us to do," she swallowed hard.

"Before I leave Nottingham in the morning I shall call on Arthur and Dorothy Cropley. We write and Dorothy replies but her hand gets very shaky, the last two or three letters have been barely legible. Francis has put a couple of photos in an envelope for them, they were good to me Mam," said Freddy with genuine sentiment.

"I'm glad that you intend to see the Cropleys, I don't hear anything of them and between calling on Sarah and Davina when I can there seems never to be time for more, but you must give them my love. It might be a kindness not to tell them of the sadness here, there's nothing they could do and at their age they would likely dwell on it."

"I really ought to be going now, dad isn't expecting me so I shouldn't leave it too late. I dare say he's tired, dad isn't used to working the shop all hours, that was always you wasn't it Mam?"

Annie smiled. "Charles has been stoic Freddy and I know he'll be so pleased to see you. I need you to give John a message, tell him that on Monday George won't be at work. If John explains to Percy Pollard that George really should be here then I'm sure Mr.Pollard will understand and present no problem. It can't be long now Freddy, try to bolster your dad's spirits, let him know we are coping. Give Francis my love, Ivy and the family too, kiss my beautiful granddaughters for me." Annie's frame shook within Freddy's arms.

"Love you Mam," he said. Freddy Eddowes walked from the back door to the street, struggling to see through a veil of tears.

Several times during the night Annie peeped at Samuel in his crib alongside her bed, she'd tiptoed on to the landing to listen at the door of the second bedroom for any sound. Finally light broke and she crept downstairs to make herself some tea. Yesterday had seen many callers, all bringing love. For Freddy to have arrived out of the blue as he did, had helped Annie more than he would ever know. She had taken the photographs from the envelope so many times and smiled down at the images of her two little granddaughters, still she sought their faces, with a cup of tea by her side on the table, Annie sat and fingered the photos yet again.

In contrast to the previous day this Sunday had produced no visitors. In a way it felt right, just Alice, George and their baby, knowing that Annie was close by.

Earlier in the day she had taken Samuel out in his pram and this afternoon she'd baked a Madeira cake, promising herself that while it was in the oven she'd cast-on the first stitches of a matinee jacket for Caroline and Edmund's baby. Concentration was too poor and after a pathetic half dozen rows she abandoned it, placing the wool and needles inside an old pillowcase to keep clean, later, it would be done later. She'd put the dish of milk out for the stray cat, which had appeared for the first time about a fortnight ago, looking half starved. Annie didn't see it every day but the milk was always gone. It had occurred to her that not for some time had she washed her hair, tending to Samuel and Alice, trying to support George in every way filled the days, so earlier she'd removed the pins and quickly washed it. Way down the list of importance Annie spent only minutes on the task, it was difficult to settle to anything this afternoon, she was anxious, something inside her was intent on undermining her confidence, her fingers had trembled as she'd pinned up her hair and the thin slice of bread and butter she'd attempted to eat at teatime had defied her appetite.

That night neither George nor Annie undressed. Samuel had obliged them and gone straight to sleep when his grandma laid him in his crib and despite his troublesome gums, which had caused him to wake most nights, so far this night he slept soundly.

The air was warm and Annie sat in a chair with a light blanket over her legs while George lay on the bed beside Alice. Not until the early hours did anything change, Annie glanced at the clock, it displayed the time as being just after two.

Alice began to stir, her fingers pulled at the bed cover, she was saying something, George listened, trying to understand her but Alice's words made no sense to him, her voice grew agitated.

"Mam's mangling clothes, I can hear her out in the yard, turn the handle dearie, mind your fingers for the cogs, always mangling, good little wife, turn the handle dearie."

"What does she want Mam? Said George, "I can't understand."

For almost an hour, in spasms of unrest, Alice mumbled those same words. Annie had moved to the bed, sitting on the edge, her chest tightening with

423

every breath she heard George take, their torment found no relief until half past three. Alice had gone quiet, she no longer fidgeted with the hem of the bed cover. So intense was the emotion that Annie hardly dare blink for fear of disturbing Alice and her distress returning. Then Alice opened her eyes, her lips tried to form speech but she had no strength remaining. With the slightest of sounds as she appeared to swallow, it was over.

Annie made no attempt to stem George's outpouring of grief. He didn't cry out with noisy, doleful misery to waken and alarm his baby son but with hushed agonies of lost love. Grief finally exhausted and bodily weak from the emptying of his soul, George lay still. Annie smoothed his brow and spoke softly.

"I need to do the very last kindness for Alice, I shall wash her, dress her in a pretty frock and brush her hair."

"Should I go and fetch Tommy?" Asked George.

"No, not until the morning. I want you to lay down on my bed, come with me." Annie held out her hand, he grasped it as he'd done when a little boy. Together they went to the other bedroom, he did as she asked, George had always trusted his mam. Annie picked the sleeping Samuel from his crib and laid him in the cradle of his dad's arm.

Alice Boucher's life was ended August 15th 1932, words now inscribed over Annie's mind and memory, engraved forever onto George Boucher's heart.

CHAPTER TWENTY-FIVE

A week had passed since the funeral. Hilda had been desperate to get back to Samuel, to fulfil the promise, which in her own heart she had made to Alice, to keep home for her brother George, to care for her young nephew.

Annie had returned to Gregory Street, to endure the well meaning but perpetual sympathies brought to the shop by every customer.

Charles withdrew to some remote place, moving about in almost total silence, bodily present but his mind elsewhere. Annie's strength was spent, she felt unable to try and follow him, to engage with him at that other place, where his spirit became bound, to ransom his smile.

They had eaten a meal, John had gone to see grandma Sarah. Charles sat quietly for a while then got to his feet and said.

"I'm going out for a bit, I won't be long."

His manner was pleasant enough and Annie didn't question his destination. It was the first time he'd made any move to go out since she'd come home, in a way she welcomed the normality of it.

At Ainsley Road, Hilda had taken her nephew up to bed, as was her habit, she read to him, as much for her own comfort as for Samuel's.

George sat at the kitchen table, in his hand lay his half of the locket, his gaze fell on the other half, which had been around his wife's neck since the day they were married, that rested on the table in front of him.

The back door opened, George presumed it was John or Annie, but it was neither. He looked up to see Charles.

"Dad," he said, he sniffed urgently, the wateriness of tears was never far away, not flowing openly but there, ever close by. He drew his sleeve across his face.

Charles carried two bottles of stout, he put them down on the dresser. "Try to drink it if you can, it's strengthening." He walked slowly to the table and sat down by George. "Is Hilda upstairs?" He asked.

"Yes," George nodded his head. "I'm sorry, it must be hard for you, bringing back such memories. The doctor said it was the pregnancy, having a baby that accelerated Alice's condition. It was already there but it was bringing a new life into the world that took her own from her. Your first wife Enid and my Alice were so similar, they died through their longing for motherhood."

Charles spoke and the tone of his voice alarmed George, he stood up, he was shaking. "Your Alice was nothing like Enid, nothing do you hear. Your Alice died bringing life into the world but Enid died through her determination to destroy life before it took breath. I didn't even know she was pregnant, she took herself to some place of evil and paid for an abortion." Charles wrung his hands in anguish. "I didn't even know if the child was mine or that of some other man, I've never known and never shall. All these years I've wondered. Don't ever think your Alice was like my Enid, my Enid!" Charles' voice was pitiful in its bare truth, "Was she ever really my Enid?" George didn't know how to respond. Charles continued to speak. "William and Freddy were told their mother died in childbirth, the baby too, they must never know any other, never, you'll not tell them." Charles looked at George intently.

"I wouldn't, I give you my word, nothing could make me inflict upon them such misery."

Gradually Charles calmed. He looked at the half locket in George's hand, almost tenderly he took it from his palm where it had lain. Then he picked up from the table the other half, his eyes studied the inscriptions as he put them together until they clicked into place, as one. Gently he lowered the locket with the chain into George's hands and said in a tired whisper.

"Your heart George can yet be whole, how I envy you that."

George's fingers curled tight around the small, gold heart, with tears welling in his eyes he watched Charles, his stepfather of twenty-five years walk away across the scullery floor. He paused at the back door just for an instant, without turning his head to look back, he spoke again.

"My heart has ever failed me."

The door opened and he left, closing it quietly behind him.